A safe place With You

César L. Baquerizo

Copyright© César L. Baquerizo, 2016
English language rights published and retained by Pen Name Publishing, LLC.

All rights reserved. No part of this publication may be reproduced, distributed, or transmitted in any form or by any means including photocopying, recording, or other electronic or mechanical methods, without the prior written permission of the publisher, except in the case of brief quotations embodied in critical reviews and certain other non-commercial uses permitted by copyright law. For permission requests, write to the publisher, address "Attention: Permissions Coordinator," at the address provided below:

Pen Name Publishing
P.O. Box 173
Bargersville, IN 46106
www.pennamepublishing.com

Printed in the United States of America
First Printing, 2016
Publisher's Cataloging-in-Publication data and copyright number is available upon request.

ISBN:
.mobi - 978-1-941541-90-6
.epub - 978-1-941541-91-3
TPB - 978-1-941541-92-0

Cover Design: Dionne Abouelela for French Press Bookworks
Interior Design: Dionne Abouelela for French Press Bookworks
Author Photograph: Joshua Degel

Distribution and Printing by Ingram Distribution Group

DEDICATION:
For you.

TO ALL THE HOPELESS ROMANTICS, BIG DREAMERS, adventurers. To those who are different, shy, weird — and especially to whoever who is still looking for, discovering, and understanding what you really are: a human being.

REFLECTION:

You should know.

I WROTE "A SAFE PLACE WITH YOU" AS A FICTIONAL NOVEL, but I was inspired by the following true events and facts:

*On May 17, 1990, the World Health Organization (WHO) removed homosexuality from its list of diseases and mental illnesses.

*Until 1997, same-sex relationships and romantic activity were illegal and punishable by four to eight years in prison in Ecuador.

*In 1998, Ecuador protected sexual orientation against discrimination in its constitution — and the protection of gender identity followed in 2008.

*In 2011, rehabilitation centers were discovered still attempting to "cure" homosexuality in Ecuador with torturous "treatments". At the time, it was estimated that two hundred such facilities were in operation. Government officials closed down more than thirty that were believed to have been functioning for ten years. These centers were not registered to the Ministry of Health, other than to provide treatment for general addictions. Like the fictional clinic in this story, the owners were often unsavory characters. Doctors would lend their names to give the clinics credibility, but only visit the patients once a week. In most cases, the families didn't know about the torture that the patients endured, but some did know and didn't care as long as there was hope of having a "normal" child. In the following years, more cases of escaped patients came to light. Despite the complaints registered against the centers, some directors are still free and justice has not been served. The Ministry of Health continues to investigate and close clinics.

***

Since the middle of the 20th century — and even continuing today, in some parts of the world — there have been a myriad of treatments to "cure" homosexuality: surgical, substance, electroshock, etc. Religious centers have violated human rights and destroyed lives, although the Bible never mentions homosexuality explicitly.

What is homosexuality? Throughout the history of humanity, it has been defined as a disease and a sexual deviation. So then, is there a cure? Others say it's a sin, an abomination. Why did God create us like this? Still others say that it's just a sexual orientation. Why can't we live a life without prejudice or discrimination?

If it is a choice, are you driven to it or are you born with it? Many still think that being homosexual is a choice, but how does one choose homosexuality? Do you know what you would have to face: the rejection, discrimination, and intolerance? And whether it's a consequence of the social or family environment, or whether you are born with it, what would you do if your child prefers chocolate ice cream and not vanilla? Or if his favorite football team is your team's rival? Would you force him to like vanilla or your favorite team?

If you don't like same-sex relationships, then don't have one. It's God's place to judge — not ours. People hate and are afraid of things that they don't understand. In order to understand the love between two people, you must first experience love yourself.

Remember: LOVE ALWAYS WINS.

INSPIRATION:

Quote.

"*If a bullet should enter my brain,
let that bullet destroy every closet door.*"
— Harvey Milk

PROLOGUE:

Untying the identities in knots.

Thursday, June 21, 2012

His Excellency,
President of the Republic of Ecuador:

As we all know, a heterosexual relationship is formed by the two sexes that exist in nature: man and woman. Its goal is reproduction, which is naturally absent in homosexuality. Today, it can be said that heterosexuality is favored by society, while homosexuality is the most rejected.

Most people think that homosexuality is a choice, a lifestyle. Why would a person choose a life that does not give the opportunity to reproduce, a life without the acceptance of others, and a life of rejection? In mainstream society today, would that be what you, or anyone, would choose? Knowing in advance your response, now I ask - why **are** there homosexuals? Simple. It's because of the attraction and love that a human being feels for another of the same sex. Why does this happen? Does it really matter? Most importantly, I think, is to wonder if all that is relevant and how it could affect or harm the personal life of everyone else.

Moreover, it should be noted that homosexual relations are not new — they have existed since the beginning of humankind and will continue to exist until the end of time. Homosexuality even manifests in other species.

Heterosexuality has a great and valuable purpose, procreation, which ensures the continuation of our species. That leads us to ask what purpose then does homosexuality have? The opposite, the extinction of the human race? Well, that is not the case because, out of the almost seven billion people who exist, not all are homosexual. It is absurd to think that. What, then, should happen with a heterosexual couple who cannot have children due to infertility or impotence? Do we get rid of them? Do we reject them as we usually do with homosexuals because they fail to fulfill their 'purpose'? No, because, in fact, they **do** serve a purpose: to love each other. Then, turning to the million-dollar question, it is very easy to realize the purpose of homosexuality, although it may be necessary to expand a little on this point.

Love is the essence for which every human being searches and hopes to experience in life. It is the most coveted and desired. It takes us away from loneliness, sadness, darkness, and hatred. Our identity is what we are, what we discover over time; it's who we are individually, with the specific characteristics of personality, dreams, goals, and tastes. What better thing than being unique!

Love and identity are two aspects that we could call causes and, at the same time, effects of homosexuality. When a human being feels something different, contrary to the majority in the society that surrounds him, then that detail is what makes him unique — in this case, the sexual orientation. This attraction to someone of the same sex develops part of our identity, but only a part; being homosexual does not define a whole, but rather only one aspect among others that makes us who we are. Love, which is both chemical and physical, is attainable, but sometimes the path to love is long and difficult to navigate. The longer and more difficult the path to love, the more valuable, and often much more admirable, the destination.

Here is the purpose of homosexuality: the acceptance of oneself, without external influences, knowing that one knows oneself and lives as one really is, not hiding the love that is felt for another human being, to testify and be an example of what love means, to know that one must not influence or force others to be as one is, or to have the same taste one has. Love can do everything. Love cures everything. Love gives more possibilities, it gives happiness no matter with whom one finds oneself, nor what age, color, race, religion, economic status, or sexuality one has. The important thing is to fulfill the purpose of loving your neighbor as you love yourself. Despite the fact that there is no reproduction, just being together is enough for a homosexual couple. Isn't this something admirable?

The purpose of homosexuality is to reveal and show our identity, free the personality from mental barriers and fears that have been in our hearts since we were children, "untie the knots of our identity". This leads to recognizing the person one loves, a healthy love without prejudice. Perhaps most importantly, this leads the individual to be happy. The homosexual is setting an example for the world.

All human beings deserve a safe place where we can be happy as ourselves and with the ones we love, whom we adore and with whom we want to live for the rest of our lives. It is a human right.

Homosexuals do not fight for the right to make the lives of others miserable. No, not at all. We are doing this to develop as human beings, to express our love for the person who loves us back.

Love is for all. It is something that we need. We deserve equal treatment and a safe place. Both heterosexuality and homosexuality share this world, whether we like it or not, this is why we have to support each other, to live in harmony, without discrimination or rejection by the particularities of one personality or another.

It is time to untie the knot within us — not only for us, but also for all those who need us.

For this reason, Mr. President, I ask for your help to close these illegal clinics operating in our country. It is believed that there are currently more than two hundred centers operating under the façade of rehabilitation, but believe me, they are not "curing" homosexuality. They are just physically, emotionally, and spiritually damaging the young people who are locked in there. They mistreat their identities and their hearts...as they did with me.

Sincerely,
Tomás Díaz

Chapter ONE:

The Romeos.
Saturday, April 11, 1987

APRIL 11ᵀᴴ FALLS ON A SATURDAY — A DAY WITH A discouraging feeling about it as clouds partially block the dim afternoon light from Guayaquil, Ecuador. The year on the newspaper reads "1987", as Tomás Díaz picks it up from the kitchen table.

    This young man is shy and distant from his parents — a personality and behavior that he recently developed to avoid spending much time with them. As usual, Tomás comes down to make his own lunch and returns to his bedroom where he likes to eat alone.

    A thunderstorm threatens to form outside while Tomás is sitting on the bed, turning the pages of the national newspaper. He sees an event that occurred two days ago but has only recently become known. It's a story about a young man, Christian Arroyo, also eighteen years old, who committed suicide with a gun that his father kept in the closet for emergencies. The Arroyo family doesn't live far away. Tomás recognizes the street name and writes down the address so that he can find out a little more. It struck him that the boy's father had announced to the press that his son was a homosexual, a "sexual deviant", which is exactly how Tomás has identified himself since childhood. He recalls that his own father, a very religious man, read from an Old Testament passage three months ago, when Tomás came out of the figurative closet. The verse was "You shall not lie with a male as with a woman; it is an abomination." Feeling that his sexuality was a sin had traumatized Tomás; he felt rejected by his parents and especially by God. Since that day, he has isolated himself from his family, not wanting to subject himself to the hatred and aversion that they so often expressed for people like him. "Doesn't God teach us to love each other no matter how different we are?" the young man would think to himself. His mother does not support him. In fact, he knows that she is considering taking him to a religious clinic to treat his "illness" and force him to change. The center is called "Grow And Live Normally" and is far away in the cold capital, Quito. But his parents don't care - they are willing to pick up everything and move just to see him "healed". Tomás asked for the chance to change on his own, but since he is unable to do so, all he can do now is keep silent in order to stay in his house as long as possible, although it doesn't feel like home; he doesn't belong there anymore.

He just wants to let his family get to know a part of him, to have the courage to make that effort to be himself after spending years avoiding the feeling of attraction toward people of the same sex. The day he came out to his parents, he told them that he was attracted to both sexes, but that he is more inclined toward men.

"Tomás, I have to go," calls his mother, who knocks and tries to open the locked bedroom door.

"Ok," he replies, without looking up from the newspaper.

"Your father is out of town because he has a meeting with some coworkers. Please don't go out and be careful. I love you very much."

His mother is concerned because Tomás is very distant from her now. He's not the same boy who used to talk nonstop and share everything with her. Everything has changed: his activities and grades in high school, the popular girl he wanted to be his girlfriend, and his desires to go to college to become a lawyer. Everything changed the day he told her about his sexuality.

She wants the best for her only son, but she cannot agree with his lifestyle. Not only because the Bible tells her so, but also because homosexual relationships are illegal in Ecuador, punishable by four to eight years in jail. She has heard whispers of others teenagers in the neighborhood being sent out of the country to protect their family's reputation. Some are signed up for a life of celibacy and groomed to become religious leaders. Others are forced into arranged marriages. Finally, she heard about Grow And Live Normally, which she thinks is the best option for her own son. Without wasting any more time, she goes downstairs quickly, turns on the car, and leaves. Tomás cuts out the article, pasting it onto the first page of a new blue notebook.

Tomás finishes his lunch and hurries outside. He gets on his bicycle and makes his way to the house of the young man who killed himself. He wants to know if he did it simply because he was different or if there was something else that led him to make such a drastic decision — one so...so final. Tomás' mother asked him not to go out, but he can't stay there, alone and bored all day, locked in his room, locked in his loneliness. He knows that it only leads to depression.

He arrives at the address and leaves his bicycle between the bushes of a house that looks empty. Crossing the street, he reaches the front yard from where a beautiful but sad garden can be seen. He looks at the garage and assumes that the boy's parents are not home because there are no cars inside. He walks around the block to see if there is another entrance through the back, always being careful that nobody sees him. He climbs the small steps to the back door and, as expected, it's locked. He sees a rug under his shoes, crouches, lifts it up, and finds what he was looking for: a key. He opens the door and enters the kitchen gently and quietly.

Surprisingly, the house is not silent. Or maybe it's just the voices inside Tomás' head, scenes that his imagination creates about the suicide of the young man named Christian. As he exits the kitchen, he sees a big photograph hanging on the wall next to the front door. In the photo, the young man and his parents are embracing each other happily. In the living room, he sees all three sitting there, chatting amicably, or at least in appearance. Tomás notes that something is hiding behind those smiles, something like nervousness, or being forced to fake a smile with someone who one doesn't like. That, hypocrisy is the word, that's what he feels there, within that family, which somehow doesn't seem to be aware of Tomás' presence. Then, in a split second, almost like a lightning bolt, Christian pulls something out from behind his back. His parents open their eyes wide. Their mouths are paralyzed in a grin that, in another context, perhaps would have seemed funny. It sounds almost like a round of applause, but only a single clap, as if all attendees in a large theater bring their hands together in unison, once. The shot - a clatter, a light, a stream of blood that invades everything.

Tomás awakes from his daydream and realizes that he is shaking. It was all in his imagination. No one else is there. No... Yes, there it is — the bloodstain, all that's left of Christian. Without hesitating, Tomás approaches the chair and passes his finger over the dry blood. A shiver courses up his spine. He sees a flight of stairs to his left and, although his feet feel like two sacks of cement, he decides to go up to search the bedrooms. On his way, he sees more photographs of the family, together and sharing. What could have happened to change that? Christian's homosexuality? Or rather, would it have been the revelation that Christian was gay? "But...but...it cannot be so," thinks Tomás. "To choose death only for that. How strange are human beings!"

This is the only conclusion that he can reach. Like windows that connect to another world, Christian's heart-shaped face stares out from the photographs with dark black eyes. Tomás likes the way he looked - short, dark brown hair styled slightly upward and a pleasant, wheat-toned complexion. Tomás guesses that Christian was quite a bit taller like him and Tomás can tell that he had a strong body. He was handsome and looks like he was a nice boy; who knows, maybe in another life, in other circumstances, they would have been able to become great friends, maybe even a couple.

Tomás finishes climbing the stairs and reaches a hallway where he sees several doors. Stickers are plastered on one of the doors, one of which reads "Chris". Tomás slowly opens the door. The bed is made and all of the boy's belongings, including his blue belt and martial arts trophies, are in their proper places as if nothing had happened, like death hadn't arrived. Tomás feels a calm lonely breeze waft in through the window. He can't take it anymore and shuts the window. His eyes roam over everything. Nothing indicates that this young man had been "abnormal". Nothing indicates that he was suicidal.

Tomás sits on the bed and a small trashcan in the corner catches his eye. His curiosity gets the best of him so he approaches it and sees that there is an envelope among all of the discarded papers. He picks it up gingerly between two fingers, as if with fear, almost not wanting to touch it at all. It's a letter, still sealed, for someone named Sebastián. He thinks once, twice, three times until he makes the decision to open it. He lies on the bed and begins to read:

Wednesday, April 8, 1987

My dearest Sebas:

I hope the postman picks up this letter before my mother has the chance to hide it or throw it away.

Right now I feel very lonely. Solitude has entered and taken over my space. I can't sleep. It's midnight and I'm still thinking about you as I write this letter. I feel very ashamed and I hope that you understand and don't hate me...

Our relationship is the best and most valuable thing in my life. You changed it and made it better. For three years, since that day I saw you at the bus stop, I could not take my eyes off you. You brighten me with your blue eyes, your smile under the freckles on your rosy cheeks... Since then, my world changed. Before I met you, I never thought that, in this incomprehensible world, there would ever be someone like you — someone so cute, affectionate, and amazing. Above all, I never thought that I would fall in love like this — to love you unconditionally as one man loves another. It was a miracle. You are a miracle.

Today, I changed the way I see things about my life. I had a horrible argument with my parents. They found a photo in my closet in which we are hugging. It was one of the photos we took while watching the sunset on the beach in Salinas. Do you remember? It was when I told you that I love you for the first time. I had never seen you so flushed and happy. You told me that I had left you breathless. I whispered you that you're mine and you answered me, "Yes, I am and you're mine, too."

We were unique, deeply, and madly in love. My parents practically disowned me. My father told me that I was no longer his son, just another faggot, a deviant in this world — that I should leave. My mother told me that I would burn in Hell if I didn't repent or change my sexuality. And worst of all, she forbade me to see you.

I've never seen them like this before. They were not the parents I've always known. I was forced to accept their help and they're going to put me in a mental health clinic. If I don't go, they say they're going to throw me out of the house. I don't know where to go. I don't want to lose you. Now that you're with your father at the ranch in Quevedo, I don't think I can hold on for the two weeks until you come back. Forgive me... I feel like I'm drowning in the humiliation of not being able to defend myself against my parents and mostly I'm disappointed because they are not able to see my true self. They don't understand me, they don't accept me, and do not love me as I am, with my differences. I don't know what else to do...

Tomorrow morning, I will be forced to go to the clinic in the capital. I have no choice. Sebastián, I'm afraid...for the first time in my life, I feel terrified. I am weak and emotionally distraught and I am in a depression that gets stronger and deeper. Just the thought that they are going to change me, and that I will never love you like I do now, makes me not want to go on living. I swear, if that is the life that I will be forced to live, then I prefer death. I want to see you so badly, to kiss you, hug you, and tell you how much I love you, again and again. I could escape right now, but where would I go? I need you to understand - I'm screwed and stuck here.

I feel that nobody sees or knows what I'm going through. I wish that you were next to me right now to stop my thoughts. I'm desperate to be in a safe place...with you. I dream of that one day when we can be together, without prejudice, without discrimination, accepted and respected by the world, but it seems that there is nothing like you and I. Our love is incomprehensible to the rest. We are like Romeo and Romeo...

I want to erase the suffering that my parents caused me with their contempt and rejection. It has affected me so much; it's the worst feeling that has risen in me and I believe that I can make a small difference in awakening the world. What would you rather have: a homosexual son or a dead son?

I am not strong. Right now I'm lost. I don't know how I will survive in the clinic, away from you, unable to see you or talk to you, and if they change me... I can't...I can't go through that. I cannot risk having that life. It's like the end of the world. I would rather stop breathing.

My decision has nothing to do with you, Sebastián, I LOVE YOU. Always remember it, please: I LOVE YOU.

I hope that my decision, as terrible as it is, may help my parents and the world understand and accept us all. That they will open their eyes and see that there is nothing wrong inside of us, there is only love and hope. It's just the hatred and discrimination of the world. It's the ignorance that hurts us and doesn't let us live fully, loving who we must love. In my case, that's you.

I LOVE YOU.

Sebastián, you are the love of my life. You're the world to me. Without you, nothing makes sense.

Perhaps you don't understand me at all and think that I've lost my sanity...

*Maybe you may see me as selfish and vindictive with my parents, but I feel that I don't deserve you. I'm not strong enough and confident enough to get through this with the rejection of my parents. I don't want to go to that clinic and be away from you. Do you remember what I told you about soul mates? Sometimes the world doesn't work the way you want it to. Perhaps I am not your soul mate, after all. He is out there, waiting for you, although it hurts me to tell you that. But, you are indeed **my** soul mate, which is why I will die complete and in peace.*

Don't give up, and be stronger than me. I'm sure that there's someone out there who will wait for you for a second chance at love. It hurts me in all my soul having to leave you, but I don't know what to do. It's too painful right now.

Forgive me...
Sincerely,

Christian

Tomás is speechless, deeply affected. He begins to understand Christian. He doesn't share his mindset, but now he understands the true intention of this young man who felt so trapped, alone, and weak. The decision he made to commit suicide was not due to his boyfriend Sebastián, nor to his sexual orientation. Rather, it was because of the rejection of his parents, society, and the world as a whole. Christian had surrendered because he didn't have a helping hand that would lift him up and open his eyes to accept himself without the need of others' acceptance.

Tomás has a revelation. He feels a strong desire, a force inside, the need to provide real help to those who, as Christian, need someone to show them the way to self-acceptance. He feels inspired and full of confidence. At that very moment, Tomás begins to love and accept himself just as he is. He accepts that there's nothing wrong with him, that he is not a sinner, a sick person, or a monster. He is different, as any human being has their differences and peculiarities, but being different does not mean "disease", it means bravery. As if by magic, the mental weight he has about the argument with his parents begins to fade. He is proud of himself. Unexpectedly, the letter from Christian made him open his eyes and made him stronger. Now he wants to fight for his basic rights to live and love without prejudice and rejections intruding into his heart.

Tomás places the letter back into the envelope, where the address of the recipient is written and, assuming that this is where he will find the boyfriend, he gets up and leaves the room hastily. He goes back downstairs, bypassing the eerie living room and leaves the house, again taking care that nobody sees him. He picks up his bicycle and heads to Sebastián's house.

He reaches the destination and hides his bicycle next to the only big tree in the yard. A gentle wind that Tomás can only describe as dark and cold blows leaves from the tree. Being careful not to wrinkle it, he puts the envelope in his pocket and climbs up the tree until he reaches the level of the window that, he is certain, belongs to Sebastián. The window is open. He sees that there is no one around and carefully creeps along a branch, jumps, and enters the bedroom.

Everything is in disarray, but what stands out, what somehow gives harmony to that disorder, are the paintings. Works of art hang on the walls, all with a signature on the bottom that reads "Sebastián Fineli". On a nightstand, there is a photo from of Sebastián, the sweet face stares at him. Tomás picks it up to see it more closely and to appreciate his physical details: his luminous blue eyes, his simple smile, freckles, and rosy cheeks. Tomás finds him just as he had imagined from the description in the letter. He puts the photo frame back in its place and notices that one of the drawers of the dresser is partially open. There is a photo album and, without thinking, Tomás picks it up and sees that on the cover it is titled *Chris and Sebas.*

He flips through the pages, looking at photo after photo. In one, he sees the two boys embracing at the beach and assumes that it is the same place that Christian mentioned in his letter, where he had told him, "I love you," for the first time.

Although he knows it's wrong, Tomás cannot resist himself and he takes the picture from the album and saves it, trying not to damage it. He needs it as a keepsake - or rather as proof or evidence that this tragic story is real, that this story with such a sad ending can occur and, in fact, that it is repeating itself over and over again all over the world.

A car! It can't be! Tomás frantically runs around the room, panicking as he realizes he has nowhere to hide. Slowly approaching the window, he peeks out a corner and sees that a car has been parked in the driveway. Its occupants get out gloomily — the owners of the house. Between the parents and brother, he easily recognizes Sebastián. He is the only one dressed in black, looking crestfallen with a tear-stained face. But didn't the letter say that Sebastián was on vacation for two weeks at his father's ranch? In any case, that won't help Tomás save himself. They are already here. He assumes that they are returning from the funeral, which means that it's the worst possible time for them to find a stranger snooping through their possessions and stealing a photo.

For a moment, Tomás is lost in his thoughts. He lingers with his blank mind, looking at the sky that still threatens to rain. The sound of the front door closing startles him and, taking advantage of the fact that everyone is now inside, Tomás grabs the branch that had earlier served as a bridge and leaps out the window. He crawls very carefully. If he falls and breaks a leg, then he won't be able to explain what he was doing on that tree, when the house was empty.

Tomás hears Sebastián enter his room and close the

door. He remains clutching the trunk of the tree, motionless, to avoid making any sound that would catch the attention of the homeowners. From there, he sees Sebastián sit on his bed, crying inconsolably. Tomás sees him turn around and stare at the nightstand, mesmerized. He sees the envelope, Tomás realizes. If Tomás doesn't hurry down, Sebastián will see him, as well, but he can't go any faster. He has always been afraid of heights and to get up, of course, he did not have to look at the ground, but coming back down is a different story and panic paralyzes him.

Sebastián picks up the letter and recognizes the handwriting. His face is a mixture of despair and horror, of disbelief, as if saying, "It's impossible that this is here." He begins to read its contents, phrase-by-phrase, character-by-character. His tears are so big and heavy that he can't finish reading.

"Hey! What was that?" *Something made a sound outside. Something made a sound in the tree!* Sebastián becomes frightened, taking his asthma inhaler and breathing in twice. He walks towards the window.

Tomás squeezes his fingers around the branch and closes his eyes. He has no other choice but to let go. The sound of his feet crashing against the ground reveals his presence.

"Hello? Who are you?"

Tomás is terrified. He stays still.

"Christian? Christian," Sebastián yells from the window in such a way that he is afraid of his own voice. "Christian!"

Tomás waits for some miracle to happen as he attempts

to hide in the shadow of the tree trunk.

Sebastián remains in his place at the window without knowing if he had a hallucination or if he just experienced an encounter with the afterlife. The sky is getting darker.

"Christian?" he asks again, without realizing that his voice is now only a whisper.

And nothing. *It must have been in his mind.* The first raindrops begin to fall.

Sebastián's tears falls like the rain. He lies down on the bed and covers his face, biting his own hand so that his parents and older brother don't hear his sobs. He doesn't know which is worse: the death of Christian or having to eventually get over it. He is devastated and his head hurts from so many negative thoughts. He will never love someone like Christian. He will never be able to hug him or spoon with him again. He will not have his shoulder to lean on or his hand to grasp strongly. Lightning illuminates the sky. Christian was unique, a miraculous human being, someone who understood Sebastián in this world full of social prejudices. The thunder makes the tree next to his window shiver. He misses Christian's smile, his kisses, his compliments, and the love he felt when he was with him.

As the lightning lights up the sky, it breaks the shadows and Tomás feels exposed. He can't waste any more time; his parents are going to return home and he's not going to be in his room. The thunder rumbles. He takes his bicycle and pedals hastily under the drops of rain. He doesn't know what occupies his mind the most at the moment: the fear of nearly getting discovered or the concern over the death of "Chris" and the emotional state of "Sebas".

He returns home, puts away his bicycle, and runs up to his bedroom. He's all wet and does not want his mother to realize that he went out so he takes a shower. Now, more relaxed, he takes out the picture he stole (although he doesn't like to use that word) from the album of the two lovers. He stares at it in detail and he can tell how in love they were. It is evident, by the form and intensity of their embrace and smiles.

Tomás pulls out the blue notebook that he started in the morning, where he kept the newspaper clipping. He pastes the picture and writes under it "True and real love".

He smiles, but just for a moment because the idea of the death of Christian tumbles into his heart and kills any spark of joy. He closes the notebook, putting it aside. He lies on his bed without closing his eyes and listens to the rain with a blank mind.

A thought eventually visits him. He remembers the trauma he felt when his father showed him the Bible verse. In fact, he gave Tomás a Bible. There it was, in his night table, the book, which contains the famous Holy Scriptures.

"Does God...love me?" Tomás wonders. "Has God accepted Christian into his realm? If God made man in His image and likeness, why did He create people like Christian or me?"

These questions run through his head. He decides to look thoroughly into those pages for everything related to homosexuality. He wants to find out everything there is about this matter. He wants his questions to have answers.

Chapter TWO:

What is Homosexuality?
Friday, December 15, 1989

"HOMOSEXUALITY IS AN ATTRACTION. A DESIRE...a sexual identity...an affection and a...a...a sexual orientation towards a person of the same sex," responds Tomás, summarizing all the theories that turn around in his mind, with a soft demeanor in order to avoid a fight.

Dr. Claudia Losala, his psychiatrist, does not seem very happy.

"God hates it. It is a disease of humanity," she answers, sitting opposite her patient with a notebook on her lap and without the slightest intention to accept or understand his definition.

"God and Jesus don't talk about homosexuality. That word is not even mentioned in the original versions of the Bible. They do not condemn homosexuality or even express an unfavorable position toward this orientation," Tomás states.

This is his second week with the psychiatrist. Her office, relatively quiet and cozy, contrasts with the life on the other side of the door. This is especially true of the sexual reorientation wing where Dr. Rutherbor's guards pose as nurses and give violent treatments to "cure" the young patients who are locked up in there.

"The Bible and the Lord Almighty say that homosexuality is a sin and a depravity before their eyes," Dr. Claudia insists with stronger tone, attempting to force the belief into his head.

"When the Bible was written, many people practiced prostitution, taking advantage of women, especially those who were considered inferior and dependent, and sexually exploited them. When the Scripture says that a man should not lie with another man as with a woman, it means that men should not treat others with the same disrespect that was shown to those women. The two people should treat each other equally and base committed relationships on love." Tomás shares his interpretations with confidence.

"That changes nothing. It says what it says there and it refers to homosexuals!"

"Have you never wondered the reasoning behind what you read?"

"There is nothing to question in this book. That's why it's sacred," the psychiatrist defends.

"The Bible wasn't written by God, but by many human beings, like you and I, who contributed at different times and places over thousands of years. When you read the Bible, you can clearly distinguish the different social environments, not references to of the morality of sexual orientation."

"It refers to homosexuals. You're confused, but don't worry — that is why we are here — to heal you."

"It does not refer to homosexuality, but rather things like prostitution and rape because of the immorality that prevailed at that time."

"That isn't true. The Bible is very clear in that homosexuality is an abomination."

"And if we assume that what *you* say is true, what about the other biblical passages where "abomination" is mentioned?"

"What do you mean?" Dr. Claudia asks, confused.

"There are many other places in the same book of Leviticus which mention the 'abominations'. In fact, there are a number of 'abominations' that are more explicitly condemned, but we continue to do the complete opposite — sometimes everyday! What about the laws relating to eating seafood, planting seeds, types of clothing, shaving, and tattoos? Why don't we treat adultery the same way we treat homosexuality today?"

"How can you compare all these random laws with homosexuality, which is much worse? Besides, they are old moral codes that are not meant to be taken literally in modern times."

"Exactly. Since all of these laws were written thousands of years ago in totally different circumstances, it would be nonsense to accept and practice them today; they concern customs and traditions that have changed over time."

"But you cannot ignore what it says about homosexuality, it is a sin!"

"Why do you cherry-pick like this? For convenience? Who gives you the right to decide which rules to follow and which to ignore? Do you know what Galatians 3:23-26 says?

To clarify, it means that, through Jesus Christ, we live in faith, not in the laws. Today, most Christians don't follow Jewish laws." Tomás stares at her, seeing the doubts that are drawn on the face of the psychiatrist.

"That is not an excuse to ignore what it says in Leviticus." Dr. Claudia cannot believe her ears. For the first time, she is beginning to consider his point of view, but she has one more point to make. "What about Adam and Eve? God created man and woman for procreation."

"That's right, He created man and woman for reproduction because the world was not yet inhabited. It was duty, obligation, for them to populate the planet, but procreation is not the same as love, which is also necessary for human existence. Today, there are many cases: couples who are infertile so they adopt, single mothers and fathers raising children. Above all, God created man to love. Adam and Eve were the example for procreation, not necessarily of love. I don't know for sure if they actually *were* in love. The right to love and commitment belongs to every one. I'm not saying that the Bible can't be used to show us how to be good human beings. The Bible does teach us how to treat each other well and give back to our neighbor. But using it only for the reward of salvation in the afterlife and using it to judge and condemn someone in the present life is more immoral thing you can do! This is how people justified the enslavement of black people, blocking women's equal rights, and other similar situations."

Tomás finally loses his friendly expression as he continues, "Think how the Bible has contributed, almost unintentionally, to the oppression of entire segments of society. Christianity is not only about believing, but also about loving others — something that is not always seen in the laws of the Church, in the Bible, or in the words of the priests who abuse children or steal from the alms. Those things happen and no one demonizes them the same way that they do with homosexuality. God is not just a religion - it's about a relationship, and is present in each of us, without judging us. Remember that the most important and valuable lesson that they teach us the Bible is what Jesus said in Mark 12:31, "You shall love your neighbor as yourself. There is no other commandment greater than these." God loves us. The Bible does not condemn homosexuality, nor does Jesus speak of homosexuals — the word 'homosexual' didn't even exist at that time." Tomás knows because he researched the origin of the word in both Hebrew and Greek. The original definition refers to prostitutes who harmed their neighbors with greed, lust, and slander.

"Well, if you won't listen to moral reason, then listen to science. Homosexuality is a serious problem - it's contagious. It's been proven by Dr. Rutherbor's tests."

Tomás isn't fooled because those who share this orientation know that it isn't some condition that can be caught like a disease. "It's something natural and normal in humans. It's present from birth and not a 'depravity' or 'malignance'. It isn't a choice — it's not something that *would be* chosen, due to the discrimination that we go through." Tomás tries his best to use it own experience to explain the truth of the matter to her.

"You're not born that way; it happens to you and it's possible that you were infected by it."

"But where I did get it from?" For Tomás, it sounds ridiculous.

"A large number of factors can contribute: neurological circuits, hormones, certain aspects of the family or culture. There is something wrong either physically or in the environment that causes homosexuality to take hold."

"That's why it's not necessarily a choice. May I ask the same question to you? When did you choose to be heterosexual?" Tomás wants to let her know how it feels like to be in his shoes.

At first, Dr. Claudia wasn't sure what to say. "I just always have been, but the difference is that *this* is natural."

"Well, I've always been like this — it came naturally for me, too. I never felt like I was doing something bad until I was exposed to the prejudices of others around me. What I'm saying is, that in the end, there are different religious and scientific theories about homosexuality, but it's something that belongs inside of us, is part of our process to get know ourselves, is a personal and private thing that should be respected." Tomás attempts to explain it one more time with physical examples, "It's like how I was born with different colored eyes or with my dark brown hair. See? And you look differently than me. You wouldn't judge someone based on the color of their skin, would you?"

Tomás is very disappointed by the people of his time because they hold on to that same mentality of the people in his notebooks — like the psychiatrists who analyzed homosexuals in an attempt to "cure" them of their "sickness", the religions who tried to convert them, the world leaders who denied them their rights, and the everyday people who abused, ignored, and discriminated against homosexuals out of ignorance. This is why he feels like it's his duty to act, to protect and help the community, so people like him don't give up, so they know they are not alone. This is why he's carrying his blue notebook, which compiles quotes, data, and reflections since he learned of the suicide of that young man, Christian Arroyo, almost three years ago.

He is positive and thinks with perseverance and patience he will be able to live in a time of changes — and not just him, but also the other young people who are hospitalized at the clinic. Tomás has always believed the cause of homosexuality is irrelevant — that none of these factors gives the right to discriminate or treat someone as "ill", "a sinner", or "crazy". For him, a homosexual is none of the above. They are simply human beings like anyone else, but with different feelings of attraction. He hopes that the day will come that he and his companions in this institution will be released and have the opportunity to love the people they want, regardless of sexual preference, religion, or race. Tomás imagines everyone living freely, but knows deep down that there is still a long way to go.

"Our time is up," warns the psychiatrist, looking at the clock on her wall, emotionally drained.

"You know very well that there is no cure," Tomás reminds her, getting up from the chair. "There is nothing wrong with us. We don't have a disease. Judging others is the real sin. When you do that, you demonstrate your lack of love and kindness for your neighbor, forcing many gay teens to commit suicide due to the lack of understanding."

"It's complicated," answers Dr. Claudia, turning so that her patient does not see the doubt drawn on her face. "I'll see you on Monday for your next sessions. Take your pills." She opens the door and Tomás steps out. Claudia breathes deeply, moved and exhausted. For the first time in her life, she feels an understanding towards the "sexual deviants", as she used to call them. She begins to question everything she has learned, even her beliefs. She brings her necklace up to her mouth, a crucified Jesus Christ, and closes her eyes. Two guards escort Tomás back to his room.

***

At midnight, the young man secretly leaves his room. As he walks, he feels a little pain in his rib and his left arm from the frequent physical abuse he receives from the guards every day. He walks to the chapel at the end of the long hallway of the sexual reorientation wing where he meets with the rest of patients.

This is the only room where patients can meet without being discovered so that they can interact, share, and support each other. Tomás tries to offer his fellow patients confidence and security so that they can relax and let go of those fears affecting their emotions and their minds. He knows that the "treatments" they receive only distort their identities and leave them marked with bruises — physical and mental. The others see Tomás not only as a support, but also as a mentor. There are twenty-three patients, including Tomás, with ages ranging from fourteen to twenty. They were admitted for their homosexuality and have been drained of all their self-esteem. But they aren't drained in there, not in that big room where they pray to God every morning. There, the patients can smile with relief and forget about the daily insults.

At twenty, Tomás is the oldest of all. He's only been at the clinic for two weeks while the others have been locked away in there for one to two years. "It's been a long time since they've seen their relatives or friends," thinks Tomás, for whom his own imprisonment is not a major concern; in fact, he feels that his priorities are the health and treatment of the others.

Tomás is very proud of his sexual orientation, happy to be different. He doesn't let Dr. Rutherbor and Dr. Claudia fool him. He is very mature, focused on helping those around him, and has the ability to calm down tense situations. He is a conventionally good-looking young man with a clear complexion. He is tall and toned, but his muscles have been atrophying gradually since he came to the clinic because the guards often deprive him of food. His oval face features well-defined pink lips. His penetrating gaze has the distinction of a blue color in his left eye and an amber color in the right eye. He sports a smooth haircut where his dark brown hair is longer on top and shorter on the sides, tousled lightly with bangs scattered against his forehead.

Many patients are attracted to Tomás but he does not get emotionally involved with any of them. His goal is to help them, to encourage them to believe in themselves, and to cope with the abuse of the security guards: Manuel, Víctor, José, and Harold, who act as the clinic's nurses. The young patients try at all costs to test the hypothesis of Dr. Rutherbor, who professes that homosexuality can indeed be cured.

The weekly routine in the sexual reorientation wing is to gather as a group in the chapel each morning to ask the Lord to cure them. In the afternoons they attend the sessions with Dr. Rutherbor and Dr. Claudia, who not only talk to them, but also prescribe them drugs and analyze them with a lie detector machine that is in another small, locked room within the chapel.

This reality is what both frustrates and gives strength to Tomás to fight for his new friends. In the short time he has been at the clinic, he has already seen too many atrocities: verbal and physical aggression, they have cut the hair off some patients, while others have been raped, and many are often handcuffed with their heads over the toilets, attached to a pipe, like the five patients who, at this moment, are being tortured in the five, locked "therapy" rooms. When the guards hit patients, they avoid hitting them on the face so as not to leave visible injuries incase their parents make one of their rare visits. This goes on from Monday through Friday without fail.

At night, the patients are subjected to more torture by the guards. They patrol the halls, looking for open doors and urinate on the patients, throw ice water over them as they sleep, force them to clean up the bathroom and the hallway, and forbid them to eat. The weekends are challenging because the clinic's professional staff is not in the building. This creates the opportunity for the patients to receive violent treatments all day long.

The combination of this abuse can easily cause an identity crisis that makes the young patients want to stop living. That is why some nights, in secret, Tomás meets them in the big room to give them encouragement and uplift their self-esteem, which has been trampled since they were admitted.

They feel protected by Tomás. He's like their rock, the only force that is left to sustain their pride and their self-acceptance. Everyone hates that idea that they can be "changed", an idea promoted by Dr. Rutherbor who manages the clinic for general addictions, but also for the other true objective of the place: to serve as a laboratory where they, the patients, are nothing more than guinea pigs that will serve to help the doctor prove his theory and be rewarded again in the scientific community. The doctors who work in the other areas of the clinic know about these violent "treatments", but are afraid to speak up as they receive constant threats from Dr. Rutherbor.

They know that the one who opens his mouth...will regret it.

Chapter THREE:

Grow And Live Normally? Part 1

THE CLINIC, GROW AND LIVE NORMALLY, WAS OPENED on Wednesday, May 13, 1953 as a public institution, but it went private with time and its new owner quickly expanded the small facilities. More areas were built on to the clinic and it became one of the biggest and most famous in the country — famous, most of all, for its treatment for drug and alcohol addiction and mental illness.

The main building has two floors. On the ground floor, there are twenty rooms, separated by a minimal distance. Each room has two beds, so the addictions area only has a capacity of forty people despite the huge demand. There are also five rooms set aside for the rotation of the twenty nurses that work there every day. On the same floor, at the end of a long hallway, is the cafeteria, which is basically a large kitchen where fifteen tables with six chairs each have been set.

The administrative area is on the second floor. It has ten offices: three for the psychiatrists, five for the doctors, a meeting room for all eight and, of course, the main office belonging to Dr. Rutherbor. He was born in 1929 in the United States and has been running the clinic for half of his life. He earned his PhD, specializing in addictions, then traveled to South America and on November 17, 1964 when he was able to transition this health center into a private religious clinic.

On Monday, October 16, 1967, he opened the new sexual reorientation wing, an experiment more than anything else. At the time, homosexuality was considered a disease worldwide and same-sex relationships were illegal in Ecuador. The clinic's claim of being able to cure this tendency grabbed ahold of the collective psyche and, most of all, the doctor's pockets. He openly loathes homosexuals.

Dr. Rutherbor will never forget his first patient in the sexual reorientation wing. Paul Gómez was introduced to the doctor by one of his former university students, Juliana Revas, his best pupil. He remembers that Paul begged him for help curing his homosexuality. He felt like he needed to change and that, at twenty-three, he wasn't happy. Paul was becoming violent, conflicted, and out of control.

Ten years later, Dr. Rutherbor announced to the media and the medical field that he cured homosexuality with his first and only case. The doctor was awarded, applauded, and revered by his colleagues at various ceremonies held in his honor. Paul instantly became the famous "ex-homosexual". The sexual reorientation wing was soon expanded to accept more patients thanks to the influx of funding. The parents of those suffering from sexual deviations began taking their sons and daughters to Grow And Live Normally by the dozen. They left their children in the lobby and didn't see them again for months at a time for two to three years. This translated to the institution consistently being filled with money as the parents paid up without asking many questions during their rare visits.

Monday, January 15, 1990

Because of the high demand and the influx of patients to the new wing, the clinic expanded even more and came to be what it is today. The most visible part, the addictions area, almost didn't change at all, but the sexual reorientation wing was radically transformed. Under Dr. Rutherbor's guidance, construction began to add twenty new rooms. One is the office of the psychiatrist, which is currently empty due to the strange disappearance of Dr. Claudia. Another room is the big chapel, used for morning prayers and by Tomás to gather the rest of the patients in the middle of the night in order to share and support each other in secret. There is another small locked room with a lie detector machine tucked inside. There are no real nurses, but the guards stay in a room with four beds — the same guards who violently abuse the "sexual deviants". There are five other locked rooms that serve as therapy rooms; that is, the rooms where the torture that Dr. Rutherbor calls "medical treatments" take place. Patients are randomly chosen and locked up, tied by their hands and feet, beaten, electrocuted, and humiliated. The other twelve rooms are the remaining dorms of the patients, each one with two beds; at the moment, there are twenty-three patients. They never leave the sexual reorientation wing with its big locked door and they never interact with the general addictions patients.

One month has gone by since that session with the psychiatrist, Dr. Claudia, in which Tomás refuted the biblical quotes she put forward. One month and two weeks since Tomás has been there and it has been insufferable. No one warned him that Dr. Rutherbor monitors all of the psychiatrists, recording all of their conversations and reviewing them each day. Dr. Rutherbor really didn't like what Tomás said that day and made sure that Tomás knew that he doesn't agree with the young man's interpretations of the Scripture. Since then, Tomás has received only one meal a day and has had double shifts in one of the five locked "therapy" rooms, handcuffed to a pipe over the toilet.

What has really terrified him is that, just before the New Year, Tomás secretly watched from his door as the guards carried out what looked like a lifeless body. A sheet covered the slight frame, but a lock of blonde hair was hanging from the side — the same hair color as Dr. Claudia.

Tomás wanted to believe that it was only his imagination, but since that day, no one has seen Dr. Claudia. That in itself is suspicious, yes, but it's even worse if one takes into account that this happened a few days after the disappearance of another patient, fifteen-year-old Bernardo. Tomás also saw what looked like Bernardo's body being taken from one of the therapy rooms by the guards. The official version from Dr. Rutherbor was that Bernardo had been partially "cured" and that he now was able to go back home.

Tomás hasn't told anyone about his suspicions, but it's inevitable to connect the dots: two deaths — disappearances, whatever one calls it. Tomás wants to investigate and rid himself of doubts. He has written about these fears in his blue notebook and tonight, as they gather in the meeting room, he begins to share these thoughts with his peers.

But something stops him: two sharp knocks on the chapel door. The occupants are completely still, paralyzed with fear. There's the sound of some keys and the knob starts to turn. Tomás tries his best to calm the others, knowing what to expect. The door opens and the guards enter, joined by Dr. Rutherbor.

"Good evening, Doctor," they all say together in a whisper, except for Tomás.

"Believe me, it's *not* a good evening," Dr. Rutherbor stares at Tomás. "And you, little bastard, this time you've really made things difficult for me. Now you're going to learn."

The guards move quickly to grab the patients and begin to hit them, not paying attention to which parts of their bodies they smash. They are all in a sea of tears, but not Tomás. He doesn't resort to violence, even in self-defense, but instead finds courage. "Leave us alone!" he finally shouts.

Dr. Rutherbor realizes that the young man has the blue notebook in his hands. He immediately knows that it's in there that Tomás keeps the notes and arguments that he has used in his sessions. He struggles with Tomás until one of the guards helps him finally take possession of the notebook. He slaps Tomás with the back of his hand, making sure that the ring on his finger hits the boy in the nose. Tomás's nose starts to bleed and Dr. Rutherbor hits him in the stomach, taking his breath away. Tomás loses consciousness.

"Listen to me," the doctor addresses the entire group. "Everything that's written here is a lie. Tomás wants to brainwash you. The truth is that he's a bad person, like most of you, who just want to destroy me and this clinic that I have built with my bare hands. But don't worry, from now on, that's all over."

Hours later, the young man opens just one eye and he already knows where he is, because he's surrounded by darkness. A light shines on his face, incandescent, burning his eyes. He tries to move, but he's tied to the bed with the straps that he knows quite well because he has visited "therapy" room number five several times before. He wants to cry, but he holds in the tears.

"Where are the others?"

"Don't worry, that's not your problem. The only thing that should concern you now is to get better. To… get… be‑tter."

"I'm not sick. You just want to toy with my mind." Tomás tries to loosen the straps, although he knows that it's impossible.

"No, no, no. This is not a game. Here you will get better for real, whether you want it or not. You know how it goes."

"Get out me of here! I'm not sick! I'm a hum—!"

"You are a freak! A medical abomination! Get it inside

your fucking head!"

At a signal from Dr. Rutherbor, the guards, Manuel, Víctor, José, and Harold, hold the young man down and open up his mouth. They shove in some pills: a cocktail of muscle relaxants, sleeping pills, and neuroleptics. Tomás sees from the corner of his eye that they're bringing in another machine — the electroshock machine that he hates so intensely. The guards, now acting as nurses, put on white gloves. The smell nauseates him — a mixture of new plastic and baby powder. Tomás already knows what's coming — his worst nightmare and his biggest fear, electric shocks.

Two guards extend his arms while a third looks for his vein. A pair of gloved hands suddenly appear behind him, massaging his temples with a freezing cold, thick, sticky liquid. Tomás trembles in fear.

"You see, this faggot thing actually comes from the mind," says the doctor, "That's why we're about to do a little work on your head, to take out…how can I put it, how can I put it…those demons, that evil that's inside of you."

A gloved hand places a tube under Tomás's tongue. He cannot resist any longer. His body is limp and he can't control his movements; that's the effect of the pills. He sees, but no longer feels, the needle penetrating his arm — the anesthesia. He sees, but as if from afar, a small red bulb in the electroshock machine. He sees, but it's blurry now, how they approach with the equipment and place it on his temples, then he sees nothing… Everything fades with a jolt.

Wednesday, January 17, 1990

Two days later, the young man awakes to an excruciating headache. As he opens first his amber-colored right eye, he sees a complete stranger standing in a white room with a smile on his face that Tomás can only interpret as…friendly.

There is something…something odd, something wrong. The man looks unfamiliar, yes, but Tomás also feels like he knows him. It's like the idea of that person has disappeared from his mind. But that's not weird enough what really makes him panic is that he, himself, has disappeared; that is, his concept of self. He can't remember anything — not what he has done throughout his life and not what has put him in the place that he is right now. He doesn't know himself. He doesn't even remember his name.

"Your name is Tomás Abel Díaz Bermeo," the stranger says to him, "And you have…well, you suffer from a disease. I'm in charge of your care."

"Who are you? What is this place?" the young man asks, not particularly afraid. Actually, he's almost emotionless; he doesn't realize that he's still under the effects of the psychotropic.

"Grow And Live Normally is the name of the rehab clinic in which you are a patient. I'm the owner, Dr. Ralph Rutherbor."

"Rehab? What…what do I have? And why can't I remember anything?"

"Well, those are two different questions. Yours is a condition that's known as homosexuality."

"Homo…?"

"Yes! Homosexuality is a kind of madness. An

imbalance. But it's worse than madness because it's not located only in people's brains, but there are certain germs that get inside the bodies of the effected. It's a horrible disease, but it's also a sin to act on it and also to spread it to others. Oh, it's quite complex." Dr. Rutherbor gives him the friendly look again. "It's better if you don't think about this right now. Stay calm. The memory loss is another topic. That's because you suffer from schizophrenia, a disease that causes all of your memories to get wiped out suddenly."

"Schizophrenia?"

"Yes, but I insist that you don't think about it right now."

"Yes...I can't remember a thing."

"Exactly. So relax —"

"But if I can't remember who I am, what things I used to do or anything...how am I going to cure myself from something I can't remember?"

"Close your eyes. Relax, It's all good now." Little by little the doctor's look is less friendly. "Now you have to take these pills."

When he sees the orange bottles where the medicine is kept, a memory comes to Tomás's mind: the odor of new plastic and baby powder. He doesn't know what it means and he simply accepts the blue pills that Dr. Rutherbor puts into his mouth. He is able to read "Prochlorperazine" on the label of the bottle.

"Sleep. You need to sleep. But don't worry - trust the treatment. You are going to get better." Dr. Rutherbor doesn't smile anymore. "With this medicine, we will treat your schizophrenia. Soon I will give you other pills to treat your homosexuality, as well. Just sleep. Sometimes you have these attacks. Last night you had one and that's why you are like this."

"And my parents?"

"Yes. They were the ones who brought you here. You see, homosexuality is something very serious that causes real problems If you don't get better...well, I don't think that they'll take you home, I don't think that you will be accepted in any university and I seriously doubt that you'll land a job."

"I don't know what you're talking about."

"Well, I do know. You just trust me."

The doctor and his "nurses" turn off the lights and leave the room. Tomás is left alone, in full darkness. What did Dr. Rutherbor mean with that homosexuality thing? What is that?

The medicine starts to work and Tomás falls asleep. The night is filled with strange dreams, in which masculine and feminine bodies dance in front of a red curtain. His emotions vary - they confuse him. He feels attracted to both of them. No...it can't be... Is this what the doctor was talking about? Is this a symptom of what he called "homosexuality"?

Friday, February 16, 1990

A month after this incident, Dr. Rutherbor appears in public with his glasses perched upon his big nose, sporting a goatee, and dressed in a formal white suit. He is always looking his best. He is mostly bald with wisps of white hair across the top of his head and above his ears. His skin is white but his round face is ruddy, a constant shade of red even without embarrassment or physical activity. His large stomach protrudes over the waist of his pants. He anxiously awaits the visit of his former student, Juliana Revas. He wants to ask her to be the new psychiatrist of the sexual reorientation wing, but the doctor also has his share of fears. He doesn't believe that she's going to want to accept his proposal. In the first place, because the other psychiatrists from the general addictions wing are a little hard on women, according to him. Secondly, because the absence of Dr. Claudia has become an out-loud-secret in the medical field and no one is going to want the infamy of being associated with such a thing.

Dr. Rutherbor isn't worried about that, though. He has most of the medical field and all of the country's politicians in his pocket. His name is so revered that no one wants to mess with someone so powerful - no one wants to mess with someone like him, that's for sure.

Juliana knocks softly at his door and Dr. Rutherbor greets her with the smile that he has mastered so well.

"Hello!" she, a youthful-looking forty-three-year-old, hugs him.

"Honey, how have you been?"

"Me? Very, very good. How have you been?"

"I'd lie to you if I told you I'm fine. You have no idea the stress I'm under."

"Why? What's happened?"

"I've been looking for a new psychiatrist for sexual reorientation for almost two months. Claudia...I don't know where Claudia is. She's not returning my calls and I can't find a replacement."

"I understand. It's not easy to handle this work environment. I don't blame her if she ran away," Juliana appears to be joking, but truly believes what she's saying.

"Some practitioners and some girls have come to ask for the job. But none of them are professionals and, most of all, I don't trust them like I trust you."

"You want to give me the job?"

"That's what this is about, yes. You see, homosexuality, sometimes, I think has a life of its own. It's an entity, a being that behaves, that reacts to specific events, that evolves like a virus."

Juliana's face reveals that she's not following the doctor's logic.

"Since I opened the clinic, or the reorientation wing, homosexuality has started to realize that we had a weapon to defeat it. That's why it doubled its efforts because, like all living things, it wants to survive. That explains why there are so many cases of homosexuals cropping up lately. That explains why even the best families have had to deal with these aberrations. Homosexuality is becoming harder to cure as well. This causes fewer successful cases in the clinic. Do you understand me?"

"Alright. Now I understand."

"I need you. The parents are losing their trust in this clinic, their trust in me. Homosexuality is the result of an unresolved trauma that causes the patients to suffer from gender confusion. No one is born like that. It is a condition that can and must be changed, as I did with Paul Gómez —

and it took me ten years to finally cure him! You trusted me to cure him and I did it! Now I need to trust in you. We must cure these kids to get back to our place at the top of the market. What do you say?"

"You know why I can't..." Juliana's smile disappears. She stares at the floor, as if thinking. "It would be impossible for me to be... No, the answer is no."

"The clinic's reputation will be ruined if you don't help me. I need you as our psychiatrist."

"I couldn't..."

Dr. Rutherbor loses his patience. "Are you okay with homosexuality? In this time that we haven't seen each other, did you...lose your course?"

"How can you say that? I'm a professional and you know very well what I think about homosexuality."

"Then, help me," begs Dr. Rutherbor, "Let's bring this project forward, together; we both have reasons for this clinic to survive..."

"I've never done it before; I've never handled that area. I've never even studied about homosexuality at university! I would have to buy textbooks about it..."

"Don't worry about it. I'll be by your side, advising you, and giving you the instructions on how to treat them and what to say them. I will be monitoring everything. You can come to me at any time with questions or doubts that you have." Dr. Rutherbor feels like she's already convinced. "You were always my best pupil, my favorite. That is not just by choice. It's because you're brilliant, because I always believed in you as a professional. Besides, it's not as difficult as it seems. The treatment actually consists of motivating the patients, in making them believe that they're able to achieve anything they set themselves to, with the help from the medicine and, of course, from God."

"Alright, alright," Juliana answers. "I accept."

Dr. Rutherbor erupts in a real smile.

"But tell me something, and tell me the truth. What really happened with Claudia?" Juliana feels there is something the doctor doesn't want to tell her. Dr. Rutherbor sighs, as if he's being forced to admit his lies and that, this time, he must tell her the truth.

"Claudia had an offer from a clinic in the United States. She left to live there."

"And what about her not answering your calls?"

"Well, honey...I had to convince you somehow." He laughs to break the tension and ease the nervousness that he feels coming from Juliana. She understands and, little by little, relaxes. She trusts her former teacher.

"That means it was all a setup for me to accept, huh?" she asks, radiant.

"Something like that."

The doctor gets up from the chair behind his desk and approaches Juliana to give her a hug. Juliana, although nervous about her new responsibilities in such an unfamiliar field, is happy.

Chapter FOUR:

The ex homosexual. Friday, February 16, 1990

"YOU MUST BE AWARE THAT NO ONE IS BORN WITH A homosexual orientation. I mean, it's not an orientation, it's a disorientation, a…let's say…a mistake."

Juliana nods.

"If we want to cure the disease, we must first focus on the main roadblock: depression. The patients feel rejected, misunderstood, and they are closed-off. They are rebellious and will block their hearts from us. That's why we must tell them what God say about the sin and what science says about the disease. So then they will understand that the only way to get out from that depression is to change, so in that way they will finally be accepted and have a better life," Rutherbor continues, while leading his new psychiatrist downstairs to the general addictions area.

"Alright. I understand. But that…mistake. How do we cure it?"

"With a mixture of two therapies as I did with Paul Gómez. For one thing, there is what we can call the physical treatment, consisting of pills that produce internal changes in the patients. But we must also work with the emotional aspect. We have to encourage the kids. We have to instill in them the spirit of initiative and the desire to achieve change, we have to convince them that they can achieve whatever they want."

"What about the spiritual aspect?"

"Well, it's very important. But, you see, we used to put more emphasis on that. We forced — we gathered — the kids every afternoon to pray and ask God to cure them, but that turned out to be a bit... How do I put it? The kids were just waiting for prayer to cure them. Now we talk to them about religion so that they understand that this isn't just a disease, but that it also leads to terrible sins. You need to talk to them about God, so that they have faith that they will be healed, but we also let them know that the hard work is their responsibility."

"Help yourself and I will help you," Juliana quotes the biblical principle, almost to herself.

"Exactly."

Juliana is excited to work for the clinic of her former teacher, it's an honor for her because she admires and respects him a lot, especially because she considers it a miracle that he was able to cure her college friend, Paul Gómez. Dr. Rutherbor and Juliana pass through the door with the big lock and enter the sexual reorientation wing. Five female nurses are attending different patients in their respective rooms, which look comfortable given the circumstances, of course. Any doubts that she could have had about her teacher and his healing techniques disappear and she trusts him completely.

"How many kids are currently in this area?"

"Ten, not counting Tomás, who I reserve as my own patient. And in one week, we'll have one more."

"Do I have to treat eleven patients?" she asks nervously.

"Don't worry. They will get better and then there won't be eleven."

They stop in front of room eight.

"Here's Tomás." The doctor gestures towards a closed door.

Juliana places her hand gently on the steel frame.

"And how is he?"

"Since I diagnosed him with schizophrenia, I've had to work with him a lot. We still have to treat him. Progress does not have a specific time frame."

"Alright. I understand. And those rooms?" she asks, confused by the five unnumbered doors.

"They're storage rooms. That's where we keep the old inventories of the clinic," lies Dr. Rutherbor.

They walk through the big room that used to be the chapel and enter to another small room. "Is this the lie detector that you mentioned?" asks Juliana, pointing to a device that is widely used by criminal and judicial authorities, and more recently, by psychologists and psychiatrists in rehabilitation centers.

"Yes, we used that machine with Dr. Claudia for reparative therapy."

"Does it work to diagnose changes in people's sexual orientation?"

"Yes, with the information it provides us on the vital signs and body functions of the patients. When we ask them questions, we can better visualize their anxieties, check their blood pressure, heart rate, etc. and that helps us to read physical reactions to one sex or the other. Do you know what I mean?"

"With images? I mean, you show them images and then see how they react?"

"Yes, and also videos...you know, nudity. But it's better to apply this treatment when the patients who have been in therapy for at least a month — that way you'll get better results."

"Alright, I understand," she nods, much more nervous than before because she has no experience with any of this.

"But it's never easy, dear. These processes are long and the kids are slow to heal. As you know, Paul took me ten years to heal. I want you to always keep this in mind - patience will be your greatest virtue so never give up."

"I won't, Doctor. I have treated many children with bipolar disorder and many manic-depressives at North Clinic. I know they take a long time to heal." Juliana looks around and feels like the room and its atmosphere feel impersonal. "Do I always have to come here for the therapies?"

"No, my dear, we'll take the machine upstairs to your office," Dr. Rutherbor answers. In fact, his plan is to move her upstairs to the administration offices and far from the sexual reorientation wing to avoid the same problem as with Dr. Claudia.

"Alright. That's better."

The sexual reorientation wing has changed a lot since that night one month ago when Dr. Rutherbor decided to remove the previous twenty-two patients to avoid suspicion and to temporarily smooth things over. Everything has changed — even the treatments and rules of conduct. In the redesigned clinic, the patients can interact outside of their assigned sexual rehabilitation area only at lunchtime in the main cafeteria. They can visit each other freely in rooms; however, it is forbidden for two patients of the same sex to be alone in the same room with the door closed, despite the nurses each having copies of the keys for each door. That's another detail: the guards are gone. Instead there are five nurses working there every morning and afternoon, plus a rotation system that keeps one nurse in the clinic every night. Two of the former guards, José and Harold, keep an eye on the clinic, but now from the outside, like a proper security detail.

There are no longer two beds in the rooms. Now only one patient sleeps in each room. The "therapy" rooms are now largely used as storage rooms, as Dr. Rutherbor told Juliana. The hallways of the sexual reorientation wing, once dirty and putrid, are now clean and bright. Only one thing remains the same: the rule about visits from relatives, which are forbidden unless specifically approved by Dr. Rutherbor.

Juliana leaves the clinic, saying goodbye to the guards. She's a mix of emotions on the inside. She is afraid, but happy. One of her dreams is finally coming true and she doesn't know if she's ready for it. They say success is the meeting of preparation and opportunity, but is she ready for such strong emotions? She spots a phone booth near the clinic and walks over to call her husband.

"Honey?"

"Yes," he answers, somewhat curtly.

"The job is mine. Dr. Rutherbor wants me to replace Claudia and to work here until 3 o'clock. In the evenings, I'll still work at North Clinic. Don't you like the idea? I'm so happy."

"How can I not like it?" he asks sarcastically. "At last, you will heal those perverts. But watch out! They may spread something to you!"

She feels nervous and is reminded how much this behavior annoys her. "Relax. Wait for me to have dinner together and then I'll explain it better. I have to rush to the other clinic right now. I...I love you."

She hangs up without actually feeling her last words. That cold, macho attitude stresses her out. She begins to open the door of her car, but she startled by a noise at her backside. She turns and senses that there is someone spying on her from behind a bush. "Who's there?" she asks, defiantly.

Nothing. Nothing moves.

"I asked who's there!"

She walks slowly to the bush, without taking her eyes off it, so that the individual cannot run away.

Something touches her shoulder.

"Aaah!" Panicked, Juliana jumps and turns to face a...a lady?

"I'm sorry. I didn't mean to frighten you like that," the stranger apologizes.

"Oh, but you gave me such a scare!" Juliana's fright is replaced with a big laugh; she laughs so much that she struggles to breathe.

"Are you ok? I swear that wasn't my intention."

"Don't worry, ma'am. I'm fine. I'm fine. How can I help you?"

"Do you work at this clinic?"

"Well, you could say that. I'm new, yes."

"Oh. It's just that…I don't know. I don't know who to turn to, who to ask for help."

"Tell me, tell me. What happened?"

"It's my son, Mateo. He has that…you know…that sin. He has the devil inside of him."

"Yes, yes. I think I understand you."

"I need your help. Cure him for me, please. I'm so desperate. He tried to kill himself last night. He is very young, cute, and clever. It's not fair that this happened to him." She starts to cry.

"Ma'am, what is your name?"

"Charol Feirro."

"Alright, Charol, calm down. Don't worry, there is still hope."

"Can I bring him tomorrow?"

"No, I'm sorry, but I will be here early next Monday."

"And I can't bring him right now?" she begs, desperate.

"Well, I won't be there. Right now I have to go to my other office. I'm going to be late."

"I understand."

Juliana reaches inside her purse.

"Here. This is my business card."

Charol reads 'Juliana Revas, Professional Psychiatrist' and a phone number on the card. "Thank you. I'll call you

Monday then. But tell me - is it true that they heal? They go back to normal?"

Juliana looks into Charol's eyes, with her mouth open and ready to respond, but the word she is looking for is not there.

"Juliana!"

A voice takes her out of her haze, familiar, from antiquity. She turns to see her college friend, Paul Gómez, approaching. She shrugs an apology at Charol and walks toward Paul.

"Paul! What a pleasure. What are you doing here?"

"Juliana, long time no see! Well, I come to help with the patients. You see, I talk to them about...about this disease. I speak about the experience of being healed."

Charol's brown eyes widen behind her thin glasses. "They really cured you in there?"

"Yes, I think so." Paul laughs in an exaggerated manner. "I once was lost, but now am found. Was gay, but now I'm straight."

To Charol, this is like witnessing a miracle and she hugs Juliana.

"Thank you, ma'am, thank you. I hope you can fix my Mateo."

"Trust me, Charol. We will definitely cure your son," says Juliana.

Charol says goodbye and leaves, on the verge of tears of joy.

"Paul, it's been so long. Give me your number or your address. I'm sorry, but I have to be at the other clinic in a half an hour."

"Ok, let me take you out to lunch to catch up. What time are you free on Monday?"

"At three."

"I'll pick you up at three then. Where will you be?"

"Here. Starting on Monday I will work with Dr. Rutherbor."

"Really? Congratulations!"

"Thank you. And what about your wife and your daughter? How are they doing?"

"Well, my wife is not working right now. Paulita is in her last year of elementary school."

Paul leans in to kiss her goodbye on the cheek and Juliana sees two things: Paul's hands are covered in dirt and a camera hangs from the open bag that he carries. She easily makes the connection.

"Paul, what happened?"

"Oh, nothing. I fell earlier." He wipes his hands on his pants, laughing nervously. "It was embarrassing, but not serious."

"Alright. You have to be careful. More than anything - for the camera. You could break it."

Paul feels exposed and adjusts the camera in his bag.

"Are you still teaching those photography classes?"

"Yes, I love them. I'll never quit. And tell me, were you just hired today? You told me you start on Monday?"

"Yes, I start on Monday, but right now I have to go, really. Meet me here at three then."

She gets into her car, puts on her sunglasses, and starts the engine. She's a storm of thoughts: first her meeting with the doctor, that call to her husband, Charol, then Paul. She drives away, without looking back at Paul, who doesn't take his eyes off her while she leaves.

Paul Gómez is forty-five years old, tall and slim. He has an olive complexion with short chocolate brown hair, attractive black eyes, and a constant smirk on his round face. He lives with his wife and his twelve-year-old daughter, and the only work he does is teaching a photography class and giving lectures at Grow And Live Normally.

"Paul! Paul, how have you been?" Dr. Rutherbor greets him anxiously, walking down the stairs.

"Hello, Doctor. Fine, and you?" They hug, making sure that all of the nearby employees and nurses see them.

"Let's go to my office," Dr. Rutherbor invites Paul, putting a hand on his shoulder.

They walk up the stairs, enter the doctor's office, and close the door behind them. At that moment, the gentleness gives way to a tense atmosphere between the two. The disguise disappears.

"Why Juliana?" asks Paul, obviously annoyed.

"I had no choice, Paul."

"Her life is in danger working here."

"But every day I get calls from the relatives of these kids. What do you want me to do?" The doctor falls down into his desk chair, tired, as he waits for Paul's approval. "I'm too old to deal with so many people."

"Couldn't you hire just anyone? Pretend? Like you have always done..."

"No! I cannot keep taking risks with the clinic," answers Dr. Rutherbor, beginning to get upset.

"I told you those plans of yours were a risk in and of

themselves. You made your bed now lie in it, but don't get her involved."

"People are already suspecting that the famous 'cure' is more a product of advertising than anything else. I had to do something, move fast. I don't know. It's getting more difficult to cure them all, but still, you're my living proof that curing them is possible. I'm not up for these tasks anymore. It's been a difficult eleven years since I opened the sexual reorientation wing to new patients. Only a few have passed the lie detector, but hardly any time passes before they are caught having those disgusting thoughts again. Some of the parents were even coming to take the patients after only two or three years of being here without being cured! At least most of them took my advice to send their children outside of the country to other anti-gay centers as the next step in curing them. I try to explain to them that it takes years and even a decade to cure them as it did with you. If I didn't start making changes, everything would have crumbled, believe me. Everything is going well now. Look at you and how far we have come!"

"You should have left the other patients here. Now everything is going to look strange. People are going to start asking where that Catholic center is."

"It all got out of control with Claudia. She turned out to be a traitor. And, also, the case of Bernardo, and that Tomás who thought that he was such a big deal. We had to put him in his proper place. Everybody was getting suspicious so we had to get rid of the evidence. But now everything's fine, trust me."

"Have the family members of the previous twenty-two patients contacted you?"

"Yes."

"And what have you told them?"

"That I could still not cure them. That the next step is to send them in anti-gay centers outside of the country or to move them to the Catholic center to receive new treatments."

"How is going there?"

"Fine. They were all admitted there without any problem."

Paul is relieved. He hates loose ends.

"Yes, but Tomás is still a problem. We need to keep an eye on him. We don't want him to get his memory back and cause another fuss. We have to leave him here. He still believes that he suffers from schizophrenia so we just have to make sure he continues to take his daily pills that prevent him from recovering his memory."

"Has anyone else come here asking for their children?"

"Some...but luckily they fell for the same story. They trust me and don't want their children to return to their homes if they aren't completely cured. They explicitly told me that they do not want — and I quote — 'sexual deviants' at home. Please, there's no need to pressure me."

"I'm not pressuring you. The One above, He pressures you," Paul points up, referring to God.

The doctor understands. He slowly gets up from the chair with a heavy body.

"Let's go. You have to give that lecture."

They leave the office, walk downstairs and go straight to the sexual reorientation wing where eleven young patients are in the former chapel waiting to hear the special guest speak.

"Hello, everyone, my name is Paul Gómez, I'm forty-five years old and I'm an ex-homosexual."

They all murmur a greeting in return. Tomás, among those present, feels something strange about Paul, something that makes him mistrust this "ex-homosexual".

"I remember that, when I was twenty-three years old, I felt different from everyone else. The word that would describe me was...weird. To think about heterosexuality disgusted me. I was attracted to people of the same sex. An emotional need steered me towards them, but...but then I realized that what I was doing was wrong. I saw and felt that I was making my family suffer. I wasn't giving them any happiness. I was selfish. I could not let them down. I had an internal struggle. I was imperfect and empty and I suffered a lot on the inside, in my soul. My homosexual stage was very sad. I fell into a depression that made me think what is the best, not only for everyone, but also for me, for my future? And the answer was to be normal. To grow and be normal, for me, became a matter of life and death. And I chose life."

As he talks, the patients listen attentively, some of them even feeling inspired by his story. But Tomás still doesn't trust him. He doesn't know why. Something tells him that not only is this story false, but also Paul is not who he claims to be.

"My only defense is the fact that I didn't choose to be attracted to people of the same sex, like many do, because I knew that I had a disease, a temptation that got a hold of me and controlled me. I chose to not succumb to it. I made a decision," he pauses, takes a sip of water and continues. "I came to Dr. Rutherbor on my own." He points to the doctor, proudly. "Thanks to him, I was able change, to heal the wounds and traumas that made me a homosexual. After ten years of his treatments, therapies, and medicine, I could go back to my true sexual orientation and I was happily cured. Now I'm free from guilt, pain, and sin. I can be a happy and healthy person. I was able to grow to be a normal person. I met my wife, who I love and together we have a twelve-year-old daughter. I live a life that's full and I have a future in front of me. That's going to happen to you, just do your part and let the doctor help you. Meet his conditions, and take every pill he gives you. Believe me, he will be able to cure you. Do not fear and never doubt. It is possible to stop being a homosexual."

He finishes his introductory speech and gets ready to start his lesson. He takes out his notes and leaves them on a table. He sets a big poster board against the blackboard. Tomás, still incredulous, feels someone grab his hand. He turns to see Sandra sitting beside him. He doesn't know how to react and decides to let her do it. He thinks maybe she needs support. He checks the entire room, the faces of all his peers, to get a sense those who agree with what the speaker says. Everyone seems to agree, except for two patients: Patricio, a seventeen year old, who tends to dress as women, and one more patient, sixteen-year-old Julio, whose dream is to be "Julia" and to get an operation and change his sex to that of a woman, a transsexual. The two of them seem to share the doubts Tomás has regarding the speech.

"What is homosexuality?" Paul asks the patients in

his audience, pointing to a picture on the poster board. "It is a sexual deviation, a disease, that is caused in humans by many factors, but it's not present from birth, so it can be changed."

Tomás is beginning to be bothered by this guy, to really dislike him; he thinks he is a fake.

"Among these factors are the divorces of parents, the absence of one parent in the family or in the growth of their children, or overprotection. Believe me, these types of trauma can cause this disease to take hold on your body and soul. Have any of you been through any of these?"

All the children and young people in the group look at each other and nod, except for Tomás, who is worried that his words will influence his companions. What this guy is saying seems absurd and ridiculous to him.

"But it is not only the parents' fault, no. That's why we have to be strong and not change our *true* selves because of these external circumstances that influence us. Another instigator is shyness and inability to socialize with others, especially with women. Am I right or not?" he asks, with the intention of lifting the mood of the room and to encourage the patients to interact with him. They don't respond. "See? You have to do your part, give your greatest effort to change. It not only depends on Dr. Rutherbor, but also on you. Anyway, putting aside these reasons, there is one that stands above all the rest put together, to avoid God's punishment!" he yells crazily. "God created a woman and a man with the purpose of procreation and as an example of the union that has to exist between human beings. That's how He defined it thousands of years ago — not a man with a man! This is why homosexuality is unnatural and sinful in His eyes. We must eliminate these trends. This disease of our sexuality is destructive!" He raises his voice, warning them, "If you do not believe me, read about the wrath of God that is HIV, AIDS. This is God's punishment for perverts who do not repent and do not want to be cured. You must heal to save yourselves from that terrible suffering and death."

The patients are already scared. Dr. Rutherbor, from the back of the room, wrinkles his face in a smile. "It's all good. Everything is under control," he thinks. The patients are already convinced. The first step has been taken. He does not want to remember the recent times, when his reputation as a doctor was almost ruined. He watches Tomás and does not like what he sees - the young man doesn't seem to be falling for it. But it can't be, it's just the doctor's imagination. Tomás does not even remember who he is.

Tomás, on the other hand, does not know why this whole situation seems so familiar. He remembers almost nothing of his past, but he has an indescribable feeling, like déjà vu. He knows that what Mr. Gómez is saying is a lie because, since the day he woke up without remembering who he is, the only feeling and piece of his identity he recovered in time, is his sexual orientation. This is something that he knows is a part of what makes him who he is as a human being, but he still has to find the other pieces so he takes his pills, even though they make him drowsy. He trusts Dr.

Rutherbor, but doesn't trust Paul Gómez.

Tomás has this desire to prove his case with arguments, to back his claims up based on analysis and study, not with myths or unfounded fears. He does not give up. He does not have to renounce his sexual identity.

Chapter FIVE:

The second encounter. Sunday, February 25, 1990

ONE WEEK LATER, A CAR IS PARKED IN FRONT OF THE main gate of Grow And Live Normally.

"Darling, relax, everything will be fine."

It's seems like a cheerful night. For any other resident of the capital, it is just another busy Sunday full of tourists, which is when businesses thrive and money enters like a shot of encouragement to face the next week.

"Now, don't cry. He's the best doctor. He is very, very good. You'll see."

Ana, the boy's mother, grabs his hand, with tenderness.

"It's going to be very good for you. This clinic is recommended in all of South America."

The boy lets go of her hand and gazes at the mountainside drawn on the horizon, lit only by the moon. He doesn't know why, but Sebastián is under the impression that…no, he doesn't want to think in absolutes, no, it's not a final goodbye.

"It's just for a little while. It's like a blink. You won't even feel the days go by."

He is a local, of course, but, for the first time, he puts himself on the side of the tourists. It's like a veil has been taken off his eyes. Now he understands the phrase "You don't know what you've got 'til it's gone". That moon? The mountains? No, it's not the last time.

"I'm going to visit as soon as possible. At first, as I understand, the doctor does not like relatives to come very often. It interferes with the treatment, he says. But don't worry, that's just at the beginning."

It's too late to realize it, yes, but now he really appreciates the city, he misses it and he hasn't even entered the clinic yet. He still hasn't crossed that door, that point of no return, but he already misses the capital. He doesn't feel it's "his" city anymore.

The tears slide into his mouth. He licks his lips and the salty taste takes him out of his daydream. He turns his head and stares through the window at the black metal door, the portal to the other world.

"Sebas, don't be like that… Look at me, talk to me, say something."

He continues to ignore her. He now realizes he has always been on the side of the tourists. How could he have forgotten! The city receives you as its own, makes you feel like you belong to it. That's why he had forgotten that not so long ago, he arrived there to study art at the university. At first, he had the financial help of his parents, who accepted his trip with the hope that the new environment would it would lift his emotional state and ease his chronic depression. He always thought he would have time to get to know the capital — that he should not have to hurry, that with patience he would have gotten to know it all.

"You're being unfair. All this is for you. It's the best for you."

He always thought that he would have more time with the city, time to know it all, to find out more about its labyrinths, its legends, its museums and libraries. He understands its everydayness, the sounds of the buses in the mornings. Not only the public transportation, but also the buses that arrive from other parts of the country or from the entire continent, full of sleepy tourists from the long ride that must have lasted all morning. And the sounds of the evenings, in silence, it sounds contradictory, but that's how the capital is. It's a silent noise, a howling of a cold wind that doesn't annoy him because the city where he was born is sunny and hot, which doesn't suit his personality very well. Yes, if he has to choose, he chooses the capital. He finds it cozier.

"Well, let's go. Don't make this harder."

Sebastián avoids his mother's eyes, disappointed.

"This is best for you, trust me."

"Nothing in this world will be good for me," he says softly and slowly, feeling abysmally alone.

"Actually, it's true. You are absolutely right. Nothing, but nothing will be good with that lifestyle you choose. If you continue to live in sin, you will never be happy. Here you will have the chance to live normally — you'll be perfect!"

"No one is perfect..." Sebastián uses his asthma inhaler, drowning in his desire to cry.

"I don't doubt that you will be much better than you are now. Look at you!" His mother loses her patience.

"I don't believe that and I've already told you, it's not a sin what I am or what I do. Do not forget that I was happy once."

"Oh, Sebas, again with the same song? It's been three years. Get over it! In fact, take this as an opportunity. Take the fact that he died as an opportunity to change your life. Have you ever stopped to think that perhaps the death — that boy's disappearance from your life — was a gift from heaven? Maybe God wanted him to disappear so you could be...normal."

"I don't want to talk about it. Just leave me alone. Leave me by myself."

His mother gets out of the car and walks to the trunk to get Sebastián's luggage. He is still sitting in the passenger seat, staring at the black metal door of the clinic. She takes the luggage out and stands next to the window. She opens the car door.

"We love you, darling, but you leave us no other option. You're not aware that you have a psychological problem. I know we raised you badly, but that's why your father and I want —"

"Since when do you agree with my father on something?"

"When it comes to your own good, of course. And this, believe me, is for your own good," his mother points to the clinic door and smiles. "It was our fault that you're like this. That's why we want to fix you. Don't be unfair."

"But it's my life. It's who I am!"

"That's what the doctor said you were going to say — exactly that! You don't realize it, but you have all the symptoms of that...that filth!"

Ana is honest in what she says. She really believes what they've put in her mind. Three years have passed since Christian killed himself and her son is still reeling from the blow. In fact, she feels that he is gradually getting worse, falling again into a depression, but this time without an end.

"Putting me into this clinic is not the solution. You'll only depress me more. My sadness has nothing to do with my sexual orientation. The only thing is that...is that...I miss him. It's a burden that —"

"Don't even mention him! That's the first step, according to Dr. Rutherbor. Not mentioning him will help you forget him."

Sebastián puts his inhaler back into his mouth. His mother gestures at him to get out of the car. "Let go, once and for all. You have to move on."

"Mom, please, don't put me in there. Stay by my side and help me move on."

"I'm sorry, darling, but it's a matter of life or death. Your father and I have tried everything to straighten you out and Dr. Rutherbor said that what is needed is for you is to be under constant observation. Work with me here."

"How long will you leave me in there?"

"That will be the doctor's decision, darling. There are professionals who can help you and the treatment costs a lot of money, so I hope you take advantage of it."

"I don't know. I don't trust that doctor."

"He will help you and you're going to live like everyone

does in the path of God!" His mother raises her voice a little to remind him once again.

"Nobody *lives*. We're all just surviving and dying each passing day." His voice is just a whisper, like he's trying to remind himself, as a tear slowly drops down his cheek.

"I don't understand why you do this to us. We want a family — grandchildren. Why don't you want to make us happy?"

Once again, Ana means what she says. She is resentful and concerned. In her mind, there are no more options. She carries her son's bags, walks to the gate, and knocks three times.

"It is not about you, it's about *my* happiness," says Sebastián from the car, in an act of courage because he knows that his time is short. He takes the opportunity to look at the mountains and the moon, perhaps for the last time.

His mother knocks again and one of the security guards, Harold, opens the door. From the car, Sebastián sees the two of them talking. She points at him and says something, not very happy. Is this when it gets violent? The guard turns around and enters the clinic. Not much time goes by, not even a full minute, before Sebastián sees a figure in white coming out with the guard. This must be the doctor everyone talks about. The figure in white smiles and walks towards him.

"Good evening, Sebastián. It's okay. Don't be afraid, there is nothing to fear." Dr. Rutherbor smiles "Come in. This will be your home…" the doctor's pause terrifies Sebastián, "for a while, of course."

The young man assesses his options. There is no escape. He has no choice but to get out of the car. His mother seems to worship Dr. Rutherbor and Sebastián does not understand why. The doctor doesn't seem nice, at all.

"Excuse us for the delay, Doctor" she says "I don't usually come to the northeast of Quito, it's too far away from the center of the city."

The city! He has to see it one last time. *No, not for the last time.* He's very confused. Maybe the others are right and he is wrong.

Now he's nothing more than a visitor. He was passing through the world, nothing more, and his time is up. Now it's his turn to leave, to say goodbye to the capital, to the labyrinths and legends, to the mountains, to the moon, to the stars.

He walks under the frame of the door and a thick shadow falls on his shoulders. He takes a look around and observes the clinic. Everything looks so new, so clean and bright. It looks like a mansion with many rooms and a large, imposing staircase in the center.

"It's so nice to meet you," Dr. Rutherbor greets him as if he were speaking to a small child. "I hope you know why you're here. It's because we care about you, because your mom and dad love you and want to help you improve your life. How old are you? Eighteen? You are in the prime of youth; you have so much ahead —"

"I'm twenty-one," interrupts the boy.

"Really? But you look younger. Don't waste the opportunity you are been given."

"I told him the same thing," Ana interrupts. "He

came here to the capital two months ago to study." She says this last part almost in a whisper, as if sharing a secret that shames her. "Art, just imagine that. He came here with our financial support until he found an office job. My husband and I thought it would be a good change for him, to be in a new environment, but we were wrong; two weeks ago, that awful thing that I told you about happened and —"

"Don't worry. I'll take care of him, I'll fix him."

"Fix me?" asks Sebastián, indignant.

"It's okay. That's what you need" The doctor moves his fingers, as if calling someone. "Right now you should rest because we'll start early in the morning. The nurse will take you to your room. You'll see that it is quite comfortable and clean. You have nothing to fear."

A nurse, Verónica, answers Dr. Rutherbor's call and pats Sebastián's head, gently. He re-evaluates his options and has no choice but to follow her. He leaves without saying goodbye to his mother, without even looking at her, disappointed.

"Doctor, excuse my son's behavior," Ana says once Sebastián disappears down the hallway. "Lately he's been like that, like he's blocked and I can't reach into his heart. Oh, I don't know…"

"Do not worry, ma'am. It's normal. The boy has a chronic depression. It cannot be expected that he would act otherwise."

"And how long are we talking about? Tell me the truth."

"At this point I cannot say for sure. I must do a lot of evaluations. But it may be a year, or months, or weeks at best."

Ana pulls something out of her purse. "Here is his admission consent form. It took a lot to convince him to sign it. And here is the first check; we'll do the rest with transfers, as we agreed, right?"

"Thank you. And yes, I'll wait for your transfers at each month's end. Remember that the money is for food and medicine for your son. We have almost no profits here; everything is sacrificed for the greater good."

"Oh, Doctor, you are divine. You have a huge heart."

"Thank you, and you know that you cannot come to visit Sebastián unless I authorize it. If you need to contact the clinic for any reason, you have the number of my office and my home. I'm always there at night. Remember - just speak with me, no one else. That is the procedure in such cases that are...special."

"Don't worry." Ana says goodbye with a kiss and a hug. She leaves the clinic with a knot in her chest — a mixture of sadness, anxiety, anguish. But she must be strong. She knows that she did the best thing. She's convinced. She has to trust her instincts.

Turning down another hallway, Verónica and Sebastián come to a door with a large lock. The nurse takes out a little key and introduces him to the world in which he will be locked. "Sexual Reorientation Wing" reads a sign, which makes him feel like he's in a prison from where he will never escape without losing his soul, or perhaps in a laboratory where he's the guinea pig. As soon as Sebastián is alone in his room, he bursts into tears. He has to use his inhaler many times so that he doesn't have a full-blown asthma attack. He bites his fingers to drown his moaning so that he doesn't draw the nurse's attention, or whoever else is out there.

He opens his bags and looks for his drawings and his photo album, his eternal companions. He hugs them tightly. He scans his room: a bed, a window with bars, a night table, bars, a clock that looks new and has the eyes of an owl, bars, dim light which will not allow for drawing at night, bars, and more bars. He strokes his photo album, which has an old and worn-out sticker on the cover that says "Chris and Sebas". He doesn't open it. He just holds it there, embracing it, as if it were he, as if it were Christi— "Don't mention him! Remember what your mother told you," his own mind tells him. "It's worse if you say his name."

Three years. Three years have passed since he decided to leave. Three years in which the same thought haunts Sebastián and keeps him awake, but maybe it's not a thought, maybe it's his spirit. Maybe it's the lost soul of...

"Don't say his name! Of...Christian! There it is! I said it! I said it and...nothing happened. I wasn't struck by lightning or anything." Sebastián walks to the barred window. He sees the moon lighting up the profile of the mountains and feels happy - happy because he hasn't lost them, because they won't be able to take that away from him. They won't be able to...

His mind is full of memories.

Friday, January 19, 1990

It's been a really busy first week for Sebastián at his new

publishing assistant job. He does everything his editor-in-chief has delegated to him in the hope that he will one day be able to work on the cover art for books. Classes have also started a week ago so the little time Sebastián has left before bed is dedicated to his drawing.

He finally has time to have a little social life and to try to meet a new friend, a gay friend, he hopes. Actually, he never had gay friend, only Christian, and it's so difficult for him to be himself with his university classmates. He's tired of pretending to be someone he's not whenever someone asks him if he has a girlfriend or asks him to comment on the girls in his class. He's disappointed and tired of trying to act "normal" — to act straight. It's not easy to come out as gay in a Roman Catholic society.

One night, as he is walking to the store, he saw one of those illicit gay bars he had heard about before he moved to the city. Such clubs are, of course, illegal, but some police officers look the other way at night in exchange for money. Sebastián is not used to going out to gay bars, much less alone. He can't even ask his roommates, his cousins, to go with him. He hasn't told any of them that he is gay because his mother prohibited him from embarrassing her, although they all secretly suspect it.

On this night, he decides to finally go to the club by himself. Sebastián is leaning against a wall, next to a small table, having a drink. He hates the smoke and his body is not used to it and he wants to avoid an asthma attack and ruin the party. But he has to admit that he does feel better; he still thinks of Christian, but the feeling is not so negative anymore. In fact, it feels good to have a fresh start in a new city. He has a job, he is no longer financially dependent on his parents, and he is studying what he has wanted to do since childhood and has always been forced to do only as a hobby: to become a great artist, drawing nature, portraits of people, everything his eyes can see. Now he is waiting for someone somewhere that could be like... Chris, but he was unique, he was the best Sebastián ever had. Sebastián thinks while he drinks and glances around. He sees three men kissing each other, a group at a table snorting cocaine; on his left is the place they call the "dark room", where people go for sexual acts. The couple that just walked into the bathroom is obviously up to no good. He begins to realize the reality that surrounds him: a world of promiscuity.

"Hello, are you in line?" someone asks him. He turns around.

"No, I'm not in —" Sebastián is pulled from his thoughts and realizes that he is standing next to the bathroom. "No, I'm just looking around. I'm not standing in line."

"Sorry, I thought you were. Hey, do I know you?"

"No, I don't think we know each other..."

"Are you new here? I don't know why, but I think I've seen you before. Hello, my name is Gustavo."

"Sebastián," he returns the greeting, shaking hands. "And yes, I'm new. I just arrived in the capital. This is my first time in 'Heaven.'"

"Well, there are better clubs here. It's a big city. Let's be friends."

Sebastián smiles and is happy to finally make a new friend.

"You're cute." Gustavo get closer, flirting with Sebastián.

Sebastián is confused and uncomfortable. Gustavo approaches him, grabs him by the waist and is about to give him a kiss on the mouth. Sebastián doesn't like his forwardness and pushes him away gently, trying not to offend him.

"Sorry, no. I don't want to."

"But you seem very nice."

"It's just that I don't want to. It's nothing personal."

"You think I'm ugly or something?"

"No, it's not that. The truth is I'm not ready to date or even flirt with someone… I'm just here to make friends."

"Oh come on, in a gay club you will never find a new friend." He grabs Sebastián's neck to give him a kiss.

"Hey! Get out of here!" A tall young boy grabs Gustavo by the arm and pushes him away from Sebastián.

Gustavo's face transforms with fear before he walks away.

"Hello, cutie." The boy greets Sebastián formally with a handshake, but he can't help but give an innocent wink of his brown eyes, calling Sebastián's attention to his lovely little smile. Sebastián is instantly interested in getting to know him and befriend him.

"Thank you for helping me." Sebastián doesn't know what else to say; he is clearly shy when he likes someone, but he at least tries to be friendly.

"You're welcome. My name is Alejandro. What's yours?"

"Nice to meet you. My name is Sebastián. Where are you from? You don't look like you're from here."

"I'm from Spain, but my mother is from here. After my parents' divorce last year, I came to live with her." He takes a cigarette, lights it, and blows an impressive smoke circle.

Sebastián begins to cough, forcing him to use his inhaler.

"Are you ok?" Alejandro is confused and worried.

"I'm fine. I just have asthma, no big deal," Sebastián is embarrassed and tries to make light of his serious situation.

"Oh, I'm stupid. I'm going to throw it. See? Gone." He shakes his curly blond hair with his hand, feeling guilty for causing Sebastián's breathing problems.

"No, I'm fine, seriously. Want to dance?" Sebastián is surprised at his own bravery. He suddenly doesn't feel shy anymore. He is not the same depressed boy that everyone used to know. Maybe moving to the capital was a good decision after all. He is moving on with his life after the tragedy of his first boyfriend that left him suffering through years of loneliness and guilt.

"I was waiting for you to ask that since I first saw you enter the club. Sure!" Alejandro smiles, takes his hand and pulls him to the dance floor.

Monday, February 26, 1990

Cuckoo! Cuckoo!

Sebastián is out of bed before he opens his eyes. It's

morning and he doesn't know where he is. The call of a... bird? Suddenly, the memories of the previous night become clear. He realizes it's just a memory that is still causing him stress. He must have fallen asleep suddenly last night, clutching his drawings and his photo album. He hears something outside. What time is it? He gets up and looks at the owl-shaped cuckoo clock. It's seven in the morning. Sebastián forgot to lock his door and rushes to...*the sound of keys!* The knob starts to turn, slowly.

"Good morning, kid," a new nurse, with an ill-tempered face, says, "Time to wake up."

"Yes, goo...good morning."

"Come on, get dressed quickly, kid. At eight, you have an appointment with your psychiatrist, but you have to eat breakfast first."

"And where do I have breakfast?"

"Get dressed, I'll wait for you outside and then I'll take you there."

The nurse, Mónica, leaves, closing the door behind her. At first, Sebastián reaches to lock the door, but realizes that it's useless, they can open it whenever they want anyway. He fell asleep without unpacking, so he opens his luggage and looks for something to wear. The nurse told him that he has about an hour until his appointment with his psychiatrist, so he doesn't think that he'll have time to put away his stuff in the closet. He takes out only what's necessary and turns the shower on, praying for hot water to come out. He waits for what seems like an eternity, puts his hand in the stream and, although it's not burning, at least the water's not freezing, either. He gets in anyway, grumbling. He had better get used to it; who knows how long he'll have to live like this, condemned to this routine.

There's a full-body mirror in the bathroom. While he dries himself, Sebastián looks at the mirror and something strange happens. Never has a mirror made him feel so afraid. It's nothing physical, nothing in the glass or in his reflection that scares him. He's actually scared for his life, for his future, for what awaits him, that he's so afraid. What he sees in the mirror is a young man who has a body with a mind, feelings and soul like everyone else — perhaps he will cease to exist after a while. Two weeks ago that idea would have seemed fantastic. He doesn't mean that he's going to disappear or die, it's more like he's going to change, to transform himself into something that he doesn't want to be. That's what scares him.

While getting dressed and combing his hair, he studies himself in detail so that he won't forget who he is. He's pleasant to look at, of medium height and slim, without being bony. He likes to comb a small amount of wax into his short, light brown hair. His skin is fair and soft and almost as if made from porcelain, but his round face has a healthy glow on his cheeks, sprinkled with the freckles that he's had since he was a baby. He looks like a child, regardless of his age, because he blushes so easily. His lips are thin and pink, his nose is small and pointy, and his eyes are of an intense sky blue color. He radiates innocence, tenderness, and, although, of course, he wouldn't be the most objective choice to judge himself, he thinks that with only with a short glance, anyone would consider him a good person. There's nothing strange or disproportionate about him, nothing evil, like his mother and father always wanted him to believe.

But in that mirror, Sebastián Fineli is not only able to see his body, his outer appearance. In fact, what stands out the most and what he's afraid of losing is his inner world, his soul. Inside he's very sensitive; he has suffered practically forever. First, because of his lifelong respiratory problems, then because of the lack of his parents' acceptance of his homosexuality, the harassment and intimidation that he often received at high school, then, because of Christian's death, and, finally, because of what happened with Alejandro Dunuel — the Spaniard he met only last month. Yes, his internal world is severely damaged, hurt. Worst of all is that, now, looking at himself in the mirror, he knows that this is something that he cannot hide easily. That pain fills him up inside and overflows him, escaping from his eyes, from his sad blue stare — more than anything because of the emptiness that Christian left him and he couldn't save him. Every day he thinks of him, misses him, cries over him. He wants him back, although he knows that's impossible. Christian was the best thing that happened in Sebastián's life. He was unique, exceptional.

He forces himself to takes his eyes off the mirror. He checks the owl-faced clock and realizes he has only half an hour left to have breakfast before his appointment with the psychiatrist. He uses his inhaler. He opens the door of his room and the nurse that came for him is standing there. Sebastián smiles and follows her to the cafeteria.

The walk is eye opening. It was dark last night, but now he can clearly see the sexual reorientation wing and the majority of the patients that will be his companions. There are several rooms in a long hallway and almost all of the doors are opened. He sees that everyone is calm, now used to his or her situation, resigned to a punishment that none of them believe they deserve.

They reach the door with the big lock and enter the general addictions area on the other side. In there, the atmosphere is quite different, heavier. There is also a hallway and rooms with their doors opened, but, in here, there are more nurses tending to the patients still in their beds. Some are being injected with some type of medicine; some are having their blood pressure taken, or their temperature. In here, in this part of the clinic, everything seems more medical.

They turn the corner and continue down a corridor before passing through a set of double doors. "This is the cafeteria, young man, now you know it. But remember that you cannot come here by yourself - a nurse has to bring you. It is prohibited for the patients of the other area to go alone through that door we just used. Please, eat something quickly because it is almost time for your appointment. I'll come to pick you up in twenty minutes."

The nurse leaves Sebastián alone in that oversized room filled with unknown people. Everything is threatening. He sees that, on a counter, there are bowls with food. People are standing in line and he assumes that he has to go take whatever he likes. He grabs a tray and walks to the end of the line. Contrary to what he thought, no one gives him any dirty looks; in fact, the other patients seem to be greeting him with friendly glances. It's his turn to order and he sees a carton of strawberry milk, but just as he is about to grab it, a hand appears from behind and takes it first.

"Oh, sorry, I'm so… I'm sorry…I didn't mean to…" the boy standing behind asks him, "Do you want the strawberry one?"

Sebastián, surprised that someone's speaking to him, turns around to see a boy who is quite attractive. He can't answer. Multi-colored eyes hypnotize him.

"Well, yeah…" Sebastián responds, nervously. "But you grabbed it first, don't worry."

"No, I was distracted, I thought that you weren't going to take it and that it was my turn. It's yours. You were there first."

"No, no, seriously, don't worry. It's yours."

Something happens between them both, an unspoken language, an invisible energy connects them in ways that even they can't understand.

"I'm having orange juice. Really, I don't feel like it. Take it."

"You sure? Don't make me feel bad about it." Sebastián's cheeks begin to flush.

"Don't feel bad," the stranger puts a hand on his shoulder. "You can have what you wanted."

Sebastián nods and smiles back.

"Thanks," he says, although what he really wants at this moment is for Christian to be there with him.

"My name is Tomás Díaz," the stranger introduces himself. "I've never seen you around. Are you new? Are you from the general addictions or the sexual reorientation wing?"

"Sebastián, nice to meet you. Yes, I'm new. I arrived

last night. I'm in the sexual reorientation wing. How about you?"

"Me too."

"How long have you been here?"

"According to what they tell me, a month and a week. I suffer from amnesia because of a problem that I have."

"Really? I'm sorry."

"There's nothing to be sorry about." Tomás responds with a friendly laugh; he wants to break the ice and make the new kid lose the fear Tomás knows he must be feeling.

"And how are you doing? Your treatment…?"

"Am I 'cured'?" when Tomás says this last word, he makes quotation marks with his fingers and laughs a little. Sebastián is afraid that someone might hear or realize what they're talking about. "I don't believe in that."

"In what?"

"That it can be cured, this thing we… 'have' — I don't even know if that's the right word. This thing we *are*, that would be the correct expression."

Sebastián feels like he has found an island in the middle of the ocean, an oasis in the desert. Suddenly Sebastián feels that he has found someone to trust and who may help him to feel safe in this new place.

"You want to sit with me and with Johana?" asks Tomás, pointing to a table.

"Yes, of course."

Johana greets Sebastián with a nod when he sits down. She looks quite introverted, silent, but her gestures seem friendly. Her oval face somehow, emits tranquility. She is thin and the same height as Sebastián. She has the same complexion as Tomás, her dark brown hair falls over her shoulders in waves, her eyes are big and gray. Her makeup is simple, but intense, emphasizing her sweet and attractive features. She looks harsh, but also like a princess from a fairy tale, Sebastián thinks, more than anything because he feels something mysterious inside of her, behind her sad gaze.

Her clothes also draw attention because they're not very feminine — they look rough. She wears a white t-shirt under an unbuttoned black shirt. She wears short pants and dark boots up to her ankles, but the only thing this does is accentuate her duality. She looks innocent and quiet, but confused and solitary.

"Which room are you in?" Tomás asks.

"I really didn't look. I think it's eleven."

Johana leans to grab the salt and that moment the sun shines upon a golden object that hangs from her neck. Sebastián is absorbed, like someone staring at a hypnotist's pendulum. He is able to see that the pendant says "Susana". Sebastián does not understand. Didn't Tomás tell him that the girl's name was Johana?

"Well, then, we are close. If you need anything, you know you can count on me. I'm in room eight."

"Thank you. How many rooms are there?"

"Thirteen rooms for the patients and now that you arrived, there is only one that's empty. There are five storage rooms, a big meeting room, and an extra room for the nurse that has to stay overnight."

"Do you get along with the other patients?"

"Yes, with everybody. You'll get to know them.

They're all nice people. There are seven that are underage: Lucas, Patricio, Julio, Sabrina, Augusto, Sofía, and Santiago — they're between fourteen and seventeen years old. Then there are three that are between nineteen and twenty-one: there is Johana who is nineteen, Fabricio who is twenty-one and…another girl whose name is Sandra who is twenty years old."

Johana finishes her breakfast and gets up from the table looking at Sebastián and Tomás with a forced little smile. She turns and her face turns to sadness.

"Why doesn't she talk?" Sebastián asks when she leaves the cafeteria.

"Johana is like that. She doesn't talk much. She has a problem expressing herself."

"She must be so alone. I'd like to be her friend."

"I already went through that; it was my first impression, too. The bad thing is that she won't let you. She doesn't let anyone enter her world. Or at least that's what she wants us to believe. I'm already used to it."

Sebastián looks at the clock on the wall and realizes he has less than fifteen minutes left before his appointment with the psychiatrist. But he doesn't rush. He feels quite nice speaking to Tomás.

"You have to stay cool. It is your first day and I know what you must be feeling. Relax. You are going to like everybody. The only thing is that you have to be very patient."

"Why?"

"Most of them are shy. The treatments and pills seem only to make them more depressed instead of curing them of homosexuality. Johana is the perfect example. But the doctor said that is how the 'cure' works."

"And how do you interact with them if they're all like that...in those moods?"

"I cheer them up, advise them, talk to them about anything." As he's saying this, Tomás takes a little bottle out of his pocket, grabs a pill, and takes it with water.

"Are you also on medication?" Sebastián asks, surprised.

"Yes, but I don't take these to cure me of my sexual orientation. Dr. Rutherbor diagnosed me with schizophrenia and I have to take these pills every day. I just pretend to take the other pills."

Sebastián see the blue pills and reads the name that is on the label of the bottle. "Prochlorperazine".

"But, to my knowledge, schizophrenia is a consequence of depression and an unstable mentality."

"Yes, exactly."

"But...forgive me...you seem normal and healthy to me."

"Thanks for the compliment, but I don't think it's true. It's because of the pills that you see me doing so well. They help me overcome my disorder and keep me from losing my memory. I don't remember so much about my past, it's still fuzzy and my memories are confusing. It scares me a lot so that's why I take this pills and I feel like it's helping me to recover little by little. I think every pills works differently for each person. I know the doctor tries his hardest to 'cure' our sexuality, even if I believe he can't. The only thing I can do is to cheer them up and give them confidence about themselves, but the more I try, the harder it is to reach them.

I have no control over that. In the end, he is the doctor and I'm a patient, too, and we are all here. I guess what it takes to survive in here is to just keep lying."

Sebastián doesn't know what to say. He can't agree with Tomás on that, but he just met him, he really likes him, and doesn't want to upset him. He can see his fears and sadness about not being able to do more to help the other patients and himself. He tries his best.

"Well, then, maybe it's true and the pills are helping you." Sebastián smiles. "I also have my medicine."

"Which one?"

"This inhaler."

Tomás understands. "Do you have asthma?"

"Yes, I've had trouble breathing since birth."

"But it should have gone away by now."

"I was born with a condition that impaired my ability to breathe. I nearly died from a pulmonary obstruction, but I underwent a critical surgery that saved my life when I was only three days old. It was hard for me to breathe when I was little. There were various scary situations in which I could have died. Now I'm fine. I breathe normally and the attacks are rare, but I'm still prone to complications. If I'm exposed to dust or cigarette smoke, my respiratory track gets swollen and I can't breathe."

Tomás is impressed by the story. "It's like a miracle. You could have died, but everything turned out fine. You learned to coexist with your problem and to move forward."

"I don't feel it like a miracle. I think it was just luck."

"Well, the important thing is that your family supports you."

"*Supported* me. Now they don't accept my sexuality."

"How old are you?" Tomás asks to change the subject so that he doesn't make Sebastián feel uncomfortable, judged, or criticized.

"Twenty-one."

"I would have guessed you were only eighteen!"

"That's what most people tell me. And you? How old are you?"

"I'm also twenty-one. My birthday was in January. Sadly, I was here without a party or cake, just a letter from my mother."

"I'm so sorry. Happy belated birthday. My birthday was two weeks ago."

"Happy belated birthday to you, too," Tomás says with a smile.

"I don't know why you look so familiar. I feel like I've seen you before."

"Yeah? I don't think so…although as I told you, I suffer from memory loss," he chuckles.

Sebastián is sad for him, to be alone without his family on his birthday, and to lose the knowledge of himself and have to live without memories must be awful. He likes Tomás and can't deny the attraction he feels toward him. Despite being locked-up in that clinic, he maintains a view towards life that's peaceful, positive, and cheerful. Sebastián turns to the clock on the wall and sees that it's five to eight.

"I think you're brave," Sebastián says, smiling his first big smile in a long time.

"Yeah? Thanks. I think you are a real survivor. I think you are a very nice guy and…cute."

Sebastián succumbs to another crush because he's always been a romantic, but on the outside, he keeps up appearances and tries not to be so obvious. He always preferred that the other one, the source of his attraction, makes the first move. Tomás, on the other hand, was never so romantic, but this time he feels a strong natural force born inside of him, his heart controlling him like never before.

"But how do you know that I'm a nice guy? You don't know me."

"I know. It's just that you look so…peaceful…and so innocent. I think it's your eyes. Yes, your soulful blue eyes, there I see tenderness and gentleness." Tomás confesses. Sebastián seems like such a charming boy.

"Don't you feel lonely in here?"

"Yes, well, it's inevitable. But I get along with all the others. I like to be aware of their needs. But tell me more about you."

"About me?"

"Why did they admit you? You came out of the closet or they discovered you?"

Sebastián, ashamed, bites his own lips. "You promise not to freak out?"

"I promise."

"I…I tried to kill myself. I'm sorry."

"Relax. Don't worry," Tomás calms him down, holding his arm. He leans forward and places a hand on Sebastián's neck. "Are you all right?"

Sebastián starts to cough and choke. He feels like an asthma attack is coming. He uses his inhaler a couple of times. He feels frustrated, humiliated. "I have to go," he says, between mouthfuls of air. "I don't feel well. I'm sorry."

Sebastián gets to his feet with the tray in his hand, but because he's choking, all of the plates fall to the floor making a huge crashing sound. Tomás feels guilty. He bends over and starts to help Sebastián pick up.

"I'm sorry, that wasn't my intention. I didn't want… wait, I'll help you to pick that up, don't worry."

Sebastián stands up, walks to the door, turns to see Tomás for a last time, and leaves the cafeteria. The nurse that has been waiting to take him to his session sees him pass like a streak of lighting. Sebastián sees that a patient is going through the little door with the huge lock and he runs to pass through it before it closes. The nurse realizes his intent and walks faster. Sebastián pushes the patient, unintentionally, when he passes by, almost running. He reaches his room and locks the door. Then he throws himself on the bed, crying, and a wreck on the inside.

The nurse opens the door with her keys. "Young man, what happened to you?"

"I want to be alone!"

"You have an appointment with your psychiatrist."

"No! I don't want to! Leave me alone!" Sebastián tucks himself under the sheets.

"It's your first appointment. You can't miss it."

"I told you to leave me alone!"

The nurse is scared. Her years of experience tell her that this behavior is a symptom of chronic depression.

But all she can do is to carry out her duties. She gets near and pulls his sheets off of him. Sebastián sobs louder. He's almost unable to breathe. The nurse becomes more afraid. Sebastián's eyes are streaming with tears. He breaks down. The nurse lowers the sheet, sits beside him and hugs him. Sebastián returns her embrace. He feels comforted.

Tomás, looking from outside the room, is a mixture of feelings, but the one that stands out the most, the strongest one, is guilt. If he hadn't opened his mouth…

Chapter SIX:

The first session. Monday, February 26, 1990

"SEBASTIÁN?"

The young man only responds with a slow blink of his eyes.

"Hello, dear, please come in," the psychiatrist invites him into her office.

It took Sebastián a while to calm down after his attack and, consequently, he is fifteen minutes late for his first appointment. He hopes that the doctor is not easily upset and that she won't punish him, at least not on his first day. He has been expected to absorb too much in such a short period. He enters the office and sits down.

"Are you comfortable? I want you to be comfortable."

He is visibly nervous. With one hand he plays with his inhaler, while drumming the fingers of the other.

"I'm your psychiatrist, Dr. Revas, and you'll have these sessions with me every morning. The only thing that I ask is that you try to be punctual, don't talk about our sessions to your new friends, and only call me your psychiatrist.

Everything here is private between us. I know that today is a difficult day for you, but look at it as the first day of the rest of your life, of your new life. Focus on that so that..."

The words of the psychiatrist become distant, slow and distorted. Sebastián analyzes her. Dr. Revas looks kind and does not seem to be a bad person, at least on the surface. He hopes that this is not a trick or an illusion. She is tall and thin with long, straight, dark brown hair, hazel eyes, and a gentle smile. *She is the perfect person to welcome new patients*, Sebastián thinks. Maybe this is designed to make him fall into the trap, to convince him. He looks around and sees an odd machine attached to leather cuffs. He feels uncomfortable just looking at it. What could it be? Will it be part of the treatments? He sucks on his inhaler. He returns to the present and continues to listen to the words of Dr. Revas.

"...so I'm here to help you return to being who you once were. We will repair your sexual orientation. "

"I didn't ask to come here. My parents locked me in."

"But why do you feel like that? Don't you think that maybe you have been a little cruel to them?"

"No, of course not. They did it because...I don't know. Because they have been deceived, let's say, by a society that tells them that it is wrong. They are Catholic and —"

"And you?" Juliana crosses her legs and fits her notebook on her lap. "You are not religious, are you?"

"I believe in God and everything, but...I don't believe in what the Bible says."

"How so?"

"Because it is a book written by human beings. It was

written by many people over a long period of time and most of the laws were intended for people at that specific time."

"Reasonable, but have you read it? In depth?"

"Some sections... I don't know, I guess not *that* in depth, I believe there are a lot of fictional parts. A snake that talks and a wooden boat with tons of big and heavy animals," responds Sebastián, uncomfortable.

"You must understand that the Bible was written by wise men, prophets and enlightened individuals, chosen by God. In fact, it is believed that God himself led their hands and their letters to leave us this gift, this holy book that contains the instructions for living well."

"Not for me."

Juliana feels that she is losing him by touching the topics of the Bible and God, but she must follow the instruction from her mentor. She has been advised how to treat her patients and what to use in her sessions, even though she sees how he is distancing himself, taking refuge in an inner shield.

"I want you to know that, in the treatment that you have with me, we will hardly touch religion. I don't want you to worry." Juliana pauses to try to read the body language of the young man, to see if her last words return any of his confidence. She decides the best thing to do is to change the subject. She reads in her papers the information she has about this patient, "How old are you? Twenty-one?"

Sebastián nods.

"You have asthma, right?"

"Yes, that is what this inhaler is for."

"And tell me, how many times a day you use your

inhaler? Give me an estimate."

"About twenty times, perhaps. Depends on the day, sometimes more, sometimes less."

"Tell me about your parents. How is your relationship with them?"

"Not very good. My father is very strict about the Bible; he follows it to the letter. My mother is the same."

"Are you telling me that…distance with your parents… is because of religion? Do you know that God loves you?"

"Yes…and yes, of course."

"But he punishes sin."

"I guess, although I don't think it's exactly as you're painting it now, but in general, yes. The thing is that I do not consider my…preference…to be a sin. The same message of God is to relieve the suffering of others and love them unconditionally, right?"

"Sebastián, I'll ask more personal things. Is that ok?" asks Juliana, with a friendly tone, "Tell me first, do you consider yourself a homosexual person? Is it how you want to be?"

"Yes, of course."

"And do you consider it a sexual deviation?"

"I feel that it is a natural inclination."

Juliana writes the answers in her notebook, making notes in the margins that describe his body language. What is clear to her is that it will be very difficult to change or repair this patient.

"I thought you would come wanting a change, but I see that you feel comfortable with your sexuality."

"Don't you think it's great?"

"Unfortunately not, as that single path will take you to destruction, to losing your life and…to hell," Juliana repeats what Dr. Rutherbor told her to say, but she also really wants Sebastián to know how serious his condition is. "We will have a lot of work, but I'm going to help you. You deserve a better life."

Sebastián is beginning to feel even more uncomfortable. He doesn't understand why the psychiatrist keeps mentioning the religion. Is that how a professional would act? What about science and medicine? Is there actually a pill to cure homosexuality? And the real question here is if there was…then would he take it? "Of course not!" he thinks, beginning to feel emotionally strained.

"I appreciate your intentions, but I don't think that you're going to be able to help me," says the young man, disillusioned by everything around him — the doctor, the session, the clinic, and his own thoughts. "Sebastián, we will help each other, I promise you," she says with a smile. "Homosexuality is a product of internal wounds and traumas. It can happen to a child because of an empty relationship with the father and an overly protective mother. Together, we will work to heal all of that and will get you back on track to a normal sexuality. But to do so, we must get rid of the influences that led you to be this way." She tries to cheer him up while she organizes some papers on the desk.

"I was born and was raised by my heterosexual parents. I grew up surrounded by a family where everyone is heterosexual. In my teens, everywhere I looked, there were only heterosexual people. I was educated and guided by the

Catholic religion. Most of my life I pretended to be straight to fit in with them. Why am I not heterosexual? Why was I not influenced by them to have a heterosexual orientation? Answer me."

Juliana doesn't have an answer so she changes the subject. "Homosexuality is a sexual deviance. To say that it's normal, is like saying that incest and bestiality is normal."

"But I'm not doing that... I'm just attracted to people of same sex. Like you're attracted to the people of different sex. I think anyone could have an incestuous relationship or partake in bestiality independently from one's sexual orientation. It's not fair to compare me to those people."

Juliana quickly changes the conversation. "Please, help me with your information, to have it updated."

She hands Sebastián a pen so that he can fill out the form. There is an uncomfortable silence in the office. She flips through her notebook, while his eyes are trained on the paper in his hands. The two of them are nervous. After five minutes, the young man gives her back the paper and the pen.

"Thank you, let me check it out," Juliana analyzes each answer in search of a key. "I read here that you've never been emotionally or sexually involved with a woman."

"That's right. Never."

"How so?"

"Is it not obvious?"

"No. I think you should get involved with a woman, to try out your options."

"But I don't like it."

"How you can know it? If you have never experienced

it..."

"It is something that you know; I just know it. I mean, forgive me, but... Have you ever been with a woman? Maybe you would like it if you tried it."

"What? No! That's different. It's wrong. Anyway, you're too closed-minded, dear." Juliana does not notice the irony in her words. "You should be open to new things to find out what is it that you want and who you want to be with."

"I already experienced it with a man. And I liked it. I felt satisfied, loved, and happy."

"But saying that makes you feel satisfied doesn't mean that it's the best. Maybe with a woman you will feel even happier and even more satisfied. This is how it works in nature, so that is how it should be. Being gay is not natural." Inside, Juliana implores her words to make the boy see reason. "In life, you have to educate yourself, shape up, create a family, and teach everything that you learned to your children. It is a cycle of life that should not be corrupted."

"I think that in the future we will have other options to create a family."

"What?" Juliana laughs quietly, as if ridiculing what the boy says.

"Adopting...just like the heterosexual couple that cannot conceive."

Juliana arches her eyebrows and re-reads the form that the young man filled out and she notices an important detail.

"Have you felt depressed lately?"

Sebastián nods. Juliana becomes concerned.

"Yes? When?"

"A couple weeks ago, it was a day before my birthday."

"And what led you to that?"

"No. I don't think I'm ready to talk about that."

"Do not feel pressured, really. Take your time." Juliana looks at her watch and notices that there are less than five minutes left until the end the session. "What I do want you to know is that you can trust me. Now I'm going to give you a bottle of pills. I want you to take one every morning."

Juliana walks up to a small cabinet in her office and takes out the antidepressants. They contain valerians, with mild effects so that they do not cause addiction and help the nervous system. She wants to see Sebastián in a good mood.

"Thanks," He accepts the pills, but doesn't really believe that he needs them. In fact, he doesn't believe that any pill or drug is really good for the health.

"It was a pleasure to meet you. I'll see you tomorrow."

Sebastián gets up from the chair and moves towards the door. He stops and decides to ask the doctor one last question.

"Excuse me, I wanted to ask you something."

"Yes, dear, anything."

"Prochlorperazine…is it a medication to treat schizophrenia?"

"Yes, it is. But how do you know it?"

Sebastián is relieved to hear the word "yes" and forgets his concern for Tomás. He apologizes with a lie.

"No, nothing. It is that my cousin was taking those pills. He was schizophrenic and they did not help him at all."

"That might have been because his case warranted another medication, perhaps Quetiapine. Although, the one you mention does work usually, just not necessarily right away."

Sebastián nods and leaves the office, while another patient comes in after him.

His nurse, Mónica, is waiting and escorts him to his room.

When he's finally alone, he lies down and watches the ceiling for a couple of minutes. He wants to draw and takes out a blank page as well as his fine-tipped pencils. He sits on the small desk that he has in the room and closes his eyes for inspiration.

The first thing that comes to his mind, of course, is the image of Christian, but he already has quite a few sketches based on his face. He tries to focus on something new and, although he is ashamed to admit it, the image that comes to mind next is the face of Tomás — his perfectly captivating eyes. He remembers the events of that morning and feels a bit badly about the way that he treated him. He takes out the folder where he keeps his previous works and reviews them one by one. He chooses the one that pleases him the most and puts it on the table to give to Tomás as an apology. He leaves the room with the gift in his hand.

Sebastián draws closer to the door number eight and sees a shirtless Tomás through the open door. Even though he has a slim waist, Sebastián can tell that Tomás works out everyday because his chest, arms, and torso are perfectly toned. Sebastián turns around, leaning against the door and closing his eyes. He takes a deep breath - worried that having seen Tomás shirtless will be a detriment to his therapy. "Enough! Stop it!" He tries to avoid the strong attraction toward him and waits until he puts a shirt before knocking on the doorframe. He just wants to get to know him more, to be his friend.

"Sebastián! What a surprise! Hello. How are you? How are you doing?"

Sebastián only smiles and shrugs his shoulders.

"Come in, come in," Tomás invites him into his room, keeping the door open so they don't get in trouble.

"Am I interrupting?" Sebastián asks, upon seeing an open book on the bed.

"No, not all. I just finished taking a post-workout shower. I'm going to read it for the second time," he says, gesturing to the book, "out of boredom. Until I fall asleep for a long nap, anyway. It's my daily routine. I know it's kind of boring. Why did you come?" Tomás is nervous, but doesn't know why; maybe he doesn't want to make Sebastián feel uncomfortable like he did earlier in the cafeteria.

"I wanted to apologize to you for what happened..."

"You don't need to apologize for anything."

"Yes, I feel like I owe you an apology."

"Well, in any case, apology accepted," Tomás says with his hand behind his head, unintentionally flexing his bicep.

"I have a detail that comes included with the apologies. This is one of my works." Sebastián tries once again to ignore his physical attraction toward Tomás and to focus on getting to know him more as who he is inside as a person. He takes another deep breath and hands over a watercolor of a colorful landscape. Tomás is excited.

"You painted this? I'm...I'm speechless. You know how to use perspective, foreshortening, depth. I don't know much about this, but it is one of the best sceneries I've ever seen."

"Thank you."

Tomás walks to his desk, takes out tape from the drawer and attaches the drawing to the wall next to his bed.

"Now, to feel like I'm outside of this clinic, all I have to do is look at your picture."

"I know that it may seem a little childish...and even stupid, but —"

"Not at all, not at all. I think it's a very nice gesture, something between you and me."

Sebastián becomes nervous and decides to change the subject.

"I did well in my session today."

"Yes? That's good...I'm glad you're already cured," Tomás says, jokingly, which makes Sebastián laugh.

"Of course not, it's only that the doctor didn't seem that bad. She has a different point of view on homosexuality, of course. But who knows? Maybe I'll get to heal *her*."

The two laugh together, breaking the nervousness floating in the atmosphere and creating, almost unintentionally, a moment of intimacy. Tomás approaches Sebastián and takes his hand, squeezing it gently, which returns them both to that cloud of feelings that hypnotized them earlier in the cafeteria. Sebastián is once again enchanted by Tomás's smile and, of course, his fascinating eyes. Suddenly, he has butterflies in his stomach and begins to struggle breathing. He releases Tomás's hand and takes his inhaler, puffing on it twice.

"Sorry, I need to rest. See you later."

"Don't think that what you told me, or what happened this morning, changed my way of seeing you or treating you. As I said, you seem like a nice person and I know that it's worth it to get to know you. We all have problems. If you need to talk — about anything — I'm here to listen to you. You can trust me. You've got a new friend in me."

"Thanks, really. I've been waiting to hear that for a long time. It's nice to have a new friend. I haven't changed my way of seeing you. You seem like a great guy."

Tomás watches him leave. He's a bit disappointed because something inside tells him that Sebastián is romantically interested in him, but his shyness or inexperience prevents him from making a move. Tomás has to get to know him better. He lays on his bed to continue reading the book, but not before seeing Sebastián's gift — that landscape, that other world where he can now escape with his imagination whenever he wants to. A smile is drawn on his lips.

***

Despite not being heterosexual, the beauty of the young woman walking towards him down the hallway actually impresses Sebastián. She has an hourglass figure and is just a bit taller than he is. She has honey-colored eyes and blonde hair, long and straight, like rays of the sun. Her gaze bewitches. She looks like a doll with her slightly pronounced cheeks, her oval face, her thin nose, and her pink lips. Sebastián sees in her someone exceptional — a perfect specimen of woman.

"Hi, did you just come from Tomás's room?" the girl asks Sebas, who feels nervous.

"Yes, I went to visit him for a while."

"And...did you only talk?"

Sebastián is silent. He can't believe that a complete stranger, and even worse in a place like this, thinks of asking that question. The words don't come to him.

"Forgive me for the interrogation. My name is Sandra Vélez," she introduces herself. She smiles and he notices the dimples in her cheeks that give her a touch of sweetness and innocence.

"A...a pleasure, I'm Sebastián Fineli."

"Are you gay?"

"I'm pretty sure I am," he responds with a smile, trying to shake the fear that he felt at the beginning.

"I'm bisexual."

"It's good, you have more options."

The two laugh openly now.

"Only Tomás and I are bisexual."

"Is Tomás bisexual?"

"Obviously! Didn't he tell you?"

"No, I just assumed he was gay, but it's not a problem. I have no problems with that."

"Where were you heading to now?"

"My room," Sebastián points down the hall, "It's room eleven."

"Room eleven? What luck you have! You got the room

with the biggest window. Well, so I've heard, I've never gone in."

"Would you like to see it? If you want to...let's go."

They walk a little and reach the room. As soon as they enter, Sandra goes straight to the barred window.

"It's true. You do have the most beautiful view. My window is much smaller."

"How long have you been here?"

"I arrived shortly after Tomás came, a month ago."

"And have the sessions helped you?"

"A little, yes. The psychiatrist has been treating us since last week. We didn't have one before and Dr. Rutherbor ran the sessions. We almost didn't talk. He gave us the pills and that was it."

"Are you happy being as you are? With your sexual orientation?" he asks her.

"No, not really...or well, yes. I don't know, I don't know. It's confusing. I came willingly. One day I want to have a family, children, I don't know," she answers, shaking her head without stopping, as if trying to assemble in her mind the countless pieces of a puzzle. "I want to feel more attraction for men than for women."

"Do you think that it is possible for a person to change just like that?"

"Yes. A man came to give us a talk and told us that he used to be homosexual, but that Dr. Rutherbor cured him."

"Really? Well, I think that it depends on each person. Or so it should, at least. Everyone should be free to decide whether to undergo treatment or not."

"Imagine that you are a parent and you have a child

who is sick, but who does not want to take the cough syrup because he says it tastes bad. What would you do in that case?" Sandra sits beside him on the bed. "You would do the best for your kid, right? Even if he feels that you are forcing him to do something that he doesn't want, to take the medicine. Do what the psychiatrist and the doctor tell you. It's for your own good."

Sebastián's lips stay still while his mind is swimming in doubts.

"We must follow the rules· from the doctors and from our parents to not suffer the consequences from our deviation," Sandra shares with him what she had learned during her stay. "Imagine that your parents warn you to not cross the street when the light is red and you ignore them and run anyway because you just feel that you're gonna make it. You know what's going to happen, right?"

Sebastián does not respond; she is really making him question his own beliefs. Sandra sees the folder on the desktop. She approaches it to see what it contains.

"What's in here? Can I see?"

"Yes, of course."

She opens the folder and is impressed by the talent of the new patient.

"Those are the works that I did at the university. I studied art, but I couldn't finish the first final. I hope that when I leave here I can get back. Of course I don't know when that will be..."

"I love them. Congratulations," she says, sharply but cheerful.

"Which do you like the most?" Sebastián gets up and

stands next to Sandra, who points out a particular drawing.

"Take it, it's yours."

"No, I can't accept it. They're part of your portfolio."

"No, don't worry. Seriously, take it. Now *you* have the more beautiful view in your room."

"You are quite sweet. Thank you." Sandra takes the drawing, as she smiles. She sees a photo album that is also on the desktop. Sebastián notices.

"It's a family album," he explains, downplaying it.

"Can I see it?" she asks with her characteristic curiosity.

"They are only pictures of me when I was a little kid. I don't think you want to see that."

He is nervous. He didn't want her to see the album, but it's too late. She turns it and sees the sticker on the cover that says "Chris and Sebas".

"No, wait! Leave that there!" He loses control.

"Sorry. I didn't think it was something so...that made you angry..." she says, afraid.

"I'm sorry. I didn't mean to...scare you," he takes out his inhaler and uses it a couple of times.

"No, forgive me. I am very impulsive and I should not have invaded your space."

"No, it is not that. It's just that...I haven't told anyone; it's my secret."

"What secret?"

"I don't know if it's good idea..."

"You can count on me for anything. I really like you. I imagine that Chris...is it someone who...means a lot to you?"

He only nods.

"And did you break up?"

"No, not exactly. He ended his life."

"Oh. I'm really sorry, really."

"Excuse me, I'm emotionally exhausted. I can hardly open up."

"Don't worry."

"Thank you for understanding."

She grabs her gift and leaves the room. Sebastián is left alone, but accompanied by thoughts that his new friend woke up in him. He lies down again and falls asleep.

Sandra finally reaches her original destination. She knocks on the door.

"Hello!" she greets Tomás when he opens the door, putting her arms around his neck. "I missed you a lot."

"I've always been here, Sandra."

She finds him a bit blunt, but she tries to soften him and kisses him on the lips.

"I was reading a book and I'm really tired. I'm going to take a nap."

"No problem, I'll stay here with you."

Tomás feels stifled, but must show her the same respect and patience that he shows to his other friends. He doesn't want to make her feel rejected.

"Okay, come in."

Sandra leaves the drawing that Sebastián gave her on the desk.

"You also have one?" asks Tomás, while Sandra observes the landscape stuck on his wall, which takes her by surprise.

"Yes, Sebastián gave it to me a while ago. He invited me to his room."

"Yes? Did you already meet him? Did he say anything about me?"

"I really liked him. But why do you ask?"

"He suffers from chronic depression, as I understand. I am concerned about his case. Did he tell you something personal?"

"No, nothing. Well, he only told me that he has a past with someone, with this Chris, who committed suicide. He seemed so vulnerable and it makes me sad because he seems like a nice person."

"And is he ok now?"

"Tomás, you can't let the problems of others affect you that way. Think of yourself first, *your* life," advises Sandra, although, in reality, what she feels is jealousy.

"You know how I am."

"I know. But you have to give people their own space, so everyone recovers on their own and we all get stronger."

"I think you're right," answers Tomás, while lying down and looking at the ceiling. He thinks that perhaps Sebastián doesn't open up much because he hasn't overcome that past experience. He can't wait for it to be the next day so that he can see him again.

"Tomás, do you love me?"

Sandra's words pull him out of his thoughts. He realizes that she is lying next to him, caressing his chest tenderly under his shirt.

"Yes, Sandra."

Tomás knows that what he says can be misinterpreted,

but he means that he loves her as a friend. He knows that she is in love with him, but believes that she is very fragile and emotional and he's afraid to be too harsh.

"I care about you very much, Sandra," he says, closing his eyes to sleep for a couple of hours, as he is used to having a lot of dreams every afternoon.

She lies still when she hears him say this. She thinks that perhaps she is wrong and that her suspicions are false. Perhaps Tomás is not falling for the new patient, after all.

Chapter SEVEN:

Buried memories.
Monday, February 26, 1990

THE SAME DAY, AT 3:00PM, AT THE DOOR OF GROW AND LIVE NORMALLY, Juliana starts to get impatient. In four hours, she has to be at her other job at North Clinic and Paul has not shown up for their lunch date. No one shows up, actually. Charol said a week ago that she would admit her son Mateo to the clinic. Since then, she has been postponing with, it must be admitted, a legitimate excuse — she says he is recovering from an illness. "Well, it's better," thinks Juliana. The last thing she wants is for all of the patients to fall ill with some virus and then blame Dr. Rutherbor for negligence or something.

"Juliana!"

She sees Paul pull up on the side of the road and she runs towards him.

"Paul! I thought you were never going to come."

She greets him with a kiss on the cheek through the open car window. He appreciates her hair enveloping his face and can smell that perfume he has longed for. Images and memories immediately come to him, awakening feelings from the past.

"I'm starving. Where should we have lunch?" she asks excitedly, climbing into the passenger seat.

"Do you remember our favorite restaurant?"

"Yes, I was hoping you would say that. I miss that place!"

It does not take long before they are occupying their old table, ordering the same dishes that they used to request, talking and laughing with a mixture of nervousness and built-up happiness.

"I wonder if anyone here remembers us. It's been so many years," she says, adopting a serious tone.

"Yes, you know. Everything got complicated."

"Forgive me, I don't know why I get so nostalgic. It's because I missed your friendship, I missed how we were before everything happened…"

"Juliana, despite all this time, the distance, I never forgot about you."

"Me neither. I never forgot your friendship."

"I don't mean that and you know it."

"Paul?" she asks, when she feels her friend grab her hand. "What are you doing?"

"What do you mean?"

"I'm talking about when we were classmates at the university, of the support that you gave me. I don't want you to get confused again. We already talked about it and you accepted it. I always saw you as just a friend."

"You still want to see me in that way?" Although things are not going as expected, the mere fact of touching on the issue already excites Paul.

"It was not my intention to make you believe that this meeting was… That encounter we had ten years ago — it was a mistake." Juliana does not want to be so hard. She doesn't want to hurt his feelings, but she has to be frank. "We have to recognize that it was wrong. We can't repeat it. You were with your wife and I was with my husband."

"But you still wanted it. That's why it was —"

"Yes, it is rather shameful for me, humiliating actually. I felt alone and I don't know, you were already cured and heterosexual."

"Oh, so now it's my fault?"

"Not at all, I'm not saying that. I am referring to my emotional state, the circumstances that, my marriage, I don't know. They are excuses. I accept it — it was my mistake. I took advantage of you because you were cured."

"Don't say that. I made the first move. Remember?"

"Yes, but I should have stopped you." It is difficult for Juliana to look her friend in the eyes. "What we did was bad. We already agreed about that."

The waitress approaches and serves the dishes that they ordered. She would ask if they need anything else, but she feels an uncomfortable silence between them and leaves quickly.

"Juliana, why didn't you accept me? I was there to help you to overcome what happened with Tommy and I was by your side when…you know…the thing…the rape… happened."

"Please, don't. Don't mention it."

"I'm sorry, but I had to say it."

"Stop, please, I don't want to talk about the past anymore. I already buried it." Unconsciously, Juliana eats faster, wanting the conversation to end as soon as possible.

"Did you ever love me?"

"Paul, it's not about you. Now I have a son, a husband, a family, and so do you."

"Are you happy with Miguel?"

"He is my husband, the man that I will spend the rest of my life with."

"You know very well that if you don't have the most important thing, happiness, you don't have to stay if you don't want to."

"Life's not that easy. Please, let's hurry; I have less than two hours to get to work."

"Ok, as you say."

Silence has never been so uncomfortable. For the next ten minutes, the two friends don't even exchange a sigh. When they finish eating, the first to rise is Juliana who makes like an arrow to the exit door. Paul has nothing left to do but to pay the check.

"I'm really sorry about lunch," Paul says genuinely while he drives Juliana back to the parking lot of Grow And Live Normally. "I should not have brought any of it up."

"Oh, we look like children. You don't have to apologize. We need to talk about it. I was the one who overreacted," says Juliana, getting out of the car.

"Sure? You're not upset with me?"

"No, I'm not. Let's just move on."

Juliana puts her head back through the window to say goodbye to Paul with a kiss on the cheek. He inhales deeply, wanting the memory of her perfume to stay with him forever.

"So, can I call you? Can we go out to eat this weekend?"

"Why not? You can call me or, if not, you know where I work," she answers behind her, while walking toward her vehicle.

Paul waits a couple of minutes to watch her leave and then drives off.

If someone was witnessing the scene from outside, they would probably think that Juliana is a mannequin or a corpse. She doesn't make a single movement or sound. Shortly after her encounter with Paul, Juliana is parked two blocks from North Clinic, where she will work the night shift. She just stares at the building while she thinks to herself. She has never felt so alone, like a tomb. She watches the birds on the branches of the tree protecting her from the sun, offering the darkness she needs at the moment.

The first tears begin to fall and threaten to pull her out of her daydream. She realizes that she has less than fifteen minutes until her appointment with her first patient. She tries to move and finds it too difficult; each finger weighs a ton when she tries to grab the steering wheel. She is thinking of calling the clinic to call in sick, of going to her house and tucking herself into bed. But she won't be alone at home either; Miguel will be there and seeing him would be even worse in her current state.

She feels like screaming. She covers her mouth with her hands so that passersby do not hear her, but it's useless because her scream is silent, a cry without a voice. She looks in her wallet for the photo that she has saved for years, holding it gingerly with her fingernails so that she doesn't damage it any more than it already is. She smoothes the edges straight again and when she looks at it carefully, the tears spurt forth. She cries, but when she sees such a nice man in the photo; she can't help but smile.

"Tommy... I'm so sorry," she says, hoping the photograph can hear her. "I forgot you and I can't...I can't hold on to you any longer. It was your decision..."

Unexpectedly, she hears her own screams from that night — a flash, a buried memory that appears right in front in her eyes, that cold fear. She feels again the pain and the brute force of the mysterious man who raped her in her youth. She takes several deep breaths, trying to regain her composure. She takes her makeup box from the purse and fixes herself in the rearview mirror. She fights to escape her emotional hole. She cannot let her patients and colleagues realize what happened to her.

***

The next day, Sebastián comes to breakfast ten minutes late. He is disappointed to see that there is no one else in line for food. He was hoping for another scene like yesterday, when he met his new friend. Reluctantly, he fills his tray and looks for a place to sit. Then he sees Tomás, beckoning with his hand, inviting him to his table. Sebastián gestures in acceptance and walks towards him.

Johana, Sandra, and a young stranger accompany Tomás. Sebastián sits next to them.

"This is Fabricio. You already know Johana and Sandra."

"Yes." Sebastián shakes Fabricio's hand. "Nice to meet you."

Johana, as usual, does not express emotions on her face. Sandra cannot hide that the presence of Sebastián makes her uncomfortable. Fabricio, on the other hand, is a young extrovert.

"The same — nice to meet you. You can sit here whenever you want. We are your new friends," Fabricio welcomes him.

"Yes. Whenever you want," Sandra repeats, almost inaudibly, crinkling her nose. "You can count on us."

"Thanks. It's reassuring to hear that. I never thought that I would find new friends in this place. Last night I didn't sleep very well."

"That's normal. The first days are always like that," says Tomás. "Some never get over that stage. The important thing is not to think too much. It can be dangerous. Don't shut yourself up either because that ends up enveloping you in a black cloud."

Sebastián, almost unconsciously, turns to Johana. He sees her looking pale, skinny, without the slightest shred of emotions.

"Hi, and you how have you been?" he asks.

She turns to him, with a slow movement that reminds Sebastián of a vampire.

"Like hell," she answers. "Trying to survive in this mess."

Johana rises and, without saying goodbye, walks with a nurse toward the door with the big lock.

"Wait, Johana! Where are you going?" Fabricio calls

to her, but does not receive an answer. He turns to Tomás. "I'll keep trying."

"I don't know why you worry so much about her. I think she has more possibilities to get out of here than us. Don't you see her? She must be asexual," remarks Sandra.

"Don't say that," says Fabricio. "We don't know her that well to judge her like that. Something must be going on inside of her. That's all."

"As if it were that simple," corrects Sandra. "Besides, all of us have something going on inside of us, don't we? If not, we obviously wouldn't be stuck in here."

A silence sets on the table, which makes Sandra even more uncomfortable. She looks Sebastián straight in his eyes.

"I want to apologize again for what happened yesterday."

"No, you didn't do anything, don't worry."

"I shouldn't have invaded your space."

"And I shouldn't have lost control like that. Seriously… sometimes I behave like a child."

Sebastián takes the pill from the pocket of his pants.

"They already diagnosed you, too?" asks Tomás.

"Yes, my attacks are produced by a deep depression. This is supposed to calm me down," says Sebas, while he takes his medication. "I don't want what happened yesterday to happen again."

Tomás looks for something in his pockets that, by the expression on his face, he seems to have forgotten.

"That's weird," he says. "First time this has happened to me."

"What?" asks Fabricio.

"I don't know where I put them. My pills, I mean. I must have left them in my room."

"Well, I don't think anything bad will happen to you if you skip one," Fabricio says with a serious tone, but Tomás laughs because he knows he's being ironic. His friend hates all medication.

"You should worry about what you were thinking of when you forgot them," says Sandra, sounding more like she's making a personal attack rather than a joke.

"Have any of the patients actually gotten out of here?"

The unexpected question leaves Sebastián's friends speechless. The three of them look at each other, without knowing how to answer.

"As they say, many patients were able to get discharged. But because they were cured, obviously," answers Sandra. "There are two ways to be released from here. One is, of course, that Dr. Rutherbor decides so, or even, that he concludes that his treatments have worked and that the patient is free from homosexuality." When she says this, the three friends burst out in laughter. "The other way is to go through the lie detector test —"

"The lie…" interrupts Sebas, his face contorted. Now he knows what the terrifying machine was in Dr. Revas's office.

"It's very common to use them in a rehab clinic like this. And this is the test that proves that you have changed your sexual orientation."

"I can't believe it. And that device…is it one hundred percent accurate?"

"They say it is, obviously, what else is there to say? But, off-the-record, everyone at this table think it's not. And, with all due respect for those patients who passed the lie detector, we also don't believe that they were cured as Dr. Rutherbor says. Their parents probably found out that they are still homosexual and sent them to another less-expensive anti-gay center to continue treatment. Very nice reality, isn't it?" Sandra asks sarcastically.

"But if you're smart, then you won't say any of this out loud...if you know what's good for you. Ask anyone and they'll tell you that everyone who met those "cured" patients insist that they saw them changed, that they spoke in another tone, that they said they didn't like men anymore, and that they wanted to get married and have children." Fabricio's tone starts to scare Sebas.

"The truth is that, thinking about it again, I heard they were cured and I *did* believe it when they told me. As they say, 'Where there's smoke, there's fire,'" Sandra reflects.

"And you fell for it?" Tomás asks skeptically, gaining a little more confidence in himself. "Look around you. How long do you think these kids will be locked up in here?"

"I would say at least a year, on average," says Sandra, but without any concern in her voice. She addresses Sebastián again, "Do you want to know what to do to get out of here? Easy. Change. Get healed. That way you'll be normal again, you'll go back home, you'll make your parents happy, etc. That's the only way to get out of here alive."

"There's nothing wrong with you, with any of us, that's what I think," says Tomás, doing his best to give Sebastián hope. "You just have to know who you are. You must be yourself and, as I told you before, be brave and survive by lying."

"Don't be manipulated and brainwashed by the doctors," advises Fabricio, knowing how long and difficult it will be for Sebastián to stay in the clinic.

"Is that so? It's very sweet to give hope to the new one." Sandra addresses Sebastián again, "Ask the psychiatrist and you'll see that what I'm telling you is true. There is no other way. Either we get cured or we'll never get out. But don't worry, deep down inside, I do believe in Dr. Rutherbor and that you can actually change — it's just that the treatment is a little long and complex."

Although these words are meant to make him feel better, on the inside, Sebastián is more worried than before. He starts feeling claustrophobic, as if the walls were closing in and he could be crushed any minute. His new friends barely say anything after talking about this last issue, as if the topic had left them all contemplative.

"Are we meeting up in the afternoon to talk more and see your portfolio?" Tomás asks Sebastián after they finished eating.

"Yes, of course," he answers. "At what time?"

"Do you play cards?" Sandra interrupts. She doesn't like it at all that Sebastián is hypnotized by Tomás's eye. The young man can only nod. "So, do we meet up in the afternoon?"

"Yes," Sebastián recomposes himself. "In which room do we meet?"

"Yours?" Sandra growls as her mood darkens.

"Ok, in my room, then," Sebastián looks at the clock

on the wall. "I have to go. I have my session."

The group splits up. Tomás goes back to his room with the nurse but as soon as she disappears, Sandra peeps out from the pillar to his left.

"May I?" she asks. "I need to talk to you."

He goes into the room and Sandra follows him. Although Tomás doesn't say it, she's starting to get on his nerves.

"You have to separate, emotionally disconnect yourself from that boy," she reproaches him. "And not just because I think so; it's for his own sake. He wants to be happy and you know that he has to be normal again in order for that to happen."

"That's impossible and you know it. No one is cured from homosexuality. Besides, you were the one who said that the 'cured' patients were a lie."

"You know that I believe it's true. I was only telling him what everyone says — that conspiracy theory."

"You told him that you believed it. You said 'everyone at this table' and I know why. I know that deep down inside you know everything is a big lie and that no one gets cured from homosexuality. What we have to do is accept who we are and live it."

"Are you out of your mind? Are you having doubts about the treatments? Are you taking the other pills? I told you that this is how it works! With that mentality, you'll never get out of here," Sandra belts, more and more furious. "And what you're doing is very selfish. Not only will you hurt yourself, but you are also going to drag him to hell with you."

Tomás loses his patience. He is becoming more confused and really wants to take a nap.

"I don't want to talk about this again. I need to be alone, please. I need to rest. I have dreams."

Sandra slams the door on her way out.

This time, Sebastián gets to Juliana's office three minutes early.

"Come in, come in," she invites. "How nice, you look a lot better than yesterday. Come on, sit down."

She points to a comfortable sofa, not the small cold chair where he sat yesterday. This improves his opinion of the psychiatrist. Sebastián lets himself fall onto the padded furniture.

"And, how have you been? Tell me. How have you been feeling?"

"Normal. I don't know. I'm still the same," Sebastián smiles. "I haven't healed, if that's what you're asking me."

Juliana can't help laughing at the boy's joke. She knows it is a long process to get to that point.

"And, did you take the pill? Do you feel any side effects?"

"Yes. I haven't noticed any side effects. I'm not sure that I would be able to tell you, yet."

"That's true. And, tell me, have you met anyone, have you made any friends?"

"Yes, I met a group of —" Soft knocking on the door interrupts Sebastián.

"Excuse me for a moment."

Juliana walks to the door and opens it. Dr. Rutherbor

is standing on the other side.

"Oh, I'm sorry. I didn't know you were with a patient."

"Don't worry, Doctor. Do you need anything?"

"Yes, dear, I need some medications I just ran out of."

"Which one? I'll get it for you."

"I'll get them myself, don't worry."

Dr. Rutherbor enters the office and walks to a small cabinet, saying hello to Sebastián with a nod and a smile and the boy returns the gesture. Dr. Rutherbor chooses one of the hundreds of bottles; opens it and pours some of the Clonazepam pills into a bottle that he brought with him, labeled "Prochlorperazine".

"Well, I'll leave you to it" he says, walking back to the door.

"Where were we?" asks Juliana, taking him out of his thought. "Alright, better yet, tell me when you first realized that you were attracted to men."

"Since forever. Excuse my saying so, but when I was a kid I masturbated to images of men. But it was weird, like not knowing what I was doing. Around me, I saw that a normal couple consisted of a man and a woman, but I…I don't know… I think I was born this way…"

"Nobody is born like that. You turn into one, dear. Homosexuality happens for many factors, but you are not born with it."

"I don't know. I'm not convinced by your theory. It doesn't make sense. But even if that were the case, is that so bad? Does it make a person bad?"

"Yes, it does, Sebastián. You choose it unconsciously. Everything you do in life is a choice. You can still choose to feel attracted to the opposite sex."

"So I choose it unconsciously? How? Can you explain to me how I can change this feeling that is so real?" Sebastián can't believe how many ridiculous excuses he hears about his sexual orientation.

Juliana doesn't answer and applies again Dr. Rutherbor's suggestion of talking about religion. "I'm sorry for bringing it up again, but it is sometimes necessary. God created Adam and Eve, a man and a woman, that's how He created us. We can't work against his designs. God created a man and a woman so that they could procreate and form a family. It's the ideal plan of a family that we must follow."

"Of course, I know, it's not that I'm against human beings reproducing and want us to go extinct, but there are billions of people in the world so that's not going to happen. As I said before, I even believe that, in the future, homosexuals will be able to have children through adoption."

"That's not going to happen, Sebastián," Juliana gets desperate. "That wouldn't be correct. We can't let that vice, that disease, spread out throughout the world."

"No…I don't know. I'm not convinced yet." As he speaks, Sebastián shows confidence. His hands don't tremble anymore nor does he make any other nervous movements, Juliana notices. "It's just that I honestly don't understand. The first serious relationship I ever had was with a boy. He treated me well, he provided me with tenderness and love, we were one for the other, and we agreed on everything. And, believe me, I never felt something wrong between us. All I felt was love, something special, unique, and something that filled my heart, changed my world and transformed my life for better."

"Sebastián, that wasn't real love."

"He did love me," says Sebastián, smiling off into the distance, remembering Christian's caresses.

"I don't understand how you can believe that is a relationship. Is it that one of you pretends to be a woman, one of you is the sensible one?"

"There's no woman. It's a relationship between two men, in which one can be more loving than the other, but not necessarily behaving as a woman. It's different. It's… it's like thinking that *you* sometimes can't love someone or can't be the one that takes the first step, by virtue of being a woman."

"How old were you when you had this first sexual encounter?"

"At sixteen."

"How did you meet him? How old was he? What was his name?" Juliana keeps writing what she hears in her notes.

"He was my age," Sebastián tries to control himself, but he can't. He has to take out his inhaler. "His name was Christian."

"And what happened? Where is he now?"

Sebastián hears everything as if from afar and moving in slow motion; he feels claustrophobic again. He uses his inhaler once more.

"He's… no longer here."

"What do you mean?"

"He," Sebastián pauses, "killed himself."

Now it is she who listens to this as if from afar; the picture she keeps in her wallet appears in her head, the image of Tommy. Juliana starts feeling very unprofessional.

"I'm sorry," she finally says, trying to remain serious. "But, do you see? That is a consequence of having taken the path of evil, the unrighteous path. It was his disease that brought death to your friend. He lived in sin and... tell me, where is he now? In Heaven with God?" she asks sarcastically.

"No, I don't believe that. He was decent, good, and caring. Yes, he's in Heaven, with God," Sebastián defends his first love, between mouthfuls of air.

"Perhaps...but he let himself be deceived and fall into temptation. You have to save yourself and stop from falling into it. You must heal yourself, change also —"

Juliana suddenly stops talking. She realizes that she's mixing up things — religion with medicine. This is much harder than she thought it would be.

"Excuse me. That was a little unprofessional on my part. I shouldn't digress like this from the treatment. Although, what I said is true — it's in the Bible."

Sebastián doesn't know what to do. He feels like an invisible and powerful hand presses on his chest, wanting to choke him. It wants to see him twitch in that office. Is it the hand of God? He doesn't have what it takes to hold up a defense at the moment, but he knows Christian's love was — is — real and strong.

"Your sexuality depends on many factors," Juliana carries on with her sermon. "Due to the relationships with your family, the absence of one of the two parents, sometimes because one of the two pampers their child too much, or because one is very strict. These are the traumas and memories you have buried within you and you should be uncovering them in these sessions to bring them into the light so that we can examine them. You must open your eyes, realize that you are different, and ask yourself why. You have to change. You have to heal to be like the rest of us — to Grow And Live Normally."

Sebastián hears without listening, looks without seeing. He's there, but absent. The hand of the clock on the wall moves and Sebastián clenches his jaw. There is still half an hour left for him to finish what is only his second session. He doesn't even want to think about what awaits him. Didn't Sandra say the treatment is long and complex? How much time did she say it lasted? A year?

Don't think of that...the buried memories — focus!

Chapter EIGHT:

The puzzle.
Thursday, March 08, 1990

HOURS AFTER LUNCH, SEBASTIÁN IS LYING ON HIS BED. The ideas won't leave him alone - not only from his sessions with the psychiatrist, but also the advice Sandra gives him. He has an emotional hangover. Perhaps they are right…that what he has is a disease… that he has to put his life in the hands of these doctors.

A knock on the door interrupts his thoughts. Sebastián gets up to open the door and see Tomás and Sandra.

"Hello. We're playing?" she asks, shaking a pack of cards to remind him.

"Where are Fabricio, Johana, and Santiago?"

"It's Fabricio's turn with the psychiatrist, Johana is resting, and Santiago has a fever," Tomás answers as they sit on the floor.

"So have you given any thought to what we talked about?" Sandra asks. "You look a lot better, believe me."

"Yes, I am. Maybe. Perhaps you are partly right."

"Healing yourself is the only way to get out of here. Do as I tell you," she insists.

Tomás, while dealing the cards, looks askance at his friend. Sebastián pretends not to notice and takes the cards that are handed to him.

"May I ask you a question, but this time, seriously?" Sandra's face is filled with curiosity. "How did you try to commit suicide?"

"Sandra, don't ask something like that! You're so inappropriate!" Tomás chastises her; worried that Sebastián will have another episode.

"I'm sorry, I'm sorry. Sometimes things just come out like that. You already know me a little," Sandra apologizes.

"No, no, it's ok. You guys, I'm fine — even though it doesn't seem like it because of my attacks, but that's normal." Sebastián sets down his cards and gets ready to tell his story. "To be honest, it was not just once, but many times that I wanted to kill myself. It started when I was only thirteen."

Tomás's face transforms. The situation is worse than he thought. Again, Sebastián pretends not to have seen anything.

The little naïve and romantic young man starts to share. "I went through a lot from infancy to adolescence. During that time, I felt very alone, confused, frustrated, in a depression that made me feel guilt and contempt for myself. I don't know how else to explain it. I felt something wrong with me. I liked men and, at the same time, felt the scorn of society towards those who felt something for people of the same sex so I thought there was no place for me, that I did not fit in this world."

Sebastián pauses when the memory of what happened four weeks ago invades hit thoughts. It was the day before his birthday, and the day he tried to commit suicide. "Last time I felt something curious, I felt that happiness, the same happiness when you see that you have achieved many of your goals. You have everything you have always wanted, but, at the same time, you feel sad because you don't have what you need. Suddenly, nothing makes sense. It's as if we're selfish — we always want more and more. I couldn't say that my life was complete. I was missing that puzzle piece, that special someone who is supposedly out there, who I am still looking for and sometimes I want him to find me, but, if that happens, am I going to be able to say then that my life is complete?"

Sandra looks at Tomás who is staring at Sebastián, listening carefully.

"Sometimes, I think that piece was definitely Christian, but he's no longer here. I've already lost him. Waiting would be useless. He left forever."

"But what happened?" Tomás asks, referring to Christian.

Sebastián doesn't want to ignore him, but he's so caught up in his words that he keeps on talking, as if no one else was there. He tells them the story of his life. He tells them that as a child, his family was always there for him. He was the baby, pampered by everyone. He was a tender child, innocent and quiet. His grandmothers, for example, were his biggest fans and would do anything for him — this, mainly, due to his frequent asthma attacks that put him on the verge of death on more than one occasion. Sebastián was a special and delicate case. His parents saw him as a priority, as someone they had to help survive. He didn't just need one, but many hands — and he had them, which is why he feels so grateful.

The problem, of course, started when he was about twelve years old. That's when things started to get tense because he always heard discriminatory expressions about homosexuality. It made it hard for him to get close to his parents and open up with them about his feelings and attractions so he used to hide them.

Outside of his home life, he was also going through a lot. In high school, he never came out of the closet, but somehow his classmates had already sensed his sexual orientation and he was always the subject of their jokes. Sebastián was friendly and caring, in a way that made other people take advantage of him often, so these offenses made him consider his friendships carefully. He'd rather hang out with his female classmates than with the boys so he talked or played with them. This didn't exactly help his situation; in fact, it made the jokes even worse so that, little by little, they would get harsher — with both physical and emotional aggression. On one such occasion, he had to approach the board in front of the classroom and the others embarrassed him. He began to choke, as if an invisible weight closed his chest and throat.

For a long time, he went through hardships at school. At first, he didn't understand why, but then he gradually got the idea that the main cause was himself — the fact that he was different than the others, which greatly affected him. It stunned him. He needed to escape from that feeling and that's why, at twelve-years old, mostly out of curiosity, he began to experiment with his sexuality by masturbating.

Perhaps this is when he first began to have trouble accepting who he was, since the images that visited him for long time were not "normal"; that is, while all the boys around him fantasized about women, he found himself attracted to his same sex. He cannot deny that he was terrified by the idea because he was already being bullied at school every day and Sebastián feared that, throughout his entire life, he would be the target of discrimination and rejection.

So he tried to fit in. He made an effort to go through the world unnoticed. He really tried to feel attraction for the girls. Back then, he was looking for answers and a direction for his life and he thought that acting like a heterosexual was the best thing to do. He refused to accept his fate and this, in the long run, became a bigger problem because he felt like he was collapsing deep down on the inside. Nobody would stand by him. So, at thirteen, he thought about suicide for the first time.

The most difficult decision, above all, was the method. He thought of a myriad of ways: tying a belt around his neck, cutting his veins with razor blades, sticking a pair of scissors or a knife into his stomach, and many others. But he couldn't find the courage; the fear of death was too much for him at the time and he dismissed those thoughts for a while, although he continued to be convinced that it was the only solution to the biggest problem: himself.

Things got worse when his parents found out about his homosexuality. He remembers clearly that he was fifteen when they found a gay magazine hidden in his closet. He couldn't find the right words to defend himself. He didn't see another choice other than to come out to his parents and it almost give him a panic attack. His brother, Gastón was also there. Sebastián could see him standing far away from his bedroom door, not saying a word and looking ashamed to have a gay brother.

What kept Sebastián alive was the feeling that perhaps what he wanted was not to die, but to be saved, and this, somehow, materialized when he met Christian at the age of sixteen.

They used to live quite close to each other. This gave them the opportunity to see each other in the street a couple of times and at the school bus stop, until they finally dared to strike up a conversation. They were soul mates. They had a lot in common and hit it off from the first moment. Thanks to Christian, Sebastián ceased to be a dark, depressed kid, full of confusion and feelings of guilt; he understood that the discriminatory behavior towards homosexuals is just the product of ignorance and prejudice. Christian was a young man like himself, but with more self-acceptance and courage. Even though he had never come out of the closet, he helped Sebastián to handle and accept his own identity. He made him start to appreciate the best of himself, as he had never been able to do before. Sebastián stopped feeling so alone.

However, Christian is dead. They were together for three years, just three years, and now, ironically, Sebastián, who had thought of suicide so many times, is alive. Christian, as brave as he was, with so much self-esteem, a fighter for his beliefs, is dead.

Since his death, everything Sebastián had overcome with Christian's help has returned. His emptiness returned.

Depression and darkness returned. The teasing, abuse, and intimidation in school returned. He could not believe that there were people like that, so heartless. But, oh, surprise, in the last year of school, a whole new world opened up for him. Some, not all, of his classmates had matured and he was able to get along with them. His relationships, or his ability to relate, were harmonizing to the point of changing all or nearly all his conceptions of that time in his life. Today, he does believe that there are good people in the world and that all human beings can change for the better, that they can treat others respectfully despite their differences, but that it is difficult to achieve.

He already, at twenty years of age, feels like a sign without any message, like he doesn't have any purpose. This is what causes him to become depressed. He loses control over his emotions, enters a dark abyss and then the desire to die overcomes him — the desire to end everything once and for all, like flipping off a light switch. He feels guilty to be alive, of not being able to save Christian from death; he even considers it unfair that he has not been killed by his asthma, when people with the same problem have died from not being able to breathe.

However, not everything is negative. There are moments or stages in his life in which he fills up with positivity. After overcoming all those moments during the hell that was high school, the loneliness and emotional distance at home, the negative thoughts and comments about homosexuality from his family, and the suicide of his first love, Sebastián gave himself another chance and decided to change his fate. He knows he only has to make the right decision. He cannot sit around waiting for the things he wants and needs to just fall into his lap or to escape him altogether. He has to leave his home, start the ride of his life, find that for which he was born, fully identify himself as who he really is.

The hard part, he knows, is leaving behind that which binds him: his relationship with his family, the death of Christian, and the city where he spent his adolescence. He already made this decision once, in part, when he decided to travel to the capital to study art at the university and start his career. It was a decision he made practically overnight. It seems being impulsive does not always end badly. In that instance, he did feel like he overcame a barrier, burst a bubble, and cut a rope that was tying him down. That's what he needed to do — to not let anyone force him to take a step back, to let no one stop him from living the life that he was born for.

"Wait, wait…" Tomás interrupts. "What happens then? I mean, if you went to Quito to study art, you had a job and you were independent, you had started again at zero — I guess that is what you wanted. How did you end up in this clinic?"

"I met a boy. Alejandro Dunuel."

"And, who is he?"

"We liked each other from the first moment we met, or at least that's what I thought. He used me and he swindled me. He made me fall for him and he stole money from me and my roommates."

Sebastián starts to narrate his relationship with Alejandro with all of the details. After two weeks of hanging out and countless dates, their relationship was starting to get more serious. But in the end, it was only Sebastián who wanted that.

Sebastián lived with his cousins, Alberto and Michelle. Alberto was letting Alejandro stay for a while, at the request of Sebastián, until Alejandro solved his economic situation. He had been fired from his job as a bartender. The owners didn't trust him anymore; they suspected that he had stolen money.

Alejandro asked for Sebastián's help, to let him stay in the apartment. But, as the days went by, the relationship between Alejandro and the other roommates became too tense. He owed them money — and even more to Sebastián. Alejandro decided to go back to his mother's house and, supposedly, ask her for the money he owed before the roommates threw him out — especially Alberto, who didn't trust him from the beginning and had warned the naïve Sebastián.

I'll be back, I promise," Alejandro told Sebastián and kissed his freckled cheek before boarding his bus at the station. "And I'll pay everything. Don't worry."

"I'll wait for you," answered Sebastián, mesmerized by that small smile which had conquered him the first time that they met.

Sebastián came back to the apartment and entered the room that he shared with Alejandro and opened the suitcase Alejandro had left as a guarantee that he was coming back to give them the money. Sebastián noticed that, on the back, there was a sticker labeled "Mauro P". Already thinking the worst, Sebastián opened it and saw that there were no belongings inside — only old newspapers and papers, as if to add some weight so that the bag wouldn't feel empty if someone moved it. At that moment, Michelle came into the room.

"Are you ok? What is it?" she asked, when she realized that Sebastián was crying.

"He lied to me."

"Alejandro? Why would you say that?"

"Look, the bag doesn't have clothes or anything — just these newspapers. And look, I think it even has someone else's name."

Michelle realized that what Sebastián was saying was true.

"He left, conned all of us and left. I'm sorry. I don't think that he'll pay us back. I was so naïve."

"How? How could you trust someone like that?"

"I don't know. I don't know what happened to me. I was disillusioned with him."

"You must be careful. Do you hear me? You can't open up and give your trust to strangers! Alberto didn't know him that well and warned us. There are bad people in the world."

"Yes, now I know," Sebastián used his inhaler once again. "I'm sorry. Now I need to rest. I want to be alone, please."

"Yes, lie down, I know it's difficult. Lie down and close your eyes…breathe. When you least expect it, all of this will be over and better things will come. Don't lock yourself into your thoughts. Try to sleep."

Some nights later, Sebastián returned to the gay bar, Heaven, where he suspected that he would find the missing

Alejandro. He saw the young man named Gustavo laughing and dancing with the very same Alejandro. Everything had been made up to use Sebastián and steal his money.

For Sebastián, reality really bites and it's difficult to get to know someone truthfully. He never thought that Christian would ever commit suicide and then he found out that Alejandro was a drug trafficker and a thief at the various clubs where he worked as a bartender. Sebastián felt like he was losing his grip on the world.

Alejandro, of course, disappeared entirely without paying them the money they had lent him.

"I'm sorry. Your roommate, Michelle, was right. There are bad people in this world," says Tomás, wanting to hug Sebastián, but holding back in order to avoid causing tension with Sandra. "However, you should know that we are not all like that and you cannot generalize all gay people because one of them is bad. For example, you can trust me." Tomás smiles, he wants Sebastián to feel better because he knows all of those memories must be weighing him down inside.

"Thanks. It's just that, sometimes, I think that I won't meet anyone like Christian. I've said a million times, he was unique."

"But it's also not that you have to forget him or that he stops being unique. We all have those qualities that make us unique — that's the miracle of life. I'm sure that you'll find someone just as good or maybe even better than him, then you'll feel love again."

"I remember, that night I met Alejandro. I felt like I was in a very different world. Just as I was leaving that bar, standing in front of the entrance with all those people there, I saw that I was in a world of promiscuity," Sebastián confesses, ashamed.

"It's true what you say, there is promiscuity, mostly in clubs, but although you may not believe me, it's like that everywhere — also among heterosexuals. Nowadays, you don't perceive it as alarming and negative, as with homosexuals. It's ignorance." Tomás gets serious. "I think that human beings, by nature, have that impulse to experiment sexual diversity by the head and in the heart in order to have stability and to find love."

"Do you think so?" Sebastián starts thinking, remembering the emotional and sentimental stability that he had with Christian.

"There's a phase of fun and experimenting that you can easily find in bars and there is another phase, which is where you are at now. And, as it happens with any other person, it's difficult because that's the only path you have available to find love."

"I think you are right. I lost my self-esteem and have fallen into that depression of not being able to find someone like Christian," he blushes with tears in his eyes.

Sebastián gets up from the bed and walks to the desk on his room, deciding to show his new friends his biggest treasure. He opens a drawer and takes out a photo album. He sits next to them again and opens it.

"This is Christian. He is the first and only boyfriend I've had."

"He's handsome," Sandra comments, hoping that Tomás dies from jealousy. "And you seem very happy next to him."

"Yes, we were extremely happy - until he killed himself." Sebastián uses his inhaler.

"I'm so sorry," Tomás says, in a low voice.

"I'm really sorry," seconds Sandra, out of mere obligation.

Sebastián turns the pages of the album and comes to one with no photos, but an envelope. Seeing this, a series of mental images surrounds Tomás in an incomprehensible déjà vu — a row of memories that appear unrelated, but feel like they are his. Something tells him that he has seen that envelope before.

"And that letter?" he asks.

"It's Christian's. He wrote it before committing suicide."

Sebastián takes out the envelope and shows the letter to his friends. It reads: April 8, 1987.

"And what does it say?" Sandra asks.

"I don't know. I haven't read it all yet. It frightens me a little," Sebastián uses his inhaler once again. "And well, after what happened with Alejandro..." Sebastián changes the subject so that his friends forget the letter. "It made me feel even worse. I had suicidal thoughts again and I convinced myself that the only solution was to disappear. I mean, if I ever wanted to be with Christian again, I had no other option of visiting him personally — in Heaven or Hell — wherever we had to meet." Sebastián pauses.

"Oh God, I remember thinking if only I could close my eyes right now and just figure out how to never open them again, to not go on anymore. But I always ended up restarting. I kept playing the game of life every morning when I woke up and I always realized that I lost the game when I would turn to look around me and there was no one by my side, no Christian anymore."

"So the night before my birthday, I cheated in the game and decided that the easy way to win is to overdose on pills. I took almost two full bottles with vodka. I don't know if it was good or bad luck, but Michelle came into my room just in time and rushed me to the hospital. She called my mother and, well, that's how I ended up in this clinic."

"Sebastián, please, don't ever do that again. You are not alone."

"Thank you." Sebastián wipes away the tears that are already covering his face. "But now, starting today, I'm thinking that it was for the best to come here."

"What do you mean by that?"

"Because I'm being given the opportunity to change. I have to be grateful."

"So, you decided to do so? Do you want to change?"

"Yes, in order to give back to my family what they have done for me, to get out of this clinic, to heal and live healthily."

"It's for the best," says Sandra. "Being homosexual is what makes us sad and, in your case, this depression leads you to think about suicide."

Tomás just observes without agreeing with what they are saying. They return to their card game and don't touch on those issues again — just have fun and forget their daily stress.

***

An hour later, Sandra picks up the cards and gets ready to

leave.

"And what do you say? Do we meet up again tomorrow?" she asks.

Both boys nod. As she gets up, she tries to grab Tomás' hand to leave together, but he pulls away.

"I'll stay a little longer," he says.

"But it's already late. The nurses are going to come and punish you all," Sandra is more jealous than ever.

"I won't take long. I'll join you shortly."

"Do whatever you want."

Sandra leaves, annoyed. Tomás wants to calm her down, but he knows that nothing he could say would do any good.

"I think you should go with her," says Sebastián, who doesn't want to see them fighting.

"Don't worry, she'll get over it soon. You just can't take it seriously."

"Are you…dating?"

"No. Not all," Tomás laughs. "Well, she is very attached to me. I just don't want her to feel bad. I don't know what to do to break the spell."

"It's going to be difficult."

"Why do you say that?"

"Well…you know…you're handsome," Sebastián smiles, shyly.

"Thank you. Although, I'd like to stand out for being a good person or for things like that."

"Well, of course you do. I see you are kind and considerate to others. Yes, you do stand out for that."

"You're cute. Although I'm sure you get it all the time,"

says Tomás, making Sebastián blush.

"I think, generally, people feel sorry for me."

Sebastián knows that he's falling into his usual pattern by putting himself down, but, at the same time, he doesn't want to sound unfriendly or smug. Deep down, he feels like he has met someone special, someone who makes him feel, if not the same, then at least very similar to how he felt with Christian. But, he is afraid.

"I don't believe you. I'm pretty sure they tell you that because it's true. You're cute." Tomás comes closer to Sebastián and takes his hand. "Believe me, you're adorable."

Sebastián becomes nervous and has to take a deep breath. He sees his own hand wrapped in Tomás', who feels the need to kiss him, to embrace him firmly. Both of them look into each other's eyes.

"I remember that call…" Sebastián feels a powerful trust in Tomás and opens up more. "My mom called my father to tell him what happened. I was on vacation with my father on his ranch. They knew Christian and I were 'friends'. My father didn't say anything, but I suddenly suspected something. Somehow, I managed to convince him to tell me. As soon as I heard 'committed suicide', I ran out of the house and shouted with all of my lungs, my being, and my soul. I had never released so much. That night I mourned and pleaded to my father. We went back the next day to wait for news of his funeral. I can't stop thinking, if I had known about it and had been there with him, would he still be alive?" Sebastián confesses, looking through the blue sky from the big window with bars.

"Maybe you could have helped him to see reason and

make him feel safe from his loneliness, but it's not your fault, you didn't know and you weren't able to be there. It wasn't in your hands — it was his decision." Tomás try to help Sebastián wipe his tearful face.

"I don't know what to say…" Sebastián turns his face away. He can't accept that wasn't his fault.

"About what you said about the pieces of the puzzle," Tomás strokes his hand and wait for Sebastián to turn up his face so that he can see his baby blue eyes and continue, "you know, I think that puzzle does exist and its pieces are out there, waiting for us to assemble ourselves." Tomás explains. "For example, what happened to you with Christian, a puzzle got formed there. A unique, original, and unrepeatable drawing was formed. You must always keep that design in your heart. I think that, in certain cases, there are second chances. The thing is that we are like those pieces and when we find each other, we form another puzzle, another image or design. Do I make myself clear? You must realize that you can be the piece that completes the puzzle for someone else. That's how love works – it's not a destination, it's a mystery…and you have to solve it."

Sebastián listens attentively.

"I think you have to give yourself a chance. No, I'm wrong, not just one, but hundreds, thousands of opportunities until you find the right one, true love. Only then you can tell yourself that you are happy with someone. I know that being here sucks, but outside there is so much more to come and it's just a matter of time until we get out of here. Don't give up. We won't give up."

Sebastián feels like he is healing just by hearing Tomás

speak. He realizes that his selfishness has kept him blind; it has denied him the opportunity to love someone, to put together another puzzle. Maybe he is just angry with himself because his life is not perfect and he doesn't want to die, but no one is perfect. The truth is that he just wants to be saved — to feel something real, true, honest, and good again, to not keep failing and to finally find his way, but now, inside in the clinic, it seems difficult. How will he survive then? That is what leads him to reconsider the treatments because he sees that there is no other way out.

Tomás is dying to hug Sebastián and express how much he has come to care for him in so little time; he wants to tell him that he has become someone very special, but he resists his impulses because of what Sandra said. He is afraid to make Sebastián suffer again when he is finally considering accepting himself and forgoing the clinical treatments to "heal" — or surviving by lying. Tomás could cause a lot of pain. He releases Sebastián's hand.

"Remember, if you need to talk to someone, to keep you company, or whatever, you know where to find me," Tomás says, with his best smile.

"I know. And you know it, too."

They hear sounds outside, like footsteps in the hallway.

"Time to separate! Too much time together!" exclaims the nurse, Verónica, making her usual rounds through all the bedrooms.

"I'd better leave," Tomás says, leaning in for a goodbye hug.

At that moment, the flood of emotions causes them to forget who they are and where they are. Almost unconsciously, their heads start spinning and their noses graze.

"Stop! Separate!" the nurse screams as she walks by again to hasten the patients.

Sebastián and Tomás let go, recovering their presence of mind.

"Ok, now I do have to go."

Sebastián only nods, looking at the floor. When Tomás leaves, he sits on the bed, more confused than before. Up until a few minutes ago, he was convinced that it was best to change — to heal, to believe the story that they are trying to sell him at the clinic. Now he doubts it. For a moment, with Tomás, he felt happy.

That same night, Tomás looks at the bottle of medication on his desk. His doubts are increasing and he feels frustrated, trapped. He takes the bottle and throws it to the floor, the pills spilling all over the room. He lies on the bed and stares at the drawing on his wall. Something's happening to him, something that he doesn't understand. The letter - Sebastián's letter. It reminds him of something, but he doesn't know what it is. Does it have to do with what Dr. Rutherbor said about that condition he has, which makes him lose his memory? His mind and his spirit have been altered; he cannot calm down.

He thinks of Sebastián, about how good he feels when he is with him. But what Sandra said is true - if Tomás gets too involved with him, Sebastián will get hurt. Sebastián wants to change. Well, he can't meddle with his decision. But…but, what if it's the other way around and it's there, in the clinic where he will get hurt? What if it's him, Tomás, who can save the boy? No, he can't listen to himself. He would love to. He would love to get out of that place — of that jail — and invite Sebastián to the movies, to walk around Mariscal Foch, to travel to the beaches, to the mountains, the lake. He hates to think like this. He hates being a victim of his own thoughts.

Knocks on the door take him out of his reverie. He knows who it is and opens the door reluctantly.

"Hello," Sandra says as she walks in. "The nurse is asleep now. I already put the pillows on the bed so they won't notice."

"Are you sure? We're risking that —"

"Yes, don't jinx it," Sandra interrupts him, walking to the bed, followed by Tomás. "I'm sorry for my behavior. I didn't want to get upset."

They lie down and she puts her arms on his chest as she does almost every night.

"Don't worry. Everything is all right," Tomás answers, resigned and ready to sleep.

He is stirred from a light sleep only a little while later, he hears a sound. He is scared and bathed in sweat. The sounds come from outside of his room and he, with bare feet, goes to find out what they are.

"Who's there?" he asks.

He's afraid because everything's different. The hallways are dirty and the doors are stained with…is that blood? He approaches the doorknob of a room and sees that it has red fingerprints. More blood?

He listens for the sounds again and walks towards

them.

"Bernardo!" Tomás suddenly hears, without knowing who is screaming.

"Who's there?" he asks again to the emptiness. He still doesn't see anyone. He hears a cry so he keeps walking. He doesn't know where, but the sounds, like screeches of a crying child, keep getting stronger; it seems they are near.

Tomás runs to the room where he believes someone just asked for help. He opens the door, but he doesn't see anything inside the room. Everything is dark. There's a puddle of blood on the floor.

"Dr. Rutherbor?" he asks. "Doctor?"

He enters the room, with hands outstretched, groping in the thick darkness. He takes a couple of steps forward and touches a lump with his feet.

He stands still in shock. It's a person. It's cold. He realizes it's dead. It's a corpse! He crouches and tries to identify who it is, but he doesn't recognize the person through the few features that can make out in the darkness. He gets back on his feet and walks towards the wall, looking for the light switch. He finds it and turns on the light. He stays there in panic at the sight before him. A dead child lying on the bed!

"Tomás?"

"Ah!" Tomás wakes up, drenched in a cold sweat and trembling.

"Tomás! Tomás, are you ok?" Sandra sounds worried.

"Where…where am I?"

"Calm down, calm down. You had a nightmare."

"Ber... Bernardo...who is Bernardo?" whispers Tomás.

Sandra is nervous. She looks for the bottle of pills to give him one so that he calms down.

"Bernardo. Do you know who Bernardo is?" Tomás repeats.

"Where are your pills? I don't see them."

Sandra gets up from the bed and begins to walk to the desk. On the way, she feels something with her foot — it's a pill. She kneels and picks it up. She goes to the bathroom, pours a glass of water, and hands the medication to Tomás. She now has reasons to worry. Why were the pills on the floor? He must have thrown them. Why did he mention that name? It was just a dream - or is he starting to remember? He wants to know if she knows who Bernardo is. Sure, how could she not know? How could she not recognize the name of someone with whom she was once so close?

Chapter NINE:

Daily harassments and threats. Thursday, February 15, 1990

THE DARKNESS FILLS EVERYTHING. He is wrapped in it. That's where he wants to be.

"Mateo! Mateo!" his mother calls.

He doesn't want to move. He would prefer to avoid the sunlight.

"Get up! Get up! Get up right now! The bus is coming and you haven't showered or anything!"

Those are the few moments that he has to enjoy life — there, in that space that is not a space, that time off time, wrapped in darkness, tucked from head to toe between two blankets and two sheets in the darker black of night that he himself has created a refuge.

"I don't want to go. I hate school."

"And what do you expect from life? To be a bum? Get up! It's past seven!"

"I don't want to go," he insists.

"You have to go to classes, as any normal child, so you get educated. Then you will go to college and study whatever you're passionate about."

"But I don't know. I don't know what I want to be," Mateo confesses.

"You'll figure it out — now get up! Don't forget to take your medication," his mother reminds him.

Mateo take his daily pill for his Hashimoto hypothyroidism. Then he starts the shower and stares at the water as if he isn't really there, resigned to having to start another week of school, and especially approaching the moment he will be forced to see his classmates. He is someone who prefers being in places with few people, or alone. If it were up to him, he would spend the whole day under those two blankets and two sheets.

As he dries himself after his shower, he puts on his glasses and looks in the mirror. The first things that stand out are the marks on his wrists. He looks at them and remembers. He caresses them. His brown eyes sadden. He puts on his school uniform, pulling his shirtsleeves down so that they cover the scars. Then he goes to the kitchen, where his mother waits for him with breakfast served.

"You have ten minutes to eat. But first, pray."

The two assume the prayer position, with their heads tilted and hands folded, while Charol mechanically repeats the Morning Prayer.

"And my chocolate milk?" Mateo asks, once they finish thanking God.

"Here it is. Hurry up, you have seven minutes left."

His mother pushes the glass closer to him; Mateo stretches to take it, making sure that his scars are hidden under the sleeves of the uniform.

"Mom? Is it possible to switch my school?" Mateo will

make the attempt to admit his real reason for not wanting to go to school; something that he has been keeping secret for a long time, but now he needs to share it.

"Don't say that, son. You are in the best school in the city."

"It's just that I don't like it. There they always —"

"What are you talking about? Hurry up, hurry up! Eat fast. This school is Catholic. I chose it myself. They will guide you through the steps of the Lord, through the path of good."

"I know, I know, but —"

"Son, that's it. No more conversation." Charol hands the backpack to Mateo. "You're going to miss the bus. Get out already."

"But I haven't finished —"

"It's late. I don't want you to find another excuse for missing school. Come on, get up and walk fast."

The seventeen-year-old young man comes to the corner just as the bus stops and the doors open with that sound that already fries his nerves. He now has a lump in his throat while his mind repeats non-stop "Be strong. Be strong. Be strong." Mateo boards with shaky steps.

Inside the bus, his eyes turn down. His soul is ready for the worst.

"Look who's here!" one of the students on the bus screams. "The crossed-eyed faggot!"

All explode into a laugh.

"Four-eyed Faggot! Four-eyed Faggot! Four-eyed Faggot!" all the passengers sing in a chorus, as if cheering for their favorite team.

Mateo hates the march down the narrow aisle. He adjusts his glasses and begins the walk of pain and shame. He feels the paper balls hitting him in the face and on his back, hands that seems to materialize in the air to ruffle him or hit him with an open palm on the back of the neck, all accompanied with the same sweet music that degrades him: Four-eyed Fag! Four-eyed Fag! He wonders what the driver feels. Does he disagree with all this but somehow not have the authority to confront the students? Or is it that he enjoys it? The only thing that's certain is that this happens every morning and afternoon, Monday through Friday, as a religious ritual, and the driver never interferes. In fact, Mateo can see him smiling through the rearview mirror. On the bus, there are plenty of free seats, but all the passengers put their backpacks or books in the seat next to them and Mateo has to make the entire trip standing up almost every day. He doesn't complain, either, which gives him an advantage — just as the bus arrives at school, around eight o'clock in the morning, he is the first to get off and run away. He takes refuge in the bathroom, where he cries and regrets having been born. The entrance bell rings at 8:20, which does not give him much time to recover himself. He comes out of the stall and walks to the sink, where he washes his face, combs his hair, and adjusts his glasses. "Be strong. Be strong. Be strong."

In the mirror, he doesn't see a bad person, or even someone ugly. Mateo Feirro has a sweet and friendly triangular-shaped face with a clear complexion. He is quite thin, weighing not much more than one hundred pounds despite his thyroid problem. His short wavy hair is a golden auburn color. He wears prominent glasses, earning him his nicknames, but, if one looks beyond his thick lenses, his delicate features make him quite attractive — and it could be said that his dimpled chin is enviable. Of course, nobody sees this. The only thing they see is the "Four-eyed Faggot", stumbling and being pushed by his peers.

There are five minutes remaining before the first class starts so Mateo rushes to grab the Geography book from his locker — which is right next to Esteban's, the most popular kid in his class. *He's* not mean. In fact, he is one of the few that treats Mateo kindly.

"How are you, Mateo?" Esteban greets him when they bump into each other.

"I'm ok. I'm ok," he lies.

"I'm glad. Did you do the homework? Last night I stayed up until three and there were still, like, two pages left. I couldn't understand a thing."

"You should have…you should have called me. I would have helped you. I was done on Friday night. It was easy for me." Inside, Mateo hopes that someday he'll be able to confess Esteban what he feels for him. Someday, who knows, Esteban could become that special someone. "No," he unconsciously repeats to himself, "just stop thinking nonsense."

"It's worth ten points. What will you do?"

"I'll finish it right now, of course," Esteban laughs. "Jaime is going to lend me his homework and I'll just copy the last part. I'll see you inside."

Mateo is now alone. The inner force he feels toward Esteban vanishes when his classmate leaves.

"What are you looking at, faggot?"

Mateo hears Jaime's voice behind him. He turns and gets ready for the emotional massacre. Jaime hits him with his opened palm on the top of his head and his glasses fall from the impact. He's all alone. He becomes scared.

"Hey! Leave him alone. He hasn't done anything to you." Esteban miraculously reappears. He forgot something in his locker and came back. Mateo smiles with relief. Esteban kneels and hands him his glasses. "Here, they're not broken. Forgive him; sometimes he forgets he's a person."

"It's just that he was giving you a weird look, while you were walking into the class," Jaime defends himself. "If I were you, I wouldn't get near him."

"Come on, come on, lend me that homework."

Esteban leads Jaime away and Mateo can't do anything but lose himself back in his thoughts. Someday he'll be able to confess everything to him and then… "No, forget it, forget it. It's just your imagination".

In the back of the middle row of desks in Geography class, Mateo writes in his notebook. They are just random words that join up into phrases, random words that just appear in his mind. Writing is his favorite hobby.

The teacher is explaining something about the Panama Canal, but he's not really interested. It's not that he's a bad student, he just learns better when he's alone in his house studying. The war-like environment he has to deal with at school is not as conducive to learning.

"Hey, Four-eyed Faggot, wanna give me a kiss?"

Mateo hears Diego taunting him. Everyone around them laughs, covering their mouths with their hands so that the teacher doesn't notice.

"A kiss, Four-eyed Fag?"

Mateo ignores him.

"Shitty Four-eyed Faggot, look, don't you play stupid." The harassment continues. "Don't you want to give me a kiss?"

"No," answers Mateo.

"No? Not at all? And, if I give you a kiss? Do you not like me?"

His classmates can no longer hold it in and laugh openly, catching the teacher's attention.

"Silence in the back!" she shouts.

Mateo breathes calmly. It's not much, but at least the teacher will make sure that there is silence around him during class. And this is the case until the lunch bell rings. For a change, Mateo waits for the class to empty before he leaves. He is going to buy something to eat, but on the way, Jaime and Diego intercept him.

"Hey, gay boy. What do you think you're doing? Where are you going?"

"Nothing. I'm going to..." Mateo doesn't know if he should tell them the truth. They will probably try to steal his money. "I am going to the bathroom."

"Oh yeah? What a coincidence! We are, too. Do you want us to carry you there?"

"No, no, I'm going on my own."

"Nonsense! We'll go arm-in-arm! Don't you know that we are good friends and just want to help you?"

"No, no, leave me alone!"

His "good friends", laughing aloud, force him against

his will — one by his arms and the other by his legs — while Mateo struggles to break free. They carry him to the bathroom, but to the women's room, where they open the door of one of the stalls and throw him next to the toilet. Mateo's ankle gets twisted and the pain makes him cry.

"You're like an insect, but ugly," Jaime mocks. "And weird."

Diego releases a laugh that terrifies Mateo.

"What will you do to me? Please, don't hurt me," he begs on his knees.

"No, we're your best friends, I already told you. We won't hurt you…much," says Jaime, which prompts another laugh from Diego.

Mateo is still crying as Jaime grabs him by his hair and sticks his head in the toilet. He holds him under the water for a few seconds and lifts his head so that he can take a mouthful of air. He repeats the process one, two, three, four times until the toilet lid falls down hard, hitting Mateo on the back of the head and knocking him unconscious.

The darkness fills everything. He is wrapped in it. That's where he wants to be.

"Mateo! Mateo!" a woman — his mother? — is calling his name.

He doesn't want to move; he would prefer to avoid the sunlight.

"Mateo?"

No, it's not his mother. It is… Who is it? Where is he?

"Mateo? Do you hear me?"

He opens one eye and everything around him is

blurry. He is able to make out the image of a girl's face. *A girl and is there someone else there?*

"Don't be afraid. Try not to move. We're taking you to the school nurse." He recognizes Esteban's voice. The girl must be his girlfriend, Fabiola. "Are you ok? Can you see? Can you see me?"

"Yes...now I can."

Mateo begins to regain his composure. Now he distinguishes everything more clearly and the memories of what happened come back to him. He realizes that he's lying on the floor, next to a toilet. Jaime and Diego — yes, now he remembers. He touches his forehead and sees blood on his fingers. He must have a cut. Esteban kneels and hands him his glasses. One of the lenses is broken. They help him up and carefully lead him to the nurse.

Once at the door to the nurse's office, Mateo refuses to enter. He has nothing against the school nurse, but he doesn't want him to see the scars on his wrists.

"You know what? Don't worry. I'm fine."

"But she has to check that wound."

"No, I'll wear a bandage and that's it — all good. Thank you for helping me, but it's nothing out of the ordinary. Believe me, I'm used to this."

"Tell me the truth. Who were they? Who did this to you?" Esteban asks.

"No. I don't remember very well. They came from behind and pushed me. I didn't see them," Mateo lies.

"You see?" the girl says. "You have to go to the doctor. You could have damage to your brain or something — amnesia."

"You know that you can tell us," Esteban insists. "I'm worried that you'll stay quiet and then something worse will happen to you. These guys crossed the line."

"I know. I'll be more careful. Don't worry about me, I am a survivor." These last words seem to reassure the couple.

"My love, I think that we should not force him to do what he doesn't want to do," Fabiola says. "If he says he already feels ok..."

"Yes, I'm better. I don't know how to thank you for this, but if you need something. Esteban, if you want help in Geography, just let me know."

Not entirely convinced, Esteban has nothing left but to accept what he has been told. He nods. "You don't need to thank us. If someone is bothering you, please let me know."

Having said that, the couple leaves to take advantage of the last minutes of lunch. Mateo goes directly to his next class. He's starving because he didn't even finish breakfast and now won't have time to go to the cafeteria for lunch.

The rest of the day goes as usual — which means more wads of paper, more hurtful taunts, more obscenities of all kinds, and the occasional "Four-eyed Faggot, Four-eyed Faggot!" Mateo lives out his worst nightmare on a daily basis; he exists in it. It's no wonder that he has contemplated the idea of suicide on more than a dozen occasions — planning in detail how he would live his last night on Earth, devising the various ways of taking his own life. He believes in God, despite being different and discriminated against by the rest of the people who say that treating him badly is what God would do. But he doesn't believe what they say to him at school and what his mother constantly repeats: that God hates homosexuals and especially those who decide to end their own life. On the contrary, Mateo believes that God loves him and is waiting for him "up there" and that is why he would prefer to hurry up and meet Him as soon as possible, running into His arms to relieve the suffering.

The only reason why he has not done so is that he knows that there are still people like Esteban in the world. He really likes Fabiola, but also he envies her because she knew how to win the heart of the school Casanova and has been with him for nearly two years. Esteban fits the stereotype of the protagonist in the television series that Mateo likes to watch: he's good at sports and attractive. What Mateo likes most is his bronze skin and his eyes that seem to change color depending on the light — sometimes green, blue, or light blue. He knows that the relationship he dreams of with him is impossible, which is why he has nothing left but to take refuge in his imagination and the idea that, if not today, then in the near future, he will have a chance to be with Esteban. He would like Esteban to be his first kiss, to finally know what it is to be with someone of the same sex.

The two o'clock bell! Finally, he can go home! Happiness dawns on Mateo's face; this time of the afternoon is always his salvation. It's as if his prayers have been answered. He waits for all of his classmates to grab their stuff and run to the buses. He doesn't like to be left there and have to call his mother to pick him up. He hates the lecture she gives him on the way home. But, as he is coming out of the classroom, he feels a weight on his back, a force that pulls him backwards. He turns and sees Jaime holding onto his backpack. Diego is standing next to him.

"Not so fast, Four-eye Faggot! Don't you want to be alone with us in the classroom for a while? I swear you'll like it."

Diego laughs and claps, as if his friend had just found a new joke that he could have never come up with on his own — quite an achievement.

"Please, I am going to miss the bus. I have to get home. My mom is sick," Mateo lies.

"Yes, yes, of course, as if your mom loves you," Jaime continues intimidating him. "I am telling you I'm going to make you happy. Stay here with me."

"Enough!" the scream of Esteban interrupts the laugh of Diego. "I already told you, Jaime. Leave him alone. He hasn't done anything to you."

All of the other students in the hall turn to see what's happening and are surprised, not only because someone is defending Mateo for the first time, but also because of who's doing it.

"I can't believe that you would lower yourself to this," Jaime tells Esteban. "What are you doing?"

"Look at his head. Did you have anything to do with the cut that he has there?"

"What? I don't know what you're talking about. Are you also turning into a faggot?"

Everyone laughs, including Esteban, although his laughter has a different tone than the others.

"I'm not a faggot or a homosexual," he responds.

"But it's the same shit. Faggot, homosexual, queer,

Four-eyed Fag. It's all the same to me."

"No. Faggot is someone like you, who is obsessed with another man — with Mateo, in your case. You keep following him everywhere. You whisper to him in the classroom and everything. That seems like a faggot to me."

Now the whole school is in an uproar, a single laugh that drives Jaime crazy, until his friend Diego laughs. Mateo, on the other hand, is silent and still, staring at the ground. Fabiola is also quiet, but because she's embarrassed to be even indirectly associated with the situation.

"What's really going on is that you hate him because, unlike you, Mateo openly accepts who he is," Esteban continues. "He assumes his reality. You, on the other hand, are a coward."

Fabiola can't stand this anymore and approaches her boyfriend. She grabs his waist and tries to pull him to the side, but he doesn't budge an inch. He stands firmly in place.

"You asked for it, faggot," Jaime accuses, while walking towards Esteban with his fists clenched.

The rest of the school forms a circle around the two of them. Fabiola is afraid of being stuck in the middle of a fight and moves to the side. She stands next to Mateo and looks him over from head to toe. She looks at him with hatred, blaming him. Mateo realizes this and with his eyes tries to apologize, saying that he didn't want any of this to happen. Fabiola opens her mouth to insult him, but thinks better of it; it's best to go get a nearby teacher to stop this madness. The rest of the students chant "Fight, fight!" dying of happiness, while the faces of the fighters are already bruised and bloodied.

***

Hours later, Jaime and Diego are at the main office talking to the principal while Mateo and Esteban are sitting in the waiting room, after having given their versions of the events.

"Are you okay?" Esteban asks, sitting beside him.

"No," Mateo responds with a voice so soft that Esteban, covered in bruises, can barely hear.

"You know?" Mateo says. "I feel guilty. All of this was because of me."

"Don't say that. Don't feel guilty. It was their fault. They asked for this. It's not fair that you have to go through the same thing every day — that you have to endure being fucked with it all the time. What I'm telling you is that you're going to have to learn to defend yourself. There's not always going to be someone there to help."

"I don't understand why you defended me. Jaime was your friend, I thought. You didn't have to get involved because it wasn't about you."

"But I think it's fair, right. Believe or not, I also consider *you* my friend. I know what you have to go through. I know the suffering they've caused you."

"But it has never happened to you. Everybody loves you. They invite you everywhere. You're the most popular guy in this school, I would say."

Esteban laughs.

"Not that popular. Don't exaggerate," Esteban pauses. "It's just that it's easy to look at your face and see that, for you, even coming to class is torture."

"I try not to think about it. That's why I spend most

of my time writing," Mateo confesses nervously.

"Do you like to write? That's awesome!" Esteban likes that, behind his classmate's shyness, there is this creative energy. He respects Mateo for finding a way to express himself, despite the risks of embarrassment or failure.

"I like it — writing, that is. In class, I write short stories that I hope to combine into a novel and publish one day. I use it to escape from my surroundings. It's like I go into my own cave. You're the first person I've told this to."

"That's the problem. I am sure that you have a lot of virtues, but you can't show them. Well, it's not that you can't, but that your environment won't let you and you have to fight for your voice to be heard. I think that you're a normal person. You just have a different sexual orientation. That doesn't define who you are or what you're capable of doing. I, for example, am heterosexual, but I'm also a son, a brother, a soccer player, a boyfriend, and many other things that don't define me by themselves, but I'm everything combined."

"I like to think of it that way. It's just that I don't understand why they hate me. What did I do to create so much hate?" Mateo puts his head down.

"They are like the bad guys. To defeat them, you have to be you own hero. How? Don't let them to use you as a victim. You are also capable of putting yourself firm and self-confident in front of them. Just say no and keep calm by ignoring them. Maybe you won't prove anything to them, but you'll prove to yourself that you are much better than them. If things get more violent, don't be silent. It's ok to ask for help, that doesn't make you weaker. You're wiser for stopping the bullying. Use your mind as a shield to protect yourself from their words. That weapon will help you to have even more power over them. Take this whole situation more like a challenge to become you stronger. Don't try to explain over and over again to the people who misunderstood you and judge you because, in the end, the only thing that determines if you're happy is…you. Don't you think?" Esteban smiles hopefully.

"You're… different," Mateo says, with a smile.

"In what way?"

"In a good way. For the first time, I feel like someone supports me, understands me, someone who can stop…"

"Stop what?" he asks intrigued.

"Forget it. I just want everyone to like me. I want to be a perfect and normal person like the rest…so I can fit in here," Mateo confesses.

"Don't think about the others. Do things for yourself and you'll inspire others," Esteban advises him. "You will never be able to make everyone happy — only those who truly value you and they are the only ones that should be worth it for you. Even though I'm not homosexual, I'm not that different than you. I'm a person just like you and I know what it's like to be bullied. I know that things may be difficult for you, because of your sexuality, but you were born to stand out. Don't be afraid and don't try so hard to be liked by the others — it's boring. That will come anyway, when you are yourself. You know, that's more fun and real. Don't try to be perfect, Mateo. The truth is that nobody's perfect. What matters is that you be yourself. And most importantly, follow your instincts, your dreams, and your heart; that's what we all have to do if you want to know what it takes to fit in here."

"I've never looked at it that way."

"You're important. Don't give up. You have a lot to give. The world is waiting for the great things that you can do."

"Thanks...really," Mateo realizes that, despite so many bad people, there are those that value him and who can understand him, even if they are heterosexual.

Mateo hugs his friend, happy that he doesn't feel like he disgusts the other person, for once. "I don't know where Fabiola is, but I think she'll be pissed. Look at my face. Oh, how my eye hurts," Esteban jokes. "But you should see the other guy!"

Mateo begins to laugh, but in a second, all the joy is wiped out. His father has just arrived.

"Mateo, what...? I just got a call from the principal," he tells his son, exasperated.

"Well, yes, but I wasn't the one who —"

"I was the one who fought, sir," Esteban interrupts. "Nothing happened with Mateo."

The father looks at the friend of his son with suspicious eyes, investigating him — or rather, looking for something, a gesture that reveals him as effeminate, but he finds nothing.

"Come on, Mateo. Let's go fix your glasses."

Mateo grabs his bag and, after saying goodbye to Esteban with a smile, walks alongside his father to the car.

"Mateo, is there something you want to tell me?" his father asks, while driving through the downtown area.

"No. I don't know. What do you think?"

"I don't know either. What do I think? Yes, I think so...maybe."

"Do you think so?" Mateo asks. And both know what they are referring to — to his sexual orientation.

"I think, yes. The truth is yes. But, do you? What do you think?" his father refuses to pronounce that word that is synonymous with sin, disease, madness.

"Well, I think..." for Mateo, this is a giant step to take. "Dad, I must tell you, I —"

"Stop! Don't say it, please. It's not necessary."

"But I have to say it. You're the one asking me."

"Not anymore. It's not necessary."

"But —"

"Forget it!" his father raises his voice, scaring Mateo. "I told you not anymore! Never mind! I don't need to know anything!"

"But you already know it. You already knew it. You've always known..."

"No, it's not true. I didn't expect this from you."

"This is me. I don't know how to change." Mateo feels his eyes fill with tears. "I don't know how..."

"I don't want to hear anymore from you. Do you hear me? Either you change or I forget that you exist. This is not natural. God hates this. It's a terrible sin."

"This is me, Dad. I can't change. I need you to support me."

"You need me to support you? Are you crazy? Well, of course, you're crazy. What am I saying? Listen to me. You are not going to be a faggot! This is happening to you because of your abnormal relationship with your mother!"

Now Mateo lets the tears flow, disappointed and scared to death at the same time. For the first time, he feels that he does not truly know his father — a new piece of him is being revealed. When the car stops at a red light, Mateo opens the door and runs away from the vehicle. His father reacts immediately and runs after him. It does not take him very long to grab his son.

"Mateo, listen to me. I'm asking you, I'm begging you, to do what I tell you," his father says, while they return to the car. "I'm going to leave you in the care of your mother, but I'm going to give all the money you need for your treatment, so you get healed. And I hope you get healed."

"Heal? But I'm not sick."

"You are sick!" His father tries to stay calm. "But you're going to heal. You're going to heal."

***

That night, Mateo is lying on his bed, reflecting on what happened. He can't believe that there are still people who believe that being homosexual is the same as being sick or insane. How can they believe that God hates one of His own creations? The day's experiences have left him with lessons learned, questions formed. He thinks of his future, he predicts himself. What will become of him in ten years? Is it possible that someday homosexuals will find tolerance and respect? Is it possible that they can live in freedom? Will they be able to love whomever they want?

To all of these questions, he has the same answer: NO. And Esteban's advice fades. Mateo no longer remembers the joy he felt next to him. In his mind now, the only thing remaining is the usual teasing and the episode in the women's bathroom. He feels depressed. It's at moments like this that the ideas of suicide usually come, but now a strange thought invades him — strange because it gives him hope. He remembers something he wrote months ago, something he had never paid much attention to, but now realizes its importance. He opens a drawer and finds the text at the end of a stack of papers covered in short stories and passages. He reads it:

> *Before I die, I hope:*
> *To know what it's like to find love and to be considered equal.*
> *To know what it is to embrace and kiss a man who really wants to be with me and who makes me happy.*
> *To know what it is to be in love, to be really happy with someone that cares for me.*
> *To know what it is to have a boyfriend, to go out and spend time with him.*
> *To know what it is to hear "I love you" from someone whom I have fallen in love with.*

He made that piece of paper, that writing, for moments like this — to give himself hope. He smiles. He would like to help others who are going through the same thing as him. Perhaps he would write a book, tell his story but, above all, he would keep learning.

But will it be worth it? Will it be worth being so... naïve? Isn't he being a little dreamy, believing something that he wrote himself? What can he know about life? How can he believe himself? Everything changes and, now, there is not a speck of joy. He's frustrated and depressed.

"I know, I'm a dreamer," he whispers aloud to himself.

He gets up and walks towards the closet, bringing with him his desk chair. He needs it to achieve the goal. He opens the doors, climbs onto the chair and from there he is able to push himself up on some shelves in order to stretch far enough to reach the rope that has been hidden for a few weeks. He comes back down and walks to the bed, leaving the rope on one side and assumes the position of meditation. He prays. He asks God to forgive him — he is aware of the despicable act that he is about to commit. If God will forgive him, he asks that he please make him an angel with big wings to fly away from his suffering.

He finishes organizing everything. He's nervous but the memories of constant teasing reinforce his decision. He returns to the closet, climbs onto the chair again, and ties the rope to a horizontal steel bar. He makes another knot and loops the rope around his neck. He cries. He shakes. He sweats cold. He is determined. He steps off the edge of the chair...

The darkness fills everything. He is wrapped in it. That's where he wants to be.

"Mateo! Mateo!" his mother calls him.

He doesn't want to move. He would prefer to avoid the sunlight.

"Mateeoooo!"

He suddenly opens his eyes. He sees the face of his mother, disturbed, covered in tears.

"Mateo! You're alive! My love, you're alive!"

"Mo...mom?" everything is so confusing.

"Why did you do it? Why?"

"Mo...mom!" suddenly, the memories come back in an avalanche. "No. I don't want to keep suffering. I hate...I hate living. I hate all this pain."

"No, my love, you don't have to suffer any more. Trust me, I know how to cure you. Today...today your father and I talked and I came into your room to give you the surprise that we will find the right place to cure you and then I found you there..." his mother breaks down again and cries, in a fit of hysterics. "You were unconscious. How could you do this to us?"

"I have nothing to live for."

"Don't worry, you will be normal again. We will find the solution."

"And when have I ever been normal?"

"Trust us, son, trust us. We have to stick together and stay positive, son. Now you'll see. We're going to put you in the hands of God."

Chapter TEN:

The Juliets.
Tuesday, January 9, 1990

IN THE EAST OF QUITO, IN A MIDDLE-UPPER CLASS SUBURB, Susana is lost in the pages of *Romeo and Juliet*. She arrived last night at her mother's house, but this morning is her first time at the Zamora residence, where her mother works as a maid. Susana is twenty years old, thin and angelic-looking. Her hair is long and black, lightly straightened but wavy at the ends and her skin is a rich dark brown. She came from the countryside the previous night after her father decided that he couldn't provide for her any longer. He sent her to live with her mother, who she will accompany to work. The patrons didn't oppose; after all, they have a nineteen-year-old daughter and they know how her mother must be feeling.

Susana is nervous, of course, as this is her first time in such a large house. At least the patrons seem nice with their constant smiles. Who knows if they're sincere, but at least they smile — what a relief! The man gives her some advice, as well the book she's reading. He tells her that she had to study, to learn as much as possible. She has loved reading since she was little — something she inherited from her grandfather.

She loves this book he gifted her already and if it's going to make her smarter, even better! She's hypnotized, on the verge of crying. She didn't know stories like this existed, stories that are so sad and extremely realistic. Of course, she would like to change the story. She would like to make her own book to give the plot a completely new twist, another fate.

"Susanna, do me a favor. Wake up the girl because it'll take me a while to finish cooking breakfast. If she says anything, just tell her that if she doesn't get up, I'll have to tell her dad. That always works."

At her mother's order, Susana is forced to leave Shakespeare for the moment. It doesn't matter; it's her first day and she's dying to discover that new world. And what better time than now, when the house is only half-lit and everyone is still asleep.

"But you've got to be quiet. Go up the stairs and the first room on your right is hers. Hurry, hurry," her mother insists.

Stair by stair, step by step, Susana gets closer to the girl's bedroom door. She gets nervous. What should she do? Knock? Her mother forgot to tell her that. Does she just open it?

She still doesn't know the girl who sleeps in the room and she doesn't know how she will react. She prefers not to makes things too complicated and turns the knob. The door opens. A whole new place greets her. The room, although still quite dark, can be described as messy. But it's a girl's room, that's for sure: purple sheets, pink walls, and the smell of girl's perfume. She likes it, she feels comfortable, nice.

She sees a round window, like a moon on the wall, over a desk with several drawers and boxes. Susana is dying to know what's inside. Her curiosity is making her tremble. She looks around her. The young girl seems to be asleep.

She can't stand it anymore so she takes off her shoes and tiptoes to the vanity. There are so many boxes! She has never seen so many boxes together. She picks them up at random and opens them: bows, ribbons, necklaces, rings, and bracelets of all colors and of different fabrics and material. Susana is in a wonderful world. She puts on a necklace and a bow. She has no bad intentions. It's not like she wants to steal them or anything; it's just that her curiosity and her fascination are so strong that she can't resist. And since it's bright enough, she raises her head to admire herself in the mirror… *the girl!*

"I'm sorry, I'm sorry! Forgive me, I didn't want to!"

Susana turns to the young girl while she tries to remove the necklace and the bow. Her heart beats faster than normal from the scare; the young girl suddenly appeared in the reflection, sitting and watching her, like an owl. She must calm down but she can't stop shaking.

"Wait, wait…no." Susana gasps in surprise; the owner of the accessories doesn't seem to be upset. "You should have seen yourself…"

"No. I wasn't stealing anything. I'm —"

"Don't worry, relax" in fact, the young girl is laughing. "I didn't mean to scare you like this. You should have seen your face."

Susana calms down and starts to giggle until she can't hold it any longer and erupts into full laughter.

"Well, actually, I did see my face. I was looking at myself in the mirror."

The two girls now laugh openly, an aura of trust surrounding them.

"You look beautiful with them."

"Excuse me?" Susana thinks she has misheard. But no, something tells her that she didn't. "Do you really think so?" she decides to ask.

"Yes, don't you? Best not to take them off."

The young girl gets up and walks towards her. Susana realizes that she's not wearing pajamas. She's wearing shorts and an unbuttoned shirt over a tucked-in t-shirt, which is how she must have spent the night. The young girl puts a hand on Susana's head and looks straight into her dark brown eyes.

"Even with no makeup, you look beautiful."

Susana feels the other hand of the young girl on her arm. She feels how she caresses her, how she tries to touch her. The girl loves the way Susana's pearly dark brown skin looks. Susana is nervous but her curiosity is stronger.

"Why do you look sad?" Susana finally asks.

"Because I'm not happy," the girl responds, pulling away.

As the young girl walks to one of the night tables next to her bed, Susana glances at the door; she's afraid her mother will appear there, furious. She hears the sound of a lighter. She turns to see the young girl sitting in front of her, smoking a cigarette.

"And, are *you* happy?" she asks, as she exhales the smoke.

"Not yet," Susana answers.

"What's your name?"

"Susana."

"I am Johana. Our names rhyme," the young girl smiles and blows a smoke circle. "Are you Laura's daughter?"

"Yes, that's right. She told me to come to wake you up."

The sun shines stronger and Susana sees mascara remnants on the girl's face, as if she had been crying. She becomes more nervous and stands up to leave, although she doesn't really want to. She starts to take off the jewelry.

"Keep them," says Johana. "They're yours."

"No, I can't. Believe me, I really didn't want to steal."

"If you don't accept them, then I will say that I caught you stealing from me," Johana smiles at her joke. "Besides, I never wear them. I'm giving them to you — I'm serious."

"No. Honestly, I can't accept them."

"Well, you should. As I told you, they look beautiful on you."

Susana wishes she could respond. But it's her first day and she's just the maid's daughter. In fact, it's the first time that a person like this — so wealthy — has treated her well. Is it a trap? It doesn't feel like a trap. The young girl doesn't seem malicious at all. On the contrary, she strikes Susana as being honest, nice, and as having a big heart. And Susana loves the way the girl bites her own lip — those gray eyes, that sad stare — she even loves the way she moves her hand while she smokes the cigarette.

"I have to go downstairs to help my mother," Susana says, coming out of her daydream and searching for her shoes.

"Wait up. What are you doing later? I was thinking of going out. Do you want to come with me?"

"I would like to, but I don't know if I'll be able to. I have to help my mother. It's my first day here."

"I want to show you a beautiful place. It's not far from here. I promise you won't regret it."

Susana finishes putting on her shoes and she sees another pair — men's shoes, too big for Johana. Maybe she has a boyfriend. Susana returns to reality.

"Ok. I'll try. I'll see what I can do."

Johana seems very happy with this and stretches out her hand to seal the deal. Susana shakes it and goes to the kitchen, with her new presents in hand. She's not wearing the new baubles so that her mother doesn't get angry.

***

That afternoon, two hours before lunch, Johana walks into the kitchen. She's dressed in her usual fashion: dark brown ankle-boots, shorts, and an unbuttoned striped shirt over a white t-shirt.

"Hello, Laura."

"My dear, do you want something?"

"Yes. Susana — is she around? We met today."

"Yes, when I sent her to wake you up. Did you give those things to her?"

"Of course, I really liked her. Those are things I no

longer use — better give them to someone," Johana knows that Laura loves her very much, but also knows that she doesn't trust anything. Johana has to be straightforward. "I wanted to ask you for a favor, Laura. I need Susana to come with me to the store. I have to buy a bunch of things and I don't have enough hands."

"But I wanted her to help me clean the patio before she serves lunch."

"Oh, Laura, don't be mean," Johana is an expert at convincing her. "It's not like the patio is that dirty. Besides, patios are supposed to get dirty."

Laura smiles and Johana knows that she has already convinced her. At that moment, Susana arrives and realizes what is happening.

"Mom, I was just about to tell you there's no more milk. I can take the opportunity to bring it." This is the line she had planned since she made the plan with Johana.

"Miss Johana, are you sure you don't mind Susana going with you?"

"I said no, since I'm the one asking *you* for the favor."

"Ok, ok, go ahead. But don't be long," Laura doesn't know what to do — if her employers find out, they may get upset. But, at the same time, this is the opportunity for her daughter to build some connections. "Come back before lunch. If not, your parents will get angry."

"Don't worry, Laura. You are the best. We're going to come back quickly, you'll see."

Johana lives in a big residential complex consisting of several buildings around a lake.

"Where are we going?" Susana asks, filled with joy.

Johana takes her by the arm.

"Let's run!"

The two new friends bolt out into the infinite, laughing their lungs out and happy simply to exist in that moment. There have been very few times that Susana has been so happy. Johana pulls her towards the lake, playfully shoving her into some trees before she leads her over a huge rock where the water seems less dirty as it forms a gentle cascade. Susana comes from the countryside, but still never imagined such a beautiful place existed.

Johana doesn't waste any time and takes off her boots, shorts, and shirts — leaving only her underwear. Susana turns, sees her, and is frozen with nerves. Johana laughs. Susana's face resembles the expression from the mirror this morning.

"Want to come?"

"Where?" Susana asks, anxiously.

"To swim!" Johana screams, running and jumping into the lake. "Come on! Don't be afraid!

Afraid? Susana also gets undressed until she's only left with her underwear. No fear at all! She runs and jumps into the lake. The water is fresh, delicious. And Johana doesn't look like the girl she met hours ago. Susana didn't know there could be someone so happy inside. She remembers the men's shoes and thinks that this is the best time to find out a little more and discover if her new friend is in love with someone.

"Can I ask you a question?"

"Of course."

"Do you have a boyfriend?"

"No, actually, I don't."

"Do you have a girlfriend?" Johana ask her directly.

"What?" Susana feels vulnerable. "That's impossible."

"Why is it impossible?"

"Because it's wrong. To think, a woman with another woman..."

"What's your opinion on love?" Susana abruptly changes the topic. But Johana doesn't respond. Instead, she sinks her head underwater for almost a minute, comes back up, and takes a deep breath. "I asked you a question. What's your opinion on love?

"Are you really asking me this?" Johana splashes water at Susana's face and laughs out loud. "I believe...I think that where there's love, anything is possible. There must not be any barriers. If two people love each other equally, then they *must* love and that's it — everyone has a right to love whomever they love. Period. Love is about people that feel an attraction and want to share everything. I also believe that love is like a cure. Where there is love, everything hurtful and bad just disappears. Don't you think so?" Johana stares at her new friend and, by the look on her face, realizes that she understands her completely. "Did I just read your mind?"

"Yes, I think so. I think I believe the same thing." Now it's Susana who splashes water, laughing.

"I think that I think..." Johana repeats with a low voice, closing in to her, ready to make the first move. "I think that I think that I believe..."

Johana places her lips on Susana's.

A SAFE PLACE WITH YOU

"You kissed me," Susana whispers. "You kissed me."

"How do you feel?"

"Happy."

There's a pause, a silence — not uncomfortable, but relaxing. Then, at the same time, they both splash each other, laughing out loud, happy for that second, for being there, simply for being. Susana can't help but to remember Shakespeare. The story comes to her mind as this moment captivates her. Her life, that moment — it's like a play, like a fairy tale.

She finally found Juliet, *her* Juliet, but she's going to have to write her own version, with another outcome. This one will have a happy ending.

More than an hour goes by and the two friends are sitting on a rock, with their feet still in the water.

"Did you have a good time?" Johana asks.

"Yes, definitely. I've never experienced anything like this."

"A pond, a waterfall?"

"No, I mean spending time like this, with you." Susana can't look away from Johana's big gray eyes.

"Would you want to," Johana pauses, not knowing if the time is right. Susana, inside, hoped that the moment would be right. "Would you want to spend another afternoon like this, together?"

"I can't wait for another afternoon like this. I want to do it again now."

Johana loves the way that Susana chooses each phrase. From the little she knows of her, she knows that she's a very curious girl, but, above all, a smart girl. Johana comes closer slowly and kisses Susana again, softly. She feels more and more attracted to Johana. She starts fearing that she'll get lost in the moment, but she lets it go by. This time she doesn't care.

"Can I ask you something personal?" Susana says.

"You know you can."

"This morning, you told me you were not happy. Remember?" Susana sees the face of her friend transform. She's back to that girl she met in the morning — smoking, with runny makeup, and a sad look in her eyes. "I'm sorry, I don't want you feel bad. I just wanted to know more about you."

"Well, it's part of being human, I think."

"I don't understand."

"Sometimes I feel pain, sometimes happiness. I can be wrong or be successful, make thousands of mistakes. Sometimes I get lost and find myself again. I'm weak or strong. I'd like to be a lot of things in my dreams…well, also in reality. I don't have friends. I have a broken heart, you know, like every human being," Johana takes a moment to twist her hair, making a knot with her hand and squeezes it. "I want darkness and evil to stay far from me. I want to find true love and, well, all those things that make us human beings. I don't think that I have to explain it any better to you. Nobody's perfect."

Susana senses that she's upset, as if the question was not well received. She takes Johana's hand, to show her that she does understand her.

"But that's the best about human beings, that we aren't perfect," she says. "People are loved for what they are — flaws and everything. The secret is that you never let sadness rule you. Today I met your smile and it's resplendent, believe me. The secret is to never stop smiling. The secret is to always show that magnetic smile to the world. One day, you'll see that when you smile, the world smiles back. The people you love, those you know, or even strangers, when they see you smile, they'll smile back at you."

"I like that," Johana is already over the feeling that she calls anger, but that she knows very well is actually sadness. "And I believe that I think," she pauses as they both laugh out loud. "I think I found another secret to being happy."

"You did? What?"

"You."

Susana can't believe her ears. She remembers the time when her father gave her the news that she had no option but to go live with her mother and she cried all night long. If she had known what she would find, what was waiting for her in the capital, she wouldn't have wasted a single tear. She decides to do what she had in mind since they got to that place. She gets up, walks to the place where she dropped her pants earlier, and takes a golden necklace out from one of the pockets. She shows it to Johana.

"I wanted to return the gesture."

"No, it's not necessary." Johana takes the necklace and notices that the name SUSANA is inscribed on it.

"My father had it made for me when he found out we would have to be separated. He couldn't keep supporting me, but spend a ton of money on this present. Parents can be weird sometimes."

"You don't have to tell me. I know all about that."

Johana loves the necklace. She knows that she shouldn't accept it, but she really likes it. "Do you really want to give it to me?"

"Yes, for when you're sad and for whatever reason I can't be there, I would like for you to feel my presence in that small detail. I can, through that necklace, make you smile every time you need to."

"I don't know what to say."

Susana sits back on the rock, with her feet in the water. They put their heads together and watch the lake, the trees, the birds. They forget about everything that's behind them in the past. Above all, for Johana, this moment is medicinal — it makes the memories of the real reason she's unhappy back home disappear.

The duo returns to Johana's house before lunchtime. The girls are about to come into the house when they remember that they should have come with their hands full from the store, which was their reason for leaving. They especially couldn't forget the milk, which was the main excuse Susana gave to her mother. Everything went well that first time. They enter the house without being seen, take showers, and get re-dressed before going to tell Laura that they had come back.

And they became used to it. The trips to the lake became more frequent over the following weeks, as well as the morning visits with the makeup and jewelry sessions in front of Johana's bedroom mirror. The two became very close. They started calling each other "the Juliets" because, after meticulously studying it twice, Susana lent the book to Johana and forced her to read it, as well. They read it out loud so many times that even Shakespeare himself would have been tired of listening.

Yes, you can now say that they are each other's girlfriend and that they are happy together. Up until that moment, neither of the girls knew that Laura had been suspecting something and is now completely sure.

Sunday, January 25, 1990

Susana returns to her mother's house from yet another rendezvous with Johana.

"Mom, are you ok? Is something wrong?"

Susana finds her mother sitting on a chair. She seems to have been waiting for her there for quite a while, due to the impatience and anger coming out of her black eyes.

"How could you?"

"How could I what?"

"I saw you both. Now I know everything. I know what's going on between you and that girl."

Susana doesn't know what to do. Her mother is known for her fits.

"I don't understand, Mom. I don't know what you —"

"Do you think I'm a fool? You think I didn't notice? Ever since you arrived at the Zamoras' house, I felt something weird. Oh, it's that the angels speak to me! My lord Jesus, thank you for being so frank with me!"

"Mom, believe me, whatever you're thinking, it's just a misunderstanding."

"And you keep lying to me? Listen to me, you are not

going to be with a woman!"

"Mother, *you* listen to me. I feel good with her. I didn't know how to love until I met her."

"No! That's what men are for! If you want to love, you have to love a man; that is correct to God — it's written! Only a man can show you what true love is!"

Susana feels a presence inside her room. She looks and sees a naked man. It's her neighbor, who is always whistling to her and saying things from his backyard. She can't believe her mother. Laura throws herself onto her daughter, grabbing her by the hair, and she shoves her into the room and onto the bed with one push. She wipes off the hairs that are still stuck to her hand. Susana screams out from the pain in her head until she feels the neighbor lying on top of her, holding her hands and immobilizing her feet with his legs. Now the pain is double.

"Mom, no! Please," she cries. "No!" A mumbled scream comes out as a final desperate plea. It falls on deaf ears. Laura closes the door behind her, indifferent to her daughter's screams. She kneels in front of a crucifix that she has for decoration.

"Lord Almighty, creator of Heaven and Earth, fix my daughter, heal her for me, I beg of you. Make her learn the path of good."

Thursday, February 11, 1990

Two weeks have gone by since the savage event. Johana doesn't know why, but she feels like Susana has changed. It's like she is doing everything to avoid her. Johana decides to demand an explanation.

"Why are you pushing me away?" she asks, after practically forcing Susana to come into her room.

"Johana, we can't keep seeing each other. Come on, they'll start suspecting that we —"

"So?" Johana can't accept it. She can't believe that Susana has succumbed to those fears. "What does it matter? Don't you remember the book? Well, this is almost the same. I thought this was all clear."

"My mom saw us."

"Your mother has nothing to do with us."

"Johana."

"This is just between us and no one else can meddle —"

"Johana."

"You can't do this to me!"

"Johana, I'm with a man now."

Johana stands there as her jaw literally drops, unable to pronounce a word.

"And the situation is more…complex…than what you think."

Johana draws nearer and tries to kiss her, but Susana steps backwards.

"Johana, I'm pregnant."

"What? You don't have to lie to me like that. If you don't love me anymore, tell me to my face, but —"

"I'm pregnant. I'm not lying to you. I'm really sorry."

Johana lets herself fall into a chair. She closes her eyes and grabs her head as it explodes.

"You were going to save me from all this!" Johana

takes one of the jewelry boxes and throws it against the wall. "I trusted you."

"It wasn't my intention…please, calm down."

"How could you?"

"My mother —"

"I know you saw the shoes. I saw your eyes. I know you saw them."

Susana remembers the man's shoes that were next to her bed.

"Do you want to know who those shoes belonged to?"

"No. Aren't they yours?"

"They're his. Every night he comes and knocks on my bedroom door, to scare me and make me realize what is in store for me, that I have no way of escaping this."

"I don't understand," Susana gets scared. "Who are you talking about?"

"About my dad. He likes to smell me. He whispers to me. He touches me."

"No…I can't believe what you're telling me."

"Do you think I'm making this up?" Johana cries inconsolably.

"I'm really sorry. I'm sorry. I didn't know."

Susana has to leap up and grab Johana before she hits the ground; she has simply vanished, broken in half, she has just let herself go. Susana puts her softly on the bed.

"Johana, do you hear me?" Susana whispers. "You're right, this is between us and no one else. We can go far away. We can find a place…a safe place for us."

"Yes? And the baby?" Johana asks, opening one of the gray eyes that Susana likes so much.

"I'll raise him with you or put him up for adoption. I want to live my life with you. Without you, nothing has meaning, nothing of what I think I see inside myself," Susana kisses her, desperately.

"What is this barbarity? What am I looking at? For God's sake!"

The two girls turn to the door, where Johana's mother is standing with her hands on her waist and eyes wide open. Suddenly, she starts moving. She walks to her daughter, lifts her by the arm, and drags her away from Susana.

"What has she done to you? What has this degenerate done to you?"

"She hasn't done anything to me! Your husband is the degenerate you're talking about! You know perfectly well!"

"What are you talking about? What are they putting into your head?"

"You've always known!"

Johana's mother slaps her across the face. Susana can't stand the situation anymore and tries to separate them. The whole house has already heard the screaming. Johana's father runs out of his bedroom to see what's happening, while Laura runs up the stairs to retrieve her daughter.

"What's happening here?" the father screams when he enters the room.

"Your daughter was making out with the maid's daughter! Can you believe it? For God's sake!"

"Please, it's not what you think," Laura says, out-of-breath from running. "It's your daughter who's been poisoning my daughter. I've been onto them for a while."

"How dare you!" the mother is completely beside

herself. "Get out of my house! You're fired! How are you going to accuse my little girl? You've brought the devil to this home! Get out of here!"

Both girls are in silence, simply watching the scene around them. They hold hands tightly and can't think of letting go for anything in the world. Johana's father tries to separate them.

"Are you a homosexual?" he asks, ashamed.

"I'm a human being," his daughter answers, "And you are a pervert."

"How dare you speak like that to your father!" her mother slaps her again and, with the impact, separates her hand from Susana's. Laura seizes the opportunity and takes her daughter and exits the room, ready to leave the house immediately.

"You've always known, Mother," Johana shouts out, grabbing her face out of pain. "You knew it and let it happen," she cries, trying to get her confess. But her mother, with a shameful face, can't say anything because she is afraid of getting beaten again by her husband.

"Shut up, stupid! We're going to take you to a clinic so that you get cured. You're insane!" her father insists.

Johana's parents leave her bedroom, slamming the door behind them. They look for a phone. Everyone in the city knows what to do in these cases. They all know who to call.

That's how, that same night, the guards of Dr. Rutherbor put Johana into a vehicle that will take her to what, from now on, will be her new home, her new world: the clinic, Grow And Live Normally. She's in the backseat of the car, with her face glued to one of the tinted windows, while the driver waits for Dr. Rutherbor to finish talking to her father. The doctor is explaining the details of the process, of the treatments — whatever one wants to call it. She has already given up. She doesn't care if she lives or dies.

She hears someone tapping her window. She turns her head and sees Susana through the glass. Johana can't resist. She unlocks and opens the door. The two women become one as they embrace, kiss, and cry. Johana whispers, "I love you," in her ear.

The guards run to separate them. They forcefully shove her back in the vehicle, putting her in the middle of the backseat with a guard on each side. The door closes and Dr. Rutherbor sits in the passenger seat. The car starts. Susana is still standing there, looking at Johana while she leaves. Johana remembers the necklace. She takes it from under the neck of her t-shirt and holds it with her fingers, reading the inscription. She holds it and, from afar, shows it for the last time to her friend, to her partner, to whom will always consider her girlfriend.

Sunday, March 25, 1990

To say that they're just memories would be too simple. They're more than that. They produce an effect that doubles time-space and Johana is capable of reliving those moments, as if they were today, as if they were right here and right now. In that room, number seven, she has lived and relived the same adventures on many occasions. Johana and Susana... "Our names rhyme," she remembers that's one of the first things she said to her.

Johana is not religious, but she is spiritual and she prays. In the clinic, she learned to pray not to the common God, product of the prejudices and satisfactions of certain characters, but to that who she considers the Superior Being, the Supreme Entity. She doesn't know how else to describe it, but she understands that part of this mystery, and of all the mysteries, is not exactly knowing or being able to describe it, otherwise it would not be Superior or Supreme. *Yes, pray, and cry, cry a lot.* She prays to get out of there, to be free and live without prejudice or discrimination. She wants to be able to live as she truly is. And she wants to see Susana again, of course. She always prays for Susana to be well so they can reunite one day.

Every single night, before going to sleep, she turns off the lights and walks to her barred window. She leans on the bars and looks out to the mountains, the sky, the moon, and the stars. That's how she feeds her hopes to be able to escape from this prison, of being able to be a human being like any other. She was able to sneak in a couple of boxes of cigarettes without anyone noticing and those are the moments when she puts them to good use. She takes out a cigarette from the last remaining box, lights it, and comes as close to the window as possible so that the smell of the smoke doesn't travel under the door and reach the hallway of the sexual reorientation wing. She doesn't finish the entire cigarette, as there are only ten left.

She doesn't stop thinking about Susana. Susana is the miracle that Johana had never thought to find in her life. She cannot believe that just as Susan had arrived, she disappeared again. All that Johana has had to live through, the physical and emotional abuse from her father, *her own father*. She can't believe that she came to heal all that and then Susana disappeared, leaving more tragedy behind. Johana needs her. She's almost afraid that, one day, Susana's image will be erased from her mind. She has no photos of her. But she doesn't worry yet. That will probably never happen. Her image will always remain. It will be the last thing she'll see before she dies. There she will be, radiant, beautiful, and happy

Johana doesn't question her homosexuality. She doesn't even consider herself a lesbian. She's simply a person who fell in love with another. Period. She's not one to look at race, age, or even sex; if love comes, it just comes, as it happened with Susana. Her father didn't make her anti-men, or make her hate men, not at all. She's conscious of the fact that, in life, nothing's ever the same. Sometimes we come up with beautiful and valuable situations, but sometimes we come up with real tragedies. She needs her Juliet.

As usual, after finishing her smoke, she locks herself in the bathroom. It's the safest place to drown the screams and moans. In there, like every single night, she makes cuts in her arm, with a small, straight razor she stole from her father. After that, she always throws up until she's weak and exhausted. These are her most dangerous vices.

Chapter ELEVEN:

In the hands of the enemy. Monday, March 26, 1990

"HE'S ALL RIGHT AND DOESN'T HAVE FEVER ANYMORE."

"Are you sure, Doctor?" Charol asks, worried about Mateo's health.

She wants to commit her son to Dr. Rutherbor's clinic, but has had to apologize to the psychiatrist, Juliana, again and again; first, the boy spent a week with the flu, then he had finals for two weeks, and he has had a high fever, obviously depressed, for the past week.

"He's not hot anymore. I would say he's fine now. His thyroid is controlled. Force him to start eating more. To tell the truth, he seems downhearted."

"And, what about his...you know," Charol asks, nervous. Dr. Ramírez has been taking care of Mateo for two years.

"No, I don't know what you're talking about."

"His homosexuality. My son is a deviant."

"What?" Dr. Ramírez can't help smiling. "Come on, Mrs. Feirro, I told you before not to call him that. Mateo has to realize it himself first. It's not our place to judge."

"Son," Charol interrupts, addressing Mateo, "do you feel you are, you know?"

"Yes, Mom. I know I am."

"See! I think he should go back to taking testosterone."

Mateo is terrified to hear that option surface again. He closes his sad eyes and puts his head down, disappointed, and tries to not to remember the nightmarish side effects that he suffered while taking hormones.

"That doesn't make sense. We tried it and it didn't work, as I told you before, Mrs. Feirro," the doctor reminds her.

"Is has to be that! His thyroid isn't producing hormones. He can't produce testosterone and he can't be a real man," Charol explains, as if she knows more than the doctor.

"I explained before that the thyroid and testosterone are both connected, but also different. Testosterone is a testicular hormone and is produced without the thyroid. The hormone does not define sexual identity or the attraction — only the *level* of sexual desire. Testosterone therapy is not for homosexuals; rather, it's for people who have trouble having sex." The doctor says the last sentence in a whisper so that Mateo doesn't hear it.

"Don't worry, son. In the clinic, you'll get healed, you'll see."

"Excuse me," the doctor doesn't want to start an argument, but thinks it's the opportune time to say something, "What is it that they are going to heal? I already told you that he's healthy."

"Healthy? Didn't you hear your own words? Didn't I already tell you that he's a deviant?"

"But that has no cure as there is nothing wrong with it. It is a sexual orientation that —"

"What?" Charol becomes more upset. "It is a disease. Haven't you heard the news? Educate yourself. It's also spiritual. He needs a guide to recover and I will help my only child."

"Ma'am, I'm a doctor and that's not —"

"The World Health Organization says it's a disease. And even the Bible says it's a disease and a sin."

"But —"

"I want my son to have a healthy and fulfilling life. I want him to join me in Heaven. I want him to be a true man."

"Look, Mrs. Feirro, I think we have different points of view. I'd rather not give my opinion on that matter."

"Then don't give your opinion." Charol addresses Mateo. "We're going to be late. Hurry up, son."

"Pay my secretary for the appointment, please. And you know you can give me a call if anything else comes up."

Before they leave the office, Dr. Ramírez says goodbye to Mateo with a smile. He has heard about those kinds of clinics and knows what they are like. He's afraid for the boy, but at the same time, knows that he can't go against the will of a patient's parents.

***

Charol and her son arrive early to Grow And Live Normally. Mateo is amazed by the size of the entrance doors and by how pretty the place looks, decorated with trees and a flower garden. Charol rings the doorbell.

"Mom, are you sure this is for the best? That I stay here?"

"I don't know how long your treatment will last, but you'll see that you'll get out quickly if you cooperate. Don't think of it like you're going to live here. It's like you're on vacation at a spiritual retreat."

"But how do you know if it's really the best for me?" asks Mateo sadly.

"Because the Bible says so," Charol says proudly.

"That's it? But what is it that you think is the best for me?" Mateo asks again, confused.

"I don't know, Mateo. But the Bible gave me the answer. That's enough for me. You need to heal and become a real man."

"But —"

"Silence! No more!" Charol is stressed.

After ringing the doorbell a couple of times, Charol sees that the doors open. On the other side waits Dr. Rutherbor. "Good afternoon. Feirro family, is it?"

"Are you Dr. Rutherbor? Oh, thank you, my God. The psychiatrist, Juliana, has told me so much about you."

"Well, I can tell you that your son is in good hands. Juliana is an angel to the patients."

At that moment, a nurse appears in the doorway. Mateo reads on her nametag that her name is Verónica.

"Mateo, please walk with the nurse. I have to talk some things over with your mother," Dr. Rutherbor orders. "Verónica is going to take you to your room."

The boy, trembling, does what he is told and lets the nurse guide him into what will be...what was it that his mother told him? A hotel? A spiritual retreat?

Once they reach the sexual reorientation wing, Verónica shows Mateo the only unoccupied room — the smallest room, his room.

"Is this where I'm going to live?" he asks.

"Yes. In that closet, you can put away your clothes. You also have that table next to the bed where you can put your personal belongings. Make yourself at home. Relax. In half an hour, I'm going to come back to get you because you have your first session with the psychiatrist."

Mateo is left alone. He doesn't know what to do. His mind is total confusion. He feels the impulse to run away and escape, but at the same time, he wants to give himself a chance, to see if there is a cure. He opens his suitcase and starts putting away his clothes in the drawers of the closet. He does this slowly. One part of his mind is not fully convinced that it's best to stay there. He hears voices outside: cheerful voices, youthful. He's filled with curiosity. He peeks in the hallway and sees that two boys and a girl are coming towards him.

"Hello, how are you? Are you new? Did you just get here?"

Mateo doesn't answer.

"I'm Sandra," she tries to cheer him up. "This is Tomás and that's Sebastián."

Both nod hello. Mateo overcomes his nervousness.

"Hello, I'm Mateo. I was just arranging my stuff. I just got here, yes."

"We can help you, if you want." Sandra sees Mateo's clothes on the bed. "We have some spare time now."

"Ok. I would like that, yes." For the first time, Mateo feels like a group of people actually notices him. "How long have you all been here?"

"I've been here for one month." Sebastián answers, while he crouches with his friends to help Mateo unpack.

"We've been here two months," Tomás says, referring to himself and Sandra.

"And how has it been in here? Did you change?"

"We're a couple," Sandra says proudly, holding Tomás's hand. "So we're actually changing."

Tomás doesn't know how to react. He wants Sebastián to think that there is a cure and that's why, a week ago, he agreed to let his relationship with Sandra be official, but deep down, the feeling of lying to his friends consumes him.

Mateo addresses Sebastián, "And you?"

"Me? Well, there are moments when I get confused, but I've learned that's normal. I think that you don't have to listen to the things that distract us from our goal, but that we have to make the effort in order to have a full and healthy life…complete, as the doctor says."

"So then, there is cure?"

"If you do your part, yes." Sandra puts a hand on Mateo's shoulder.

Half an hour later, Mateo walks to his first session in the clinic. He is walking up the stairs when he sees that a very nice-looking young man is coming down. He's physically average, neither fat nor skinny, and with olive skin. Mateo almost trips at the distraction and uses his finger to push his big glasses up on his nose. What catches his attention — and keeps it — is a delightful smile in the boy's square face, his enthralling green eyes, his thick black eyebrows, his kissable red lips, and his gorgeous, medium-length dark, curly hair. Mateo tries to make a good first impression despite his shyness and nervousness. The young man thinks it's ridiculously adorable how Mateo almost fell, but it's his nerdy appearance with his little cleft chin that he thinks is even cuter so he approaches him.

"Hello, I haven't seen you here before. Are you new?"

Mateo nods his head and smiles.

"I am Fabricio Irrantia."

The young man stretches out his hand and Mateo returns the gesture. He loves Fabricio's outgoing personality. Fabricio, on the other hand, likes the opposite. He sees that Mateo is shy and quiet, but also attractive, with his glasses and his puppy-dog face.

"I am Mateo Feirro. Nice to meet you."

"Are you going to your first session?"

Mateo nods once again. He's hypnotized and can't produce a single word. He already likes this Fabricio — even more than his former classmate, Esteban.

"Be yourself. Don't let her fool you. Stay strong," Fabricio advises him, "I'll see you later." He pats Mateo on the shoulder and keeps walking down the stairs, while Mateo stays, thinking about Fabricio's words. "Fool? Why would they try to fool me?"

Juliana picks up her purse, as this is the last appointment of the day. Her coworkers at North Clinic are annoyed at her recent tardiness. She has struggled a bit to adapt to the new schedule. Mateo enters the office.

"Hello, how are you? Are you the newcomer? Feirro? Mateo Feirro, right?"

Mateo nods.

"I am your psychiatrist, Dr. Revas. I'm here to help you with everything, to guide you to the path of good. Please, from now on, everything here is private, between you and me. It is very important to remember this."

"They told me the doctor and you can heal me...in here."

"Well, yes, but *we're* not the only ones going to heal you. You have to make the effort and act on our orders. It will be a long and difficult process, but with your attention and all your effort, believe me, it can be achieved." Juliana has not yet witnessed a single successful case, but has the words of Dr. Rutherbor and the case of Paul Gómez to reassure the patients and also her self. "First, tell me. Do you consider yourself a homosexual?"

Mateo nods.

"And, do you want to be a homosexual?"

"I don't know."

"Do you consider yourself a person who has a 'sexual deviation'?"

Mateo nods as he remembers the mockeries and harassments he had suffered in school. He doesn't realize this, but he's forgetting Fabricio's advice. He's already emotionally drained.

"I think this is a good start. I do believe I can help you change."

The young man now thinks of his father and his

mother and is happy. He thinks they'll be finally be proud of their son.

As soon as the session ends, Juliana runs out to grab lunch with her husband. Her relationship with her husband is getting worse. They almost never speak to each other and, when they do get to say a couple of words, or even a few whole sentences, the same topic always comes up and everything goes to hell again.

"What took you so long? It's always the same with you." Her husband gets up from the couch, where he has been waiting for her.

"I'm sorry, honey." She leans over to give him a kiss, but he pushes her away roughly. "You think I don't have to work? I only have an hour a day for lunch and you're never here on time and in the kitchen and in…in…"

Miguel stumbles and Juliana has to rush to catch him. He's thin, but quite strong. He looks old, with gray hair, but he's only forty-three years old. His bad attitude has aged him.

"My love, haven't we talked about this? You shouldn't drink so much."

"I'm not drinking. I have to go to work in half an hour."

"My love, did you forget again? You haven't worked for two and a half months."

Miguel stands motionless, in silence. It's as if he has heard the news for the first time.

"What are you saying?"

"That you don't have a job. They fired you. Don't you remember?"

"Don't be disrespectful to me. I am the man of the house. Why aren't you cooking? You're going to make me late!"

"I'm the one who's going to be late! Don't you realize? Are you already drunk?"

Miguel slaps her with all of his strength. The blow causes Juliana to fall onto the glass table where the phone is.

Juliana is frightened and, suddenly, the shock from the hit leads her to see that she is again trapped by a violent man, like that tall stranger whose face she never got the chance to see — only his silhouette when he raped her that night as she left the university library and walked home alone.

"Now get up!" Miguel screams at her and Juliana returns from her dark memories.

"Why don't you divorce me?" she asks, sobbing.

"I would if I could, but it's a sin. Now, we have nothing left but to live together. This is what we deserve."

"No! I don't have to put up with this hell anymore! I'm out of here!"

"You are an abomination! You don't even respect the Holy Word. But…but I shouldn't be surprised. I should have read the signals that Heaven was sending me. It's all your mother's fault for rushing me to marry you to avoid any rumors of your rape that could damage your family's reputation!"

"You are the abomination!" Juliana screams while she gets up, ashamed.

"Don't you remember Tommy anymore? You don't

remember a thing anymore!"

"Don't bring him into this!"

"Homosexuality is genetic. Don't you see it? Why do you think your own son turned out like this?"

"I already told you not to bring him into this!"

"I'm out of here! I can't stand you any longer!"

Miguel leaves and slams the door behind him. His wife is shaking from panic. She doesn't know what to do. She doesn't feel capable of going to North Clinic to treat her patients. She's all broken inside like the table behind her. She can come up with nothing else but to kneel and start picking up the pieces of glass when the doorbell rings.

"For God's sake! What happened here?" this is the first thing Alexandra says when her neighbor opens the door.

"Don't worry, it's over."

Alexandra sees the bruises on Juliana's face.

"What happened?"

"I'm all right."

"And, what did you do to provoke this?"

"What? No one deserves this, Alex. I'm living with a monster."

"Remember what Father told us on Sunday. We have to respect and obey our husbands in everything. It says so in the Bible."

"What? And in which part of the Bible does it say that he can hit me and scream at me like this?"

"That's a consequence, of course. That's what you have reaped by not following the Lord's instructions."

Juliana has always liked Alexandra, although she has

also thought her a little naïve. Nevertheless, in that moment, her words are the last straw and she's not willing to let her Sunday companion see her out of her mind.

"Look, Alex, living with Miguel is like living with the devil! Believe me, God is going to be happy if I'm happy. As long as I am with Miguel, that's never going to happen. Now, excuse me, I have to —"

"Whether you like it or not, you are bound to him until death."

"Alright, no problem. I'll get a divorce, but never remarry and that's it."

"Do it and you'll lose the happiness of sharing your life with someone else."

"Better alone than in bad company."

"You're messed up, my friend. You really are."

"Let's make a deal. You don't judge me and I won't judge you either. Because at least I make men respect me and don't let them —"

"Don't say it…"

"— be unfaithful to me. I don't know how many times with his secretary, huh?"

"I already forgave him! And I learned!" Alexandra is hurt. "I learned that that's what marriage is about. It's about forgiving and moving on together, as a couple."

"You do whatever you want with your life, but I'll decide over mine. Ok?"

"Do the same as your son, run away!"

"Don't mess with my son. I'm warning you. I don't want to see you anymore. Get out! Get out of my house!"

Now her neighbor is really angry. Juliana slams the

door behind her. She is left alone and lies on the couch. She stays there, not moving, without even calling in to her other job. She is just there, feeling the absence of her husband, her brother, her son, and herself.

By nightfall, Juliana stands and walks to her room. She collapses on the bed, motionless. Miguel still does not return. She removes her wedding ring and stares at it. She doesn't know what to do. She's afraid because she knows that divorce is frowned upon by God and does not want to be in the same position as her patients at the clinic. She doesn't want to be an abomination. She tires of the thoughts spinning senselessly in her mind and she puts the ring back on her finger. She stays there staring at the ceiling for a couple of hours. Miguel does not return and she worries. He had been drinking. Did something happen to him? It's late.

Juliana pulls out her wallet from her pocket to find the phone number of her husband's best friend. She wants to know if they are together or if Miguel told him where he would be. She opens her wallet and sees the photo of Tommy. She stares at the photo, forgetting the phone call. Tommy, her younger brother, was gradually distancing himself until he disappeared from her life altogether. But she does not remember the last year. She prefers to stay in those moments when they were close together and found any opportunity to have fun, but that was when they were young, so long ago...

Then, a bang, like that of iron hitting wood, takes her out of her memories. She springs up and runs towards the sound. She finds Miguel next to the front door, facedown on the floor, next to a broken bottle of beer. She doesn't think twice and picks him up.

"Leave me alone!" he says, with a grunt.

"Miguel, you're lying on the pieces of glass. You're going to cut yourself. Please, get up."

"Leave me alone!" Miguel repeats, while his wife tries to carry him. He takes a piece of glass lying on the floor. "Leave me alone, I tell you!" He holds the glass against her neck but without cutting her. "You have to do as I tell you!"

"Let go of me!" she screams.

Juliana is afraid to move because she had never seen him so drunk and doesn't know if he would really kill her. But the thought itself, contradictorily, compels her to move. She is able to turn and kick her husband in the groin. He closes his eyes from pain and a sound like a drowned scream escapes from his throat. He falls onto the sofa. She doesn't want to keep watching. She runs to her room and locks the door. She sees Tommy's picture on the bed and puts it back in her wallet, but now in the front pocket, so that it can be seen through the plastic. She lies down. She remembers her wedding band and takes it off, putting it in the drawer. Now her mind is made up.

***

Mateo wakes up with a jump. He had the same dream all night and although he was aware that he was asleep, he is now just able to wake up. It's dawn already. It's now officially his second day in Grow And Live Normally. He doesn't like the idea very much, but he is relieved to have made it out of the nightmare he was living. He no longer has to live in the world where everyone screams at him, "Four-eyed Faggot, Four-Eyed Faggot."

He takes the glass of water that the nurse left on his table earlier in the morning while he was sleeping and washes down his thyroid pills. He then turns and looks at his watch. It's seven in the morning. He had better get ready for breakfast. Already in the cafeteria, one of the kids he met yesterday hands him a tray so that he can serve himself breakfast. It's Sebastián.

"This is Johana," he says, pointing at a girl who looks like a character in a scary movie. Mateo greet her with a smile and, to his surprise, she returns the gesture. "And, tell me, how do you feel after your first day?"

"Nervous. Pretty nervous."

"And confused, I suppose. That's normal, don't worry, we all go through the same thing," says Sebastián, remembering his first day.

"And what happened? Are you over this…fear?"

"Yes. Of course one misses the life out there, but…I don't know. The sessions and the pills the psychiatrist gives us, the friendships…it's like all of this is making us feel better."

"And the other thing? Are you over it, too?" Mateo lowers his voice. "You know, you don't like men anymore?"

"Just ignore it." Sebastián uses his inhaler and makes a sad face. Then he shakes his head and comes out of his thoughts. "Come on. Let's sit there, with my friends."

Mateo accepts, but his doubts have not dissipated at all. He walks with Sebastián and sits with his new friends. The first thing Mateo senses is an unspoken energy between them. He notices that Tomás touches Sebastián's hand when he hands him the strawberry milk and he also realizes that this infuriates the other girl, the one who claimed to be in a relationship with Tomás. Something about all of this doesn't put him at ease. He feels like life in the clinic will not be that different from the world outside. He smiles. That's when Fabricio arrives.

"This is Fabricio," Sandra introduces them. "This is Mateo. He just arrived yesterday."

"Yes, we met," Fabricio addresses Mateo, "And, how are you? How was your first night in here?"

"Not so good."

"Yes, I know. It's hard to adapt, but we have to be strong, not surrender, and, above all, we don't have to let them fool us, remember this."

"Don't give him false hope," Sandra interjects. "This is a prison. We obviously have to change or we'll never get out."

"Guys, let's change the subject," Sebastián says, "Don't scare Mateo. Life's not so bad in here."

"And…what do you think of the psychiatrist?" Mateo asks, wanting to change the conversation.

"She has helped me a lot," Sebastián answers. "I'm not so tense anymore and she helps me control my depression."

"I haven't had any sessions with her," Tomás says. "I'm being treated directly by Dr. Rutherbor. I don't know why."

The conversation reminds everyone that it is time to take their medication and they simultaneously take out their bottles. This scares Mateo.

"Every…everybody takes pi…pills?" he stutters.

"Obviously. It's part of the treatment and it is just as important as the sessions with the doctor," Sandra responds, as if she were the official voice of the group. "Soon they will also prescribe you something."

"What about you?" Mateo asks Fabricio when he notices that his new friend doesn't actually put any pills in his mouth.

"I pretend to take them, but I don't."

"Don't listen to him, Mateo. You have to take them," Sandra warns.

Mateo nods, but sees that Fabricio winks at him, as if telling him that he could keep the secret. Beside him, Johana holds the pill in her hand, staring at it.

"Take it. Don't set a bad example," Sandra says to Johana.

"Don't take it. Nothing's going to happen to you. Why do you think I'm never sad?" Fabricio encourages her.

"Don't listen to him. If it wasn't good for you, they wouldn't have prescribed it," Sandra insists.

Johana has her doubts, but finally makes up her mind. She throws it on the floor and crushes it with her shoe.

"I'll trust you," she says to Fabricio. Her face is courageous, but inside, the sadness invades her from the memory of Susana.

Mateo ends up exhausted by the secretive energy, that tension in the air. He gestures to indicate he had finished eating and gets up from the table.

"Don't leave! Stay with us for a while. Do you have something to do right now?"

"No...actually, I don't," Mateo answers, as he sits

again.

"Tell us a little about you. What made you come here?" Sandra asks.

"My homosexuality."

Everyone laughs.

"Obviously, we're all here for that. But what is it you did for them to put you away?"

"Commit suicide... I tried to commit suicide."

This seems to destabilize Sebastián, who immediately brings his inhaler to his mouth. Tomás, who is sitting next to him, becomes concerned and tries to comfort him by placing a hand on his shoulder. Mateo notices that it bothers Sandra.

"I think that you're all lying to me."

Sebastián, Tomás, and Sandra look at him intrigued.

"You're not a couple," Mateo hates lies and has the courage to confront Tomás and Sandra. Then, he addresses Tomás and Sebastián, "To me, it seems that you like each other. You are just pretending or avoiding your true feelings."

The three, as well as Johana, are left with their mouths hanging open and Fabricio laughs out loud. He likes the directness of his new friend.

"How dare you try to analyze us?" Sandra is furious and jealous. She approaches Mateo and, with one slap, knocks his glasses to the floor.

"Sandra!" Fabricio yells, as he picks up the glasses and hands them to Mateo.

"So, is it true?" Mateo asks Sandra.

"I don't have to explain anything to you. I finished my breakfast and I'm leaving."

Sandra exits like a lightning bolt, while the other five remain at the table, shocked by her reaction.

"Can you see me now?" Fabricio asks Mateo, pointing at his glasses.

"Yes, everything's all right."

"It better be," Fabricio responds with a smile.

Half an hour later, while the five of them walk down the hallway toward their rooms, Mateo takes the opportunity to clear one of his doubts.

"Can I ask you something?" Mateo asks Tomás.

"Sure."

"Do you feel something for Sebastián?"

"Is it that obvious?" Tomás jokes.

"Yes, as well as Sandra's jealousy," Mateo answers with a smile.

"Don't pay attention to her. She's just like that," Tomás lowers his voice so that the others can't hear him. "And, well… Yes, I do like Sebastián."

"I can tell. Your face lights up when you see him and talk to him. When I see you together, I get the impression that neither of you are really here. It's like you are both in another universe, with all the freedom of the world. But what are you doing with Sandra?"

"She knows I only want to be her friend. I don't know. She's emotionally weak, I guess. And I don't want to hurt her."

"But you're lying to her."

"I *am* bisexual…"

"Really?"

"I do it for Sebastián. I thought that this way, he

would feel that we can actually be healed and then, well, sooner or later, they would release him."

"But if he gets out, he's going to be even more confused. Don't you think? I think he's going to be living a lie, right?"

"I know it's hard but —"

"He will marry a woman. Imagine it. He's going to have children with her. But he'll cheat on her. Behind her back, he'll look for some man because that's where he'll feel good and that's worse - to live a double life." Mateo thinks about what his own future might hold.

"You're right. But I'm afraid he'll feel trapped and —"

"It's all the same. It already feels like we are trapped in here," he says to himself in a low whisper.

"Tomás?" Sebastián's voice interrupts their conversation. "Fabricio just came up with a theory."

"What?" Tomás asks, curious.

"Do you think Dr. Rutherbor could be a repressed homosexual? Think about it: we've never heard if he has a wife or children. He must be over sixty but there's no trace of any family."

They're all silent for a couple of seconds.

"Seriously, don't you think it's suspicious?" Fabricio asks.

"Well, thinking about it, yes, that's a little weird," Tomás reflects.

"Why don't we investigate?" Johana asks, which surprises all her friends as it's the first time that she has expressed herself so openly.

"And how are we going to be able to find out something like that?" asks Tomás.

"You," Fabricio says, pointing at Tomás.

"Me?"

"Yes, you." Mateo seems to understand the plan already. "You're the only one who sees Dr. Rutherbor every single day. Didn't you say that he treats you personally?"

"It sounds logical," Sebastián says.

"Well, I'll try to find out something." Tomás is nervous. He doesn't like the sessions with Dr. Rutherbor, much less the idea of prying into the man's private life.

Later, when everyone separates to go to their rooms, Fabricio decides to walk with Mateo. They enter his bedroom, leaving the door open.

"You look sweet with those glasses…and handsome."

Mateo blushes. No one had ever told him something like that.

"What are those pills?" Fabricio points to a little box on the desktop.

"Those are my pills to control my thyroid. I suffer Hashimoto hypothyroidism," he explains.

"But I thought that made you gain weight. You're very skinny."

"It doesn't necessarily happen to everyone who has it and no one has *all* the symptoms — especially those who start treatment early. Also, I guess I have a fast metabolism. What I have is an autoimmune disease and I will take these pills for life to control my thyroid. Sometimes I have dizziness, poor concentration, a desire to sleep a lot, and I have a lot of depression. I also have an increased sensitivity to cold most of time. Feel my hand," he extends his hand to Fabricio.

"Well, you can warn your hand with mine," Fabricio tries to make him feel better. "Believe me, I understand how you feel. It's going to be difficult being around here. I'm telling you now, the treatments, the pills... But I insist, don't let them fool you and don't take those drugs. They're the worst. Mateo. You have to be faithful to yourself."

Mateo feels the ground disappear under his feet. He feels desperate.

"How am I going to live here?"

"It's not easy, but you have to be strong."

Mateo takes the Bible on the table next to his bed and throws it with hard against the wall.

"Mateo, calm down!"

"Everything is that book's fault!"

"Relax, relax." Fabricio softly grasps his arm and guides him to sit down. "Look I'm atheist. In fact, I think that religions should not meddle or influence or force other people to believe in their beliefs, but I can understand it and I respect people who believe. Do not take it out on the Bible. It has nothing to do with this. It is the people who use it for their personal purposes and to justify their prejudices. Don't fall into their trap. Don't fall into anger. The trick is to feel good about yourself."

"Do you know what I ask God when I pray to Him?" Mateo asks, now more relaxed.

"What?"

"I pray. I pray for Him to turn me into an angel. So I can have wings and fly. Fly far away from here and...I don't know...so that, from up there, I can help other kids so they don't feel like this, so they don't suffer like we do, and guide them so they can be safe."

"That's the most beautiful prayer I've ever heard." Fabricio is deeply moved. He takes Mateo's hand again. "Maybe I'm wrong and there is a God after all and, in that case, I'm sure that God loves you. It's just that He takes a while to help you because...well, because there's so many of us."

The two of them laugh. Fabricio loves when his new puppy-faced friend smiles.

"I just want a boyfriend," Mateo confesses. "Someone I can cuddle with, someone to be with me, to kiss me, to make me smile and feel loved. Is it wrong to wish for that?"

"Absolutely not."

"Sometimes I think I'm cursed. When I love someone, that someone never loves me back. Is there anyone out there for me?"

"Absolutely. I believe there is someone for everyone."

"Maybe not for everyone. Maybe some people like me...just end up alone."

Fabricio doesn't know how to react anymore. He has never heard such intimate words before.

"Once, I dreamed that I was a gray bird in a cage. From there, I watched a landscape through a window in the room where I was locked. And outside the window, I saw another bird — so beautiful, with bright colors, and happy. That bird whistled and called me and asked me to be with it out there, but I couldn't. I felt connected to the bird somehow, but there was just no way to escape. I was still locked in the cage," reminisces Mateo.

"And how did the dream end?"

"It never did, I guess. I was never able to get out." Mateo has a lost look on his face. "It's hard to find a meaning for life. I don't see a purpose if I don't have someone beside me."

"It's easy, Mateo. You don't need someone next to you to discover that purpose. The secret of life is finding, discovering, and knowing yourself for what who you are - a human being. And to love yourself the way you are. Don't forget that. Only then will you be able to meet someone who you can spend your life with."

"You think so?"

"Absolutely. You know what hurts the most about living? Not being able to speak your own truth. For that, don't give up on your beliefs. Stay loyal to your dreams and especially to yourself."

A hopeful smile stretches across Mateo's face.

"Always be faithful in what you believe because, when you stop believing, you won't have a reason to live and you will have lost everything."

"I admire you." Mateo tries to say this without sighing. "I wish I could believe it. You really inspire me."

"And, do you know what else I think? I believe that soon — very soon — common sense will finally come to humans and we will all be treated as equals. We have to be patient and wait for time to pass. There will be people who will help us, give us strength, be with us, without being homosexuals themselves. I'm talking about everyone: a new generation in which all people, regardless of race, sex, or religion, will realize that they are in the wrong to treat us like this."

"I hope for that, too, deep down inside. I hope we can all live our lives without feeling any prejudices around us."

"I'm going to help you," says Fabricio, who is inspired by Mateo, too.

"How?"

"I don't usually do this, but I will make an exception. I'm going to pray with you. That way, our prayer will be stronger and God will listen sooner."

"Thank you for cheering me up. You're a good person."

"No, thank *you*. Thank you for your trust."

Fabricio is really happy after helping Mateo, but, of course, feels even more lost from the new feelings he has for him.

Outside of Dr. Rutherbor's office, Sebastián is extremely nervous. The nurses have just told him that Dr. Revas will not be able to come to the clinic today and that Dr. Rutherbor will have to treat him instead. He's having an anxiety attack and his hands and legs move uncontrollably. At the same time, he thinks that this might be a good opportunity to find out about what Fabricio suggested earlier this morning. Still, he doesn't like being the one in such a risky position.

"How have you been feeling, Sebastián?"

"Good, Doctor. Better than before."

"What about your homosexuality?"

"Better, also. I don't feel those…temptations anymore."

"That's good. That's good. And which pills has Dr. Revas been giving you so far?"

Sebastián takes out the bottle he keeps in his pocket and shows it to Dr. Rutherbor. The doctor analyzes its contents.

"I'm going to talk to her so that she switches the medication. There are other pills that will make you feel better."

"But am I ok?"

"Yes, it's all good. Don't worry, it's nothing bad. It's just a step forward in your treatment."

Sebastián becomes nervous. The doctor sets two bottles down on his desk, but is distracted by the ringing of his office phone. After he finishes the call, he opens a bottle and shows its contents to Sebastián.

"These are the ones that you'll take from now on: Fluoxetine."

Sebastián recognizes the colors of the pills and knows that it's not true, but he also notices that the bottle is labeled "Clonazepam", which doesn't make sense to him, either.

"Excuse me, but, isn't that Prochlorperazine?" Sebastián remembers seeing Tomás's pills in the cafeteria on his first day in the clinic.

"What?" The doctor becomes nervous and checks the bottle, finding out he made a mistake. "No, no, here it says 'Prochlorperazine'," he covers the name on the bottle with his hand, but Sebas' suspicion is already too visible for him. "Don't worry. It's easy to get confused with so many pills that we have here in the clinic. But these are not the ones that I'm supposed to give you." He picks up the correct bottle, labeled "Fluoxetine". "Remember, if I'm recommending them, it's going to be good for you. Do as I tell you."

"What will that do to me?"

"Nothing bad. It's going to help you ignore that

attraction for people of the same sex. Take two a day."

Sebastián nods and accepts the bottle, still nervous. Dr. Rutherbor, on the other hand, is used to pretending like this and is unfazed by lying to the boy because he already knows that what's in the bottle are amphetamines and will only help him to disrupt and distort his behavior and his mind.

Sebastián decides to go to Tomás's room. He finds him there with Sandra, who is wiping away tears.

"Sandra, are you all right?" Sebastián asks, worried.

"Are you happy now?" she screams. As she leaves the room she hits Sebastián's shoulder with her own.

"What happened to her?" Sebastián doesn't know if he did something wrong.

"Nothing. I just broke up with her," Tomás explains. "Things weren't working between us. The truth is that I still like men." He decided to take the advice of his new friend Mateo and tell the truth.

"I thought you had changed."

"I didn't want to. I'm still attracted to men. I know that it's the way to survive here, but I can't keep on lying. It's killing me inside. And you? Have you changed?"

"Well, the truth is that I did…or not. I don't know what to say. Actually, I didn't change. I also still like men. But I'm feeling a lot better." Sebastián is more than just confused. The truth is that he hasn't changed anything other than his sexual conduct and behavior, but he feels some sort of responsibility for his friends and prefers not to kill their faith. "Tomás, the reason I came…there's something I have to ask you."

Tomás is nervous. Is it possible that Sebastián wants to start dating him?

"Tell me."

"Can I see the pills you're taking?"

"Sure. Why?"

"I want to double check something."

Tomás searches for his bottle of pills and shows it to Sebastián.

"I knew it!" Sebastián exclaims.

"What happened?"

"How long have you been taking those pills?"

"Since I got here. Why do you ask?"

"These are not Prochlorperazine. They're giving you Clonazepam."

"What? What are you talking about?"

"Have you felt any changes? Have you not felt weird somehow?"

"Well, I'm not sure…"

"Today the doctor made a mistake and showed me a bottle labeled 'Clonazepam' and they were the pills looked the same as the ones you have there."

"What?" Tomás doesn't want to believe Sebastián. He becomes scared. "Are you sure? Why would the doctor give me different pills?"

"That's what I'm trying to tell you. I don't know why he would do that. I'm sure of it, though," Sebastián sits on the bed and is lost his thoughts as he tries to crack the riddle before him.

"I think you're too paranoid." Tomás is nervous and

having doubts about everything around him.

"Let's do something." Sebastián is so involved in his hypothesis that doesn't even hear what Tomás says. "Why not stop taking those pills, but only for a little while. Don't you remember what Fabricio said? He doesn't take them and he doesn't feel depressed anymore. And Johana...Johana didn't say a single word, but today... did not you see it? Today she didn't take the pill and she spoke." Tomás and Sebastián both laugh at the latter. "It's true. She is...I don't know how to put it. The pills have us in an unhealthy state of mind."

"It's not that I don't trust you, Sebastián, but I have to think about it. There are many pills that look the same. I don't think the doctor would do that. He's a professional."

"You're my friend and I'm just warning you. You can do whatever you want, of course, but in this, I ask you to trust me."

"I'll think about it, really. It's not that I don't trust you, but I'm scared. I don't know...to suddenly stop the treatment and have to start all over again, locked in here. Then, I'll have to be here twice as long."

Sebastián stands up and, a little disappointed, walks to the door of the bedroom.

"I'm telling you this because I worry about you," he tells Tomás before leaving. "Open your eyes."

Sebastián exits the room and leaves Tomás alone, thinking, "What just happened?" Now, Tomás is the confused one. Sebastián is depressed or something...that's why. But if he *is* right, then...no! *It's impossible.* He is becoming paranoid.

Sebastián locks the door behind him in his own

bedroom. Now he feels bad. He shouldn't have worried Tomás like that. He begins to doubt himself and thinks that maybe everything is just in his imagination and, in reality he is just immersed in one of his bouts of depression. He feels frustrated, humiliated. He lies on the bed, opens his bottle of pills, and takes out one. He stares at it - the enemy in his fingers. What if Tomás loses confidence in him? What if he is disappointed him? What if it's himself, Sebastián, who is crazy? What if Dr. Rutherbor is right and *he's* the mistaken one?

Sebastián takes a deep breath from his inhaler. Once again, he's afraid. He looks at the pill with big eyes then takes out two more and shoves them into his mouth.

Who is the real enemy?

Chapter TWELVE:

Opening the eyes.
Tuesday, April 3, 1990

JULIANA HASN'T BEEN TO WORK FOR ONE WEEK. Dr. Rutherbor suggested that she focus on settling her divorce and then return to work when she's ready. She thinks it's strange that he readily gave her so many days off, but the truth is that the nights in North Clinic and the mornings of going over divorce paperwork with her lawyer are consuming both her time and her spirit.

"Don't you say a single word," her lawyer tells her. "I'll take care of everything."

They're waiting for Juliana's husband, Miguel, to arrive in order to finish the separation of goods deal. She is somewhat absent, glued to the window, lost in the bright blue sky.

"Can I ask you a question?" she addresses her lawyer. "Do you think God always forgives us?"

"What do you mean by that?"

"I've always heard and read that divorce —"

"Don't think about that. Not now. I know that you're fairly religious, but sometimes you have to take drastic decisions in life. We have to watch out for our happiness and do what is best for us.

"But I feel like I'm doing something wrong — breaking His laws."

"Don't compare the laws of killing and stealing with a divorce, please." Mauricio smiles to console her. "Look, for me, to kill is to the opposite of love. To steal is to the opposite of respect. That's why it bothers God. I don't see divorce in any of those categories, especially in this case between you and Miguel. What do you think God wants for you? If you ask me, I'd say you deserve happiness. We all deserve to be happy, right? Don't focus so much on some book written by human beings in different time, culture, and context. Focus on your well being, your life."

Juliana likes her lawyer's words. She takes the opportunity to ask his other opinions.

"What do you think about homosexuality?"

"About homosexuality?" Mauricio laughs. "Well, I'm indifferent. It's not as if it bothers me, if that's what you're asking."

"But the Bible prohibits a relationship between two people of the same sex."

"I'm aware of that. These are more interpretations than anything else. What the Bible does state as wrong is prostitution, rape, sex without love — those kinds of things. From what I've read several times, I believe that God will never forbid us to love someone as long as it is mutual and consensual. It would go against what God really means or should represent. God is love, isn't He?"

"I've never seen it like that. Thank you." Juliana is calmer now.

"My son is gay. He confessed to me recently. I…at the beginning, I freaked out. After that, I asked him if that's how he identified and if he was happy. He's my son and I love him. He's still the same kid: kind, respectful, smart. The same kid I raised with my wife — he's a human being just like you and me."

When listening to her lawyer's confession, Juliana feels like she has been mistaken for a long time. She feels like she has misinterpreted the Bible. She feels like she has been intolerant.

"Let's go. It's our turn," Mauricio grabs her hand and helps her get up from the chair.

Sunday, April 8, 1990

It's been now two weeks since Juliana last saw her patients at Grow And Live Normally. Dr. Rutherbor told her that he was giving her the time to finalize her divorce, but the real reason is that he realized how much he missed providing the treatments himself. Most of the patients have not been happy with this change. The atmosphere in the sexual reorientation wing is getting gloomy. Tomás has gone almost four days without seeing Sebastián. During the three daily meals, Sebastián sits alone at a separate table. Tomás can't stand it anymore and decides that the best thing to do is to visit him in his room to talk to him.

"Sebastián?" he calls, knocking the door. "Are you here? Can I come in?"

He doesn't get an answer. He becomes worried and decides to enter anyway. He sees Sebastián sitting on a chair, opposite the barred window, with a strange look on his face. Tomás scans the room with anxious eyes and he panics when he sees an open bottle and a bunch of pills spilled on the desktop. The label on the bottle says "Fluoxetine". Tomás knows that it's an antidepressant, but he sees that his friend is sad, pale, and haggard. Tomás approaches the chair and puts a hand on Sebastián's shoulder.

"They're right — Dr. Rutherbor, the psychiatrists, everyone. There is no place for us in this world," Sebastián's scares Tomás. It sounds so drastic.

"You know that's not true."

"I tried, Tomás. I really tried. You are witness that I wanted to. I gave my best, but I failed. I lost. I threw in the towel. I don't know."

"And that's it? In a moment of weakness, you're going to throw your life away? Is that all? End of the road? No, Sebas. You cannot give up."

"I'm exhausted. I can't do this anymore. I hate this clinic, the sessions, the talks, the pills. I can't depend on them anymore."

"Then don't take them."

"What? *You're* telling me that? The defender of —"

"Lately, I've been thinking a lot about it. Maybe I'm wrong and you are right. Fabricio is right. When you first told me, I was in denial. I felt weakness and fear, but since

I met you, I'm starting little by little to have more strength, confidence, and trust."

"No, no, no. You were right."

"I'm telling you. No —"

"We have to take them!"

Tomás is even more frightened. He has never seen Sebastián in this state.

"It isn't right the way we are. Here they are helping us, Tomás. Seriously." Sebastián gasps and needs to use his inhaler. "The pills show us the right path."

"I don't...I don't recognize you, Sebastián. You're another person."

"There is no hope. There is no life, there is no love, and there is not a place for all of us if we choose to be that sin and disease. Either we change or we just rot in here."

"No, Sebastián, no." Tomás is running out of things to say, but he still feels a need to be the rock, to protect Sebastián, and to help him find self-acceptance. "I know it's hard to believe it, especially being locked up here, but it's just that simple. There is still hope if you have the bravery to keep fighting for it. If you want, listen to what the doctor and the psychiatrist have to say, just nod, but don't fall for their lies. Don't let them get into your spirit. I mean it. There is still life if you have the courage to be just you and there is still love if you keep loving yourself. And I believe there is still a place — a safe place — for all of us out there. It's just a matter of time before we find it. This is your life, yours and nobody else's. With your mind, your soul, your feelings, your decisions, it's all up to you. So what if you don't get everything you want. At least you'll live your life the way you want to. At least you'll live with dignity."

"Stop, stop." Sebastián's face is covered in tears. "Leave me alone!"

Sebastián starts to cough and choke. Tomás helps him tilt his head backward so that he can breathe deeply.

"Okay, Sebas. I'm going to leave you alone so you can rest. But promise me that you'll calm down."

Tomás extends his hand so that Sebastián can get up from the chair and he walks Sebastián to the bed. There, he lays him down, tucks him in, and kisses him on the forehead.

"I care about you, Sebas," he says, but Sebastián has already fallen asleep.

Tomás leaves the room with a clear purpose. He is determined to investigate the drugs that they are giving to patients, to clear his suspicions. He has to find out the truth about Dr. Rutherbor and the psychiatrist who treats his companions and…now that he thinks about it, he realizes that he doesn't even know her full name. He has never even seen her. He just knows her as "Dr. Revas".

Tomás is deep in his thoughts when he encounters Lucas, one of the younger inmates. He hasn't seen Lucas in a while, but Tomás greets him with a nod and keeps walking until he suddenly notices something. Lucas has been increasingly sad, but now he looks skinny and pale, with sunken eyes. Tomás looks around and analyzes the picture before him. All of the patients seem emaciated and listless. Many cannot even walk alone and are accompanied by their nurses. *Things have changed around here,* he thinks. Things have changed since Dr. Rutherbor as begun treating all the patients himself. Smiles are dwindling, one might say.

Tomás sees Johana walking down the hallway, speaking with another young inmate, Sabrina. After Sabrina goes into her room, Tomás approaches Johana.

"Come. Come with me. We have to talk to the others," he tells her in a whisper.

Mateo is in his room with Fabricio. He's writing the first words that come to mind to see if he can create something he finally likes. He's having a revelation. This is what he wants to be in life: a writer.

They hear some soft knocks on the cracked-open door. Fabricio gets up to see who it is and Tomás and Johana gently push their way inside.

"How are you? What are you doing?" Tomás asks, as he sits on the bed next to Fabricio.

"Relaxing. Soon it's my turn with Dr. Rutherbor," Mateo answers.

"You should read Mateo's writings," Fabricio says, handing some papers to Johana to read.

"Really? Do you write? I didn't know," Tomás is surprised. "It's excellent that you know what you're good at."

"No, not like that. It's just a hobby. I write because it relaxes me, that's all."

"Did you tell me you were up for a session with Dr. Rutherbor?" Tomás asks, remembering his reason for visiting.

Mateo nods.

"I need your help."

Mateo puts aside his stories. Tomás gets up and closes the door as much as the nurses will allow as his three friends listen to his plan.

***

Hours later, Tomás enters Dr. Rutherbor's office and is greeted with, "Come in, come in, Tomás. How do you feel today?"

"I'm okay." Tomás sits on the sofa.

"That's good, that's good. I know that it was Mateo's turn, but it seems like he's not feeling well so I decided to change his appointment for yours. I hope that's not a problem. Tell me, how are things with Sandra?"

"Good."

"Really? That's not what she told me." Dr. Rutherbor can't stand having Tomás in the clinic any longer, but he doesn't know how best to get rid of him.

"We had a little argument, that's all. You know her. She overreacts and dramatizes everything. But we're still together and we're improving our lives, just like you told us."

"And, what about Sebastián?"

"Nothing. We're friends. That's it. Why do you ask?"

"Well, one finds out everything in here."

"I don't know what you may have found out because he and I are and always have been just friends."

Dr. Rutherbor scratches his head. He's about to say something, but he keeps it inside, as if he changed his mind.

"It's all good then." Dr. Rutherbor finally says, "Fix your relationship with Sandra. Remember that it helps you to improve your behavior patterns, to straighten up that sexual deviation you suffer from. Look at the example of

Sofía and Augusto, who are together and improving their relationship." The doctor refers to former patients, but he knows that they faked their relationship in order to more easily pass the lie detector test and be released from the clinic.

"I know, don't worry. Things are going to get better."

"Are you taking the pills?"

"That's what I wanted to talk to you about. I dropped the bottle in the toilet and all the pills got wet."

"When did that happen?" Dr. Rutherbor doubts this story.

"Last night."

The doctor, upset, gets up and walks to the small cabinet. He opens the doors. "I'm going to give you two bottles."

Dr. Rutherbor starts to separate the pills that he's going to put in Tomás's bottle, when a scream interrupts him.

"Doctor! Run, run! An emergency! We have an emergency!"

Dr. Rutherbor rushes to open the office's door. He sees one of the staff nurses, Verónica, with a panic-stricken face.

"It's Mateo! Young Mateo!"

Dr. Rutherbor doesn't think twice and runs with Verónica to Mateo's room, hoping that it's not something so serious that it would risk the continuity of his clinic. Dr. Rutherbor completely forgets Tomás and the fact that he left the doors of the medicine cabinet unlocked.

The plan worked. Tomás doesn't waste a second and

goes to the closet to read the names of the labels on the bottles: Prozac, Venlafaxine, Zoloft. Under each drug name, he reads the name of one of the patients in the clinic. These are the bottles that the doctor hands out daily. On one side of the cabinet, he sees others bottles and half of them are empty. He sees that the label says "amphetamines". He opens one of the full bottles, takes a pill, and sees that it is exactly like those that were scattered on the table in Sebastián's room. *It can't be. Those were supposed to be Fluoxetine.*

A door of the cabinet is filled with empty containers and labeled Fluoxetine. Could it be that Rutherbor fills all those bottles with amphetamines? Other bottles are labeled Clonazepam and Tomás finds the same pills that he takes daily — the same pills that Rutherbor says are Prochlorperazine.

Tomás again considers his initial suspicions that day when he woke up without any memories. The reality of his treatment has suddenly become clear. "Those pills are just crap. They are destroying us inside. They are destroying our heads," he whispers. "This is real and serious. The doctor is secretly switching the drugs of all the patients, risking innocent lives. This is a crime!" He thinks.

Sebastián was right when he mentioned his own suspicions. What was Tomás thinking when he didn't believe him? He was just scared and in denial! Tomás hopes Sebastián can forgive him for that. There is no doubt anymore. Apparently, Dr. Rutherbor isn't what they thought. He's not doing what's best — he's doing the worst: manipulating and fooling all the patients and their families. Tomás can't stop thinking about how much physical and emotional damage the patients have had to suffer, especially now.

The door opens and Tomás runs to sit down.

"Tomás," Dr. Rutherbor calls with a smirk. "Forgive me, I forgot about you. I have to lock my office. Please come with me. Let's go see Mateo."

Tomás has no other option but to follow him. When they get to the room, Mateo is on the bed with his eyes closed.

"What happened, exactly?" the doctor asks, somewhere between worried and annoyed.

"He went crazy. He was screaming and then he started to take things and throw them around the room. I got scared. I was so scared, Doctor," Verónica is filled with anguish.

"It must have been an episode," Dr. Rutherbor says softly, more to himself than to the others. He raises his voice. "Let him sleep. I'll take care of him later and readjust the medication."

Dr. Rutherbor signals for them all to leave the room. He is no fool. He knows that he made a mistake by running away like that. He shouldn't have left Tomás in his office alone. What if the two boys planned this emergency? What if they were looking for a way to find out what he hides in the closet? He wipes his forehead with a handkerchief and returns to his office. He will check that all the bottles are full and that none are missing from the closet. It must just be his own paranoia. Tomás hasn't recovered from forced amnesia. He doesn't have to worry about him.

***

Juliana comes home and jumps on the couch. She has no shred of feeling in her body, mind, or spirit. The divorce completely consumes her. She starts reviewing in her mind a conversation she had with one of the patients of Grow And Live Normally.

"Haven't you thought that you're the same as me?"

"What do you mean by that, Sebastián?"

"That within us, we harbor the same desire. We both want to discover our identity — who we are — and want to show it to the world. We both want to find love and share it with another person. And it's difficult for both of us. *All* human beings find it difficult. The road is long and full of mistakes, we trip and fall."

"That's why you have to find love with a woman, not with a man."

Juliana repeats the phrase out of habit, but, truthfully, the boy's words get to her. At that moment, she stopped seeing him as a just another patient and started to identify with him, to see him as a person, as someone equal to her with the same needs but different tastes.

"I think that one doesn't choose who to love." Sebastián continues, "But the beautiful thing is that we can choose to stay, to remain with that person, no matter what *they* say around us. Who's to say that what I had with Christian wasn't love if we felt it and lived that way?" Sebastián is more confident about his past and the life he shared with Christian after the conversation about the puzzle pieces with Tomás.

"Life doesn't work like that."

"We all want someone. No one wants to be alone. I, personally, want someone who embraces me, who holds my hand. I want someone who makes me smiles and loves me for whom I am. Do you want it? Do you want it, too?"

Juliana feels like she will never forget that conversation, the words of the young man. Thinking about it again, what he wants is not so different from what she wants. She wants it, too.

She notices the time and hurries to work at North Clinic.

***

Later that afternoon, Mateo enters Dr. Rutherbor's office.

"Mateo, you had an episode. How are you doing now?"

"I really don't know how..."

"Depression. It was an episode of depression."

"Yes, I think so," Mateo tries to play along. If not, the doctor may discover that it was all part of Tomás's plan. "The truth is that I haven't been feeling good, but I'm better now, calmer."

"And your deviation? How have you been feeling sexually?"

"More or less the same, to tell you the truth. Although I have to admit that when I take the pills, it's like the attraction diminishes," Mateo lies.

"I'm going to the bathroom. Wait for me here, please," Dr. Rutherbor gets up and walks to the bathroom in his office. It's all part of his plan to see if Mateo is going to search the office.

Dr. Rutherbor has just closed the door and Mateo makes a beeline towards the desk. He starts trying to make sense of the stack of random papers on the doctor's messy desktop. On one paper, he sees what appears to be a registration form, listing several names that Mateo does not recognize. The letterhead of the form says "The Light of Christ Center" and it seems to be Catholic-affiliated. Mateo becomes scared when he sees that, at the end of the list, there are two names crossed out: Bernardo and Tomás.

Mateo tries to shape the various ideas that invade his imagination. What comes to mind is that all of these names were once patients at Grow And Live Normally, but, for some reason, they were transferred to the Catholic center. That explains why Tomás's is crossed out. Mateo doesn't know anyone named Bernardo, but maybe he's was released because he was cured or something.

Mateo hears the bathroom knob move and runs back to the couch. He sits, crossing his legs. Mateo expresses tranquility on his face, but inside his mind is racing thinking about the papers he was able to read. Dr. Ruther is now sure that what happened earlier was planned by the boys. The session continues normally.

At nightfall, Mateo, Johana, and Fabricio gather in Tomás's room.

"And the paper was addressed to a María Rutherbor, I think," Mateo tells them what he read.

"So he does have a wife?"

"Maybe. It was definitely the admission form for a

rehabilitation center — religious, Christian, Catholic, I don't know."

"Maybe Dr. Rutherbor's wife does the same job he does, but in another way. Maybe not with drugs, but with other types of therapies," Fabricio suggests.

"Makes sense," Tomás nods.

"Then he's not a repressed homosexual, as we thought," Johana concludes.

"But I saw something that was even stranger. There were names - probably from the patients that used to go to this center. And, Tomás, your name was there, too, but it was crossed out."

"My name...crossed out?"

"Yes, two names were crossed out: Tomás and Bernardo."

Hearing this name, Tomás is paralyzed. He feels déjà vu, dizziness.

"Bernardo? Bernar...? You know, I've had several dreams where, I don't know why, I hear 'Bernardo, Bernardo'. Sometimes it's even me who screams the name, but I have no idea why. I don't know anybody by that name."

"Perhaps you did meet him, but you don't remember," Johana adds. "Once I read that, in dreams, we remember things that have been blocked from our subconscious. Which means that if you dreamed of him, it's because once you met him or at least you saw him pass by. Maybe it's someone you were introduced to some day and didn't make a big impression or —"

"It definitely could be that."

"As I always tell you, the solution is not taking that

shit," Fabricio refers to the pills. "Starting today, stop taking them and let's see if…I don't know…something comes back to you, some memory."

"I think you're right," Tomás takes one of the pills from his bottle and stares at it. "We have to keep investigating."

***

At night, Juliana finally drifts off to sleep, but even there she suffers. She sweats, kicks, tosses and turns. It's the same dream that haunts her, the one where her brother won't stop yelling at her.

"Tommy? Is that you?"

"Sister, long time - no see."

The whole scenery changes and Juliana is back in her childhood home, during her teenage years.

"I've missed you so much!" she yells, running to hug him.

"I love you so much, Juliana."

"I love you, too, Castor," she calls him by his nickname. "Where are you? Why don't you come back?"

"I can't. They won't let me."

"Who? God? Are you in Heaven?"

Tommy nods.

"And did He…forgive you?"

"Of course, He opened His arms to me, His heart. He told me there was nothing to forgive me for."

"Did He accept you just as you are? With your orientation and everything?"

"He showed me that there was nothing wrong with me, just like there's nothing wrong with your son."

The image of Tommy starts to fade. The house where the two siblings spent their adolescence is getting darker and darker, as if clouds packed with rain suddenly appeared inside. She sees lightning bolts and hears thunder. Juliana realizes that she's in a nightmare.

She opens her eyes, scared. She takes several deep breaths. She thinks of her brother. She thinks of her son. She thinks of the…similarities.

***

That same night, Sebastián leaves his room careful not to make any noise. He has to speak to Tomás. He needs to see him. When he reaches Tomás's room, he knocks softly. He receives no answer. Remembering that it's forbidden to lock the doors at night, Sebastián turns the knob and enters in complete silence.

"Tomás?"

"Sebas? What happened? Are you all right?"

"I don't know what to do, Tomás. I don't know who I am anymore," Sebastián chokes.

"Your inhaler?"

"I didn't bring it with me."

Tomás worries. Would he have done it on purpose? He holds Sebastián tight.

"I feel as if I'm losing my mind. I don't know if I should change or not. I feel a huge weight on my shoulders. I can't do this on my own anymore. I feel like nobody cares what I really feel inside," Sebastián cries and struggles to breathe. Tomás grows scared and wraps his arms around his friend. "Hug me harder. Keep it tight. Don't let me go,"

Sebastián begs as if he wants to be broken by the stronger arms of Tomás.

"I care about you. I really do. Everything is going to be okay. You matter to me. I'm here with you."

After spending a minute in their embrace, Tomás looks down at Sebastián and tries to console him, but Sebastián becomes distant and moves to sit on the bed.

"I'm really sorry about this afternoon. I was really depressed, negative. I think it's the pills. I think they do something to me that —"

"It's the pills. I believe you. Sebas. I promise that, starting today, I won't take them anymore and you promise me you'll do the same."

"I'm no angel, nor a devil. I'm just a human being," Sebastián is relieved and continues, "I always try to have a special connection with another human being, nothing more. I try to make things right, I try to make my dreams and goals a reality. I want to overcome the past, I want to forgive Christian and move on. I want to learn from my mistakes, stop trusting people like Alejandro. I don't want to just *survive* anymore. I want to breathe, live and love again, but I can't. I keep taking steps back. It's like, no matter what I do, I will never be good enough for anything."

"Realizing this is proof that you really want to do your best — and you can. That's what matters."

"I have these feelings I can't get rid of. I thought I would make them go away. I just…I can't fight this feeling anymore."

"What feeling?" Tomás asks, hoping that Sebastián will open up to him and that their feelings are mutual.

Sebastián is unresponsive. His fear and concern come back. He has to be cured. He can't just succumb whenever life tempts him. He has to change if he wants to leave that clinic. Tomás, on the other hand, walks over and sits beside him. He decides that maybe it's best to make the first move so he puts his hand on Sebastián's back and caresses him, providing comfort.

"There's nothing wrong with you. It's ok to be afraid. Just let it happen because you got me here next to you."

Tomás brings his face close to Sebastián, closes his eyes, and finally kisses him for the first time. Sebastián remains motionless, shocked, nervous, but also has a tingly feeling that he has been craving. Tomás kisses him again, this time for a longer time, but suddenly Sebastián pushes away.

"No. I can't let you do that. It's wrong, an abomination. I am bad."

"That's not true. You're not bad. You're just confused by the pills. Stop taking them."

Tomás puts his hand on Sebastián's flushed, freckled cheeks. He's falling more and more for his light blue eyes. He's moved by the expression of guilt and fear. He wants to make him feel better.

"I think you deserve someone better than me," Sebastián says.

"No. I think *you* deserve someone better…and I know that it's me. Sebas, I care so much about you. I want to make you happy, to cheer up your life, I want you to feel cared for, to feel affection. I want it to come from me."

Sebastián brings one of Tomás's hands to his face and

caresses it. Those are the words he had been waiting for so long to hear again. Tomás slowly approaches and kisses him again. Sebastián is in a dream that he doesn't want to wake up from.

"Why me?" he asks.

"Because I like you. I see in you that person who I want to share every moment of my life, but..."

"But what?"

"I don't want to force things. Tell me the truth. Do you like me? Do you want to share your life with me, too?"

"Yes, of course I want to. Since we first met, all I wanted was to get to know you more and I like you more with each passing day. It felt right, but lately things were confusing and it felt wrong, I didn't know if you liked me. I am afraid —"

"You don't have to be afraid of anything. I know it's hard here in the clinic, but that's also something that we will be able to overcome together."

"And if, in the end, the treatments work and we are cured?" Sebastián asks, emotional once again.

"They won't work. It's impossible. No one changes, no one gets healed — there's nothing *to* heal!" Tomás recovers his own strength and is smiling from ear to ear; his dream is also materializing.

"What about Sandra? What's going to happen with her?"

This makes Tomás think. He takes his hands off of Sebastián's face and stares down at the floor.

"She was just an excuse not to hurt you. I thought that if you saw that change was possible — I don't know...

that you would be filled with positivity, hope. The truth is that it was me who was lying to myself. I just felt confused, too, and started to have doubts, but not anymore. Trust me." Tomás caresses the back of Sebastián's head. "What I feel for you is stronger and better than anything that I could feel for Sandra or anyone else. And I know we can make this real and good enough." He grabs Sebastián's hand and draws it to his bare chest so that he can feel how strong his heart is beating. "We can try. We have to be careful, but trust me: we can make it work."

"Tomás, for years I clung to my first love, Christian, thinking that I would not get another chance in a world so discriminating. But now I realize that you are the most romantic, loving, and friendly guy I have ever met since Christian, but also so unique and different. I don't know if I'm going to wake up and realize that it was all a dream. Can you pinch me?" Sebastián laughs through tears.

"I would rather do something else to keep your dream alive forever."

Tomás kisses him once again, but more passionately, while he takes off his shirt and starts to takes off his belt. He wants to have Sebastián all to himself, he wants to make love to him, but Sebastián moves away, scared.

"I can't. Not now. Forgive me."

"No, no. You forgive me." Tomás realizes that he has made a mistake and dresses himself. "I shouldn't have acted like this without consulting you first. I don't even have condoms here." Tomás laughs embarrassed.

His attitude leads Sebastián to trust him even more.

"No, really, forgive me if I get nervous. It's just that I

haven't had sex with anyone since Christian died three years ago."

"Not even with Alejandro?"

"Not even. I just wasn't that comfortable with him. I didn't trust him."

Tomás is relieved when he hears this confession. "I didn't mean to scare you. I don't want to rush things either. We have plenty of time and a long road to walk. We can wait for the right moment. It's no problem. For now, we can just sleep next to each other. I just want you in my arms. That's enough for me."

Sebastián places a soft, tender kiss on Tomás's lips.

"I want to do so many things with you and escape from this prison. I want to live with you in a safe place," Tomás confesses.

"It seems we won't have that opportunity."

"Yes we will. Someday soon we'll get out of here, I promise. We will find out the truth about this place."

As the boys lean their heads together for another soft kiss, the bedroom door suddenly jolts opens and a loud voice screams, "What are you doing?"

Their blood rushes to their cheeks when they see Dr. Rutherbor standing in the doorway. Sebastián begins to choke as Dr. Rutherbor grabs his arm and shakes him.

"You're going to be punished for an entire month!"

"It's not his fault!" Tomás yells. "Let him go! It was me who provoked him and brought him here to tempt him."

"Do you think I'm stupid?" Dr. Rutherbor is offended to see how the boy wants to deceive him, yet he thinks this is the perfect excuse to submit him to some punishment.

He yearns to mistreat him again. He just needed a reason. "Nurses!"

Two nurses and a guard walk into the room and drag Sebastián out, while the other patients wake up and peek out their doors to see what is happening.

"You're coming with me," Dr. Rutherbor tells Tomás. "You're going to regret this for the rest of your life."

The guard, Harold, holds Tomás, while a nurse takes a syringe from the pocket of her white coat. The young man tries to get loose, but it's useless. The nurse gives him the injection. Tomás frees himself enough to take a couple of steps, but then the world is blurred and he loses consciousness. He falls, banging his forehead against the floor.

Contained in his room, Sebastián finds it increasingly difficult to breathe. The nurses try to convince him to use his inhaler, but he refuses, with tears streaming down his cheeks. He wants to die, as he has wanted so many times before.

Dr. Rutherbor enters the room, hysterical. He grabs the inhaler and forces it into Sebastián's mouth. "Breathe in, dumbfuck! Breathe in!"

As a reflex, Sebastián inhales the air and the medication from the inhaler. He coughs. He is still choking, but, little by little, his breathing stabilizes. One of the nurses takes a syringe from her pocket.

"This will help calm you down. Relax."

Sebastián opens his eyes wide; needles have always terrified him. In the doorway of his room, he is able to distinguish Mateo, Fabricio, Johana, and Sandra, staring at him with anguished expressions.

"I'm going to my room. I hate watching these scenes," Sandra tells her friends, before leaving.

They not only inject him, but the doctor also shoves two pills into Sebastián's mouth. The boy falls on the bed, unconscious.

***

He dreams of Christian. He can feel him, listen to him, and even smell him. He feels alive.

Sebastián wakes up, surrounded by darkness. He looks at the clock to see it's two in the morning. How frustrating. He does not want to be awake. He prefers to stay with Christian there, in that other world. It takes him a couple of minutes to recover the memory of recent events. Tomás! What has happened to Tomás? As much as he wants to, he won't be able to sleep; he's too paranoid. Surely it's a side effect of the pills that the doctor gave him. Sebastián had promised Tomás that he would not take them again — that promise didn't last long. He is so disappointed in himself that he decides to take the bottle and take two more pills.

He stands up, walks to the desk, and opens one of the drawers. The cover of his photo album reads "Chris and Sebas". As he lifts the album, the letter Christian wrote to him falls under the bed. He feels even sadder now and stares at the white wall in front of him, distracted. He cries until he has an idea. He starts to take the photos from the album and tapes them on the wall: he's going to make a collage of his life with Christian and display it where everyone can see it.

By 2:45, he is finished. He's exhausted...or is it not normal fatigue that he feels? His body is weak, his mind distant. He feels a pressure coming down. The world goes dark.

***

When Juliana leaves her house the next day, she inevitably feels like she is being watched and judged by her neighbors. Most of them belong to the same group of ladies who meet every Sunday to pray and socialize at the local church. Juliana knows that the gossip of her divorce must have already passed down the block and even around the neighborhood. It's likely that they will no longer allow her to go to the meetings. She doesn't care. The important thing is herself and her happiness. But she is depressed to see how the husbands of her other friends say goodbye to them with tender kisses on the forehead or lips — those moments or those expressions of affection that she never had with Miguel. Well, life goes on. She remembers her dream from the night before, the words of her brother, and again feels confident in herself.

Meanwhile, Tomás is just waking up in his room at the clinic. He cannot stop thinking about Sebastián. He doesn't know what Dr. Rutherbor may have done to him. He leaves his room and sees that Sebastian's nurse, Verónica, heading towards his room. Tomás recognizes the opening and falls quietly in step behind her.

As the door to his room opens, they stand frozen, eyeing the scene before them. The walls are filled with pictures and the young man is lying on the ground, apparently asleep. Tomás rushes in and tries to rouse him but the boy does not respond.

"Stay with him. I'm going to get the doctor," Verónica forces.

Tomás is left alone with Sebastián. His body is trembling with fright. He keeps trying to move him, but he can't muster any reaction. He leans down onto his knees to hug the limp body and spots Christian's letter under the bed.

"Sebas. Sebas…please tell me you're okay. Tell me you're going to be all right."

"Whe…where am I?" Sebastián's voice fills Tomás with joy.

"With me. Don't worry, you're with me."

Sebastián gets up, clutching his head and signaling that it hurts.

"Sebas, what happened last night? What did Dr. Rutherbor do to you?"

"Did you do this?" Sebastián asks, pointing at the wall and looking at Tomás with bulging eyes.

"Me? No. I don't know who did this. I thought it was you."

"Christian?" Sebastián smiles, but his face looks more frightened than happy. "Christian? Could it have been Christian?"

Tomás becomes scared. He's never seen Sebastián like this. He walks to him and hugs him, but Sebastián pushes him away.

"Leave me! I want you to leave me alone, please."

"Sebas, please." Tomás doesn't know if his friend is listening or not. A few seconds ago he seemed to be laughing, but now he's crying. "You were right, Sebas. Yesterday at the doctor's office, I discovered that it was true — that he is mixing the pills. The ones I've been taking are really Clonazepam."

"Are you making fun of me?"

"No, no. Why would I do that?"

Then Sebastián explodes and begins to rip the pictures off the wall, furiously, but laughing out loud, jumping around the room and throwing the pictures up in the air. Tomás feels that he has lost him, this time the pills have won the fight. Sebastián jumps on the bed, pulling his hair. Tomás looks over and sees that, from the doorway, they are being watched. Not only by Dr. Rutherbor and the nurse, but also Mateo, Fabricio, Johana, Sandra, and the rest of the patients.

And also...no. It's not possible. Her? She's here? She works here?

"Mom?" Tomás looks Juliana in the face and he almost faints. He hasn't seen her in such a long time.

Everyone, except for Sebastián, who is delirious, turns toward the psychiatrist. It is a completely unexpected revelation for everyone except Dr. Rutherbor who regrets being so careless and letting this happen. It was planned that this boy would not find out about the presence of his mother at the clinic.

Juliana sees Tomás place his hand against the wall to

support himself and she is overwhelmed by the instinct to comfort her son. Dr. Rutherbor stops her by grabbing her arm. The serious look on the doctor's face reminds her that she must continue to follow the plan, to stay away from Tomás so that he will be cured.

"I completely agree with your diagnosis, Doctor," she tells Dr. Rutherbor, feeling a guilty for not having taken care of Sebastián's mental health lately.

"Mom, what does Sebas have?"

"Bipolar disorder, my love. He's maniac depressive."

"And what are you going to do with him?"

"We're going to move him to North Clinic. I'm going to leave him in the care of a friend of mine who is good at dealing with cases like this."

Tomás nods, looking down at the floor. He's devastated. Just last night they were finally together and now they're going to be separated, potentially forever.

The nurses grab Sebastián and inject him with a sedative. Dr. Rutherbor doesn't even want to look at Tomás. By now, he considers him a threat. Tomás sees how the doctor ties Sebastián's hands to the edges of the bed and he cannot take it anymore. Without saying goodbye to his mother, he leaves the room.

"Tomás. Wait," his mother calls, walking behind him. "We need to talk, please."

Tomás stops.

"I'm really sorry, honey." Juliana forces herself to hold back tears. "For all of this. I...the truth is that I made mistakes. I don't know what I did wrong."

"Mom, you didn't make me like this. I just *am* like

this. I'm your son. I don't know why you see me as if I'm a monster or if there was something bad inside of me."

"It's complicated."

"It may be. But this is not the way to solve things. We need love, we need to get rid of the prejudices."

Juliana tries to hold his hand, but he lets go. He sees Sebastián being carried out from the room on a stretcher, seemingly conscious. Tomás walks to him.

"Is Juliana your mother?" is the first thing that Sebastián asks him. His voice is low and barely audible, probably an effect of the sedative.

"Yes." Tomás tries to make sense of it.

"What's going to happen with us?" Sebastián asks, worried.

"This is not the end. I promise I'll come look for you — no matter what it takes. I'm going to do everything I can to get you out of there, you'll see."

"Am I going to be okay in that place?"

"Yes, they'll take care of your depression there. They will fix the damage caused by all those pills but not your orientation. You will be safe there."

Tomás doesn't know what to do. He wants to crouch next to the stretcher and kiss him but he knows that everyone is looking, including Dr. Rutherbor. He has to contain himself.

Sebastián says goodbye, seeing that Verónica and another nurse have come back to take the stretcher.

"Take care of yourself. And don't worry. Everything will be okay. This is not the end," is the last thing that Tomás is able to tell his new love as he is rolled out of the clinic.

Sebastián is relieved to feel fresh air again, to see the rays of the sun showering him, to appreciate the blue sky with its white clouds. He is coming alive again slowly, but he is increasingly losing the closeness of Tomás. He falls into a deep sleep when exhaustion takes over his mind.

Juliana, who witnessed this scene, realizes that there is something between the two young men, some kind of relationship. She feels guilty. She is sorry for having participated in the emotional upheaval of her patients, but she is mostly sorry for having made her own son in a patient.

Tomás walks back to his room. He doesn't want to see his friends, much less his mother. He is disappointed with the whole world. He remembers everything that happened the night before — the abuse, the syringe. Now he knows the truth: that he doesn't suffer from schizophrenia at all. He decides to stop taking the pills for good.

That same night, Sandra walks around her room, biting her nails and pulling her hair. She is furious and dizzy. She has not stopped vomiting all day. She feels betrayed by Tomás because he cheated on her with Sebastián. Nausea. Nausea in the morning, afternoon, and night. And the dizziness. She doesn't understand why unless…no, it's not possible… is it? She has been late for two days. Could it be? A smile is drawn across her lips.

Chapter THIRTEEN:

Is this how love is supposed to feel?
Saturday, May 12, 1990

IT'S BEEN A LITTLE OVER A MONTH SINCE SEBASTIÁN LEFT the clinic and everyone seems to have been affected by the event. Mateo, for example, made a radical decision and that is why he does not hang out with his friends or sit to eat with them. Fabricio doesn't understand why Mateo ignores him because he thought they were on such good terms and that the relationship was moving forward. He misses him too much so he decides to go to Mateo's room.

"May I come in?" he asks.

"I'm going to sleep for a couple of hours. I'm exhausted and I forgot to take my thyroid pill," Mateo answers, taking off his glasses.

"It's ok," Fabricio resigns, closing the door slowly, but then stops. He cannot stand his doubts anymore. "Did I say something wrong? Did I do something that pushed you away from me?"

"No, you didn't do anything."

"So?" Fabricio can't stop moving his fingers. He's an outgoing person, but, in moments like this, he always becomes nervous.

"Have you realized where we are?" Mateo puts his glasses back on and gets up from the chair. He walks towards the barred window, as far as he can from Fabricio.

"Well, yes, we already know that, but —"

"And, do you know why we are here? To get healed, to change our deviant identity."

"Do you really believe that? Do you believe in those speeches by the doctor and —"

"That doesn't matter, Fabricio. It's not important whether or not you believe what they say. It's irrelevant. The only real thing is that we are confined to this new world...a new world, yes, but the same as the one outside. It has the same mistreatment, the same rules, and the same prejudices. What do you want me to do? What are our options?"

"Option? There is just one option, the only one. Not giving up."

"Give up? Give up?" Mateo's mind is flooded by the memories of that night, the image of Sebastián pulling his hair and jumping on the bed, acting crazy. "Don't you see that we already gave up? That they defeated us? That they won? You saw what happened to Sebas."

"The thing with Sebastián happened because of the pills and you know it," Fabricio is outraged by the words of his friend. He doesn't want to leave, so he decides to try again, "Look, I don't know if you feel the same that I feel for you. That's what matters, not the rest. Please, you can't deny the truth."

"And, what is it that you feel for me?"

"I feel so much. Every time I see your sweet, nerdy face I feel this strong desire to kiss you — not just on your lips that tempt me madly, but also on both of your cheeks so that I can cheer you up and make you smile. Every time I get the chance to hold your hand, to warm you, I feel a trust that I want to grow within us. Every time you see me through your eyes, I feel this deep, chemical connection and this crazy physical attraction toward you. And every time I feel your presence, or I'm just next to you, I just want us to stay together. It's something unexpected and astonishing that alters me and can't ignore it any longer. I just want to experience it so desperately. I can't control myself." Fabricio sits on the bed and Mateo starts to walk towards him. "It really motivates me, it opens my eyes, and it wakes me up, makes me breath, and feel intensely alive. I just want to be with you — see you, kiss you, hold you, trust you, to be connected in every way with you, to be next to you and take care of you in a unique and special way."

Mateo wants to sit next to Fabricio, but he can't move. What he heard has left him stunned.

"And I've never felt this before, in any previous relationship," Fabricio continues. "That's why, for me, it's a blessing, a privilege, to be able to feel all of this for you." Mateo sits next to him. His words... Mateo never thought that he would hear such romantic and passionate words. He has to take off his glasses because he feels like he's going to start crying.

"Me, on the other hand, I feel like I'm cursed," Mateo says as he fills with courage. "I only want a place where I can be safe. Out there, my life was a living hell, especially in high school because they didn't accept me, because I didn't accept myself. In here, I thought that I would be safe and that I would find peace, but it turned out to be a double living hell! On the one hand, I cannot be who I really am and, on the other hand, I have these feelings for you, which I can no longer hide and I can't make them go away, I can't replace them by thinking about a woman. I want to be able to express my feelings for you and to say those words that are in my heart. I want to give you back everything I feel for you from my soul."

Fabricio listens attentively. He's happy to hear the confession. It clarifies all his doubts. He offers his hand to his friend.

"And now? How do you feel?"

"I feel good…very good. And safe."

Fabricio, with his fingers, caresses and warms the cold hand of the fearful young man in front of him.

"I'm scared," Mateo confesses.

"There's nothing to be afraid of."

"My spirit is exhausted. I don't want to still be inside here. I want to be who I am, make my own decisions, forget all of the insults, the cruelties, and those disgusting medications."

"Don't worry, I'm here with you. Together we can overcome this stage. But you have to listen to me. If you want to survive in here, you have to stop taking those pills. And forgive your past."

"What do you mean?"

"Forgive your past, let go, and release it. Only then

you'll be able to be yourself, freely."

"But if we get out of here and find that out there everything is still the same? Or perhaps even worse."

"No, this time it will be different. This time you've got me...you'll be with me."

"Yes?"

"I really like you, Mateo."

"That much?"

"That much."

Mateo radiates happiness. Lights come out of his brown eyes and his sweet face is one big, innocent smile.

"Is this how love is supposed to feel?" he asks, falling in love even more watching the enamored and attractive light-green eyes of Fabricio, who caresses his neck under the golden auburn hair.

"Yes, now you know."

"It feels so unique. I'm suddenly aware of my heart beating..." Mateo puts his hand on his chest and smiles as a tear of happiness slides down his cheek. He now feels more grateful to be alive and, most of all, relieved that he hasn't yet given up on his life and is still breathing in this special moment that he never thought he would have. "It makes me feel — and realize that I'm still here. I'm still alive. Love is supposed to be about feeling alive, not just with yourself, but with someone else. I've never been in this situation."

"What? Have you never kissed a man?"

"No."

"A woman?"

"Nope."

"So, how do you know you're gay?"

"Well, what I feel for you tells me something, doesn't it?" Mateo smiles.

"Believe me, that's more than enough for me. That's the only thing that matters," Fabricio assures him.

"Oh, and not giving up. Remember that." For the first time, Mateo feels confident and like he is a part of something unbelievable with someone.

"Yes, but Mateo, you also remember that things are not going to be easy. It's going to be very hard. We're going to have to work for it every day — if we want our relationship to survive, of course. I, for one, want it to."

The young man nods and an uncomfortable silence is created between the two of them. Fabricio assumes that this is the right moment and puts his face near Mateo's, little by little, until their lips come together.

"I feel the same as you."

"Yes?" Fabricio asks, relieved.

"Yes, I want to be us and stay together."

Both join in a single embrace.

"Do you think you can sleep here tonight?"

"Absolutely," Fabricio answers, excited. "Just give me a few minutes to go to my room and put pillows under the covers so that the nurses won't notice."

"I'll wait for you."

Fabricio leaves the room and Mateo feels like he has just been reborn.

Down the hall, Tomás hasn't taken a single pill since Sebastián was transferred to North Clinic and now he is going through withdrawals. He hardly sleeps at night. He has cold sweats, and, at times, he shakes. He doesn't know anything about Sebastián. There's no one to give him any information. Tomás is going to resist. He knows that he's going to make it and he knows that, as soon as the worst of this hangover passes, when all the effects of the medicine have come out of his body, he will uncover the truth. Dr. Rutherbor may have won the battle, but Tomás will win the war.

Chapter FOURTEEN:

How to say goodbye?
Sunday, May 13, 1990

AT FOUR IN THE MORNING, THE GUARDS, HAROLD AND JOSÉ, talk in their usual spot outside of the clinic, as they do every night.

"I'm telling you, there are the copies of all the keys in the doctor's office."

"What if they catch us?"

"Catch us? It's the word of those lunatics against ours. Who are they going to believe? Don't you get bored just walking up and down all night long? Without any fun?"

"Well, yes, it used to be more fun," José nods. "Before, we used to use electricity on the patients and the faces they made were hilarious."

"It's just that they were terrible. Do you remember that they went into the rooms to sleep together? Two men sleeping together... How disgusting!"

"Do you think they still do that?"

"We could find out. If you want to, of course."

"Are you sure? What if the nurse wakes up?"

"Tonight it's just Mónica. She's a friend of mine so

she won't say a word." Harold knows that he already has José convinced. "Look, we just have to take the keys and go room by room checking. If we catch one, we shove him into the storage rooms, where the torture rooms used to be. The doors of those storage rooms are so strong that no sound gets out."

"I don't know. Honestly —"

"Okay then, don't be scared. Let's go now before it gets light and then they will see us."

José agrees and the two guards walk towards Dr. Rutherbor's office.

For Mateo, it is dreams come true. It is the first time he is spending the night with another man, with the man he loves. It's the first time he has shared so many hugs, kisses, and caresses with another person. This is such a romantic moment. It's so perfect that he feels like he has discovered heaven on earth.

"How do you feel?" Fabricio asks him.

"Happy. Really happy." Mateo rests his head in Fabricio's chest. He takes the opportunity, "Tell me one thing…if you can and if you want to, of course."

"What do you want to know?"

"Who put you in here?"

"My father. It was my father," Fabricio's tone of voice changes and becomes serious.

"Did your mother support you?"

"No. She died a long time ago, when I was ten, in a car accident."

"I'm really sorry." Mateo didn't mean to get into such

heavy topics, but now that he's there, he decides to keep asking, "And how was your relationship with your father?"

"Difficult. We didn't speak much. We didn't understand each other. After he learned about my homosexuality, when I was nineteen years old, we didn't have a good relationship. One night, he followed me to a gay club. I got even with him and I became a rebel by doing whatever I wanted and never listening to him."

"I understand. It's the same for me. Last time I saw my father, he called me a faggot."

"My father wrote me a letter…a farewell letter."

"When?"

"A couple of days after they locked me in here," Fabricio takes from his pocket a wrinkled paper he always carries with him. It's a weight that goes wherever he does.

"If you don't want to talk about it, we can stop. We could talk about something else."

"No, don't worry." With the paper in his hand, Fabricio says, "I really want to show it to you. I want you to really get to know me. I trust you."

Fabricio hands the wrinkled paper to Mateo who reads:

Friday, February 23, 1990

Son, I don't know how else to say goodbye to you…so I'm writing you this letter to tell you that you won't see me again. I'll always keep our memories as father and son in my heart — of when I really knew you and knew who you were: my worthy son, on the right path, and guided by God. But now, with your confession that you are a homosexual, a sexual deviant, I don't know you anymore. I don't know who you are. The only thing I know is that you are no longer my son.

If you manage to get out of that clinic and heal, then we can resume our relationship. But, in the meantime, I'm really sorry. You have made your decision. I neither respect nor accept it — and God also does not accept the path you have taken, with that unnatural sexual identity. You are an abomination.

If you don't change, forget about me, don't look for me, don't call me, I won't take anything from you, you won't be welcome into my home. You, for me, no longer exist.

As I say farewell, I hope to see my son in you again — not this abomination or sin.

Goodbye

When Mateo finishes reading, he realizes that Fabricio is crying.

"I'm sorry... I didn't mean to..."

"In the end, I was left all alone," Fabricio sobs.

"No, you are not alone. You've got me."

The two boys sigh as their hands find each other. Fabricio starts to caress Mateo's arm until he feels something strange on his wrist. "What is this? What happened here?"

"Nothing. Nothing happened to me." Mateo tries to hide his scars.

"Yes, there's something there. Let me see."

Mateo has no choice but to show him his wrists.

"What happened here? Did you cut yourself?"

"Yes, it was the only thing I came up with to escape

from everything, from the whole world, from my parent, from my classmates, from the teasing."

"Please, promise me you won't do this again."

"I won't. I promise. I don't need to do it anymore. Now I have you."

"You know, I just realized that it's you I've been waiting for. Remember? To love yourself first then you'll be able to meet someone you can spend your life with. You make me see things differently. You're someone real, conscientious, intelligent... I'm thankful for having found you." Fabricio leans and kisses him on the lips. "I'm thankful for having you by my side, close to my heart."

"You're also here in my heart," Mateo confesses. "As you said, it's not going to be easy, it's going to be rough. We're going to have to work at this every day. Just like you, I also want to be together."

Fabricio loves to see him like that, with so much willpower, but is really surprised when he sees him stand up and start to undress.

"Let's do it," Mateo says, suddenly sure of himself.

"What? Are you ready?"

"Yes, I am."

"Wait, wait...are you sure? I don't have condoms. We have no reason to rush things."

They both laugh and lie down again in each other's arms. They kiss, rubbing their cheeks together. Fabricio caresses Mateo's bare chest.

The bedroom door slams open and bounces off of the wall. Harold and José appear on the other side with happy looks on their faces. They finally found their victims.

"Nasty faggots! What are you doing?"

The two young men cannot believe what is happening. It cannot be real — it must be the product of their imagination! The guards stomp to the bed with wicked smiles on their faces.

"José, dress him and take that faggot to the storage room, I'll take care of this other one."

"Please, don't punish us! Don't hurt us!" Mateo implores, while José grabs him by the arm and drags him outside of the room, "No! Please, no!"

"Relax, Mateo, relax. Don't do anything," Fabricio is able to say before the other guard closes bedroom door.

Mateo doesn't know where José is taking him, but he's sure that it's not good. He has never been so scared, not even when his classmates harassed him on the school bus.

Fabricio, meanwhile, knows that if he doesn't cooperate with the guards, it's possible that he won't even survive the night.

"Do you like giving it or taking it?" Harold asks Fabricio.

"Please, don't hurt me. I'll do whatever you ask."

"Yeah?" Harold pulls down his pants. "So suck it."

"What?"

"Suck it or I'll beat you. I swear."

"Please, I don't want to…"

"I know this is what you like, pussy. Either you suck it or I'll tell the doctor we found you and the other pussy sleeping together. Do you hear me? Suck it, fucker!"

"No, I can't…I don't want to!"

Harold punches him in the face with a closed fist and Fabricio falls to the ground on his back, hitting his head against the wooden edge of the bed. The guard takes him by the arms and turns him over. Fabricio tries to resist but his efforts are useless. Harold pulls down Fabricio's pants, opens his legs, and takes the boy's pride with ease. Fabricio is reduced to tears and cries of pain. Just a few minutes ago, he felt like he was in paradise. He can't believe how quickly everything went to hell.

Mateo is very skinny and fragile. Although he tries to get away, José has no problem shoving him into one of the storage rooms.

"Please, don't hurt me."

"Shut up, you faggot. I'm going to show you what's good."

José turns on the little light in the room, spits in Mateo's face, and kicks him in the side. Mateo tries again to get away, but the guard grabs his wrist with one hand and uses the other to pull Mateo up by his hair, throwing him to the floor.

"Please, don't hurt me!"

Mateo's glasses fall and he can't see anything. José turns around to lock the storage room door and the young man assumes this is going to be his only chance to escape. He gets to his feet and runs as fast as he can towards the door, but José hears him and turns, punching him in the nose. Mateo falls onto his back. His whole face is a puddle of blood. José is hysterical and takes a knife out of the back pocket of his pants.

"Listen, spawn of the devil. I can't waste much time here with you, so you'd better —" José doesn't finish his sentence because Mateo's adrenaline rush prompts him to stands back up and try to escape. José makes a move to stop him and, when he stretches his arm, his knife is buried in the boy's stomach.

The two stand motionless, mute. José draws out the knife in a single motion. His fingers are covered in blood.

"Ah... ah," Mateo mumbles, the shock has rendered him to where he can barely speak. "My...my stomach..."

"It wasn't my...I didn't mean to..." The face and personality of José seem to transform in that tragic second, not because he cares about the young man, but because he believes that this will cost him his job. "I told you to stay still, shitty faggot! Now, what am I going to do? What am I going to say?"

Mateo puts his hand over the wound. The blood flows in spurts.

"He...help..."

"Yes! Yes, that! Help...help...where?" José walks in circles, hitting his forehead, trying to think of some solution. "I know, I know! Stay here. Wait for me. I'm going to wake Mónica up. We'll call the hospital and they'll treat you. You're going to be fine, don't worry. Be patient, of course. Wait for me."

José leaves and locks the door. Mateo remains alone in the dark room with only the dim light, holding his hand over his stomach, feeling the warm liquid seeping through his fingers.

Harold is oblivious to the screams next door as he enjoys the torture he is placing upon Fabricio, paying no attention to his cries and sobs, until he hears soft knocks on the door. He guesses that it's José. He reluctantly stops, giving the boy a break, as he opens the door with a wicked grin.

"We're fucked. We're fucked."

"What? What happened?" Harold responds, shocked by the state of his friend.

"I stabbed the knife… I stabbed the knife…"

"What are you talking about? Calm down and explain it to me. What happened with the knife?" Fear begins to take hold of Harold.

"That faggot ran away and…I…didn't want to…I stabbed the knife into his stomach!"

Fabricio, still facedown on the ground, hears the words and his blood freezes. "Mateo! What did this asshole do to Mateo?"

"You're kidding, right?" Harold asks with a smile.

"No! I'm telling you, that faggot is bleeding all over the storage room!"

"Are you crazy? What did you do? It can't be…we're going to lose our jobs. They're going to turn us in to the police!"

"What do we do? What do we do?"

"Let's go. Let's get out of here."

The guards start to leave the room but quickly stop in unison as they remember one is still alive.

"What about the other one? We can't leave him there, he'll wake up the other patients and we won't have time to escape," José warns.

"It's true…it's true. Let's take him to the storage rooms."

The two grab Fabricio, who is so scared and hurt that he can't even move. They drag him to the storage rooms.

"Where did you put the other one?" Harold asks.

"In the third room. Do we also put this one in there?"

"No. Let's separate them. Open the second door to put him in there."

José takes out the key and opens the second room. The guards shove Fabricio in and lock the door.

"What do I do with the keys?" José asks.

"Let's take them with us. That way, no one will be able to open the doors until we are far away."

The two guards make sure that the second and the third storage rooms are locked and run to the door of the clinic. They know they have no choice but to leave and go as far away as possible.

Fabricio feels around in the darkness as his hands settle upon the damp floor. He heard the guards lock Mateo in the third storage room. He knows that he needs to find some way to talk to him, to comfort him. Still in pain, Fabricio pulls the cords to turn on the almost-broken light. He walks to the wall and starts desperately probing it with his palms and fingertips.

"Mateo, are you all right?" Fabricio screams at the wall, desperate to find some opening, some little hole or crack to see Mateo. He finds a small hole where the wall joins the floor. He slides down, still groping the wall. He feels cold air on his fingers, as if death lived right next to him. It seems there is a gap between the floor and the wall through which the two rooms connect.

"Mateo? Mateo!" he calls to him.

"Fabricio?"

"Mateo! Are you there? What happened? Are you okay?" Fabricio is glad to hear his loved one, but is scared by the tone of his voice.

"No, I feel weak... I'm scared..."

"What happened to you? Are you all right? Answer me!" he asks again, but faster and more desperate.

"Fabricio...I'm hurt..." Mateo answers him.

"Where? What did he do to you?"

"He stabbed me."

"Where? Tell me!"

"In my stomach."

"How big is the wound?"

"I don't know. I can't see very well. I can't find my glasses. I can't see it... I can't... everything is red..."

"Can you cover it with something? Are you bleeding a lot?"

"I am. I think I'm all covered in blood. I'm so weak. Fabricio, I don't want to die..." For the first time, Mateo is afraid to die.

"You're not going to die...you're not going to. Let me see if I can open the door." Fabricio jumps up. He doesn't feel any pain anymore, or rather, he knows in the back of his mind that his pain is still there, but he has no time to worry about it. Right now he has to save Mateo.

"No, please, don't go. Don't leave me alone."

"I'm not leaving you alone," Fabricio cries out in

between gasps for air. He's pulling and pushing the door, trying to make it give in, but it's useless.

"Come here. I don't know if we have much time. Stay here, close by."

"We have to do something. You can't just stay like this. You could bleed to death!"

"The guard told me he was coming back. He told me he was going to ask for help and that he would come back. It might be true." Mateo tries to calm his partner of just one day, because deep down, feels that he has little time left.

"Did he tell you that? Okay, don't move, just hang in there." Now it's Fabricio who tries to calm Mateo, but he heard the guards plan their escape and he knows that what Mateo heard was a lie. "Hang on, please. In any case, it's almost dawn and the nurse will wake up. Does it hurt?"

"I'm cold, but it doesn't hurt. It doesn't hurt much anymore." Mateo feels the cold take control of his body more than he ever felt and he feels his skin becoming clammy and the blood that fills his veins slowly draining.

That's...that's good," Fabricio consoles him. He knows it's not a good sign. He knows he's going to lose him. "Try to cover the wound with something. Try to stop the bleeding."

"I'm trying, but it keeps coming out."

"Come a little closer. I'm going to stick my arm though here — see if you can reach me."

Mateo can barely see the hole next to him, but he can see the blurred hand and he smiles at the hand he longs to hold. He slowly approaches, careful not harm himself any more, while his vision becomes even more blurred. He trains his eyes upward to avoid seeing the blood and moves until he reaches the hand of his love, grabbing him immediately. Fabricio tightly squeezes his hand and pledges to not let go, not even for one second. Fabricio wants him to know hat he cares for him and that he's not alone.

"So many times I wanted to kill myself and my whole life perspective changed when I met you," Mateo slowly slurs. "You made my life better…and that's why I didn't think my life would end at seventeen. I thought I would have so much to get to know, to learn, and to give back. What happened?"

"Mateo, save your energy. You're not going to die. Hang on."

"I never imagined that I would die here, alone, and without being able to see properly. I'm scared."

"You're not going to die." Fabricio denies the reality in front of him. "You're not alone. I'm here. We're together. The nurse will wake up any minute."

"Is this it? Do I have to say goodbye?"

"No. You don't have to say goodbye. You have a future ahead of you," Fabricio assures him.

"It seems I no longer have that. Destiny brought me here. Do you think you and I would have been more?"

"We are, Mateo. We're more. You came into my world and owned me from that first moment. I love you, Mateo."

"I…I love you, too." His face lights up when he hears those words for the first time and is able to say them back to the love of his life.

"Close your eyes," Fabricio tells him.

"No…I'm afraid that I won't open them again…"

"That's not going to happen. Trust me, close your eyes. Breathe."

Mateo trusts Fabricio and does as he says.

"Where do you see yourself ten years from now?"

"Graduated from university. I'm a writer…I publish my novels." Mateo answers, smiling in the darkness.

"Are you happy?"

"Yes…with you…we're inseparable…in love."

"Mateo, don't leave me… I need you."

"Do you think it could happen?"

"Absolutely. This is all going to happen. We'll be happy together, we'll live in a world without discrimination. The rest will even understand us. You and me against the world."

"I like that plan." Mateo coughs quietly. He has to wipe the edge of his mouth with his hand to remove the blood. "Fabricio, I'm dying…I have to say goodbye to you."

"No, please, don't say that."

"Thanks for your love."

"It's just the beginning. We have so much love ahead of us," Fabricio affirms.

"I can't breathe very well. I feel like I'm suffocating." He coughs harder.

"Mateo, are you there?"

"Yes. I'm still here," he answers, breathing slower to avoid the pain. "I can hardly breathe." Mateo coughs louder and he has to wipe the blood from his mouth again.

"Don't say goodbye…"

"I don't know how to," Mateo speaks softly.

"Just hang on."

"No, no…I don't know how to say goodbye to you because I don't want to. I want to be in your arms again,"

Mateo confesses.

"I'm dying to have you in my arms. Don't say goodbye to me. Please tell me we'll see each other later...because we will see each other again."

"You believe so?"

"Yes. I believe in us."

"Fabricio?"

"What?"

"I'll see you later." Mateo smiles again. "Do you know what's the best thing that could happen to me in this clinic?"

"What?"

"You. For me, it was you, Fabricio. You are...the door I never thought would open... before you, I was lost..."

"Mateo, I'll never meet someone like you; you're unique and special."

"Am I?"

"Yes, for me, you are," Fabricio confesses, squeezing his cold hand even tighter.

Mateo coughs once again, louder, spilling blood onto his chin. He removes his other hand from the wound and sees that his palm is red. He covers the wound again and tries to keep confessing more things to Fabricio.

"Out of all the hopes and dream for which I could have prayed for, you are here."

"I'm still here with you," Fabricio tells him, not removing his hand.

"Promise me something. Promise me that you'll get out of this clinic and be yourself...that you won't give up. You'll fight for your rights and won't let anybody discriminate against you...and...promise me...that you'll fall in love again..." Mateo requests.

"We're both going to get out of here...both of us."

"Promise me...promise me, Fabricio..."

"I promise."

"And, if you ever get to meet my parents...tell them I don't blame them, that I love them...that I regret not being the perfect son they wanted..."

"Don't leave me, Mateo. You can't go and leave me like this..."

"I would like to stay...I would like to turn eighteen and be an adult...to start a whole new life...to live a safe place... to create a home with you in this world so bright...and be part of a generation that can be accepted and understood by the world...to be me with no discrimination towards me because of my sexuality, but...I can't."

Fabricio is crying so loudly that he can't keep Mateo from noticing. Mateo, on the other hand, doesn't cry. He smiles with true happiness laced with a pinch of resignation.

"Do you think I'll go to Heaven?"

"Yes, don't doubt that," Fabricio answers in between sobs, emotionally defeated. "You are a good person. God is going to welcome you with open arms. He'll turn you into an angel just as we prayed for, remember?"

"Yes? Would have God listened to my prayers? Will I become an angel?"

"Yes," Fabricio assures him, anguished that he is so close to losing him.

Mateo is hopeful that it will happen, confessing to him, "Do you know what I will never be able to explain?"

"What is it, my love?" Fabricio asks him.

"The way you opened up to me today and how it allowed me to open up to you."

"Why?"

"Because you were the first one. I had never done it before. You were the exceptional one that conquered me. I felt so alone before. I only hoped and dreamed that someone would come and change my life the way you have. I never thought I would be able to find a place to call home, and, for that, I'm grateful to you because I felt at home with you. You made me see where I belonged and it was in me…and with you. All I wanted was to find someone special, someone different, and someone meaningful. I like having known that sensation before I leave."

"Please, don't leave!"

"Now I believe in what they say: that true love exists. You are my only one, my true love. Tha…thanks for…tha…"

"Mateo? Mateo!"

His own name is the last thing Mateo hears. He drops his head back against the wall with his eyes open, the last of his tears fall to his half-open mouth and mix with the dried blood on his lips. His hand loosens over his wound, creating a pool of blood around his slumped body. His other hand releases that of his true love as the lightbulb in the room fades, too, like it is passing away along with the boy.

In that instant, Mateo vanishes. From the absolute darkness of the room, everything becomes bright white.

"Mateo! Are you there? Mateo, talk to me, please! Don't… don't go," Fabricio howls. In his mind, he goes through all of the moments together with Mateo: the first time he saw him when he almost tripped on the stairs, his wonderful smile, his sweet cleft chin, his sad, puppy-dog eyes. He promises himself that he will never erase these memories.

"Mateo..." he calls for the last time. "Mateo, do you hear me?" He realizes that their fingertips are still touching but that Mateo's grip has released. Mateo's hand is no longer just cold, but frozen.

Outside, everyone is still asleep. No one knows about this terrible event, about this tragedy, the dramatic ending to the new Romeos.

Chapter FIFTEEN:

The story of Castor and Pollax. Sunday, May 13, 1990

IT'S HER MOTHER'S BIRTHDAY AND JULIANA HAS TO TRAVEL several hours to reach the city where she spent her youth. The city at dusk makes her sad. It brings back memories.

"How is Tomás doing? Did he cure his…?" her mother asks, with a grimace of revulsion on her face.

"Very good. He's getting better." Juliana tries to changes the subject as fast she can.

"But he isn't cured yet?"

"That takes time."

"I always knew he wasn't going to turn out normal."

"Mom! Please, he's my son."

"No, I don't believe that. That kid is the product of sin, of a rape. I warned you something like this would happen. The most humane thing, the best for the boy, would have been not having him in the first place."

"One thing has nothing to do with the other. You had Tommy and he also turned out like that…"

"The difference is that your brother chose to take the

deviant path. Do I make myself clear? He was a normal person that got lost along the way, but your son. Oh, ever since he was a baby, I noticed. He was born like that — he has a malignant mark."

"Mom!" this is why Juliana hates visiting her. The worst of it is that she's going to have stay there for one more day because she has vacation at the North Clinic and Dr. Rutherbor also unexpectedly called to give her Monday off. Juliana thought that he sounded anxious, like he wanted to keep her away from the clinic for some reason. "I already told you he's my son. We'd better change the subject."

"It's just that I'm worried about you. How could you get a divorce? Marrying Mr. Díaz was what saved you from your sin. You were able to raise your son with a man worthy of God! You're going to be all alone. That wasn't God's plan for you and now...how are you going to look the Holy Father in the face when the time comes? You have committed one of the worst sins. What went wrong? You were very quiet and disciplined with us, especially good at following the Bible passages in my class — you were my best pupil!"

"Mom, please." Juliana leaves her cup of coffee on the kitchen counter. "I'm going to lie down for a while. I'm tired from driving so much."

Juliana doesn't wait for her mother to respond and walks to the living room to take the stairs to the second floor. Her mother doesn't respond. She just drinks her coffee and continues her internal monologue, reproaching her daughter for having twisted the family that way. She's devastated.

"What did I do wrong? What did I do to deserve this

nightmare?" she eventually asks herself out loud. Would things have been better if she had done something more to help her son or would have made her daughter get an abortion? Would she not have sexual deviants for her son and grandson? But abortion is also a sin — she can't believe the horrible things she is thinking! She is more confused than ever.

Juliana is filled with nostalgia when walking by the closed door of her brother Tommy's bedroom. Something attracts her, forces her to turn the knob. She goes in. It's dusty and there are cobwebs in the corners. Apparently, it is just as he left the last time he was there...before they put him into that rehabilitation clinic. The memories hit her, but being there again, in that room, reassures her. It's as if his very memories were stored in there.

She lies on Tommy's bed. The sadness overwhelms her. Tears start to fall from her eyes almost involuntarily. She wipes her eyes with the back of her hand. She remembers Tommy. He was four years younger than her and both were born in late May. They always called each other by their nicknames: he was Castor and she was Pollax. This was Tommy's idea.

They were so close, one for the other. People even thought that they were twins because they looked so much alike with their hazel eyes and straight, dark brown hair. Where they did differ was in their hobbies. Tommy was fascinated by astrology, horoscopes, and the esoteric in general. He said he was proud to be a Gemini and, after a while, Juliana realized that that's where he had gotten her nickname, although the original name was "Pollux" and he changed it so that it sounded more feminine.

Tommy was always there for her through thick and thin — always protected her from strangers and defended her to their parents. But everything changed one day, when he was about seventeen. He, despite being so attached to her, could not tell her the things he felt inside. In that home, it would have been difficult for anyone because of their mother's religious teaching that bordered on fanaticism. But that one day, the truth had to come to light.

Sunday, June 11, 1967

The whole family gathers in the kitchen at the small table with the checkered tablecloth. Their father reads the news.

"How disgusting to see this…these perverts doing their business."

"What perverts?" Juliana asks, curious.

"These homosexuals. Here it says that there were thirty caught by the police only this month. Imagine that. How many will they catch in a year? A thousand? One thousand homosexuals in just one city — imagine that."

"And what do they do with them? Do they just lock them away? We should organize a march so that they can eliminate them once and for all," Juliana's mother jokes, but, in truth, she doesn't think that it's such a bad idea. "They are an abomination to the eyes of the Blessed."

"Why are there homosexuals? I don't understand," Juliana says, confused. "They know that they are wrong and that God won't love them."

"They're committing Lucifer's sin," her mother

answers her seriously. "The rebel before God, before His laws, before everything that was created. They think that —"

"Did a homosexual tell you that? Or are you just saying it because you think that's how it is?" Tommy interrupts her.

"What are you saying?" their mother is indignant.

"That you're passing judgment on people you don't even know. You're drawing conclusions —"

"Honey, I understand that, at your age, you see it like that, but in time, you'll realize that those people…well, if you meet one, you've met them all."

"But that is the exact definition of prejudice!"

Juliana stops her fork halfway to her mouth, scared by the volume of both, while their mother worries about the tension.

"Enough! Stop talking about this. We don't talk about vile subjects at the dinner table. Eat, eat," their father interrupts, banging on the table with the palm of his hand. The dishes rattle and drinks spill.

"Calm down," his wife pleads. "Son, just eat," she warns Tommy.

"No, I'm not hungry anymore, for real." Tommy sets his silverware down on the table and goes to his room.

"I don't understand that kid," the father says, irritated. "How long do I have to be patient? I don't know, but he better watch out because he's not going to want to see me blow up." Infuriated, he steps outside to smoke his tobacco, the only thing that calms him down.

Juliana rushes to finish her breakfast because her

brother worries her. He usually talks back to his parents, but this time she noticed something different…some deception.

"I'm done. I'm going to Tommy's room to ask him what's with him," she tells her mother, getting up.

"And tell him to cut that hair."

"That's the fashion now, Mother. Men let their hair grow to the neck."

"Whatever, I don't care. He's going to look like a girl before too long. Tell him I say he has to cut it. That's why I give him his allowance. And mention how badly he behaved with us. He must apologize to his father."

Juliana nods and quickly runs up to Tommy's room. She knocks a couple of times, but he doesn't answer. She opens it without an invitation.

"What just happened in the kitchen?"

"Nothing. Leave me alone," he answers, lying on his back, half-covered with his sheets and facing the wall. "You won't be able to understand me. Leave me alone."

"I *will* understand you. I've always understood you. Come on, don't be like that, tell me."

"No. Leave me alone."

"Come on, I'm your sister. I'm Pollax. I know all your secrets. You can trust me."

"There's something about me you don't know," Tommy says, turning to face her. "I…I don't…how do I say it?" Tommy sits on the bed, next to her. "I don't think about women."

"What? What are you saying?"

"I think it's what you think. I like men."

Juliana opens her eyes wide. Then she frowns and

realizes this must be a joke. She laughs.

"No, don't laugh. I'm being serious. I'm telling you the truth. I'm gay."

Juliana stops laughing. "Seriously? No. I can't believe what you're —"

"It's true. I'm gay, I'm homosexual, whatever you want to call it." Tommy smiles widely. Despite everything, he's still the same Castor.

"But...but..." Juliana is stunned. She moves a little to the side, away from Tommy. "Are you sure? Maybe you're just confused."

"Why are you backing away? I'm not going to hurt you. It's not like I have something contagious."

"Yes...that's a disease. It's a terrible sin. It's in the Bible —"

"That's not true. You can't believe those things they tell us. Look, since I accepted who I am, I'm happy, I don't feel angry at the world, and I don't feel less than anybody else. I accept myself and that's it. I'm happy and I'm not alone."

"You are not alone? My God, are you with someone?"

"His name is Jason. He is a classmate —"

"What! No, don't say that, Tommy. You can't be like this. You can't! You are not homosexual!"

"Juliana! Juliana, calm down. I don't want them to hear you. Promise me...promise me you won't say anything."

"We...well... only on one condition. I want you to change. That thing must have a cure! I want you to try hard to —"

"I don't think there is a cure, actually, but I can

promise you that I'll try to —"

Tommy's promise is interrupted as the door of the room opens and both siblings turn, hoping that it's not the worst thing that could happen to them.

"What are you saying? That you're a faggot? It is that what I'm hearing?" their father screams, furious.

"Honey, calm down please," their mother asks her husband, wiping her tears.

"No, I'm not a faggot. I'm homosexual and I'm your son!" Tommy says, standing up.

"How dare you shame this house, this family, this way?" their father screams as he walks towards his son. He slaps him hard and returns to stand next to his wife.

"No! Please, no violence!" their mother yells, emotionally ruined.

"Listen to me, you degenerate, I promise you that you'll get cured because *I'll* cure you — whether you want it or not!

Tommy starts to tear up. His hands are clenched in fists. Anger consumes him. He is alone against the world, against his family — not even his Pollax is by his side. They look at him with contempt, like a stranger. He has lost them. He no longer has a home. His loneliness gets darker when they leave him locked in his room. Only Juliana looks back out of sympathy, but her father calls up the stairs to take her to the clinic to intern with him.

Sunday, July 09, 1967

A month later, Juliana throws a rose on Tommy's coffin. The

day is quiet, not even the birds sing. The air is warm, but the Revas family is cold; the cold comes from within, from inside each of them.

"Goodbye, Castor," Juliana mutters, looking at the coffin descending into the hole with her rose. "Goodbye, Tommy."

The girl turns and sees her parents walking towards the car. She feels guilty. Could she have done something more for him? Something…different? Or perhaps it was the fault of those doctors and psychologists at the clinic? The only thing that comforts her is that after they found Tommy hanged in his room, they closed up that center and the authorities are investigating the matter. That's what they told her, at least.

"Juliana!"

For a moment, the girl believes that it's Tommy who is calling her, but she returns to reality and turns to her parents. She says goodbye to the coffin one last time. It has been covered with dirt. She walks to the vehicle in the drizzling rain.

"That's why the birds don't sing," Juliana says to herself. "They're crying."

"Juliana! Hurry up, it's raining!"

Or maybe it's Tommy that sent the water, as a message to tell her that, in the end, he did make it to Heaven and that God accepted him among His kingdom.

"Juliana!"

The girl walks faster. Juliana - that is her name. No more Pollax. Pollax is dead, buried with that coffin…just like her rose.

Months later, to move on from the tragic loss of her brother, she decides to move to the capital. She enrolls in college to study psychology, against her mother's wishes, where she attends classes with Dr. Ralph Rutherbor. She quickly becomes his best pupil. She befriends Paul Gómez, a student of photography, and introduces him to the doctor so that he can cure his homosexuality and not end like her dear brother.

Sunday, May 13, 1990

The memories vanish. She gets up from the bed and walks towards the closet. If the whole bedroom is just as her brother left it, then it's probable that she'll find something of value, something she may keep.

She opens the closet and looks in drawers, but she only sees clothes. She bends down and looks through the shoes on the floor — a black box. She thinks that this may be what she is looking for although she doesn't know for sure. She picks it up sit back on the bed. First, she makes sure the door is locked. She doesn't want a repeat of what happened so many years ago.

She opens the box: papers and photographs, pictures of her brother — and he looks so happy in them! Most seem to have been taken some time before he confessed his secret - before their father decided to commit him so he would be "cured". What about this one? Tommy appears in a photograph embracing another boy and the two are smiling. Is it *him*? Juliana turns the photograph over and sees that faded writing in pencil: Jason and Castor.

"He is...Jason."

She sets the picture aside and picks up one of the crumpled papers. It's a letter. Painfully, she decides to read it.

Tuesday, June 13, 1967

From: Castor
To: Jason
My parents already know. I have no way out. The decision is already made.
My sister couldn't understand me. I don't blame her. I know, deep down inside, she loves me and thinks that it's the best for me, but I know it's not. Even so, I forgive her, because she'll always be my Pollax.

Juliana stops for a moment, with tears on her face. Already hurt, she has been touched. She feels relieved little by little from the blame she has carried since his death, but, on the other hand, is haunted by the thought of having failed him, of not having been there by his side. She takes a deep breath and continues reading.

I don't know what will happen to me. I only know that they'll put me away in a clinic...to cure me...or at least that's what my father tells me.
I hope I survive this stage. I hope I can get out of that place and keep on being as I am and be with you again.
I'll be strong. I hope so. I love you so much, Jason... I already

miss you.

This last phrase tells Juliana that Tommy simply couldn't take it any longer — and that was *before* they sent him away. Who knows what kind of treatments they subjected him to in that clinic? Then she thinks of Tomás. What if her son...

"No! Don't think about that," she says to herself. "Doctor Ralph is a good man, a professional. He would never let Tomás reach those extremes. He would never let me down." Or at least, that's what she hopes, of course. Her head hurts. She is emotionally drained. She lies down and closes her tearful hazel eyes.

Chapter SIXTEEN:

The exemplary man with a double life.
Monday, May 14, 1990

JULIANA WAKES UP ON THE BED THAT USED TO BE HER BROTHER'S. She fell asleep next to the pictures and the paper she read the night before. Her thoughts soar again: it's inevitable to compare Tommy with Tomás and that thought tortures her. She doesn't know if she's doing the right thing, if having her son secluded is a way out for the dilemmas that haunt her mind. She doubts her previous decisions. Now, she is not even convinced that homosexuality is a disease. The only thing that *is* certain is that she loves him. What if it's best to take him out of the clinic? No, maybe not. She, as every other mother, wants the best for her son...

"Jason." She reads the name on the letter that her brother wrote. "Jason." She turns the paper over and sees an address written there. Why would her brother do that? Why did he put the address on the back of the paper? Could it be that he suspected that he would not return from the clinic? That he wanted someone to see the letter and deliver it? She's unsure. She knows the neighborhood by heart, but she hesitates. She doesn't know if going is the right thing to do. Well, he wrote it for some reason, didn't he? It's what Tommy would have wanted her to do, but what if Jason doesn't live here anymore? What if he got sick, if he died or something? It's been so long…

She gets up and walks to the closed window and watches the new day, closes her eyes, and takes a deep breath before making her decision. Upon opening the letter, a curiosity about delivering it wakes up in Juliana. She inexplicably feels that the answers to all of her questions will be with this man, Jason. "I hope he's alive," she tells herself. She feels the need to see him, to see if he managed to change, or to find out how he lives his life nowadays, if Tommy is still an important part of his life after everything they went through.

She makes up her mind. She turns, puts the box back in its place, leaves her brother's room and stealthily walks to hers. She doesn't want her mother to wake up and ask her where she's going or what she's doing. She takes a shower, changes clothes, puts on makeup, and goes downstairs.

"Aren't you going to eat before going out?" her mother asks, blocking the doorway.

"No, I'm in a hurry."

"And may I ask where you are going in such a hurry?"

"I'll try to come back for lunch."

"I never liked those little secrets."

"Alright. To Norma's. I'm going to Norma's. Okay? Happy?"

"Say 'hi' from me."

Her mother steps aside and Juliana leaves without saying goodbye. She starts her car, reads the address again, and turns off the engine. She's nervous. What if Jason forgot about Tommy? What if he had a hard time overcoming his disease and she suddenly appears with that letter? What is she going to get out of this? Reopen the wounds, the memories? "This is what Tommy wanted. That's why he wrote the address on this paper," she repeats to herself. "I have to do this." She turns the engine on again and drives to Jason's, trying to keep her mind blank so as not to question what she's doing.

***

At that same moment, a man with a mustache rings the bell of the clinic Grow And Live Normally. Verónica opens the door.

"Good morning. I need to speak to Dr. Rutherbor. Is he in?"

"I wouldn't know. Wait here at the reception. I'll see if he's here. Who do I say is looking for him?"

"Rodrigo Losala."

Verónica nods and goes up the stairs to the doctor's office.

"Someone's looking for you downstairs," she tells him.

"For me? Who?"

"A man…Losala, he said."

"No, no, no… Tell him I'm not here, that I won't be here for the whole week. I don't know, tell him that I'm in a seminar outside the country, whatever…"

"Very well, doctor."

"And not only him — anyone who comes looking for me, unless it's Mr. Iñeziz…"

"Don't worry. I'll take care of Mr. Losala."

***

Before ringing the bell, Juliana thinks a thousand times about what she's going to say. She is already starting to believe she has lost her sanity. What is she doing in that place? How will she start the conversation? She decides to stop thinking and simply act. She rings the bell.

"Good afternoon," a woman greets her.

"Goo…good afternoon. Excuse me, I was…looking for a man…Jason."

"Yes, my husband?"

"Perhaps, yes." It's a little weird for Juliana, but it would be too much of a coincidence that two people by the name of Jason live or have lived in the same house. "I have a delivery. I have…I have to give him something. Is he home?"

"Yes, hold on for a moment. I'll get him."

The woman leaves and Juliana is left alone at the door. She seizes the opportunity to take the paper from her pocket.

"Yes? Are you looking for me?"

"Yes. Hello, I am Juliana Revas," she expects that he will remember the name. "I'm Tommy's sister."

"Tommy…" Jason whispers, evidently affected.

"I'm sorry. I didn't want to —"

"No, don't worry. It's…it's a pleasure. Believe me,

Tommy always talked about you...about Pollax, as he called you. You were his heroine, his other half."

"It's good to know, thanks."

"And...why are you here? Can I help you with something?"

"You were a good friend of my brother, right?"

"Yes, you could say that. I suppose."

"He...before they took him away," she can't help feeling guilty, "before the clinic, he told me...he told me about you two. I don't want to make you uncomfortable. I...I no longer have anything against that. I just came to —"

"Look, for me, that's all in the past," Jason lowers his voice so that his wife doesn't hear him. "I mean, I did love Tommy; I still do, but now...now I have a family."

"Did you love him a lot?"

Jason looks back and closes the door behind him to make sure that his wife can't see or hear him.

"He was my world," he says, finally. "You have no idea how much I loved him. He changed my life. He saved me. I...I would have done anything for him, whatever he asked for. Yes, if I had found out they were going to lock him away in that hellhole — I don't know how, but —I would have avoided it. I would have...I don't know..."

"You have nothing to feel guilty for," Juliana realizes that she's making him feel bad and wants to change the topic a little, to liven the conversation up. "And I see you've started a family. You have a wife...kids?"

"I know what you're trying to do," Jason answers, on the defensive. "But it's not that I've changed my sexuality. It's just my sexual conduct. I'm still the same. My wife...

well, she was my friend and was able to console me when the thing with Tommy happened and you could say I love her. Not the way I loved Tommy, or how I would like to love someone. It's hard to explain. I love her as you love a friend, a good friend. I care about her, I respect her —"

"I didn't want to meddle like this in your privacy."

"Excuse me, forgive me for getting like this. It's just that seeing you has brought back many repressed memories."

"But, are you happy? Are you content…comfortable with your life?"

"My children are the best things in my life. They're a gift from Heaven. But no, I can't say that I'm completely happy. You see, I do cheat on her…on my family."

"You cheat on her?"

"I mean that sometimes I'm unfaithful to my wife. Something happens to me and that anxiety comes back, that need to be with men."

Juliana unconsciously makes a face of disgust. She realizes this and has to make an effort to regain composure.

"You can get a divorce," she tells him, remembering her own experience and, deep down, already identifying with the man in front of her.

"Sadly and ironically, this is indeed the life I chose or, I should say, this is the life society chose. I wouldn't want to deal my wife that blow. As I already told you, I love her very much. She's been with me through all the hard times. I couldn't be so ungrateful."

"It's just a suggestion because with everything you're telling me, well, I think you're not only hurting her but also yourself."

An awkward silence follows in which Jason just stares at the ground.

"I know, I'm a coward. I wasted my one and only life. I can't believe it," he dares to say. "I've thought about it, yes, I've thought about telling her, but she... Always. I've always been a coward."

Juliana can't resist herself and gives him a hug, squeezing him with all her might.

"The important thing is to do what will actually make you happy, whatever it may be," she comforts him.

"When I was with Tommy, nothing like this happened. I mean that. I had courage. I wasn't afraid of anything." Jason's eyes are watery. This entire experience has been tough on him. "And, by the way, how did you find out where I was living? How did you get here?"

Juliana realizes she has forgotten the one thing that brought her there, although she had the letter in her hand the entire time. She shows it to Jason.

"Through Tommy," she answers, confusing him, while she hands him the paper.

Jason reads the letter. He feels young again, like he's that same boy who fell madly in love with Tommy. He is briefly swept back in time, but quickly returns to his life in this prison that he built himself as he finishes reading the letter.

"I think he wrote it a little before they took him to the clinic. He had no time to give it to you," Juliana explains, seeing his tears and suffering. She hugs him again to console and support him.

***

Dr. Rutherbor is alone in his office. He has no reason to be there at that time but the situation with Mateo and Fabricio has wrecked his nerves and he prefers not having contact with anyone. He doesn't like to be seen like this. He's afraid that the others will find out his weaknesses.

Someone knocks on the door, pulling the doctor out of his thoughts. He knows he can't delay and moves to the door quickly.

"Sandrita!" he greets her cheerfully.

"I'm ready. I don't want to be here anymore."

"Well, yes, I also believe it's time. I'm proud. Thank you."

"You're welcome, Dad."

"I'll call your mother now to tell her to pick you up tomorrow. And next Wednesday we will go to the media: newspapers, TV stations, radio, all of them. We're going to make a fortune, just like I did with Paul Gómez, you'll see."

"No, Dad. Look, I've been thinking. I want — rather, I don't want — to be part of your show or your experiments. I want to go stay with my aunt and live my life, that's it."

"What? You don't know what you're saying. I know that it can be really stressful in here and —"

"No! You don't know. You don't know anything! No, the worst is that I think you *do* know! You know it and you do everything on purpose!"

"Girl, don't raise your voice at me."

"You know very well there's no cure. You play with people, you abuse them, and they're kids, teenagers!"

"Don't talk to me like that, ungrateful girl! Go back to your room! Go back this instant!"

"And Mateo? Where is Mateo? See what you did?"

"This is the last time I tell you…"

"What about Dr. Claudia?"

"You're giving back to your father, to your family. You have no idea what I had to do for you, for your mother, for —"

"I'm not giving my back to my father. I'm giving my back to the doctor, to the owner of this clinic."

"If that's how you want it then don't even think you'll get out of here!"

Sandra cries. She decides to mention what was forbidden since the first day she entered the clinic as a patient.

"There was nothing wrong with him, there was nothing to cure in him. That's why he ended up dead."

"He died because he didn't let anyone to cure him!"

"What really makes me sad is that he died without anyone by his side…without being understood."

"Don't mention him anymore! What makes you think I'm going to let you leave?"

"With everything I know? Do you know the problems I could cause?"

"What do you mean?"

"Today I saw Mr. Losala. You were in your office, but apparently, Verónica didn't see you because she told Mr. Losala that the doctor was off on a trip."

"I know where you're going with this."

"You let me out and I won't say a word. It's that

simple."

"Well, aren't you clever?"

"I got it from my father."

Dr. Rutherbor doesn't answer, but it looks like he agrees. Sandra leaves the office and walks back to her room, rubbing her belly, connecting with the baby growing inside of her. She knows that her father's macabre plans could end badly — that, in a moment, everything might crumble. She doesn't want to be there when it happens. If someone is going to end up winning, then it has to be her.

Chapter SEVENTEEN:

Following the signals.
Tuesday, May 15, 1990

SHE HAS TO BE BACK AT THE CLINIC IN A FEW MINUTES, but it requires too much effort for Juliana to move, too much effort for her to ease her feelings of emptiness and guilt. It's a beautiful day. The sun falls on her face and numbs her, makes her think less, which is really what she needs. Remembering her brother and the visit to Jason has her convinced: there is no cure. It's not a disease, but what to do about her son? She has thoughts and feelings that seem too difficult to overcome. She knows they won't stop until she does the right thing. She has to make things right with her son and get him back. She knows that she no longer has the support of Dr. Rutherbor, Paul, or much less her mother. She is alone. Alone. No, she's not, she realizes, she only *feels* alone.

Tommy…

She feels the presence of Tommy next to her. She takes a deep breath and feels relieved. She has a shoulder to lean on. He is her rock. Yes, she feels him and knows. She knows her brother will guide her.

She gets out of her car, which has been parked outside of Grow And Live Normally for nearly half an hour, and she feels like a different person, changed. She walks to the building, but, as she reaches for the door, and she feels a tap on her shoulder.

"Doctor Juliana, right?"

"Yes, that's me."

"I'm Teresa, Paul's wife."

"Nice to meet you! How are you?" Juliana is surprised, but the fear she feels is stronger. What an odd visit!

"I've heard so much about you."

"Really? And I feel like I already know you. Paul doesn't stop talking about you. We're friends from college —"

"Yes, I know. That's why…that's why I came to see you, Doctor."

"Juliana. Call me Juliana."

"Juliana, it's just that you know him better, I think. The truth is that I'm worried. Paul has changed. He's practically unrecognizable."

"Tell me about it."

"Well, he's distant — literally, physically — sometimes he doesn't even sleep at home or he sleeps at home, but not with me. He's always sleeping down in the basement and I don't know what's in there because he won't let me go down. He tells me he's studying or working on material to teach in his class that —"

"In the basement?" Juliana has never heard something so strange, but she laughs so as not to worry Teresa even more. "How so?"

"I don't know. He says it's his study, his office, I don't know... I don't believe him anymore. I'm pretty sure he's hiding something."

"And why don't you go down?"

"That's why I came. I think...I'm thinking of going down and, since you're a good friend of my husband, I wanted to consult you first."

"But what is it that really worries you?"

"That he hasn't changed — that he's still a homosexual." Teresa speaks covering her face with both hands. "Juliana... is there something you know that I don't?"

Juliana thinks hard. She's afraid for Teresa's emotional health and doesn't dare to tell her the truth, the secret — perhaps her best-kept secret — the one-night affair she had with Paul ten years ago while they were both married to other people.

"No, nothing," she finally says.

"I'm afraid to confront him. Last time I did, we had a bad argument. He hit me."

"Paul? That doesn't sound like Paul."

"Maybe we don't really know him." Teresa starts to cry. "And I'm worried about our daughter. I don't know what to do."

Juliana also doesn't know what to do and the situation is uncomfortable. After all, she's a professional and being a psychiatrist means being there when another human being needs her, unconditionally. She hugs Teresa and lets her cry on her shoulder.

Juliana dares to say, "Go down. Go down to the

basement. Take the opportunity when he's not home and go down. If you want, I'll help you. If you want, I'll go with you, but you have to get rid of those doubts, break those emotional chains. I...I went through something similar. My ex-husband mistreated me and, well, it's still hard for me to talk about that."

"Did you get a divorce?"

"I know it's complicated, that it's frowned upon...but I had no other option and...you know what? I feel like I have done nothing wrong. On the contrary, I feel lighter, as if I had taken a weight off my back. I even feel like God is happy with me."

"You. Can you help me?"

"Yes, I'm going to help you. Or at least, I'll do what I can. I promise."

The new friends exchange numbers, hug again and smile goodbye. They're both afraid. They know that the basement situation is not normal. They would have liked to evade that fact but know it's impossible. They've made a pact.

"Hi, Dear. How have you been? How was your weekend?" Dr. Rutherbor greets her in the entryway of his office.

"Very, very well. That extra day felt great. I took the opportunity to visit my mom." Juliana greets him with a smile from ear to ear, but it's all part of a performance, a character she is portraying to hide the fear she feels. She's beginning to doubt everything in the world.

"Yes? That's good, that's good. Here, on the other

hand, wasn't good. I'll tell you. Oh, how sad… "

"What happened? When I left, everything was fine."

"Mateo…he escaped from the clinic."

"Impossible. Mateo didn't seem like he would do something like that."

"Yes, we're still piecing things together, trying to decipher how he did it, but believe me, he escaped. I'm the most surprised, but Harold and José, the guards on duty that night, seem to have left the door open. We're not sure because they, realizing what they did, also left and we have not seen them since. The nurse was asleep and —"

"No, Mateo isn't like that." Juliana doesn't fall for the story he's telling her. "At any rate, he's only seventeen — he can't be roaming the streets alone. Have you contacted his family?"

"Yes, I already talked to his parents." Dr. Rutherbor is worried that Juliana sees through his lies, but it worries him even more that he saw her talking to Teresa through his office window. "They reported him lost. I hope the police find him. It's our only hope."

"Poor kid."

"But, that's not everything."

"There's something else?"

"Well, it's not that bad — sad, you might say. Fabricio's parents came to take him home."

"That's not so sad. If he only reunited with his family —"

"What? It's terrible! His father told me that he had found another way of curing him and that he didn't want anything else to do with us. Imagine that. Where would they take him? What treatments? Oh, people are crazy."

"Well, if you say so."

"Yes, I say so." Dr. Rutherbor's facial features transform from a scowling grin into an open smile. "Something else happened. You know me — I always save the best news for last."

"Is there any good news?"

"Sandra healed. Last night, her parents came for her and took her home. She's going to start her new —"

"She got cured? All of that happened this weekend?"

"Yes. I was also in shock, but she passed the lie detector test and, believe me, she's not a lesbian anymore. She likes men, just like you do." Dr. Rutherbor picks up his briefcase.

"Are you going out?"

"Yes, I'll be back in half an hour or so. I have a meeting." Dr. Rutherbor opens the door, but stops and turns to Juliana, "I know that things became tense the other day, with Sebastián and your son. But now, the last thing Tomás needs is to see you. I hope you understand. He's still not ready. Am I clear?"

"Alright, Doctor. You know I always listen to you."

"Perfect."

A short time later, Juliana decides to break her word. She needs to see Tomás. It's her son! They've been apart for too long and she knows that, at any time, she can completely lose him. Also, there is a strange air in the clinic. She feels like hidden things are about to come to the surface and knows that none of this can be good.

She leaves her office and goes to the sexual

reorientation area where, to her surprise, she discovers that Verónica know guards the small metal door with the big lock that separates the two wings.

"I need to see a patient."

"Did Dr. Rutherbor give you permission for that?"

"Yes, but…I don't need the doctor's permission. I'm the psychiatrist."

"Forgive me, Doctor. But it's just that after everything that happened with young Mateo, things have changed a little. It's for the patients' sake, you know."

"May I come in?"

"Okay, but the doctor didn't say anything to me…"

Fearful of Dr. Rutherbor's potential reproach, Verónica finds it difficult to accept, but, after all, Juliana *is* the psychiatrist and has more authority than she does. She opens the lock and Juliana immediately walks to room number eight. She knocks softly.

"Mom!" Tomás greets her, as he opens the door.

"Hello, Tomás. I wanted to talk to you."

Her son steps aside to let her enter the room.

"How is Sebastián doing?" he asks, worried. "It's already been a month."

"He's recovering. He's calmer. He rarely gets depressed anymore."

"I…I miss him." Tomás stares at the drawing on his wall.

"Do you care about him a lot?"

"I do."

"I felt it when I saw you together — that time, before they took him."

"Did he seem 'abominable' to you? 'Depraved'?"

"Honestly, no." Juliana sits on the bed, next to her son. "I found it worrying, though."

"There's nothing to worry about. It's love."

"Have you fallen in love with him already?" Juliana asks, with a smile.

"I only know that I miss him, I want to see him, and spend more time with him."

Juliana takes her time to say what she wants to say.

"Son, I've also realized some things. When I saw you with him, yes, it's true. I did worry, but then…I could see beyond. I understood something. I saw something I didn't see before, that I couldn't see. I think it's true, there's no reason to be worried. I felt that connection between the two of you."

"What do you mean?"

"That we're not so different. Maybe on the outside it seems like we are, but, inside, we all feel love for another person, another human being. I saw that love is possible between two people of the same sex."

"And what made you see that?"

"Many things, but especially you, Tomás." Juliana holds her son tightly. "You are my son. I love you. If that's how you want to be, if this is how you identify, I don't care because it's still you…and you're not hurting anyone. I'm going to ask the doctor to only treat your schizophrenia from now on. I'm going to take you back home with me, but it's important to take care your health so you'll still have to come for your appointments."

"Thank you, Mom." They hug each other.

"Mom, how long have I been here?" Tomás takes the opportunity to clear the doubt that has followed him for days.

"Since early last December."

"But, no…that doesn't match my calculations."

"Why do you say that?"

"I must have come here in the middle of January."

"No, it was early December. At the beginning, Claudia Losala was your psychiatrist and —"

"Who?"

"Claudia. Dr. Claudia. Don't you remember?"

"No, I've never met any Claudia."

"This must be what the doctor mentioned — the schizophrenia and the memory loss. Are you taking your pills?"

"It's just…I think that's what this is all about, Mom."

"What are you talking about?" Juliana is intrigued.

"Since I've stopped taking the pills, I dream of a lagoon, a dead woman in the hallway, and a dead kid in a dark room."

"Those are nightmares."

"What did Claudia look like?"

"Short blonde hair, tall. Why do you ask?"

"It's her. I'm sure it's her." Tomás gets up from the bed and starts pacing in circles. "The girl in my dreams…she's just like you describe her. Did she have dark eyes? Did you say she used to be my psychiatrist?"

"Tomás, are you sure of what you're telling me? They must be things you dream of because you're not taking the pills."

"No, Mom, it's her. Claudia is the dead woman. Don't you see that it all makes sense? She used to be my doctor, but I don't remember it. Don't you think it's strange? I take the pills and I forget everything. I stop taking them and I start to remember. Dr. Rutherbor is hiding a lot of things and he manipulated me with those pills. He even lied to me that my last name was Bermeo. That's why I never recognized you while you were here: everyone called you Dr. Revas."

"He did that? It can't be!" At first, Juliana refuses to believe Tomás. Although she has doubts about her teacher, she doesn't believe Dr. Rutherbor capable of killing anyone or concealing a death. But lately she has to admit that she feels manipulated by her mentor.

"What about Mateo and Fabricio? They just vanished into thin air." He tries to convince his mother.

"The doctor told me that…well, their parents took them out of the clinic."

"Do you believe him? Why would their parents do that? Considering they didn't get along at all."

"But why would the doctor lie?"

"Mom, you have to help me…but in order to help me, you have to trust me."

"Alright, my dear, yes."

"So, then you have to find proof of what I'm telling you."

"I don't know, Tomás," Juliana is nervous.

"The doctor is manipulating and using all of us by changing the pills!" Tomás tries to make her understand that the situation is serious. "On the doctor's desk, there was a paper with a list of names. Mateo told me that 'Tomás and

Bernardo' were crossed out. I think Bernardo is the kid in the dark room from my dreams."

"Are you telling me that the doctor put pills in mislabeled bottles? A list on a piece paper? What was that?" Juliana can't believe it.

"Yes! Fabricio thought they were patients who had been transferred to another clinic. The paper had the letterhead of a Catholic center somewhere. Those patients had been transferred, but what a coincidence that, of the two names crossed out, one is mine and the other is Bernardo. Since he's not here anymore…"

Juliana is a whirlwind of thoughts. What if Tomás is right? Could it be so serious? But then, Tomás…she's risking losing her son.

"Alright…I will," she agrees. "I'm going to see if I can get any proof, at least to clear any doubts."

Juliana holds her son's hands and puts them against her heart. Tomás smiles in a way that he hadn't for a while.

**

The nurse on duty doesn't know how to control the man who is at the front desk. He's hysterical. She feels a huge relief when she sees Juliana approach.

"Yes? What is it?"

"Doctor, look, this gentleman won't believe me that Dr. Rutherbor is not in. And it's not the first time he has accused the doctor of something."

"I'll talk to him, don't worry. In any case, the doctor told me that he wouldn't be long."

Juliana leaves the nurse at her station and walks

towards the man, signaling him to go with her outside of the clinic. She wants to talk in private.

"Excuse me, you're looking for the doctor?"

"Yes, I am. Who do I have the pleasure?"

"Juliana Revas. I'm the clinic's sexual reorientation psychiatrist. Are you the father of one of the patients?"

"Did you fill in for Claudia? I am her brother —"

"Losala? Claudia Losala? Nice to meet you! How is she doing in the United States?"

"What? What are you talking about?"

Juliana doesn't know why, but feels like she just made a mistake. The man is getting angrier.

"My sister never left the country. That's absurd! And I don't think she ever left this clinic."

"I don't understand."

"You don't know? No one has heard anything from Claudia for months — not my family, or me, or anyone." The man gets past his anger and is invaded by sadness. "Not a single trace. The last person to talk to her was my mother, on the phone. Claudia was working here at the clinic and… she just vanished."

"And the police? They haven't found anything?"

"No. They're still searching, but nothing. They even inspected the clinic."

"And? What did they find?"

"Nothing. But because they gave notice in advance — or maybe he blackmailed them. You know there's widespread corruption in the police force. That's why I think this doctor, who refuses to talk to me, is hiding something."

Juliana starts feeling sick. How many things have

happened under her nose and she didn't realize? She doesn't like the idea of having replaced...a missing person? Is that her official status? Why then did Dr. Rutherbor lie about the work in the United States? How many more lies has he been feeding her? She realizes that her son's theories may not so crazy after all.

"Here's my number," she tells Mr. Losala, writing it on a scrap piece of paper. "Tell me anything you find out, any news at all. Claudia and I...knew each other."

She doesn't waste any time and barely says goodbye. Juliana goes back into the clinic and walks up the stairs to the doctor's office. She turns the knob and, to her surprise, the door opens. She knows she has to act fast. The nurse at the front desk saw her going up and may come to look for her any time. There are no papers on the desk so she has to go through the drawers. She finds the registration form with the list of patients and the names of Tomás and Bernardo are, in fact, crossed out. Tomás was not lying, he was not exaggerating, and he was not delusional. A María Rutherbor is listed as the owner of the Catholic center.

"It's crazy how a life can change in just one weekend," she thinks. Her brother, Jason, Teresa, Mr. Losala, and Tomás...they have all led her to this point. They have all accompanied her on her way from the beginning, without her even suspecting. Juliana puts the paper back in its place, closes the drawers, and gets up. A whole new person leaves the office.

***

Meanwhile, in another part of the capital, Mr. Iñeziz has

no other option but to let the doctor into his office. He has been avoiding him all day, but the doctor is still waiting there…as if Iñeziz would *want* to know every little problem at the clinic.

Dr. Rutherbor is pale when he walks in and sits in the chair facing the desk. Iñeziz resigns himself. He lights a cigarette and leans back.

"Another dead kid." Dr. Rutherbor swallows audibly. "One of the guards stabbed him it seems. We don't know, we haven't found the guard yet."

"The body?"

"In one of the storage rooms. No one knows anything… yet, but it's already starting to smell."

Iñeziz opens one of the desk drawers and takes out a gun. He sets it on the desk.

"And what's your plan? I mean, if you have one." Iñeziz treats him like a child. "Are you going to spray it so it doesn't stink?"

"We can dump the body in the middle of the street, in a neighborhood where drug addicts go, gang members…" Dr. Rutherbor was waiting to meet up with him to figure out what to do and get his approves while he grips his briefcase tightly to hide his shaking hands, "We'll say he escaped from the clinic and that…I don't know…he was murdered there."

"Was murdered there? Does anybody know?"

"Only Juliana, the psychiatrist, but I already told her the same story. I don't think it will be a problem." Dr. Rutherbor starts to relax, "I have the footage. We can also drug another kid, dress him in Mateo's clothes, and make him act like if he's escaping. We can blackmail the officer police as we did before, that's easy."

"That's fine. Nothing else? Have they told you I am a busy person?"

"There's something else, yes," this is the part that Dr. Rutherbor has been dreading. "There's another kid, but this one is alive...he's unconscious, that is. He's in another one of the storage rooms. You could say he was present during the thing with Mateo. He's a witness."

"Didn't you say that no one knew anything?"

"I can do the same thing I did with that other kid, Tomás. I erased his memory..."

"I'm not convinced. Isn't it better if —"

"I don't like that. Killing a kid with my own hands? That's not my thing. I'd rather have him there, even as a zombie. Tomás was a success, relax."

"Well, we'll see...but we all have to do it someday. You know, using our own hands." Iñeziz takes a long drag on his cigarette and looks straight into Dr. Rutherbor's eyes. He smiles sarcastically, "And how is Juliana doing?"

"Okay. She's okay. You recommended that I hire her and I did so she's working —"

The office door opens and Paul, Mr. Iñeziz's son, enters. Dr. Rutherbor turns around and addresses him.

"I needed to talk to you, Paul."

"What happened? What are you doing here, Doctor?"

"Nothing, just a meeting with your father. Listen to me. Is your wife friends with Juliana?"

"No, not that I know of. I'm not so dumb as to —"

"Well, today I saw them talking outside of the clinic, in the parking lot. Are you taking care of her? She seemed worried."

"Don't worry about her." Paul decides that he hates Dr. Rutherbor right then and there. He could have chosen any other occasion but in front of his father? "On my side, everything is in order. It's in your clinic where things are getting out of hand."

Paul realizes deep down that he's lying. These last few days, his wife has been asking him questions more than usual. She seems anxious, worried. Juliana would notice something. Could she also be in danger? He has to rush home. He can't leave the basement unguarded.

Juliana drives her car to the address she saw on the paper: The Light of Christ Center. She asked her evening job to give her the day — or rather the night — off because she is "sick". She decides that she has to discover everything she can and if possible, to somehow repair the pain she has caused her own son.

She arrives at the center, which was formerly a large residential house, and rings the bell several times.

"Good evening, how may I help you?" asks Mrs. Rutherbor. Juliana recognizes her immediately from the pictures in Dr. Rutherbor's office.

"Good evening, my name is Aurora Cortés." Juliana uses the name of one of the patients' mothers from Dr. Rutherbor's list. "I am Antonio's mother."

"Mrs. Cortés, it's so nice to see you!" It's obvious that the woman is hiding something, like she doesn't want Juliana to come in, but she has no alternative. "Come in, come in. It's been a while since you came to visit us."

"Yes, I've been abroad. Has he made any progress?"

"Well, he's still not cured, but he's a good kid. He makes the effort."

"I don't remember exactly. How long has Antonio been here?"

"Since the middle of January, ma'am. It's not much. This is a long and complicated process, but a cure is attainable."

"I want to see him. May I see him now? Do I just wait for you here?"

"Sure, sure. Wait for me here and I'll bring him to you."

The woman never stopped smiling, but Juliana could sense that it was a fake smile. It's the first time that Mrs. Rutherbor has had to face one of the patients' mothers. She walks down the hallway to the room of "the deviants", as she usually calls them.

"Antonio!" she screams after opening the door. "Come over here!" The boy gets up from his bed, a piece of cardboard on the floor. He's frightened to death, thinking it's another therapy session coming, another session of beating and electrodes.

"Your mother came to see you. Listen to me, you freak. You won't say a single word of what you have seen or heard in here. Am I clear?"

The boy nods, looking down at the ground so that he doesn't accidentally give away the joy he feels knowing that at least one of his parents was interested in his existence. María Rutherbor, who looks like a witch with her large, pointy nose and her voluminous, curly gray hair, grabs him by the hand and practically drags him to the room where his mother is supposedly waiting for him.

"Did you paint that?" Juliana asks María as soon as she walks into the foyer.

The woman turns to see the painting and Juliana has time to signal the boy, who of course immediately recognizes that that person is not his mother.

"No, that was done by my son, Bernardo. Beautiful, isn't it?" the woman answers proudly.

"Yes, very stunning."

Juliana gets up from the sofa where she had been waiting, like she is going to greet a son she hasn't seen for quite some time.

"Can you leave us alone?" she asks with a smile, but then the smiles disappears and her hazel eyes grow wide — the name!

"I'm sorry, I can't. I have to be here."

"I have something very intimate to tell him, please." Juliana doesn't come out of her shock. Did the woman say, "My son Bernardo?" She manages to think of an excuse. "It's about my health…something very delicate."

María doesn't know what to do. She's worried that if she opposes too much, then she's going to make Mrs. Cortés suspicious.

"Well, okay, since it's you."

The woman leaves.

"Antonio, I'm here to help you." Juliana can tell just by looking at him that the boy has been severely mistreated. He only nods as an answer. "I need you to tell me how long you've been in here."

"It must already be four months. But before that, I was in a clinic just as horrible as here."

"Grow And Live Normally?"

"Yes, that's the one."

"And how do they treat you in here?"

Antonio remembers the warning that Mrs. Rutherbor gave him, but he can't keep it in any longer. Nothing can be worse than what he has already suffered. He silently pulls up his t-shirt and shows the marks on his arms and stomach. Juliana is horrified. The boy is covered in bruises and scars, needle punctures, and the trademark burns from electric shock treatments.

"But this is not just from here," the boy says. "In the other clinic, the treatments were worse."

"Do you know someone named Bernardo?"

"No."

"And someone named Tomás?"

"Yes, but we don't know what happened to him. He stayed at the other clinic when they brought us here."

"And was Tomás also mistreated?"

"Yes, he was — much more than any of us. He was the doctor's favorite. Do you know what happened to him? Is he dead?"

"No." Juliana hears footsteps approaching. "Antonio, listen, I need you to cry, to say that I'm your mother. Tomás is all right. He's still in the clinic. I'll tell him that you're al...all right. I promise I will get you out of here, all of you. I'm going to get you all out of here."

"I'm sorry, ma'am, but it's time to pray and —" the woman says as she walks back into the foyer.

"I want to be with you, Mom. Don't go." Antonio plays along.

"Son, don't be a baby. This is best for the entire family. We need you to be cured".

Juliana is only acting, but she suddenly feels a pang of guilt when she remembers that she once said something similar to her own son. She doesn't have to act very much, after all. Then she remembers the name, Bernardo, and what she promised her son - to get evidence to corroborate his theory. She notices a picture under the painting, a portrait of a child.

"Is that your son, Bernardo?" she asks, as she approaches the painting.

"Yes, my Bernardo. It's a shame. He was…sick."

"What did he have?"

"He was a deviant. Poor thing. He killed himself when he was just fifteen."

"No! I'm so sorry. But how? I don't understand. Why at that age?"

"I threw him out of the house." The woman is a stone. Juliana notices that she doesn't even blink as she speaks, as if such a sad incident doesn't affect her. "I offered him help. I wanted him to go to rehab, but he refused. I had no other option but to throw him out. I couldn't let him contaminate my home. Imagine, a sexual deviant under my own roof! So I did what I had to…they found him dead a month later."

"And don't you feel guilty?"

"No. He knew he was ill, that he had to get cured, but he didn't accept God's path. That's why I operate this center now - to help kids like Bernardo. God gave me another chance. He gave me these kids to care for and love. God gives. He doesn't take."

Juliana doesn't mention it but she notices that the woman's eyes start to water. No one can be that cold all the time. Next to Bernardo's portrait is that of a girl — someone Juliana knows very well.

"And her?"

"That's my daughter, Sandra. She was also a deviant, but she turned out fine. Her father got her a scholarship and she studies in the United States."

"Have you talked to her?"

"No, she and I aren't very close, but her father tells me she does call him on the phone and they talk."

"Wouldn't you like to talk to her, too?"

"No. We grew apart after her brother's death. It was hard for her. She blamed me. I don't know why."

"It's getting late. I better go."

"Of course, of course," the woman says, relieved that the mother is leaving, but also for having talked to someone about the pain she bears inside. "Come back anytime, but please, next time, tell us you are coming. Do you have our phone number?"

"Yes, I have it. Next time, I'll call first. I promise."

"May God light your way."

The supposed Mrs. Cortés leaves and Mrs. Rutherbor calms down.

Dr. Rutherbor has just finished checking the security camera footage at the clinic. He can't believe his eyes. He sees Juliana walking into Tomás's room, chatting for quite a while, and then they hug and cry. *It can't be possible! Think of the information they could have exchanged!*

Apparently, that's just the beginning. His blood freezes when he sees another video of Juliana walking into his office and looking through his desk drawers. She finds the paper with the information about the fictitious Catholic center. This is too much. He runs to the telephone in his office. Mrs. Rutherbor is breathing a sigh of relief when she hears the phone ring.

"María!" Dr. Rutherbor yells through the receiver. "Did Juliana come to visit you?"

"Who? No, no Juliana has come."

"Are you sure? No one came to the house today?"

"Well, a person did come, a woman."

"What did she look like, what did she look like?"

"Tall, hazel eyes, dark-brown hair —"

"That's Juliana!"

The woman hangs up the phone indignant from the treatment she received from her ex-husband — a reality she won't accept because she hates the idea of becoming a divorcée.

Dr. Rutherbor, on his end, is hysterical. He feels as if he has been stabbed in the back. He hates betrayal. Although, if he really thinks about it, it's for the best that Juliana found out about everything. He'll be able to do what he has always wanted to do. He's going to wipe out that patient from hell once and for all. That Tomás...

It's the only solution, the only path that his mind shows him.

***

"Paola, right?" Juliana asks the twelve-year-old who opens the door. "Are your parents home?"

The girl shakes her head.

"Did they leave you all alone in here? Aren't you afraid?"

She nods. Paul and Teresa's daughter is pale, as if she had seen a ghost.

"Are you all right?" Juliana caresses her cheek, but little Paola steps backwards. "I'm not going to hurt you. I am a friend of your father. If you like, I can stay here until your mother and father come back."

"She's not coming back because now she knows," the child finally says.

"I don't understand. Who isn't coming back?"

The girl doesn't answer. Instead, she takes Juliana by the hand and pulls her into the house. She leads her to the basement door and Juliana remembers the conversation with Teresa.

"This is it."

"Is this where your father works?"

The girl only opens the basement door in response.

"Do you want me to go down?"

The girl nods once again.

"Alright, but stay here…and don't open the front door for anybody except your father or mother, understand?"

Juliana walks down the stairs and everything gets darker and darker until she's in a soft light. She reaches the end of the stairs and she finds herself in front of big metallic doors that she can only assume lead to a storage room. But where Juliana is standing, there is a chair and a table covered with folders, like an office. Juliana is shocked by what she sees on the walls: photos, photos, photos...of her! All of those photos from the places she's been lately — no, not just lately! There are photos from various stages of her life: college, her engagement, her wedding, but also...*it can't be!*

Juliana covers her mouth with her hand. The most important revelation of her life is before her eyes. She's there, half naked, in a photo when she was young and...*asleep? No...unconscious...raped! But how? Was Paul her rapist? He was still homosexual at time....or was he?*

It feels like the floor drops from under her when she realizes as she stands there, looking at the photo of her being raped, that Paul is Tomás's father!

She can't accept this fact. She's devastated. She rushes to take the pictures off the walls. This is all the evidence she needs. She puts them in her purse with her heart beating so fast that she feels like it's going to burst out of her chest. She immediately walks up the stairs to get out of that place where her worst memory has been turned into a shrine.

"Juliana! What are you doing here?"

She bumps into Paul as she shuts the basement door behind her.

"Paul, I'm sorry. I came to look for you." Juliana closes her purse so that he can't see the photos. "I needed to speak with you."

"With me? About what?" Paul's eyes are bulging out of their sockets and his lip trembles. Juliana becomes scared. She has never seen him like that. "If you avoid me, ignore me, treat me like a dog..."

It's only then that Juliana looks down and realizes that Paul's hands and shirt are all red, dripping with blood.

"Paul? What did you do?" Juliana starts to walk backwards, slowly so as to not anger him. "Where is Teresa? Did she come with you?"

"Why? Are you two best friends now?"

"What's that on your hands?"

"Paint." Paul takes two steps forward for each step Juliana takes back. "I was teaching the students to...paint."

"Look, I'm sorry to have come like this without telling you or anything...to come into your house...but little Paola was alone. It was rude of me. I'll go."

Juliana stutters out her apology and gestures towards the door. In a flash, Paul grabs her by the arm, hurting her with his angry grip and staining her with blood. Paola runs to her parents' bedroom.

"Mom! Mom!" she screams.

"Now you know, right? You discovered me," Paul whispers to Juliana, who is struggling in vain to escape his grip. "You discovered me. Tell me the truth."

"I don't know what you're talking about. I have discovered nothing. Please, you're hurting me. Let me go."

Paul takes something out of his pocket. It's just a handkerchief, but the smell makes Juliana dizzy. Paul presses the handkerchief against her face, forcing her to inhale through her nose and mouth. It doesn't take much time before Juliana is unconscious in the living room. Satisfied, Paul walks to his bedroom where his daughter hides, crying in fear.

"Mommy! Mommy!"

"Relax, my love. Your mommy will be taking care of us from Heaven."

"I want my mommy!"

Paul sits little Paola on his lap. He caresses her cheeks and stains it with blood. He quietly sings her a lullaby, waiting for her to fall asleep.

Chapter EIGHTEEN:

The last night. Part 1. Tuesday, May 15, 1990

VERÓNICA IGNORES HER DUTIES AS THE NIGHT NURSE and buries herself into a novel. Tonight was her turn watch the patients in the sexual reorientation wing, but she prefers to stay in her room. A dragging sound echoes down the hallway and breaks her concentration. Her curiosity wins and she sets aside the novel and walks to the door.

She doesn't want to be seen so she opens the door just a little. She is shocked by what she sees. Paul is dragging the seemingly unconscious psychiatrist down the hallway. Did something happen to her? Verónica wonders what she can do.

"Maybe he's taking her to the doctor," Verónica thinks. She lies back down on her bed and continues reading her novel.

"Put her there! In the next room — not that one!" Dr. Rutherbor directs Paul. "I'll look after her. You go ahead and look for your father."

Paul obeys and goes out to look for Mr. Iñeziz. Juliana starts to wake. She blinks, holding her head in her hands. Her eyes are blank and she looks like she's coming in and out of this world, until she is able to focus her gaze on Dr. Rutherbor.

"Whe...where am I?"

"Relax, dear. You had an accident. You slipped and hit your head."

"Doctor? What am I doing here?" Juliana feels like her skull has been replaced with a rock. Her head has never hurt so much and her vision is still a bit cloudy.

"You passed out. You slipped. Don't you remember anything?"

"I don't...I don't remember." The memories come flooding back all at once. Antonio Cortés, María Rutherbor, Bernardo...Paola...Teresa! *No! It was no accident!* Juliana tries to get up, but the doctor holds her down with one hand.

"Doctor, listen to me, you have to reconsider. You still have time. You're not helping the kids, you're harming them."

"Yes? You think so?" Dr. Rutherbor's sarcastic tone scares Juliana even more. "What made you change your mind?"

"The way is to understand them, to get into their hearts. With those violent treatments —"

"It's all good, calm down. You're delirious - no doubt a result of the blow to the head. You don't know what you're saying, Juliana. And it hurts me, it hurts me because I trusted you so much." Dr. Rutherbor prepares a needle.

"But, Doctor —"

"Shut up! Homosexuality is a disease! Homosexuals are degenerate sickos who deserve everything they get!"

"What happened to Dr. Claudia? What did you do with her?" Juliana knows that it's risky to talk about this in her current situation, but if not now there may never be another chance.

"I already told you, she got a —"

"That's a lie! You lied to me and it must have been for some reason. There has been no trace of Claudia for —"

"Those are just stories! People make things up to destroy us. Oh, too bad, Juliana. I always thought you would be on my side."

"What did you do with Claudia?"

"Okay, okay. Do you want the truth?" Dr. Rutherbor sits next to her with a needle in each hand. "She betrayed me, she was going to expose the treatments at my clinic. Imagine that…I couldn't allow it."

Dr. Rutherbor shrugs his shoulders like he has nothing left to lose and starts to tell Juliana what really happened on December of last year.

Wednesday, December 20, 1989

"Doctor, it's not my intention to criticize you, much less attack you, but I think these treatments are a little tough on the kids." Claudia is nervous; for the first time, she has to confront her boss with such a delicate matter. "The beatings, the electricity, all those pills, depriving them of food and water…even the lie detector. I think it's a bit much."

"What makes you think that? Did someone say

something to you?" Dr. Rutherbor monitors all of the psychiatrist's sessions and knows about the conversation Claudia had with Tomás, but plays dumb in an attempt to determine how much his employee actually knows. "Have you been talking to someone outside of the clinic about what you're telling me?"

"No, of course not. You know, Doctor, I would never do that. What I'm telling you are my own thoughts — no one else's."

"But you know very well that there's only one way to help the patients. You know that this is the only way. Remember Paul Gómez, remember I cured him?"

"I know, but the rest...the rest have been here over a year and none of them have been cured. You could even say that they're worse."

"It took me ten years to cure Paul. There's no time limit. Each patient is an individual case."

"I don't know... something tells me this is not the way."

"You doubt me?" There's a threatening tone in Rutherbor's voice, a tone that scares Claudia.

"No, of course not. You know I would never doubt you," she answers immediately.

"Look, I'm going to think about what you're telling me. Maybe because Christmas is coming, who knows, we can decrease the intensity of the treatments a little bit, then we'll see how the kids develop."

"Thanks, Doctor."

Wednesday, December 27, 1989

"Things have gone too far!" Claudia yells, with Bernardo's body in her arms.

"Calm down, Claudia. Accidents like this always happen."

"Acci...? Accidents? Your own son just died and you don't even flinch!"

"Lower your voice, lower your voice. We don't want the others to find out."

"We don't want? What do you mean by we don't wan—"

Dr. Rutherbor approaches Claudia and grabs her by the neck with both hands. "Exactly. We don't want..." Dr. Rutherbor starts to squeeze.

"Doc...you're...hurting me..." she manages to say.

Dr. Rutherbor lets her go. It was an impulse. He doesn't know what got into him. He doesn't like using his own hands to...

"You have to stop all this." Claudia recovers her breath. "Listen to me, Doctor, you still have time to reconsider."

"You are not the boss in here. Things will be done my way!"

"Then I quit. This is my last night here."

"You are under my command!"

Claudia is devastated and is afraid for her own life. Little by little, she gets up from the floor, leaving the body. She runs towards the door to escape.

"You're not going anywhere! You will ruin my career!"

Dr. Rutherbor takes her by the neck again, another impulse. His son…his son died of an overdose. It was his mistake. "I had nothing to do with it," he repeats to himself. And if Claudia dies, it would be an extension of Bernardo's action, too. It's not Dr. Rutherbor who's acting; it's the shadow of his son. He's not to blame. It's just an impulse.

"Doc…doc…tor, ple…ple…ase. I ca…can't bre…a…the… You're hurting…me…"

"Shut up!" he tells her, without releasing his grip. He whispers in a malicious voice, "You won't quit, but this will be your last night!"

Claudia loses her strength and stops breathing. Her hands fall.

"Finally!"

Chapter NINETEEN:

Grow And Live Normally? Part 2.
Friday, November 10, 1967

THE DOCTOR WASN'T SUCCESSFUL WITH THE YOUNG MAN'S treatment. He diagnosed Paul Gómez as bipolar, manic depressive, and even slightly schizophrenic, but not with a sexual disorder.

Frustrated, he decides that the best thing to do is to end the treatment and close down the sexual reorientation wing. When he told Paul this, Paul confessed that his last name is actually Iñeziz and persuaded the doctor to call his father, Mr. Ignacio Iñeziz, who was willing to help the clinic out financially. The doctor, knowing that the Iñeziz family was one of the wealthiest in the country, called Paul's father right away.

The night of November 15, 1967, the life of Ralph Rutherbor would change forever. At first, what he saw in the basement of the Iñeziz house didn't seem fair or reasonable. It was a disturbing place! There wasn't another way to describe it.

Ten kids between fourteen and seventeen years of age were admitted there, receiving a "therapy" that consisted of drugs, insults, beating, and all kinds of abuses. Three boys were chained to the water pipe of a shower. The doctor got chills when he first saw it. He knew that these methods would cause terrible repercussions for the patients - not only physical bruises and scars, but mental and emotional injury, as well.

The doctor's first impression of injustice, though, changed the moment that Mr. Iñeziz told him about his son. Paul was the living proof that homosexuality could be cured, that the treatments that they were applying on that basement were effective to "eliminate that disease from the physical, psychological, and spiritual organism of people". According to Mr. Iñeziz, Paul used to be a homosexual. He was treated in that basement and was now healed.

Paul convincing his classmate to introduce him to her teacher was only a scheme designed by his father in order to get close to Dr. Rutherbor. Paul's father was desperate to propose a business plan that would make both parties rich and famous.

Iñeziz knew that there was a lot of money to be made this way: locking-up young people with the pretense of curing homosexuality. But he needed the doctor's help. He needed a façade, a legal image that would allow him to convince the parents of the patients that the best thing to do was to admit them to the clinic to "fix" them. The parents would think that they were entering a decent place and that a doctor backed the treatments, approved by the scientific community.

Another reason that Mr. Iñeziz needed Dr. Rutherbor was that he knew that, at any moment, justice was going to catch up to him. Everyone knows that the Iñeziz family fortune comes from the black market and extortion. One of the wealthiest families in the country was also one of the most corrupt. As a well-known mobster, Iñeziz's days of freedom were seemingly numbered. The military had frustrated many of his operations and they were spying on him. The last thing he wanted was for them to discover that, in the basement of his house, he was running a "clinic" to make even more illegal money.

At that time, the doctor also had nothing to lose. If what they told him about Paul was true, then he not only had to accept because of the money, but he would be contributing in a big way to the wellbeing of all of humanity. He would have in his hands the secret to curing homosexuals. He would be remembered throughout history for his contributions to the field of science. He would be awarded in so many... His mind didn't stop to imagine all the flattery he would receive. He accepted the offer.

On October 29 of 1977, all of Iñeziz's predictions came true. When the military inspected his home, they didn't find anything in the basement. The boys were already sent to Grow And Live Normally, without leaving personal traces or suspicions. At the clinic, the patients weren't to stay at the main area, the addictions section. They were taken to the sexual reorientation wing, reopened that same year, on a side wing of the building where one gets in through a small metallic door with a huge lock. Inside, the patients weren't in the hands of the certificated doctors, but with the same group of guards that used to work in Mr. Iñeziz's basement. The three psychiatrists from the main rehab clinic also didn't treat them, but Dr. Claudia Losala treated them instead.

On Wednesday, November 9, 1977, Dr. Rutherbor completed his end of the deal by claiming to have cured Paul Gómez's homosexuality to the media and the medical guild. The following year, he was awarded, applauded, revered by his colleagues in various ceremonies in his honor. Paul instantly became the famous "ex-homosexual". Then, the sexual reorientation area began accepting more patients. The parents of those suffering from "sexual deviations" began taking their sons and daughters to Grow And Live Normally. They left them one day and they didn't see them again for months, even years. It translated to the arcs of the institution being filled with money; all of the parents paid up without asking many questions and with only rare visits

Chapter TWENTY:

The last night. Part 2. Tuesday, May 15, 1990

"YOU KILLED HER? DID YOU KILL HER?" JULIANA IS BESIDE herself. She can't believe what she hears.

"Me? I had nothing to do with it. Bernardo put me in this position. And Paul…so it was your fault, yes! Your fault! If you hadn't introduced me to Paul when you were a student, none of this would have happened."

"Paul? But Paul… Didn't you cure him?"

"Don't be silly. He was never homosexual. We needed that story to justify the existence of the sexual reorientation wing."

"What?"

"Paul is Ignacio Iñeziz's son. Yes, the one in the news — the thug, the mobster. His name is Paul Iñeziz Gómez."

Juliana can't believe her ears. She's been living a lie for most of her life, a lie concocted by the people she trusted the most. Paul returns to the room in time to hear the doctor's confession.

"What are you doing? Why are you telling her this?"

"Relax, it's not important anymore."

"Are you an Iñeziz?" Juliana asks the newcomer, looking him straight in the eyes.

For Paul, this is a blow below the belt. She, the person he has always loved, now knows everything about him.

"You're an asshole!" he screams at the doctor. "You betrayed me."

"It's not important. Aren't we going to wipe her memory?" Dr. Rutherbor takes the cap off one of the syringes. He presses it slightly and a little liquid squirts out of the needle.

"And what's with that injection? Be careful you don't make a mistake."

"You didn't find your father? Didn't I tell you to go look for him?"

"No, I didn't find him —"

"Maybe he didn't want to see you. He gave me precise instructions a long time ago. Maybe he told me that if this happened, then I should —"

"You're going to kill her, right?" Paul becomes upset. "What's in that injection?"

"Be objective, Paul. We have no other option. She already knows too much." Dr. Rutherbor starts to walk toward his former psychiatrist, waving the syringe like a sword.

"Don't even think about it." Paul is becoming desperate; Dr. Rutherbor doesn't seem to be listening to him. "I'm warning you…"

But Dr. Rutherbor doesn't stop. Paul has no other option. This whole game has already cost him his wife. He can't lose the true love of his life, too. He pulls a gun from his belt and, without thinking, pulls the trigger twice.

Verónica, who had fallen asleep with the book on her chest, jumps up at the sound of the gunshots.

"You...shot me?" Dr. Rutherbor is a mixture of astonishment and fear. He breathes heavily.

"You crossed the line. You got involved where you shouldn't have. I have control now. I don't need you any longer."

Paul puts the gun to Dr. Rutherbor's temple. He pulls the trigger again and kills him instantly. Juliana wants to scream, but her voice doesn't come out. She had never been so afraid before. She leans against the wall, as far away from Paul as she can get.

"Please, don't hurt me anymore," she begs.

"Juliana, but I would have never hurt you. You know this very well."

"It was you! You raped me that night!"

"I love you, Juliana. You gave me no other choice. I wanted you so badly. I was so obsessed with you."

"Monster!"

"Well, you know how I feel about you. You know I'm crazy for you. Of that, I am guilty. I couldn't control myself."

"I don't want to hear any more of this, please..."

"When you married that guy, Miguel, you destroyed me inside, Juliana. I was the one who was supposed to be by your side." As he speaks, Paul comes closer to Juliana and starts to touch her, to kiss her hands and neck. "But...but you do love me. That's why you accepted my advances that night we had our little affair. Well, that was actually our second encounter if you count the night that I —"

"Stop! No! I never wanted you. It was a mistake."

"You love me! I was always by your side. I helped you overcome the death of your brother, when you felt alone in your marriage, when you discovered your son's disease. I've always been present and now…now I saved you from what that doctor was going to do to you. Don't be ungrateful!"

"Leave her alone."

Both hear a voice coming from the doorway. It's Ignacio Iñeziz, escorted by two of his guards.

"What happened here?" he asks. "Paul, did you kill him?"

"I had to. He was going to kill Juliana."

"Paul, there are things you'll never understand."

"What? So it was true what he told me? Did you bring Juliana here to kill her?"

"Paul, I'm telling you there are things you'll never understand."

"Yes? And what are those things?"

"For example, Juliana is never going to love you! That you are an obsessed freak!"

"She does love me!"

"You're making me lose my patience."

"I'm telling you she lo—"

In a fraction of a second, Ignacio takes out a gun and fires it at his son's leg. Paul falls to the ground, twitching in pain.

"You're sick in the head," Ignacio says.

"Da…dad! You shot me!"

The roar of the last shot echoes through all of Grow And Live Normally and stirs the patients from their sleep.

Most of them decide to lock themselves in their bathrooms. They assume it is the safest place. But Johana doesn't hide. She recognizes the sound and decides to run to Tomás's room, one of the few friends she has left.

"Did you hear that?" she asks Tomás as he opens the door. "It was a gunshot."

"A gunshot? How do you know?"

"What else would it be? I've already heard more than one."

"You heard...where?"

"Here! Just now! React! Something's happening!"

Tomás had never seen Johana so nervous or heard her speak so much, so he lets her go on about her version of the shootings and thinks that it's best to lock the door. Before closing the door, he sees a figure in the dark: it's the nurse, Verónica, walking quickly down one of the hallways. Is it true what Johana is saying?

***

"Help me," Paul begs his father. "It hurts…"

"I can't stand you. You're a useless crybaby."

"I'm your son!"

"Yes, I know and you have given me enough shame."

Verónica enters the room. She sees the scene in front of her: her dead boss, Paul with a gunshot wound, and Juliana in tears. She understands what's happening. She doesn't even need to take the time to identify the other three people before she turns and runs for help.

"Grab her!" Iñeziz commands.

Verónica doesn't run far before she is caught. One of Iñeziz's guards covers her mouth and drags her into one of the other storage rooms. Johana and Tomás watch the scene from the bedroom door. They jump in their hiding place as a loud noise rings out, echoing down the hallway. Another gunshot! The pieces start to add up… someone killed the nurse!

"We're in danger," Johana tells Tomás. "We have to leave. If we stay here, they're going to kill us, too."

Inside the other room, Ignacio signals his remaining guard to take his son away. "He's driving me crazy with this crying and complaining," he states firmly. "Now, we need to take are of this one," he commands, pointing towards Juliana.

"No, Dad, please don't kill her!" Paul implores him to spare Juliana.

Iñeziz doesn't answer. He waits for Paul to be carried out of sight before he faces her. Since hearing the shot that killed Verónica, Juliana is practically in a catatonic state, shaky and looking as if she wanted to say something, but she only emits senseless sounds.

"You will be dead and I will have to take care of my grandchild, right?" Ignacio smiles. "Tomás is an Iñeziz."

"No…never. He'll never know that."

"Excuse me, dear, but," Iñeziz points his gun at her, "it's me who'll decide that."

While he struggles with the guard, Paul's gun falls from its holster as he is carried outside of the clinic.

Tomás and Johana are worried as they watch the

strength of the man taking Paul away. They know they are in danger and their only choice is to sneak out of the room and check on Verónica. As they tiptoe down the hallway, Iñeziz's guard reemerges from the storage room. The duo turns to run back to the safety of Tomás's room, but Johana slips, twisting her ankle. She cries out in pain as the joint spasms.

"Johana, watch out!" Tomás yells, as the guard reaches for her. "Run!"

Tomás turns back and places himself in front of Johana, acting as a shield. The guard punches Tomás in the face, knocking him to the floor. He stomps on Tomás's right leg, grinding him into the floor. He turns to a frightened Johana who, seeing herself with no way to escape, spots Paul's gun on the floor and pulls herself to it, reaching it just in time. She takes aim, trying to control her shaking body. "Stop! I don't want to shoot!"

But the guard doesn't stop. Johana becomes desperate. She points the gun toward the ceiling and fires a warning shot. The guard isn't deterred so she runs to the nearest storage room and desperately yanks the door open.

Johana is shocked by the scene inside the room and fires the gun impulsively.

Chapter TWENTY-ONE:

May 17 of 1990.
Tuesday, May 15, 1990.

THE SHOT IS STILL RINGING IN HER EARS. HER HEART IS about to burst out of her chest.

"Johana, are you okay?" Tomás screams from the hallway.

Johana doesn't answer. She can't believe what she just did. In a split second, she felt so much control, unbelievable power. She realizes that the weapon is still in her hands and drops it. The subject is alive, at least, which puts her mind slightly at ease. She distinguishes his figure in the dark, twisting and moaning. She doesn't know who she shot.

"Guys, are you okay?" Juliana calls out.

Johana pulls herself together and tries to speak, but she is still trembling and only stutters incoherently.

Iñeziz's remaining guard takes advantage of the confusion and runs out of the clinic.

"Mom." Tomás walks towards Juliana, in disbelief of what he sees.

"Tomás! Thank God!" Juliana rushes to embrace her son, happy to find him alive although he is limping with bleeding lips and with a black and blue eye barely open into a slit.

"What have I...what have I done?" Johana finally manages to ask. "Did I kill him?"

"It was in self-defense." Juliana wraps her arms around the girl. "And he's not dead...not yet."

"And who is he?" Tomás asks.

"Ignacio Iñeziz."

"Iñeziz?"

"One of the most-wanted gangsters in South America. He's the true owner. Let's say...the head behind this clinic." Juliana motions toward the floor and Tomás realizes who is moaning and twisting on the floor of the storage room.

"What are we supposed to do now?" Johana asks, almost in a whisper.

"Call 911...and the police."

"The police?"

"Don't worry, Johana. You're not to blame."

The girl nods, fighting with herself over shooting a man. She shakes her hands to clear the feeling of the gun from her subconscious.

"Go on, quickly — before he actually dies or escapes. Use the phone at the reception."

Johana nods again and quickly walks away in complete silence. Juliana turns to look at her son. Tomás is in very bad state. He wobbles as if he were going to faint. Juliana grabs him at the waist and sits him down against a wall.

"Mom?"

"Yes, son. Please, I ask you to forgive me."

"There's no reason to forgive you, Mom."

"Yes, yes there is - for leaving you, for not trying to understand you, for bringing you to this hellhole. There is nothing wrong with you. I should have...I should have listened to you."

"It's not your fault, Mom. Don't worry."

"I don't know how I could think that this was going to be the best for you. Forgive me."

"We'll be alright," Tomás answers, without feeling obliged to forgive her because, to him, there is nothing to forgive. She's his mother and she did what she did because she believed was the best for him. "What matters now is that you know now what's best for me and for both of us," he tells her and she cries on his shoulder.

She strongly returns his hug, remembering who his father is, and she promises herself that she will never tell him. "It wouldn't be good for him to know," she thinks.

Tomás is relieved, not only because the events of this evening have come to an end, but also because his entire stay in the hellhole is finally over.

***

The officers arrive on the scene quickly. Juliana tries her best to describe the details of what has happened to the police officers.

"This is Dr. Rutherbor's office," she tells them, while she shows them around the clinic.

Tomás notices a blue notebook in the bag hanging from the doorknob and reaches for it out of curiosity. As his hand touches the cover, Tomás's mind is flooded full of forgotten memories. His head begins to pound and the room spins. He is forced to sit down as he suddenly recalls everything. He opens the notebook and reads various where he wrote his Bible interpretations and other notes about homosexuality. He flips through the pages until he stumbles upon the picture he glued there, the picture of Sebastián and Christian. On another page are his suspicions about the disappearance of Claudia and Bernardo, even the places where he thinks their bodies are buried so that he could tell the police.

During all of this, the police officers, in their search for evidence, insist on viewing the security footage screens.

The scene that unfolds on the small television screen stuns everyone in the room. Playing like a horror movie, events both known and unknown become evidence. The room gasps as they notice that there is a person locked up in one of the storage rooms, also known as the therapy chambers.

"There is someone there now!" another police officer says.

"It's Fabricio!" Johana cries excitedly. "Quickly, we have to go get him!"

Despite the pain from their injuries, Tomás and Johana rush to go to the rescue of their friend as the officers follow closely behind. They fly down the stairs and down the hallway to the storage rooms. It doesn't take them much to open it with the help of the police. They find Fabricio lying on the floor with one hand stretched through an opening in the wall.

"Fabricio!" they call, as they run to his side.

Fabricio doesn't react. He is pale; his lips are dry

and blue. One of the officers notices that he is holding something. Upon closer inspection, they realize that it is an arm connected to a person on the other side of the wall. This can only mean one thing - there is another person on the other side of the wall.

"Please, Fabricio," Johana begs. "Wake up."

The police waste no time in knocking down the other door while Tomás remains by his friend's side. He places his hand over Fabricio's and can feel Mateo's cold, still arm through the hole in the wall. He already knows what it means, but doesn't want to say it out loud and alarm his friends. Fabricio blinks.

"He's alive!" Johana shouts.

"Mateo?" Fabricio asks. "Mateo?"

"Shh, the police will get him out of there," Tomás explains.

"Is he alive? He's...he's hurt. Is he alive?" Fabricio cries. "I want to see him. I have to talk to him."

"They'll get him out. Calm down."

"What the hell happened here!" one of the officers shouts.

Tomás knows the reason for their alarm. Fabricio tries to get up.

"No, don't move too much," Johana implores. "You are very weak."

"I need to see him." Fabricio starts to get up and Tomás holds him so that he doesn't fall. "Help me get over there..."

Tomás wishes that he doesn't have to experience what

happens next, but he also doesn't have the courage to deny Fabricio the truth. With the help of Johana, Fabricio is carried to the next room. The scene shocks everyone.

"No!" Fabricio shouts, pulling away from his friends and running to Mateo. The young man is slumped against the wall with his arm still in the opening connecting him to the other storage room. The entire floor is covered in dried blood.

"Mateo!" Fabricio kneels and embraces his body. "Mateo!"

Johana wipes away tears while Tomás holds his breath to avoid crying He knows that there will be time for proper mourning, but now he must be strong to, on one hand, console Fabricio and, on the other, explain everything to the police so that justice is served.

"Fabricio..." Tomás crouches next to him and touches his back. "Fabricio, please, let the officers do their job. You need to drink water, to eat —"

"No! I can't leave him!"

"I know, I know, Fabricio, but —" Tomás sees something shining on the floor, reflecting the light from outside. "His glasses..."

"Whe...? Where are his glasses?"

Tomás picks them up and hands them to Fabricio.

For Fabricio, it's difficult to touch the pale face of his loved one, but he uses his fingers to gently close Mateo's turned-off eyes. He adjusts the glasses on the boy's face. Unable to resist, he hugs the body as tightly as he can, continuing to cry over his regret at not having been able to save him.

"Fabricio, I'm so sorry," Johana tells him, her own heart shattered.

"I couldn't save him."

"It wasn't your fault and you were by his side," Johana reminds him.

"I never let him go...I never let him go... I didn't leave him alone."

"You did what you could," Tomás says. "You did your best. He didn't suffer...he didn't suffer much. He left quietly because you were there with him. He felt loved."

"He had so many dreams and goals and now...he's gone. Life turned its back on him."

"Maybe...but I see it like life gave him to you. It gave him a Fabricio because Fabricio was what he was missing. Life joined you and he stayed with you until the last second of his life." Tomás puts a hand on Fabricio's shoulder. "It is not up to us to decide what happens around us. This is how it works. It is difficult to understand, yes, it's complicated. Some make it, others don't."

Fabricio thinks about what happened that night. He doesn't understand it; he cannot understand it. He knows that Mateo was a miracle for him, a gift that life gave to both him and Mateo. He felt that they loved deeply and that the affection and the connection they shared was unique. Life had been beautiful once with Mateo, even for such a short time, but with memories that would last forever and that relieves Fabricio.

"What will happen with...with his body?"

"It will depend on his parents' wishes, I imagine, but his soul will always be with you."

"You think so?"

"Yes, I believe so, but you have to believe it, too. It's up to you."

"I believe it. He always prayed to become an angel, to have wings and fly."

"Perhaps now he is one."

"He would be very happy."

Fabricio finally weakens and faints. One of the policemen stoops to take his pulse. He is not responding and his state is quickly deteriorating.

"How long was this kid locked up in there?" he asks.

"It must've been at least three days...without any food or water,"

"Is the ambulance here yet?"

"I think so," the other policeman answers.

Wednesday, May 16, 1990

Grow And Live Normally is filled with soldiers, police officers, health ministers, reporters, and activists. They crowd outside holding banners mixed with messages of support for the kids being removed. The place is a scandal. In the midst of the crowd, one of Ecuador's most respected reporters begins her transmission:

"Good afternoon, viewers. We come to you with news of a very tragic event and one of the most shocking revelations of recent times. We're here at the scene: Grow And Live Normally, a well respected and nationally recognized rehabilitation clinic, where, for more than a decade, treatments have been administered in an attempt to cure homosexuality. There's news of corpses, patients imprisoned for days on end in complete darkness...and this is only the beginning of the story. The testimonies of the patients with whom we have already spoken are indeed heartbreaking. They describe their stay in this center as demeaning, where they withered away. Instead of food, they received shock therapy and dangerous drugs of all kinds.

Here is an exclusive interview we conducted with one of this center's previous patients:

"I just wanted to be fixed. To be normal, you know? To overcome my weakness and the sickness, as my father used to call it." An anonymous man speaks out, hidden in the shadows.

"Why did you father used to say those words to you?" The worried voice of the reporter is heard from the background.

"For being...a homosexual. I felt like I embarrassed him. Not only was *he* ashamed of me, but so was my mother."

"How did you end up in the clinic?"

"I remember the day very well. It was Saturday, February 21, 1976. My parents set up a trap. They sent me to the corner store and, when I was walking back home, a van stopped and people took me — kidnapped me — and drove me to that place, to that Iñeziz's basement. It's been hell."

"Can I ask what they did to you there?"

"They locked me in the basement, they stripped me and chained me to a water pipe where they continued to just beat me, insult me, and drug me. Even worse, they threatened that, if I didn't change, they would go after my family. I remember clearly feeling the blood gush over my face."

"Did you end up fixed? Cured?"

"No, the truth is that I ended up broken — on the outside *and* the inside."

"How long were you there?"

"I believe one year in the basement and then one year and some months in Grow And Live Normally."

"How did you survive?"

"It's so sad to think about it. Because we were so many, you know? Just kids. Even before I was in the basement, I had heard so many stories of the previous inmates who managed to escape and still others who were found dead with their families washing their hand of the guilt, saying that they had just lost their path with the sin and deviation. Some of us managed to get out of there, but the rest were sent to Grow And Live Normally. We knew that the only way to survive was to pretend, to keep lying. We never changed our sexual orientation, just our sexual conduct. We were able to pass the lie detector and get out."

"Why now? Why now you are telling and sharing your experience? Why not before? You could have stopped this from happening to others." The interviewer doesn't intend to make the man feel guilty, but wants to be as direct as possible for the viewers at home.

"Of all of the kids who were there with me, only five survived. The rest…they killed themselves." The anonymous man starts to cry. "Over the years, we had to keep quiet or we would risk the safety of our family. They warned us that no one was going to believe us, much less defend us. Every one sees us as a criminal, a disease, a sin — just for being who we are."

The interview ends and the camera returns to the reporter.

"At this time, we're still waiting for the full truth to come to light, but we know that the body of Dr. Ralph Rutherbor was found last night. His is one of five bodies that have been discovered so far, but more may appear as the investigation is still underway. Among the dead is a former psychiatrist here at the clinic, Dr. Claudia Losala and, unbelievably, a child identified as the very son of Dr. Rutherbor. These two bodies were already in a state of decomposition suggesting that they had been buried for nearly five months.

"As terrible as it already is, the story gets even more complicated. Twenty-two young men were transferred to a so-called "Catholic center", managed by María Rutherbor, the separated wife of the head doctor here at Grow And Live Normally, where..."

Sebastián has to turn off the TV the news makes him dizzy as he relives some of his own experiences. He takes a breath from his inhaler. He thinks that, in the end, he was the luckiest one, but he feels guilty for not having been able to help his new friends. He doesn't know if he would have been able to escape from the clinic with his life if he hadn't been moved to North Clinic. It's the best thing that could have happened to him, not only because of the way he is being treated for his depression, but also because it has even improved his relationship with his parents.

A nurse peeks into his room, "Excuse me, you have a visitor."

Sebastián gets out of bed and looks in the mirror. *Who can it be?* Sebastián isn't sure he even looks presentable enough to accept a guest. As he assesses himself in the mirror's reflection, Sebastián sees Tomás standing in the doorway.

"Tomás! You're here! Just like you promised…"

Sebastián runs to hug him. "Yes, now I have you," Tomás tells him, kissing him several times on his rosy cheeks.

"And I have you, too," Sebastián returns.

As Sebastián wipes the tears from Tomás's face, he notices that Tomás is wounded. "Are you okay?"

"Last night…I don't even know how to start to explain…but I will be fine. We'll all be fine!" he says, happy to have Sebastián in his arms again.

"And the others? I heard that they don't know how many have died…"

"Most of them are fine…but not all of them. Sandra left the clinic shortly after you left. She said that she had changed, that she was no longer bisexual."

The two friends smile in complicity. They know that Sandra was an expert liar.

"Johana is under observation. A friend of my mom is taking care of her. She was the hardest hit, but she saved us. She pulled the trigger on Mr. Iñeziz…"

"Will she have to go to jail or something?"

"No, it was in self-defense. Besides, she didn't kill him. She shot him in the chest, but he's still alive."

"Mateo? Fabricio?"

"Mateo...Mateo is..."

"What?"

"He's dead."

The news leaves Sebastián frozen. He uses his inhaler so that he doesn't choke.

"Yes. They stabbed him with a knife, a pocketknife... one of the guards. He had been dead for four days when we found him."

"But...but he was so young..."

"Yes, and you can imagine how Fabricio is? He's devastated, well, he will get better eventually, they say... although I have a feeling that it's going to be really difficult for him. They fell in love and Mateo died next to him."

"I don't know what to say. Mateo was such a good person. He had a very bright future ahead of him."

"I know. We are all very heartbroken. I...I can't believe that so many things happened so close to us. It was all right under our noses and we didn't notice anything."

"We don't have to start blaming ourselves," Sebastián tells him as he sees Tomás rub the pain in his leg. "Are you ok? Would you like to lie down for a while?" Sebastián helps Tomás to the bed. He was exhausted and they quickly fall asleep, wrapped in each other's arms, to ease the memories from the previous night's events.

An hour and half later, Sebastián wakes up and sees Tomás at his side, awake and serious.

"Is everything okay?" Tomás doesn't answer him and only stares back at him. "Why are you silent?" Sebastián worries and turns to face him.

"I have a confession." Tomás finally says.

"What? Are you heterosexual?" Sebastián laughs. He's happy, ecstatic, to have Tomás in front of him — to be able to touch him and hold his hand, to see his eyes and even his bruised face. He never stopped thinking about Tomás, day after day, after he had been transferred from the clinic.

"No, it's that...those pills that Dr. Rutherbor gave me...they made me lose my memory."

"You don't need to explain anything to me. I mean you don't have to apologize or justif—"

"No, that's not that what I'm trying tell you. The thing is that I started to remember everything, little by little, when I stopped taking those pills. When I learned the truth about what was happening, memories began to come back..."

"Thank God." Sebastián kisses him on the lips, but that doesn't seem to clear concern in Tomás' face. "I'm glad."

"Do you remember that you once asked me if we had already met? If you had seen me somewhere?"

"Yes. But we agreed that it was just my imagination."

"Actually, it wasn't."

"Really?"

"You did see me before. Not much, but you did see me..."

"What are you talking about? When? Where?"

"Just days after Christian..." Tomás pauses to analyze how Sebastián would react to hearing his name. He feels like Sebastián is calm so he decides to continue, "I was the intruder...that day in your house, next to the tree. I left the letter on your bedside table."

Sebastián drops Tomás' hand and gets up from the bed. Suddenly, his face transforms. He feels deceived. He backs away from Tomás, who stands up and approaches him.

"How did you get into my house? How did you know where I lived?"

"Sebas..." Tomás begins to plead. Sebastián is still motionless and confused. He's speechless. "I'm sorry, I —"

"I'm sorry, Tomás. It's just that I do not understand how —"

"No, forgive me. I just felt like I had to tell you. And the truth is that I want so badly to take you away from the loneliness and the darkness. I want to be that essence you hoped to find that would fill your heart once again because I care about you so much. You're the only person I've cared for this much. It's from you that I learned that it doesn't matter what everyone else thinks. What matters is to be the best version of us. You make me realize that the love I feel for you is completely perfect. You never threw away or denied what you felt for another boy, another soul, another human being. You kept it alive in your memories, in your heart, and I saw you protected it in your photo album. I never met Christian, but I have no doubt that he was a good guy and that he is someone important in your life. You're the answer of what it means to be a human being: to live true to your imperfect self, to love another human being perfectly. That's what I adore even more about you. You inspired me and teach me to how to be me, to be us." Sebastián is still speechless. Tomás grabs his hand and holds it to his chest.

"I need you. I want you. I desperately want to have you

to be a part of my life and build some new and wonderful thing with you, but in order for me to have you, you have to heal first. Do you understand me?" Tomás pleads.

"The doctor says that I'm recovered. I don't suffer from bipolar disorder — that was a misdiagnosis. I don't have those episodes anymore."

"No, I mean heal your heart."

Sebastián tries to control himself, but tears roll down his face anyway. Tomás pulls the paper that he found under Sebastián's bed from his pocket and places it in his palm. Sebastián realizes that it's the letter from Christian, the letter that started everything between he and Tomás and brought them together.

"This time you have to read it all...all the way."

"I can't."

"Yes you can. I'm here with you. Trust me." Tomás holds his hand tight.

Sebastián knows that Tomás is right. It's the key to moving on with their lives, to letting go of their pain. Tomás smiles. Sebastián lifts the paper and places it in front of his eyes. He read everything to himself, until he gets to the last paragraph, which he reads aloud.

Don't give up, and be stronger than me. I'm sure that there's someone out there who will wait for you for a second chance at love. It hurts me in all my soul having to leave you, but I don't know what to do. It's too painful right now.

Forgive me...

Sincerely, Christian

A teardrop falls onto the letter, smearing the ink.

"Are you okay?" Tomás asks.

"I will be with you." Sebastián smiles once again. He knows that Christian was right. He would have a second chance at love. It was right in front of him. Even though Christian left him, Sebastián finally forgives him and the remaining resentment in his heart disappears. He silently vows to never leave him; he will always keep him in his heart. He will be part of his life forever. Just like Tomás. "Thank you."

"Sebastián?"

"Yes."

"I have to confess something more and I'm sorry if it's too soon."

"Tell me."

"I love you." Tomás' eyes radiate love. A feeling of relief rushes over the flushed young man, just like the day when Christian said the same words for the first time.

In that moment, Sebastián understands that love is everything, love cures everything. In particular, he finally understands what Tomás told him that day when he first opened up to him. For the first time, Sebastián doesn't feel like he can only have one soulmate. He is free to have another chance at love with Tomás. He feels like he could fall in love with him, to get to know him, and develop a relationship with him. He feels a new phase in his life is coming.

The two young men embrace. Sebastián now feels that all the pieces of the puzzle are in place.

Thursday, May 17, 1990

"Good news! The doctor just told us that you can come home today," Sebastián's mother tells him.

"Finally. You don't know how much I wanted to get out of here and be independent again."

"Again we...we want you to forgive us," his father tells him, ashamed. "Your mother and I feel really bad. We didn't know that you would have to go through all this..."

"It's not your fault. I love you and I'm glad that you understand...and that you get to know me as the person I am. That's the most important thing."

"You are our son. We love you and if you're happy like this, and you identify like this, then that's how we will love you." Sebastián's mother hugs her son.

"Your brother, Gastón, couldn't make it to come to visit you," his father adds.

"It's ok. I'm going to be out of here and see him soon." Sebastián is happy to finally reconnect with his parents and older brother.

"This boy who came to visit you...he's very handsome, huh? We must invite him to eat at the house," his mother teases, looking at Tomás.

"Yes, I am very lucky."

"I am the luckiest here...for having found you," Tomás sighs, sitting next to Sebastián.

"So, would you like to have dinner with us?" Sebastián's mother asks him.

"Sure. Thank you very much."

A nurse enters the room. "I'm sorry for interrupting,

but you have to see this..."

The nurse turns on the television and the same reporter from the other day appears on the screen.

"...so you can say that today, Thursday, May 17 of 1990, is a day that will change humanity forever. Tolerance and equality come together today against homophobia. The General Assembly of the World Health Organization has removed homosexuality from its list of mental illnesses. From now on, any member of the homosexual community should expect to be treated like any other person and their individual rights must be respected. The decision comes after years of studies and it's possible that Ecuador will also remove the crime status of same-sex relationships. Many of the supporters of this decision think that it was time to take these measures to stop the discrimination, rejection, and intolerance towards homosexuals. We can remember how the Stonewall riots made history and now, June 28, will forever be celebrated as the LGBTQI pride day. In a few moments, we will return with first-hand testimonies from the members of the Commission..."

Sebastián can't believe how everything has changed overnight. He is happy. After all this time, he can finally say that he is happy. He also sees his parents happy. He feels fingers slip between his own and is pulled out of his thoughts.

"Now we can say that we love each other and no one is going to think that it's a symptom of a disease," Tomás tells him.

"No, now they will know that it's a symptom of love."

Sebastián understands now that it was all part of a

plan. His coming to the capital was necessary for his dreams to materialize. It was what he needed to grow, to get to know himself and overcome his fears, to overstep the obstacles that prevented him from moving forward in life. He had to turn the page and start a new chapter. Despite the horror that he felt and his lack of hope, he managed to survive. This is the best lesson that life has given him: no matter where we are taken by destiny — or our own decisions — we must not lose our identity, we must be as who we really are, we should get to know ourselves to know our truth. From then on, simply be, without masks or costumes, and proudly live the only life we have, without fears and with hope.

Sebastián finally manages to heal and overcome his past. He turns his blue eyes on Tomás, embraces him, and kisses him on the cheek. From now on, everything will get better. Life will get better for his loved one and for himself… for everyone. He feels it.

EPILOGUE:

The new generation. Sunday, June 24, 2012

FOR THIS REASON, MR. PRESIDENT, I ASK FOR YOUR HELP TO CLOSE these illegal clinics operating in our country. It is believed that there are currently more than two hundred centers operating under the façade of rehabilitation, but believe me, they are not "curing" homosexuality. They are just physically, emotionally, and spiritually damaging the young people who are locked in there. They mistreat their identities and their hearts… as they did with me.

>Sincerely,
>Tomás Díaz

"Mr. President? It's time now."

"Yes, yes, in a moment." The president leaves the paper on his desk. "You have no idea how this letter has moved me, Carlos."

"Are you all right?"

"Do me a favor. Do you think you can locate this Tomás? What was his last name? Díaz? I want to meet him."

"Was he the one who wrote that letter?"

"Yes."

"I'll take care of that today. Don't worry." Carlos picks up the envelope and reads the address of the author, but he can't act now because and the president is about to give his speech.

The president gets up from his desk and his guards escort him up to the palace's balcony. A crowd eagerly waits for him outside.

"Dear country, dear citizens, here I stand as a leader," the president starts his speech. "I officially announce my candidacy for this year's elections. I announce my commitment to begin a new period and further bolster our collective welfare. We have a challenge and this challenge is to fight for the rights of each and every one of us — our human rights." The crowd cheers and raises their posters in support.

"I believe that all human beings have the right to be treated fairly, with dignity. We have the right to be respected, even if we are different on the outside. Our physical features, disabilities, skin colors, race, whatever it may be, do not dictate who we are on the inside. We also have the right to be treated equally if our tastes, or our ways of seeing things, are different from the rest. These pieces of our lives are our beliefs, ideologies, religion, or even our sexual orientation. Being different does not have to mean being a freak, or that we should be marginalized, forcibly grouped together in some rejected minority, discriminated against and with no opportunities. We all have the same rights." The crowd is now silent and listening carefully.

"Inside, we are all equal. We long for the same thing. We long for love, to find our own identity, to achieve our dreams and goals, to live a life where we feel safe. We can all relate to these feelings and by dong so, realize that we have much to share with our fellow countrymen. Therefore, dear citizens, I firmly promise to fight for the individual rights of each of us. I promise we will advance not alone, but together, as a group, fighting for our individual rights."

The cloud explodes in applause and cheers of support. For the president, it is a proud moment, but also one of relief. He didn't know how they would react to his words, to the speech that he just improvised.

"Never stay silent. Raise your voices and we will be here to listen to you. I promise this. I won't let you down. It's time we do the right thing!"

The press doesn't waste a second and as soon as the president is finished, reporters have moved through the crowd to find spectators to interview. The first is Samuel, a homosexual activist.

"I feel so lucky to be part of this generation. I feel blessed. I think the community feels a little more understood, integrated. Finally, someone acknowledges us, they think about us. It seems like a miracle. This is what we have dreamed of and what we have been asking for in our silent prayers for decades. Let me tell you. We did it!"

Interviews are also being conducted in television studios and the last words of the president are being analyzed.

"Now, the question is: does the president have the

support of all the sectors of society? Or are we talking only about a few minorities?"

"Well, although it sounds strange or ironic, most people *are* minorities," states one critic. "And why not? Why refuse to walk the path that the president proposes? Minorities also are made up of people and, at least until now, they have not been given the attention they deserve. We have not been concerned that people with disabilities have the same opportunities as everyone else. We continue to turn a blind eye to social discriminations dealing with the matter of race or skin color. We know that, in this country, there is a large LGBTQI community, but we have been looking the other way and pretending they are not there."

In another station, it's the president himself who is being interviewed. "I firmly believe that all people need a safe place where they can be happy. We all live in this world and we have to understand each other and interact harmoniously. We cannot continue rejecting each other, discriminating against each other simply because certain people like certain things and others don't. Or because one group of people holds certain beliefs that we don't share."

"And how exactly will you provide the support that you mention, with regard to the homosexual community?"

"I can't share any details right now, but we are organizing a televised event for June 28. We chose the date because it celebrates gay pride."

"In two days?"

"That's right. Now, please, will you continue with the

next questions?"

Thursday, June 28, 2012

The young man says goodbye to his mother on his way to watch the event at his girlfriend's house. His middle name is his dead uncle's first name, "Bernardo". He lives with his mother, without knowing the whereabouts of his father. They never met and never will, if it's up to his mother. She thinks it's safer.

"Are you going to be okay here by yourself?"

"Obviously. Go on, now."

"If you want, I'll stay here with you."

"I'll be fine, I'm telling you. Go on, say hello from me." Sandra knows where her son, Isaac, gets his protective personality. He's exactly the same as Tomás.

He kisses his mother and leaves.

Minutes later, the image of the president with his wife and his two children appears on the television.

"Good evening, dear citizens. This is both a warning and a call for understanding, which we hope reaches all corners of the globe. We want to start changing things. Gay Pride Day wouldn't be celebrated today if it weren't for those who once fought for these changes and showed the world that they had nothing to be ashamed of. So today, we thank the heroes of Stonewall, who never gave up and who began to write their own story. It has been forty-three years since the day they broke their silence and started working towards gaining civil and human rights in the United States and around the globe. And for that, we are gathered here today to begin working toward the same goal, but in our own home, in our country."

Every time the president pauses for breath, the crowd applauds and chants, as if winning a battle or encouraging a sports team. Sandra can see on the television that the place is packed. There are hundreds, perhaps thousands, of people carrying banners and rainbow flags.

"I would like to first acknowledge the source of my inspiration and courage to stand up and support the 8 community during this re-election campaign. For those of you who don't know, Harvey Milk was an openly gay American activist who fought for the recognition of the rights of gays in San Francisco in the 1970s. After several failed political campaigns, his perseverance and courage finally won out and he was elected to the post of municipal supervisor. With that position, he did his best to makes a difference in the lives of all citizens, but above all to fight the anti-gay initiative, a concept that became popular in the most conservative sectors of American politics.

"Milk was the creator, or at least the leader, of an integrated political movement that inspired a new generation. He accomplished a lot in a short time. It is thanks to him that a law was passed prohibiting discrimination based on sexual orientation. He could have done much more for human rights, but, unfortunately, he was assassinated within the year. Discovering Harvey Milk has also inspired Mr. Tomás Díaz to fight for his own rights in the hopes that he, too, will be inspirational and remembered as a significant public figure in the LGBTQI community here in Ecuador. In fact, today's event would not have been possible if it had it not been for the help of Mr. Díaz, who, fortunately, is here among us now."

With a gesture, the president invites Tomás to the podium to give his speech. Tomás, who is now a lawyer, thanks him with a handshake and a broad smile.

"Good evening, everyone. First, I want to thank Mr. President for this unique opportunity."

This is why Sandra didn't want her son to watch the broadcast with her. The memories come like an avalanche and it is impossible to separate them from her emotions. First comes her doubt, but she makes the decision to turn off the television. She instead walks to the kitchen, opens the third drawer from the bottom, and grabs the bottle of pills hidden in there. She has been fighting for years with her emotional state. It's better if she just goes to bed and lets the memories continue to be buried.

"At eighteen, I used to wonder: does God love me? Would God accept me into His Kingdom? If God made man in His image, why did He create people like me? My questions were answered and, without wasting more time, I will tell you how." Tomás continues, "God never spoke ill of homosexuality, nor declared it as a sin. That lie was assumed in the more recent interpretations of the Bible — when we should be sticking with the original version. God loves me as I am because I am His creation, a human being like you. God gave me the desire to know and accept myself. I have nothing to be ashamed of and I shouldn't hide who I am. I follow His word, which is love Him and love your neighbor as yourself." The audience applauds and waves their flags.

"A couple of weeks ago, I started writing a letter. I

only started it because I couldn't finish it. It seemed like a waste of time. I set it aside for a few days. I had lost faith that I could make any difference with it. I'm talking about the letter I sent to our president." Tomás turns and smiles at the president, then looks around for Sebastián Fineli, whom many in the audience recognize as a talented painter. "I think I would have not recovered that hope had it not been for my partner. He persuaded me to continue, giving me a reason and reviving the spirit of not giving up. Thanks to him, I finished the letter and sent it. Thanks to him we are all here today.

"That's what this is about. We need to insist, not to just bow our heads, to fight for our rights to the end. I love my partner and I would do anything for him. I do not see myself getting married, but you never know…I would if he wants to, although I already know that he does." Tomás laughs and the audience laughs with him. "And if I agree to marry, it would not be to harm others or break the current marital tradition. I would do it for love because I know it would grow our love and be worth a lot to us."

The audience breaks into applause. Tomás takes a second to check on Sebastián and notices that he's crying. Tomás must hold his breath for a moment to keep his own composure, as he feels the tears coming. He doesn't know if they are tears of happiness for the present or sadness for the memories that start to come back.

"We all know that it is very difficult to get married, especially in our country. But something extraordinary happened in the United States when it held the first gay marriage. When I saw that, my eyes filled with tears. I know it must not have been easy for that couple, but the fact that they achieved it — that...that inspired me. Two people were not allowed to marry just because they were gay. It seems unfair, absurd, and wrong. Who are the others to decide if I can do this or if I can do that? Do homosexuals go from house to house to decide whether heterosexuals can marry?"

Tomás has to stop to take a sip of water. "Please, let's reflect. Miraculously, my letter came into the hands of the president and his purpose began to materialize. Now, we have the law, justice, to close once and for all those false rehabilitation clinics that supposedly cure homosexuality. But there is nothing to cure. There is no disease. We are human beings with a different sexual orientation. Period."

Now the crowd is in heaven. Not all, but most of those present, are gay and the fact that Tomás is saying all of this publically makes him a revolutionary.

"Now, I have the pleasure to introduce and invite to the microphone my great true love, Sebastián Fineli."

Sebastián is received by the same applause that greeted Tomás, who is forced to limit himself to a hug on television. He still has to save his kiss in order to avoid scandal.

"Hello. It's a pleasure to be here tonight and support our president. It is truly an honor." Sebastián has to use his inhaler before beginning his testimony. "I confess that I...well, I tried to kill myself, not once...several times. At thirteen, I was already feeling lonely, frustrated, guilty, depressed. I felt hatred and contempt for myself because, of course, I liked people of the same sex and that was banned, hated by everyone around me. How else would I feel?"

The festive mood in the audience suddenly disappears and is replaced by a respectful silence, with looks of understanding and empathy.

"I felt I did not fit in this world, that there was no place for me. My first boyfriend, Christian, he changed my life, made me see what love is. Unfortunately, he committed suicide. He couldn't take it anymore...and I couldn't save him in time." Sebastián uses his inhaler again. "I fell back into depression and into the suicide attempts. Worst of all, I was admitted to Grow And Live Normally, where my life really became a hell." Tomás, still standing behind Sebastián, caresses his hand to give him courage.

"Looking back at the past, I can say that every cloud has a silver lining. I survived all of those experiences and I met Tomás. Next to him, I became strong and brave, I didn't give up, I managed to find myself, to be myself. After all those years, I realized that it's not about your race, color, sexuality, gender, or economic status that makes you different and unique, but how you act and respond. It's about how you are as a person that makes you stand out. If you are faithful to yourself, you will shine and inspire others to live their lives as themselves. To discover what being different means is something unique and special. To show it without fear is the best we can do in our lives. Let's remember that there are still kids in the world, even today, who are committing suicide from the mental and spiritual disorders these treatments cause them." Sebastián reaches his least favorite part of the speech, those memories he wishes he could make go away. "I remember my high school days. I always denied being gay and I pretended that I liked women so that I could feel and understand what the others felt. I mean taunts, insults, and intimidation. Anyway, all of that not only affected me emotionally, but also worsened my disability. I was the loneliest boy in the world, I was ashamed of who I was, I didn't fit in." Tomás puts his hand on Sebastián's shoulder, supporting him.

"But I must admit that the last two years of high school were different. Things improved and I began to relate better to my colleagues. People *can* change for the better. It's a process for everyone. It takes time. The reality is that we can improve our coexistence. We can generate values of respect and tolerance in our schools. Believe me, it's possible. What we must know is that it is completely normal to feel alone and rejected during adolescence. It happens to everyone, even to heterosexuals. Do not fall into the simple solution, to escape. Better be an example for others. Let's delete the option of suicide of our minds. It's not easy, but I can say that I am an example of this. I survived.

"Of course, I will not deny that coming out is difficult. In many instances, the decision takes time, not just for the one coming out, but also for others. My family had a hard time accepting me, but they did it. Now they love and understand me and are there when I need them. I'm saying the way from the starting point is long and difficult, but if you keep walking, when you least expect it, you realize that you have crossed the finish line.

"As I said earlier, it's a process for everyone. It takes time to improve things. In fact, it takes time to find who you are. It's a process — it's a difficult process — but, believe me, when you get to that point where you find and know yourself, it is a great and extraordinary thing. It really is. You'll see it and feel it. To know who you want to love is amazing because that's what it's all about, to know which sex you are more attracted to in order to know who you want to spend the rest of your life with, loving and receiving love from that person. I am proud for having accepted and having told the world, aloud, who I am. Now I am very positive about my future. I have my profession and I have the one I love beside me. Perhaps it's necessary to go through terrible things to then get grand, good experiences. Who knows? The truth is, now the world is changing. There are thousands of people who understand us and speak for us, who want to help us. Many are here tonight."

The audience breaks the silence, which was beginning to turn uncomfortable, with chants and cheers.

"I ask that you don't let society define you. Everyone has their own dreams and goals — just like I have mine. I'm a painter and it wasn't easy for me to make my dream come true. I received a lot of rejections. Trust me, a long list of them. No one cared about my paintings. People criticized me and they never stopped speaking badly about my works and my decision to become a painter. But I just put them there and left them, while I moved on with my new experiences and adventures to achieve my dream — and they missed it. After years of trying and a lot effort, I finally managed to hold my first exhibit in an art gallery and the rest is history." He laughs a little along with the proud public, most of them have seen his paintings.

"Not everything is about luck, but also about the perseverance and effort to make your dreams a reality. Never forget the rejections that you will get along your road because the moment you receive a 'yes', and you are living the success expected, all those same rejections will make you see how far you have come.

"So smile. Let everyone see your smile, enjoy your life as you really are. There is nothing better than to make a difference and improve the world. Let's be ourselves. Prove to the whole world how unique and special you are. Preach that life is beautiful and there are so many amazing and unforgettable experiences to go through. Being gay, lesbian, bisexual, transgender, transvestite, intersex, queer, pansexual...it's a significant part of who you are, but you're more than that. You are a human being, with great expectations and dreams to materialize. Do not give up! Have patience that things will get better!"

To the applause of the audience, Sebastián and Tomás sit back down in the seats set out for them.

A young black man stands up and takes his place at the microphone. "Hello, everyone. My name is Benicio and I am twenty-two years old. I am the son of two lesbians." He points to a couple sitting next to Tomás and Sebastián. Johana and Susana are in their forties but still look young. They are beaming with pride because he decided on his own to participate with a speech at the event. "Oh, and I forgot — I'm straight."

The audience erupts with laughter.

"My girlfriend must be watching me on television." Benicio laughs along with the public. "Well, as I was saying, I was raised by two mothers and yes, I'm heterosexual. I have a degree in math and physics, I am currently finishing my thesis in business administration, and I plan to do a postgraduate course in Germany. I work in a bank where I am the Head of Finance, which is what I've always wanted and, best of all, I'm making my mothers proud. A lot of people would think that someone raised like me would not have a prosperous future, but what do you base this idea on? It's just ignorance. I am here before you to prove that I was not hurt at all. Inside, I have the same love and affection that all people have. I have an identity, I have my dreams, and I have goals that I'm sure soon I will fulfill. I cannot ask for a better family than the one I have."

Johana can't stop crying. It's a rare scene because a smile is drawn on her face, but the tears roll down her face. Susan grabs her hand.

"That's our son," Susana whispers.

"I'm proud to be different, if I could call it that. I am proud to come from where I come from...although I must admit that it was not easy. And not because of my mothers, no. It was because of the outside world, because of social prejudice. Having lesbian mothers did not influence my sexuality — it had no effect. I discovered my sexuality for myself by being attracted to the girls in my school. One day, I came home and told my mothers how I felt and I had no problem. In fact, they were so happy when they met my first girlfriend. I remember they told me excitedly, 'If that's what you feel, that's fine.' It was good to feel that desire, love, and affection for another person.

"Of course, having two lesbian mothers caused me emotional problems during my school years. It was hard to explain the situation to my peers. Many parents forbade them to hang out with me. They said I was an abomination, the result of a sin. Some argued that the Bible said that, others that the teachers had told them, and still others said that because they were told by their parents so it must be true."

Tomás turns to look at Johana. In silence, they share an entire conversation. As if by telepathy, they had exchanged all the memories of their stay in Grow And Live Normally.

"But that also served as a good thing. I opened my eyes. I didn't care what they said. When I came back each day to my house, I saw my mothers and that was good enough for me. The truth is - we were a family, and not so different from the ones I saw in the houses of my classmates. We did the same things: we had lunch, watched TV, went out for a ride, and all the other activities of a family. Of course, we also had our fights or arguments, as any traditional family, but, at the same time, I also received something extra, the double love of a mother".

"Yes, that's our son." This time, it's Johana who whispers to Susana.

"And, well, it saddens me that despite all of the struggle, despite all of these years of having shared this life, society still discriminates and argues all kinds of irrational excuses for not allowing them to marry. They are forbidden to legalize their commitment. They are not given a chance to belong. Let's stop the ignorance. The happiness of my mothers is not a threat. It won't affect anyone or influence a heterosexual child to magically switch sides, if that is what they fear. These are just superstitions." Benicio feels that while he speaks he is being filled with anger. He pauses and takes a deep breath. "Who are you to decide who can fall in love with whom? Let's ask ourselves how we would feel if a third person came to forbid us to marry the person we love. We would feel it like an injustice. Well, that's how they feel!

"Put yourself in the shoes of others, under the skin of those that we are banning things for being different. Love is love. Let's respect and love our neighbors. In my case, I am able to say that I am happy and grateful for what is the best gift God could have given me: my two mothers.

"Mr. President, I kindly ask for your support, not only for my mothers, but for all people who are going through the same situation. Although I'm heterosexual, I consider myself a member of the LGBTQI community. I know what it feels to be rejected by the world. I know what goes on inside a person who feels that they do not have the same rights or the same consideration as others. Again, who are we to take away the rights of another human being? Help us, Mr. President, to have equal treatment and justice, to let people know that marriage has nothing to do with color, age, social class, or even the sexuality of a person. My desire is to see that gay marriage is legalized and, if it's not asking much, to see my mothers happily married. Remember that family is family. Love is love. It can be for all those who have a mature relationship, with love and mutual consent and true commitment. Thank you."

Among the applause, whistles, and shouts of support, Benicio waves and returns to his seat. It is another speaker's turn.

"My name is Fabricio. I was one of the patients at Grow And

Live Normally and I am HIV positive. Many must think that I am a carrier because I'm gay, by a divine curse or something, but that's not the case. The reality is that during my stay in the clinic, I was raped by one of the guards and he infected me with the virus. Of course, it was not the only consequence. I still wake up at night, terrified by the memories. I had no help and no one could save me from him. I did my best. I tried to defend myself." Fabricio stops, he cannot continue without breaking down. "I don't have AIDS — make no mistake — I'm just carrying the virus and I can live normally like anyone else. But I rely on medications to regulate my body. I take a dozen pills daily. However, I am grateful to see the years pass by and know that I'm still here. I am alive and happy. I will not be giving up."

The audience is silent again, this time struck by the strength of spirit of this speaker.

"I ask all of you to always protect yourself, to take care of yourself, and as soon as you feel the slightest doubt, go and get tested for HIV. Start the treatment. That's the only way to defeat AIDS and prevent it from being transmitted. The funny thing — because, in the middle of 21st century, that the idea still exists is funny — is that there are still people who claim that this virus only affects homosexuals like me. They don't realize that there are also heterosexuals infected. And a person is not only infected by unprotected sex, no, this must be clear. The virus is also transmitted by the use of unsterilized needles or by the exchange of bodily fluids such as blood, breast milk, semen, and more.

"The carriers and those who have AIDS are forced to fight daily against others who ignore, reject, or fear them.

Believe me, it's exhausting. Mr. President, this is why we need your help — not just yours, actually — that of every citizen. We need your help to feel that we have a chance to live with the same rights as any other person. We need the love of all of you to access and participate in medical care, to have the ability to marry and start a family, for security, education, work, freedom of speech, participation in the political life, and an adequate standard of living. And, most important of all, we need you so that we are not being subjected to cruel, inhuman, or degrading treatment.

"No one can be infected just from touching us. Mr. President, I'm not here for my situation, but for that of others. There are many infected who are not only ignored by society, but they themselves are often unaware they have the disease or what they can do to have a decent life. We have to lift their spirits and let them know that, yes, they have a life ahead of them."

Silence is broken again with the applause of the crowd. Fabricio feels weakened. His emotions are stronger than he imagined.

"And there's another reason why we are all here." Fabricio closes his eyes, feeling the silence all around, and remembers him, the darkness of his eyes. He sees Mateo with his glasses, the memory of his face, his essence, and his smile that lights him up like an angel, like he always dreamed of being. Fabricio can see Mateo happy, as he always prayed to be, and feel him at peace, which makes Fabricio smile. But then he opens his eyes, turns around, and sees them: Tomás, Sebastián, Johana, and Susanna, holding hands with watery eyes, inseparable.

"We are here to show the world that we are not a bunch of freaks, that we are human beings with a different sexual orientation. We have to stop the abuse, the distorted reality that these so-called rehabilitation clinics show, where they don't cure anyone and are solely dedicated to ripping people off. Those who survived the nightmare, we are here to make those torture centers disappear once and for all!" Fabricio take a deep breath.

"And, one last thing. Remember to be loyal to your beliefs without hurting your neighbor and always...always say and live your own truth." Fabricio concludes.

Fabricio steps down from the podium and walks to where his friends are seated. They all greet him with a hug. They all want to talk, to say something, to congratulate each other, but no one can find the right words to express their happiness. The president stands before the microphone.

"The decision is made. I will shut down all of the illegal clinics in this country. Any rehabilitation center, legally established, that is selling false ideas or boasting to cure homosexuality will have a maximum period of one month to close that area and return their patients to their homes. Not only that, but also, all centers that have been working in the subject will undergo an audit. These centers will be audited for economic accuracy and at the patient care level. We will analyze their physical and psychological state. And if one — even one — has suffered a setback of any kind, then the clinic will have to pay for the damages."

His voice roars over the sounds of applause and chants from the audience.

"And with this new mandate, I will also preside over the legalization of marriage between people of the same sex. Count on me! It is time that our environment is a safe place. It's time that we learn to love, to live, to respect freedom of expression of others. It's time to create a new generation of human beings, without prejudice, with acceptance, understanding, tolerance, and integration. These are human rights! To fight for a new generation! To be mature enough to accept others and let them live in peace with their beliefs and lifestyles, opinions, tastes, and thoughts, however different from ours they may be. We must not give up on life, love, dreams, and hope — that's the secret to achieving our goals and happiness! Remember, together we will succeed!"

As the crowd breaks into applause of congratulations for the current president, a woman has to cover her face with her hands because is crying so much. Does she cry from pride, happiness, or sad nostalgia? Juliana squeezes the hand of her second husband so hard that he yelps in pain. They hug and she continues to cry.

And on the stage, there is satisfaction — satisfaction for having reached the goal, the end of the road, or perhaps, more than the end, a *new* beginning.

"Now everything is going to be better," Sebastián tells Tomás. "Everything will be better."

"We did it," Tomás responds. "You and me…we did it." The couple embraces and shares a long kiss, projecting all the intensity of that eternal moment of success and happiness.

ACKNOWLEDGEMENTS:

Thank you.

THIS BOOK IS A DREAM COME TRUE.

Since I was a small child, I have dreamed of writing a novel in order to provide examples of personal values and give inspiration to the world — a desire that is the result of my own experiences finding, discovering, and knowing myself or what I am: a human being.

First of all, I want to thank the heroes that inspired me to move forward with my novel: those who fought that historical night, June 28, 1969, in the streets of Stonewall, USA, who showed bravery and gave an example to the whole world that you have to be proud of yourself and you do not have to give up while searching to find what you are as a person, that we should act and fight for human rights. To the mathematician, Alan Turing, for his unique genius as well as for his bravery in being true to himself during a difficult time to be homosexual. To the politician Harvey Milk, whom I admire and who keeps inspiring me to take initiative for the LGBTQI rights. To Ellen Degeneres, for being one of the first public figures to come out of the closet and, most of all, for setting a good example while serving as proof to the world that you can live a normal life both personally and successfully regardless of your sexual orientation. She kept the inspiration and always found the strength and the courage to stand up for what I believe – we all deserve a safe place.

This book is also for all of those who have had the bravery and courage to stand up and defend our rights and our equality. People like Zach Wahls, Jacob Rudolph, Shane Bitney Crone, and Hudson Taylor. All of you are empowering and continue to be valuable inspirations for me. You've unknowingly give me the will to help others to widen their perspective of the LGBTQI community. I wouldn't have been able to move forward with this dream if I hadn't discovered all of you.

I also dedicate this to my grandparents: Papi Cesar and Lucho. Without them, I wouldn't be alive. They took a chance and paid for an expensive operation that saved me because, from the second I was born, I was on the verge of death. Thanks to them, today I can live proudly and feel free to be myself while carrying both of their names. In addition, I want to thank my grandmother, Mami Dolly, and my grandmother, Fanny. May they rest in peace.

To my mom, who, since the day I was born, has given me tender love and faithful support. I am especially thankful that she always believed in me, and understands and appreciates me as her son - just the way I am.

To my father, for teaching me to value myself and to be independent, for opening up my eyes so that I can build my life with success.

To my first editor and writer of poetry, my brother, for being the first member of my family to ever listen to me, to support me in my fight for who I am and who taught me not to give up.

To all of my uncles, aunts, and cousins, for always giving me their care and concern, for always being mindful of my health and for thinking about my welfare.

To my best friends, Leslie Ayala and Valeria De Cesareo, who I first trusted, and who were my first support system and a rock for me to lean on. I love them. They are special and a gift that God and life gave to me.

To my incredible best friends: Juan Pablo Corral, Daniel Valdivieso, Joshua Degel, Michael Tanner, and my dear friends from high school, Milton Santamaria and Ricardo Iturralde. I don't know what my life would be like without you guys. I think it would probably be boring and with no unforgettable moments. I love, admire, and cherish you a lot for your successes and, mainly, for your friendship. I'll always be thankful for the support and trust you deposited in me.

To my dearest friends and advocates of the first Spanish edition of this book: the economist Humberto Mata and the lawyer Silvia Buendía. I'm so grateful for your support and your trust when you joined me on my national book tour, especially for standing up for our beliefs and for the rights of the LGBTQI (Lesbian, Gay, Bisexual, Transgender, Queer, and Intersex) community.

There are people that I give thanks to: Lala Piscicelli, Rossy Rodas, and Lizette Troya. You have given me a hand to keep going despite my hearing disability and my sexual orientation. You were one more inspiration for me to write this novel.

A big special thanks to my bosses from my previous job: Yesenia Riofrio and Valeria Cortés. For their advice and for always believing in my book. For helping me with a lot of permissions to travel to promote my book in Spanish and their presence at the event launch. You were very patient with me and I would not have been able to do the promotion for the national Spanish book tour without your support.

Thanks again to all of these people. They have opened my eyes and, despite so much discrimination and prejudices in this world, made me aware that there are people like you, with such a heart and that distinct touch of humanity.

I would also like to thank the team of the CAUSANA foundation, for the opportunity to visit their office in 2013, where I delivered my first-edition Spanish copies of this book to many of the young people who were forcibly interned in those clandestine centers. I especially thank the members of the team, who took their time to let me interview them and who answered my questions.

Their interesting and factual information served as my reference for the text in the opening reflection. You should know this, because this story is not only based on truth, but also IN truth. Thanks to the foundation's surveillance and monitoring work, young people are more aware and turn to CAUSANA to avoid being admitted against their will to centers like Grow And Live Normally. Now, most of the complaints have ceased.

For more information about this incredible support organization, visit their official blog: http://desafiandomitos.blogspot.com

The biblical interpretations and conclusions that I wrote for Tomás' blue notebook are based on my own reading of the six scriptures that supposedly refer to homosexuality as a sin. I realize that there are different interpretations and I do not intend to offend or disrespect anyone. For my research, I used The Bible of the Americas (1986) and my ideas were also constructed by following the Bible studies of Gary Lynn and Rev. Adermin Diaz Flores. I thank them both for permitting me to use their websites.

For more information from my official sources and for a searchable online Bible in over 100 versions and 50 languages, visit the follow websites:

    http://lakeweedatarrowhead.net/ **Author:Gary Lynn.**

    http://www.libresporsugracia.org/ **Author: Rev. Adermin Diaz Flores.**

    http://www.biblegateway.com/

I want to thank the twenty-three rejection letters and even more unanswered letters from publishing houses and literary agents in the U.S. that made me fight harder to be published. To my translator, Diego Rendón, for the time spent working together on the first English edition of this novel that allowed me to continue writing and editing over the next two years until I began working with my editor.

To all the people I know and have befriended on my

incredible journey through New York, Los Angeles, and Dallas. An extra special thanks must be given to my friend, James Kaechele, for his kindness and advice that inspired me to move forward with my novel. To my dear friend, Rebecca Spencer, for her awesome support in this unexpected dream come true. To my friend, Ben Starr, who is down to earth and really fun to be around, for his incredible encouragement. To Iván Aguila for being such an amazing friend to hang out with and for persuading me not to give up publishing this book in English. To my best friend from Argentina, Lis Figarola, you are like my sister; I love you so much!

To my extraordinary editor in the U.S., Rachel Edgell, I could not ask for a better editor! I'm so lucky to work together with you and especially grateful that you were a part of this incredible project. You were so amazing, patient, and so helpful to me. I definitely wouldn't have made it without your huge effort to make this book look great! An enormous gratitude to the wonderful editor-in-chief of Pen Name Publishing, Dionne Abouelela, for believing in my novel and trusting me to be part of their incredible authors' team.

After five years of struggling in writing, editing, rewriting, more editing and translating my novel Spanish into English, all I can say is that it takes a lot of courage and perseverance, but hard work pays off and dreams really do come true.

If I made my dream come true, you can, too!

AUTHOR BIO.

Hello there! My name is César L. Baquerizo. I was born on Sunday, April 6, 1986 in the warmest, largest, and the most populous city in Ecuador: Guayaquil.

During my birth, I suffered a condition that impaired my ability to breathe. I was at a high risk of dying from a nasal obstruction. My grandparents paid for an expensive operation that brought me to the U.S. in the very beginning of my life. Eric M. Kraus at The Ear Center of Greensboro, P.A, performed the operation. Thanks to him, I survived.

After the operation, I suffered a high-percentage loss of hearing. When I was four years old, my parents took me to Buenos Aires, where I received special language classes at the Instituto Oral Modelo (IOM) and successfully developed my speech and understanding in Spanish. I also started to use my hearing aids.

Despite my disability of being 90% deaf in both ears, I have not limited myself in work. Before I started my new career path as an author with this book, I worked in various jobs and positions: I worked as a real estate sales executive, as a freelance graphic and web designer, as a waiter, as a retail salesperson in a shopping mall, and as a human resources assistant in a bank and in an insurance company. I have worked in franchise companies, as a host for customer service in Cinemark, as an administrative assistant in Subway and as a cashier in Forever 21. I gained a lot of work experience, but I still needed to accomplish my dreams.

As every dreamer out there often wishes, I always wanted to make something different, to do something special, to have something meaningful and to share it to the world. Now, with this book, I have just that.

During my teens, I went through an internal conflict with my sexual identity in a society in which homosexuality is often treated with discrimination and rejection. What gave me strength was my faith in God. Also, activists like Ellen Degeneres and Harvey Milk helped me to find the courage to fight against the constant struggle and to discover myself: a human being who has the right to live and love exactly as I am.

Ever since I was a little boy, I would write stories as a hobby — and as a means to escape from reality. I dreamed of the day when I would publish my own book and inspire others. After everything I have been through in life, I am blessed to have the opportunity to help others realize their life's dream. Through my words and my main characters (that aren't so different from me), I hope to make a huge difference in the issues facing our communities today. Because of these desires, I have the courage to make my dreams come true.

A Safe Place with You is my gift to you.

Did you like this title?

Let the author know!

The best present you can give to an author is to leave them a review. We recommend GoodReads or your favorite online retailer such as Amazon, Barnes & Noble, IndieBound, or iTunes.

Our entire family loves to talk to readers, writers, and bibliophiles. You can reach this author, César L. Baquerizo via his website, https://cesarluisbaquerizo.wordpress.com/, on Facebook - https://www.facebook.com/asafeplacewithyou, or on Twitter - @asafeplacewithu

Pen Name Publishing is a modern publisher looking for bold stories by bold voices. This title you've just finished is one of many that we've published - and plan to publish!

Connect with us on Twitter - @pennamepublish, Instagram - @pennamepublishing, or on Facebook under Pen Name Publishing.

CPSIA information can be obtained
at www.ICGtesting.com
Printed in the USA
FSOW01n2023240516
20778FS